By Della Borton
Published by Fawcett Books:

FADE TO BLACK
FREEZE FRAME
SLOW DISSOLVE

SLOW DISSOLVE

Della Borton

FAWCETT BOOKS • NEW YORK

A Fawcett Book
Published by The Ballantine Publishing Group
Copyright © 2001 by Lynette Carpenter

All rights reserved under International and Pan-American Copyright Conventions. Published in the United States by The Ballantine Publishing Group, a division of Random House, Inc., New York, and simultaneously in Canada by Random House of Canada Limited, Toronto.

Fawcett is a registered trademark and the Fawcett colophon is a trademark of Random House, Inc.

www.randomhouse.com/BB/

Library of Congress Catalog Card Number: 00-110102

ISBN 0-449-00705-7

Manufactured in the United States of America

First Edition: February 2001

10 9 8 7 6 5 4 3 2 1

Acknowledgments

The author wishes to thank the following for various kinds of assistance and information: Kathy Amato, Kim "Ask-Mr.-Chemistry" Lance, Craig Ramsay, and Judylynn Ryan. Last but not least, she wishes to acknowledge the support of Beany and Cleo, who spent many long, boring hours on the job.

Prologue

FADE IN

1 Ext. Modern suburban house—Day—Present day

EXTREME LOW ANGLE of a body, arms and legs spread, which seems to be floating in space. The bright light coming from behind the body obscures the details, but it is definitely a body, definitely human. As the CAMERA HOLDS for a few seconds, we can determine that this is an UNDERWATER SHOT, and that the body is floating in water. Perhaps it undulates slightly. A swimsuit and cap account for the distinctly human silhouette.

(Faint music can be heard, but the tune is unrecognizable.)

2 Poolside, Modern suburban house

REVERSE ANGLE of the previous shot from the deck of a small-sized private swimming pool. Along the perimeter of the deck are large redwood tubs overflowing with colorful flowers—petunias, geraniums, marigolds, and the like. In the background, on the opposite side of the pool, is an empty lounge chair, a beach towel draped over one arm. Next to the chair is a small plastic table where a pair of sunglasses and a plastic bottle, probably sunscreen, have been placed.

(In the background, music is playing: Lili Marlene.*)*

We can now see the swimmer more clearly—a woman whose age is difficult to judge but whose body is not the slender, well-toned body of a young woman. She floats, face down, in the bright blue water.

*   *   *

1

The camera TILTS up, PANS left, to reveal the back of a modern suburban ranch house. The camera begins a SLOW TRACK up a small flight of flagstone steps, across a patio, and in through an open patio door, where a sheer curtain flutters in the breeze. We are now in a living room, comfortably but neither expensively nor newly furnished, showing a certain amount of human clutter—mostly magazines and newspapers, a cookbook, small framed photographs and memorabilia, a vase of dahlias on the coffee table and several photo albums on the table's lower shelf. The camera TRACKS past all of this, through a door and into a hallway. The right-hand wall is covered with framed photographs, typical records of family life—graduations, marriages, children. At the end of the hall, framed against the light from an open doorway, is a tall gate of the kind used to contain large dogs or small children.

(The doorbell rings. Lili Marlene *has ended, and Ella Fitzgerald is singing* Night and Day.*)*

The camera TRACKS down the hall, over the gate, and into a moderately sized master bedroom. Like the living room, it is comfortably furnished, with two single beds, a nightstand, and two dressers—a tall chest of drawers and a low dresser with a mirror, very obviously his and hers. One bed is turned down, the sheets mussed as if someone had just been sleeping there. Three large packing boxes, labeled "bedroom," are stacked against the far wall, under a window. Past the beds, on the right-hand wall, a closet door stands open.

A MAN is standing in the middle of the room. We can only see his back, but he is thin, apparently elderly, with wispy white hair. He is wearing only boxer shorts.

(The doorbell rings again.)

> WOMAN'S VOICE
> (Tentatively) Mother?

The MAN turns his head toward the camera, giving an almost furtive glance behind him. Then he turns back toward the closet, and moves in that direction with a heavy-footed, shuffling gait. He disappears inside the closet, then reappears, one arm inside a jacket he is struggling to put on.

> WOMAN'S VOICE
> (Calling) Mother! Mother!

The MAN gets his arms into both sleeves and begins to button the jacket. A button falls off onto the floor. He stoops to pick it up, and stops, halfway down. He straightens and crosses to the mirrored dresser. The camera FOLLOWS, and MOVES IN for an OVER-THE-SHOULDER shot.

The MAN in the mirror is wearing an old military jacket, a brown bomber jacket that hangs loosely on his frame. It appears to be the same jacket worn by a younger man in a black-and-white photograph clipped to the edge of the mirror; in the photograph, the young man in full military uniform stands awkwardly, arms at his sides, in front of a World War II bomber.

> WOMAN'S VOICE
> (Fainter, farther away, but alarmed) Mother?

The MAN smiles at himself in the mirror. It is the kind of smile that involves his whole face, pulling his chin down, pushing his eyebrows up, spreading his ears wide. It is a wolfish smile, showing a protruding set of even white teeth. He shows no sign of having heard the voice. His eyes stray from his image to the photograph and back again. Slowly, he salutes himself.
FADE TO BLACK

1

I was in the dark. Not a new state for me, either literally or figuratively. This time it was literal, preceded by a clap of thunder that could have been God's Foley artist answering George Lucas. The boom launched me off my stool and precipitated my knee into a close encounter with the makeup bench. I cursed the darkness, pressed one hand to my throbbing knee, and reached for the flashlight with the other one. I felt it bump my fingertips. Then I heard it hit the floor with a crack, and roll.

"Oh, hell!" I shouted, the sound bouncing off the walls of the projection booth and hurting my own ears. In every direction, I knew, lay obstacles waiting in the darkness to trip me, stab me, bash my shins, and fall on top of me. In one direction only lay the door, but I would have to feel my way to it.

I took a deep breath. Aloud, I muttered, "Think happy thoughts, Gilda. This is no time to be cranky. You're an independent theater owner about to be visited by the box office darlings of the summer season, who will leave their dino-prints all over your ticket sales reports. Better to have the power outage tonight and get it over with than to send everybody home from *The Lost World* on Thursday night. As your cousin Faye would say, chill."

My knee still smarted as I limped in the general direction of the door. In the dark, I was more acutely aware of the smells of the old theater—a faint mustiness, the scents of the cleaners and oils used to keep the antique projector and the newer platter system running, the rich, buttery odor of more than half a century of popcorn. A deep silence inside the theater answered the rumbling storm outside. As my eyes adjusted to the disorienting blackness, I realized that a few photons had made their way into the booth from the exit signs at the front of the theater.

I took the stairs slowly, surprised by the darkness of the lobby below. The late afternoon thunderstorm had crept up on me while I was working in the booth, but it must be some storm, I thought. A sudden flash of lightning lit up the lobby, and I cried out. Two feet away from where I had frozen on the bottom stair, a man was standing. A clap of thunder rattled the glass doors on the front of the theater.

Training, my Aunt Lillian always says, counts for everything in situations like these.

"May I help you?" I croaked.

Out of the darkness came a sigh, barely audible under the sounds of wind and rain outside.

"I used to be in pictures," a voice said softly.

Poised for flight, I considered my options.

"Yeah?" I said.

"Long time ago," the voice said. "Before the war."

At that moment, Central Ohio Power seized the upper hand, and the lights flickered on. The ice machine resumed its contented purr.

The man before me looked to be in his seventies. He was slightly stoop-shouldered and had white wispy hair retreating along both temples. He wore dark green polyester pants and an old brown military jacket, even though the day was warm.

"I'm Leo," he said, turning to look at me.

Then he smiled. He had a jawline shaped like a boomerang, and his smile widened his mouth into a V. A row of front teeth protruded like an awning over his lower lip. If ever a grin could be called wolfish, this was it.

"Gilda Liberty," I said, putting out my hand. He looked at it, then put out his own. "I own the Paradise."

He nodded, and continued to grin at me.

"Did you want to, uh, look around?" I asked hesitantly. I had work to finish upstairs before the early show.

"I'm waiting for my girl," he said.

"Your girl?" I echoed. I didn't think any of the summer help could be in this guy's range, romantically speaking, and none of them would tolerate being called a "girl," much less with a possessive pronoun attached to it.

"Gladys," he said, beaming at me. "You know Gladys?"

"I haven't had the pleasure," I said.

"Glad's a real peach," he assured me. "Works at the engine plant. She's crazy about the picture show, she is. She can't get enough of Ronald Colman and that other guy—you know who I mean? I forget his name. I say, what do you need those guys for, when you got me? But she just laughs, and I keep shelling out the dough."

I nodded, wondering briefly if perhaps the storm had somehow precipitated me into the past, and I was having some kind of weird *Back to the Future* experience. The engine plant had been closed for years; what was left of the building was as dusty as the inside of Ronald Colman's coffin.

"Say, I got a picture of Glad," he said, snapping his fingers. He reached into his back pocket, but came up empty-handed. His face crumpled into panic. "It's not there!" His frightened eyes circled the lobby as if he thought a thief was lurking in the shadows.

Now I knew which one of us was experiencing a flashback.

"That's okay," I said soothingly. I took him by the arm and guided him to a chair. "You can sit down here and describe her to me. That way, it'll be more personal."

I stole a peek at his back pockets before they hit the seat of the chair. Sure enough, I saw no telltale bulges there. I wondered how I would find out where Leo lived if nobody came looking for him.

"About Gladys," I prompted him.

His worried expression cleared. "You know Gladys?" he asked eagerly.

"I don't think so," I said. "What does she look like?"

I was just making conversation. I didn't expect Gladys, if she walked in the door now, to look like she'd looked in the Ronald Colman years.

"Aw, she's a sweet kid," Leo told me. "A real peach."

That appeared to be all the information I was going to get about Gladys, at first. His gaze circled the lobby again, and he sighed.

"Gladys?" I said again.

"Gladys?" he echoed. Again he seemed momentarily confused, then clarity returned. "Oh, Gladys, why, she, she's got me wrapped around her little finger, I can tell you. Hold on! I've got a picture—"

I interrupted before he could get his hand in his pocket. "You live around here, Leo?" I asked.

"Around here?" he echoed. His gaze swept the lobby again as if I were suggesting that he had a bachelor pad back behind the concession stand. "No, I don't think so," he said slowly. Then he brightened. "No, I live over on Lenox Avenue with Shelly." He gestured over his shoulder with his thumb. Something glinted on his wrist when he raised his hand. It looked like an ID bracelet.

"Shelly?" I asked, faintly hopeful.

"You know Shelly?" he responded eagerly.

"I don't think so," I said. I fished out a cigarette and lit it. His eyes followed my hands. I should have offered him one, but I hesitated, not knowing whether he would be able to manage it without catching himself on fire.

"Shelly, he don't have time for movies," Leo told me. "He's all the time practicing, or playing gigs. That's what they call it—playing gigs. Say, maybe you saw his band! They played over at the park for the Rotary Club." He gave me more thumb action, this time in a different direction.

"Sorry, I missed that concert," I said.

There was a moment of silence as we contemplated my missed opportunity.

"I want to go home now," Leo announced abruptly, and stood up.

"Okay," I agreed. "Let's see if we can figure out where you live."

"I want to go home," he repeated, not whining, just stating a fact.

"Believe me, Leo, I'm all for it," I said, stroking his arm reassuringly. "But—"

"There you are!" A woman's voice, sounding tired and exasperated, came from the front entrance.

"Hello, Pauline," Leo said. "I want to go home."

"That's good," she told him. "At least we agree on something." She turned to me. "I'm sorry if he bothered you. I was around the corner at the optometrist, and I just took my eyes off him for one second. Honestly! It's like having kids all over again."

Pauline was a graying brunette of medium height, about my age and looking it. She had the same middle age spread at her hips, the same thickening of her upper arms. She wore a nondescript cotton skirt and a white cotton shirt, and she kept running a hand through her short, curly hair. Her hair might have been styled when she left home that morning, but it wasn't now. I couldn't afford to criticize; mine wasn't styled, either. It was on its own, which might explain why it was always reaching out to everything I passed as if I were running a strong electrical current up from my toes.

"I'm trying to help out while my mother's in the hospital, but I don't have a lot of practice at this sort of thing." She waved a hand in Leo's direction. "Leo's my stepfather. Leo Mayer is his name, in case you ever find him here again. I'm Pauline Kline. He wears an ID bracelet, so you can always call the number on there." She hauled up Leo's hand to eye level to show me the bracelet on his wrist. Then she shook her head at him. "I don't know how you can stand to wear that jacket in this weather, Leo. It must be eighty-five degrees." To me, she said, "I know I shouldn't let him wear it in this heat, but he's so attached to it. My mother says let him wear it if he wants to."

"I never sweat," Leo announced. "My brother Shelly, he sweats something terrible, but I never sweat." Leo trailed off as if uncertain again what the topic of conversation was.

Pauline was playing on my sympathy, but for all I knew, she deserved a little sympathy, so I gave it to her.

"I'm sure your mother appreciates your help," I said politely.

"Yeah, well, at least *she* does," Pauline admitted truculently.

I let that go. I wasn't about to play Joanne Woodward to her Sally Field, so I turned to Leo.

"Nice talking to you, Leo," I said. "I hope you find Gladys."

"He was talking about Gladys?" she looked at him. "Leo, that was two wives ago. She's probably dead by now."

"Dead?" He looked alarmed. I could see that Pauline was definitely not cut out to nurse the senile.

"Come on," she said, tugging at his arm.

"I want to go home, Pauline," he was saying as she led him out. And then, when they were almost out of earshot, I heard that voice again, wistful: "I used to be in pictures."

2

"Leo Mayer, Leo Mayer," my mother said. She looked thoughtful—or as thoughtful as a person *can* look who is wearing one of those hair-coloring caps pulled over her head like a leaky rubber glove sprouting hair. "I think he's related to Oliver."

"Leo Mayer?" my aunt Adele repeated, fingernail polish poised in midair. She looked at my mother. "I thought he was related to you somehow. Isn't he a cousin of yours, Florence?"

My mother, who would have passed muster in a *Star Wars* bar scene, shook her head, and all the little sprouts of hair waved back and forth. Her daisy-print plastic smock bulged with a gesture we couldn't see.

"I don't think he's anybody's cousin," she said. "At least,

not anybody in our family. I think he's related by marriage. We'll ask Gloria."

My aunt Gloria, former hairdresser to the stars and wife of the aforementioned Oliver, was in her little chef's pantry off the kitchen, mixing up hair dye like Frankenstein in his laboratory. The ammoniacal smell of hair dye waged war with my aunt Adele's L'Air du Temps cologne and fingernail polish, making for a potent assault on my olfactory nerves. How Adele could see to paint her nails through the heavy curtain of her false eyelashes I couldn't imagine, but she'd had lots of practice so maybe she could do it blind.

My mother, the female half of the Dancing Liberties in her own Hollywood salad days, still attended dance recitals at the Eden Academy of Dance, which she and my father had founded when they retired from the screen. She prepared herself for them as carefully as for the Academy Awards, and Gloria took them just as seriously as she did. In general, my mother assumed a more casual approach to beauty than either of her sisters-in-law; "presentable" was a word she liked to use, as in "I just have to look presentable" or "Gilda, if you'd only try to make yourself presentable." But tonight was a special occasion. And since my aunt Adele, the former set designer, had been permitted to design the recital sets and decorate for the reception, she would also be attending, in full costume. I'd be attending, too, wearing whatever hair I was wearing now and whatever I could find in the closet that fit.

The campaign to "do something" about my hair—a campaign waged vigorously by my aunts and mother—had abated now that I'd permitted Gloria to cut my hair short. A week or so ago, I had needed a disguise for a small Liberty family production. As soon as it was over, I'd washed the dark rinse out of my hair, returning my wavy locks to their original light brown streaked with gray. But even I had conceded that something needed to be done with the hair I had left, and I'd reluctantly yielded to a body wave. Gloria had shown admirable restraint—she'd even kept quiet when I'd fended off the hairspray—and the results were, in my opinion, an improvement, even if I did look like a Fuller brush on legs.

Gloria probably viewed her recent actions as only the first incursion on my hairline, with the major battle yet to come. I suspected that she was stockpiling chemical weapons to that end. But at least I wasn't in line for Gloria's services today; I was just hanging out, trading gossip.

I wasn't about to insinuate myself into Florence and Adele's negotiation of our family tree. It was immense and intricate and it stretched back to God, the original *auteur*: he'd produced and directed, written the script, and designed the set. The only thing he hadn't taken on was costuming, but all the Liberties except me had made a point of remedying that oversight. Whole branches of my family tree—including myself—were now populating the town of Eden, garden spot of Ohio, where my grandparents had moved when they retired from the movie business. Most of the rest of the family lived in the Los Angeles area, several states west but only a beeper away. I'd spent much of my life trying to distance myself from my relatives, so my grasp of the family tree was pretty shaky.

"Here we are," Gloria announced, returning from her laboratory.

She was wearing a lab coat given to her by my uncle Wallace, Adele's husband. Uncle Wallace, who had once played bit parts in horror movies at RKO, still had contacts in the business, and this coat had a movie title printed over the breast pocket: *Revenge of the Mad Scientist.* In the old days, it was widely acknowledged that movie people made more money than anyone could justify, and it was therefore assumed that they should be happy with salary, meals, and limo while they were making a movie. These days, everybody who works on a production gets a souvenir. Industry execs claim that rising ticket prices are due to rising advertising costs, but I want to know whether raising the *Titanic* would pay for the presents James Cameron gave out to the cast and crew who sank it. On the other hand, nobody's proposed lowering ticket prices for *The Lost World* because most of the stars aren't getting salaries, let alone presents. If the dinosaurs needed something else to tick them off, this would be it.

"Gloria," Adele said, "do you know Leo Mayer?"

Gloria raised a gloved hand to her own hair, dyed a color my sister Betty had dubbed "radioactive white," and prodded a few damp curls with the back of her wrist. She brought a lot of intensity to her work. "Leo Mayer?" she said. "Sure, I know Leo. He used to be married to a cousin of Oliver's."

"I knew there was a cousin in there somewhere," Adele remarked.

"He moved back to town, oh, about a month ago," Gloria said. She handed my mother a towel. "He's got Alzheimer's disease."

We all observed a moment of silence. The oldest Liberties, including these three women, were all in their seventies or eighties. So far, we'd been lucky: nobody had been stricken with Alzheimer's. But secretly, we all watched for it, expecting it to show up like Death in *The Seventh Seal*.

"She's the one I really feel sorry for," Gloria continued. "His wife, I mean. She's got family here, too, but they met down in Florida. I don't know how long she'd been there, but he'd only moved down there, oh, maybe six or seven years ago. And they meet, and get married, and the next thing you know, bam! He's got Alzheimer's disease. They moved back here to be around family."

As she talked, Gloria lifted strands of my mother's hair and squirted them with a dark, acrid solution. I could feel my eyes flinching sympathetically as my mother pressed the towel to her face.

"I don't think Alzheimer's hits you like that—bam— Gloria," Adele objected.

"And *then*," Gloria said dramatically, ignoring her sister-in-law's correction through force of habit, "she almost drowns, in her own backyard swimming pool. Now isn't that something? She always wanted a pool—that's what Oliver's sister Margie says. And here she gets one, and nearly drowns! She's still in the hospital."

"Where do they live?" My aunt Adele frowned as she screwed the lid back on the nail polish. Adele, the former set designer, claimed she could never really understand a story until she could picture the setting.

"In that subdivision out by the new clinic," Gloria said. "Eden something—Eden Falls, Eden Lake, Eden Pond?"

"Eden Springs," my mother said.

Gloria nodded at her in the mirror. She'd had a large mirror installed behind the dinette so that she could pursue her art at home. Oliver said it gave him the impression that they were feeding twice as many people as they were, every time they sat down at the table. "I feel like I've walked onto a De Mille set," he'd lament.

"So they live in one of those new ranch houses?" Adele persisted. She was now using an aerosol spray on her nails, and I turned my head away from her field of operations. The chemical industry owed its livelihood to women like my aunts, who never met a beauty product that wasn't worth trying.

"Well, I guess they're not so new anymore," Gloria conceded. "When did they put that subdivision in? Was it before or after they built that McDonald's across from the hospital?"

"That was a dreadful summer!" Adele exclaimed. "Dust all over everything! That's when Edna moved the dress shop out to Eden Square because she said the construction dust was ruining the merchandise. Remember, Florence?"

This was how their conversations always went. One sign that they didn't have Alzheimer's was their conversational dexterity; they could follow endless digressions, yet still return unerringly to the original topic. And whether I wanted to admit it or not, my own conversational style owed something to theirs.

"I think Eden Springs went in before that, though," my mother said.

"It's hard to keep up," Gloria said. "New housing developments just seem to sprout up overnight."

"That's exactly how I feel sometimes," my mother confessed. "One day I wake up and there's something new, something that just seems to have appeared where I didn't expect to see anything. That's when I think maybe *I'm* getting senile."

"That happens to me, too, Mom," I assured her.

"So maybe *you're* getting senile," my mother countered.

"Anyway, they're just renting," Gloria said. "The owners got transferred right after they bought it. And I think the new Mrs. Mayer, Shirley is her name—I think she didn't want to buy a house right now."

"I don't blame her," my mother said. "I don't know how far along he is, but eventually she'll have to put him in a nursing home. That means she should start giving her money away so he can qualify for Medicaid."

I glanced at my mother in surprise. What did she know about nursing homes and Medicaid?

"Hand me a wet cloth, Gilda," Gloria said, holding out a wet, brown-stained hand. "I guess she could always divorce him."

"That's what I'd do," Adele said. "When you marry at our age, your spouse should come with a warranty."

"I think there are rules about divorce, too," my mother said, closing her eyes and pressing a towel to her forehead. "I don't know what they are, though."

"How did we get onto Leo anyway?" Gloria asked.

"Gilda was asking about him," my mother told her. "He wandered into the theater yesterday."

"He said he used to be in pictures," I said. "Did he?"

"In pictures?" Gloria looked surprised. "Well, I guess in a way he was. He was freelance. He made television commercials mostly, I think. He was pretty successful."

"Not in Hollywood, though?" Adele asked.

"No, no," Gloria said quickly. "Not in Hollywood. In Columbus." Her tone made it clear that real movies were made in Hollywood; everything else was a home movie.

"So, Gilda, speaking of pictures, is this dinosaur movie really starting tomorrow night?" Adele asked.

"Unless Central Ohio Power interferes," I said.

"Ooh, Oliver can't wait to see it!" Gloria enthused.

"Wallace either," Adele said, "even though he's not usually crazy about science fiction."

Gloria set a timer and sank into a padded dinette chair. She wiped her hands absentmindedly on a towel. "Maybe I should offer to do her hair," she said speculatively.

"Whose?" my mother asked.

"Shirley Mayer's," Gloria said. "Poor thing! There she is, stuck in that hospital bed, practically drowned, for heaven's sake! And then, you know how it is, people come to see you, and you can't stand to have them look at you. I wonder if she was wearing a cap."

"When I had gallstones," Adele recalled, "I hated to have people come—except the family, of course." She patted her tawny coiffure primly. "The whole time they were there, all I could think was, 'I look like you-know-what!' "

"Something the cat dragged in?" my mother suggested.

"Maybe I should offer to do her hair," Gloria repeated.

They never did get around to explaining how Leo's wife nearly drowned in the first place. That was the part that interested me.

3

"Gilda, I wish you'd talk to your aunt Clara."

My uncle Valentino, former Hollywood gaffer and the youngest of the Liberty brothers, was rewiring a plug in the theater lobby on Wednesday. Cousin Duke, my seventeen-year-old business partner and theater manager, had blown it the night before when we'd plugged in the VCR and monitor we'd set up to show the educational video about dinosaurs. We had to get it fixed, Duke insisted, because the video was the most respectable item we were selling in our collection of dinosaur kitsch.

"You don't think the dinotapes are cool?" Faye had asked. "Those roars are awesome!"

"They may be awesome, Faye," Duke had said sententiously, pushing his glasses up on his nose, "but they're hardly authentic. Nobody knows what dinosaurs sounded like, if they sounded like anything."

We had every tacky dinosaur item ever invented. We had dinosaur key chains, pencils, erasers, bubble blowers, plastic cups, foldout sunshades for cars, coloring books, kids' sunglasses, stamp sets, and a pair of metal bookends so heavy they must have been made for a brontosaurian library. We had vinyl blow-up dinosaurs and stuffed dinosaurs. We had pterodactyl mobiles. We had big rubber dinosaur flippers you could fit on your own feet to make dinosaur tracks. We had special flashlights that cast dinosaur shadows on the wall and dinosaur cutouts that glowed in the dark. We had small hand-held devices made in Japan that emitted a loud roar touted by its packaging as "Bloodcurdling! Terrifying! Very realistic!" We had ice cube trays that made dinosaur ice cubes. We had Barney backpacks. And we had T-shirts: "NEXT TIME, THE LIZARDS WIN," "DINOSAURS ARE OUT OF SIGHT," and, for the militant vegetarians, "BRONTOSAURUSES WERE VEGETARIAN, AND LOOK HOW BIG THEY GOT."

Duke pretended reluctance, but it had been his idea in the first place, and he was secretly proud of this stuff. He was even prouder of an educational display he'd set up across the lobby. It was about Gertie, an animated dinosaur and the first cartoon superstar, predecessor to Felix the Cat and Mickey Mouse. Created by pioneer animator Winsor McCay, Gertie had proven that animated characters could have personality; the ads had proclaimed, "She eats, drinks, and breathes! She laughs and cries! Yet, she lived millions of years before man inhabited this earth and has never been seen since!"

"Gilda, will you please pay attention?" Val said impatiently.

"I heard you," I said. "You want me to talk to Aunt Clara." I sighed. Why my family members couldn't just talk to each other when they had a problem was beyond me. Why they invariably picked me as the go-between was an even greater mystery. Tact had never been my strong suit where my family was concerned, and after so many years away I was out of practice.

"You know she has a bee in her bonnet about making a comeback," Val said.

"I thought it was supposed to be a 'return.' "

"Whatever. The point is, she's been pestering Toby to write her a screenplay."

The light dawned. Val's partner Tobias was a writer of some stature. He had two National Book Award nominations to his credit, and a host of other awards. He had written a few screenplays, worked on a few others, and even taught a class in screenwriting at the local cultural arts center. The class had been heavily populated by my relatives.

"She even has some ideas for him," Val continued darkly.

"Ah."

"Which one would you like to hear? There's the one about the great actress who retired from the screen when her beloved husband disappeared, only to encounter him years later, at a romantic site to be named later, and discover he's suffered from amnesia all those years and didn't remember her until he saw her again."

"Kind of a *Sunset Boulevard* meets *Martin Guerre* kind of a thing? Or if she does it on a ship, it could be a remake of *An Affair to Remember*. Shipboard romances are hot right now, but I think that one's already been remade with what's-her-face."

"Anyway, that's the best one," he said. "There's another one where she joins a Himalayan expedition, and heroically saves several expedition members—we don't know who yet, but probably a romantic male lead and a couple of cute kids, though why the kids are on this expedition in the first place has yet to be worked out."

I nodded. "Kind of a *Lost Horizons* meets *Nurse Edith Clavell* kind of a thing." A thought struck me. "Unless—she's not planning to sing, is she? We're not talking *The Sound of*

Music moved to the Himalayas, minus the Nazis and plus an avalanche or two?"

"You're getting the picture."

"She'd not only need a stunt double, she'd need a voice double," I objected. Clara was probably the least musical of the Liberty siblings.

"Unless she's planning a comedy," Val agreed. "So anyway, will you talk to her?"

"Why doesn't Toby talk to her?" I asked.

"And say what?" Val countered.

" 'No' strikes me as an appropriate response," I said. "It has the virtue of being honest, unambiguous, and concise."

"He's tried that," Val said gloomily.

"And?"

"She offered him more money."

I received this in silence. It told me everything I needed to know about Clara's lack of perspective. Tobias didn't need money as long as he and Val were together; Val's sister Mae, former owner of the Paradise and benefactor to the whole Liberty clan, had left Val well provided for. And since Val and Tobias had been together for more than forty years, a separation at this point hardly seemed likely. And even if they did separate, I suspected that Toby would be financially secure; his career as a writer had been as lucrative as writing careers could be if you weren't Stephen King or John Grisham.

"So will you talk to her?" Val persisted.

"What do you want me to say?" I asked in exasperation. "You know that nothing will have any impact, short of a claim that Toby is a lousy writer, and she knows I don't believe that."

"Tell her he's retired," Val offered.

I snorted. "She won't believe that either. When did he retire? After he wrote that essay for the *Atlantic* last month?"

"Remind her that Ronnie's new wife, what's-her-face, is a writer," he said. "Pearl? Jade? Sapphire? I can never remember her name but it's something to do with jewelry. Tell Clara she needs a woman's touch."

"Hmm. A woman's touch. That might work," I conceded.

"Except that what's-her-face is in California so that Clara can't look over her shoulder and boss her around."

"So, convince her she needs to take an extended vacation in L.A. to see this project through. She can't seriously expect to launch a comeback from the middle of Ohio anyway. And frankly, she's getting on everyone's nerves around here."

That much was true. "Okay, I'll talk to her," I said crabbily. "But why you think she'd listen to me I can't imagine."

"Because," he said, plugging the VCR into the newly rewired outlet and lighting up the screen with big green lizards, "you have your finger on the pulse of the American moviegoing public. You own a movie theater."

I hadn't wanted to own a movie theater. I never asked for one. Up until six months ago, I'd been living what passed for the good life in New York as a well-established insurance executive with no worries on my mind except parking, physical safety, high blood pressure, incipient asthma, and the cost of movies and dry cleaning. Then one day, the woman I expected to spend the rest of my life with had abruptly announced that she'd fallen for a biker with spiked hair and a Harley-Davidson tattoo on her muscular forearm. Liz had rounded up her three bewildered children, formerly thought of, by me at least, as our bewildered children, and departed. Three months later, my Aunt Mae, Lillian's twin sister, had died, and I'd packed up what shreds of myself I could find lying around and headed home to Ohio for her funeral. I had already made it clear to my mother that I was not staying to run the Paradise, Mae's special legacy to me. Here it was, not two months later, and I was not only running the Paradise, or, more accurately, helping Duke to run the Paradise, but I was living at ground zero in Liberty House, the family mansion Mae and Lillian had inherited from my grandparents.

On the up side, I spent so much time running around for the theater and worrying—about bills, about special programming, about the films we could and couldn't book, about film breaks and equipment malfunctions, about gum in the carpet and tampons in the toilets—I didn't have much time anymore to mourn the departed Liz and her kids.

On the down side, after spending a lifetime distancing myself from my family, I suddenly seemed to be in business with all of them.

They began arriving at six-thirty on opening night. You wouldn't think they could work up this much enthusiasm just one night after the big recital at the Eden Academy of Dance, but they were troupers. My uncle Wallace and aunt Adele arrived first, probably because Adele wanted to rearrange the lobby displays. Wallace leaned on the ticket counter, breathing whiskey in my face, and reminiscing about the special effects designed for the Val Lewton horror unit at RKO.

"One time, I remember, they had my hands and face painted with this phosphorescent paint," he said. "I couldn't touch anything, couldn't even go to the john, or else, well, you know. Then my skin started to itch. Well, I couldn't scratch it, you know. Couldn't get the paint off, or I'd be another two hours in makeup getting it back on again. Brother! Was I miserable!"

"Now, they'd just color you in with computers, I bet," my father said, behind him.

My mother was still wearing her recital coiffure. "Everybody I know is going to be here tonight, Gilda," she told me. She was more a critic of mine than a fan, my mother was, but tonight she looked excited and pleased.

Aunt Lillian arrived with Ruth Hernandez, her longtime housekeeper-companion. These were my housemates. They were arguing as usual.

"Your aunt, she pretends she isn't interested in prehistoric lizards," Ruth said to me. "But don't you believe it. If I don't watch her, she'll bring home some of those dinosaur ice cube trays. How do they work? she keeps asking me. How should I know? I said. Do I look like a person who would know about dinosaur ice? It's probably the same way they make those ducks out of concrete."

"One is never too old to learn," Lillian said with dignity. "Besides," she added wryly, "I'm of an age to identify with the dinosaurs."

Val and Tobias arrived with a bottle of champagne.

"Congratulations on scoring Godzilla's grandkids," Toby said, giving me a peck on the cheek.

"Thanks," I replied. "It was an act of God, believe me."

"I am pretty curious to see those computer-generated dinosaurs again," Val confessed.

Toby winked at me. "Yeah, he thought *Jurassic Park* was the bee's knees," he said.

"I'm not *that* old-fashioned, I hope," Val protested. "I said they were keen."

Gloria appeared, her silver-white hair frozen so stiff with hair spray that it looked like a wig. She was leading somebody dressed in a plush Barney costume. Barney stomped into the lobby, flashing an insipid grin and leaving a little trail of purple hairs in his wake.

"Oliver, you're shedding," my mother pointed out.

"Aw, how did you know it was me?" came a muffled voice from inside the purple grin.

"Don't let 'em rag you, Uncle Ollie," my cousin Faye called from behind the concession stand. "That Barney suit is a killer."

"She must be in a good mood," Val murmured.

I was surprised, myself. Faye, with all the impatience of youth, usually had an even lower tolerance than I did for Oliver's shenanigans.

But there was no disputing the celebratory air of this particular opening. Even Duke couldn't hide the slight smile he reserved for those movies, few and far between, that stood a chance of letting us pay off a good portion of our overdue bills. But tonight he was actually showing signs of enjoying himself. He was even wearing his own commemorative T-shirt: REX RULES! on the front, and TYRANNOSAURUS ROCKS! on the back.

Aunt Clara arrived with the first of the ticket buyers who were not members of the clan. Tobias made himself scarce, I noticed, but Wallace and Oliver both made a beeline for her. She had waded into the lobby crowd, greeting people with an air of gracious condescension, as if practicing for her next premiere. She was wearing one of those dropped-waist dresses reminiscent of the twenties that she favored—the kind that was designed for flat-chested flappers. She herself hadn't been born until 1925, but she had always considered the Jazz Age the height of glamour, and it was true that between the times of Clara Bow and Twiggy, fashion designers hadn't designed much with boyish figures in mind. She wielded her long cigarette holder like a stage prop, a dangerous practice in close quarters.

"Are you going to tell her to put that thing out, or am I?" Duke growled.

I just cut my eyes at him and turned back to the next customer. He stalked off in Clara's direction.

There was a limit to how much attention I could pay my family because the lower mathematics of ticket sales required my full concentration. I also did my best to discourage some of the younger clientele whose parents were dumb enough to think they'd enjoy a movie about rampaging gigantic lizards with teeth like scimitars—or rampaging little, fast, vicious lizards, for that matter. Nobody was discouraged, and in the end, we lost several of the rugrats during the early show. The rear view of several of these as they departed suggested that we would need to search the house for wet seats at the end of the night. Mind you, some of these kids were the same ones who'd screamed their heads off when confronted in the lobby by Barney. Because we were mature businesspeople, we didn't say, "I told you so." We sent them home with a free box of popcorn to watch *The Little Mermaid* reruns.

"Catch the clue bus," Faye would mutter as soon as the parents were out of earshot.

My parents helped out by selling dinosaur merchandise between shows. Barney had appropriated a stamp set and was stamping any kids' hands that were offered to him. Gloria was down on her knees showing the kids how to blow dinosaur bubbles; I caught myself wondering whether the ones that burst against her hair were causing acid rain to fall on our carpet and whether our insurance covered damage caused by internally generated weather. Wallace and Adele were deep in conversation with Clara, who had gone outside to smoke one of her clove cigarettes. I eyed her wistfully over the heads of the ticket buyers; I could use a cigarette break myself. Police detective Dale Ferguson, my high school chemistry lab partner, showed up for the late show with his ten-year-old twin boys, and assured me that his beeper was turned off.

Once the second show started and Clara had gone off with Lillian and Ruth Hernandez, Val and Tobias appeared at my elbow.

"Toby has an idea for a sequel," Val said. "Don't tell Clara."

"See, it's about these dinosaurs who get shot into space," Tobias said. "They end up in the middle of the war between the Empire and the rebels when their ship is captured by the Death Star. What do you think? Think Lucas and Spielberg will go for it?"

"I guess you're calling it *Star T. rex*," I commented.

A figure with the body of Barney and the head of my uncle Oliver popped up on the other side of the ticket booth. "Hey! That's good, Gilda! Star Trex!"

"If they do go for it, let me know," I said. "I'll buy stock."

Oliver wound up a small T. rex, and set it on the counter. It marched around, pawing the air. Ollie made roaring sounds.

"Pipe down, will you?" Duke fussed, as he emerged from the projection booth and crossed the lobby. At family gatherings, he was shy and reticent—but in the theater, his word was law, and even at seventeen, he didn't hesitate to correct his elders.

Oliver softened his roars.

Wallace wandered over and cleared his throat. "Can I talk to you, Gilda?" he asked, adding, "In private."

As I led Wallace to the small room behind the concession stand, Oliver shot him a suspicious glance that I didn't understand.

"What's up?" I said.

"Gilda, I wish you'd talk to your Aunt Clara," Wallace began.

Here we go again, I thought.

"What about?"

"Well, you know she wants to stage a comeback, and I'm all for it," he said. "In fact, I've written a screenplay for her. It's quite good," he assured me, as if I were skeptical, which I was. "It would really be perfect for her, but she needs convincing. It's about a woman who rents a house after losing her husband when he accidentally falls off a cliff."

"Is the house haunted?" I guessed. "Or just surrounded by vampires?"

He looked disappointed. "You've been talking to Adele. I told her not to say anything."

"It was just a lucky guess, honest," I said.

He brightened. "The twist, you see, is that the widow becomes the head vampire, with three men vampires to do her bidding."

"Like Dracula's girl group," I said.

"Right. And then the climax comes when the husband, who is supposed to be dead but isn't, happens to come to the house one rainy night when he loses his way in the fog—"

"I thought you said it was raining."

"It's sort of doing both. Anyway, he comes to the house, but here's the thing: he doesn't recognize his own wife."

"Being that she's now a vampire."

"Right. Well, you can imagine how she feels when he shows up."

"Thirsty."

"Yes, and vengeful."

"I can't believe Clara said no to this, Uncle Wally," I said.

He obviously shared my astonishment. "Can't you just picture Clara, little Clara, with fangs and wild black hair? She'd be riveting!"

"I take it she doesn't want to do horror," I said.

"She says it reminds her of Davis and Crawford in *Whatever Happened to Baby Jane?* But that wasn't a vampire movie!" His voice expressed indignation. "So, would you talk to her, Gilda?"

"Why me?" I asked.

"Well, she, she respects your opinion, Gilda," he answered. "We all do."

This was the first I'd heard of it. If they respected my opinion so much, how come they were always telling me how to live my life?

"Just talk to her, Gilda," he pleaded. "That's all I ask. Just put in a good word for me."

I sighed. "I'll see what I can do, Wallace," I said.

Faye stuck her head in the door. "Late show's out, Gilda," she reported. "Dale's looking for you."

Dale also wanted a private talk with me. So while his kids pawed through the dinosaur T-shirts, we sat down at one of the tables next to the concession stand. I just hoped he didn't have a screenplay he was peddling. But he wasn't even interested in Clara's career plans.

"Your detective pal, Styles," he began. "She working for Shirley Mayer?"

"I wouldn't know," I said, a bit snippily. "She doesn't discuss her cases with me."

It was bad enough that everybody in Eden knew who my relatives were. It was bad enough that everyone held me responsible for the actions of my own family. When they started expecting me to keep tabs on a Lone Ranger like Styles, a private investigator whom I'd first laid eyes on at my aunt's funeral, they really pushed my buttons. Just because we'd been involved in two cases together didn't mean she had my number on her automatic dialer. I'd had enough trouble keeping track of her when we were supposed to be working together. Now that those cases were closed, she could pursue her detecting while I ran my theater. Unless she was keen on dinosaur flicks, I didn't expect to bump into her in the near future.

"Anyway," I said, "what do you know about Shirley Mayer?"

"That was supposed to be my line," he responded evenly.

"I don't know anything," I said. "She's married to the man who used to be married to Oliver's cousin. I've met him. Leo. He has Alzheimer's disease, and he wandered into the theater one day. I heard she was in the hospital after she almost drowned in her backyard pool."

"Off the record," he said, regarding me keenly, "it was more than a drowning. She was poisoned."

"You mean, before she fell in the pool?" I asked, shocked.

"The pool water was poisoned," he said. "Somebody dumped a load of copper cyanide in the pool. Could have been a mistake, but probably not. There's a chemical used to treat pools that resembles copper cyanide in appearance, but it's not one that a pool service would have on hand. Anyway, I saw Styles there in the hospital room with Mrs. Mayer. I don't know what's going on. I don't even know if her work for Mrs. Mayer has anything to do with the attempt on Mrs. Mayer's life. She should be careful, that's all. Just talk to her, Gilda."

"Okay," I said. "Do you know who did it?"

He shook his head. "The woods are full of suspects."

He tapped my arm as we stood up. "Just Styles, Gilda. Nobody else should know about this. Officially, you don't even know. Understand?"

I felt tired. I turned to see my family clustered around the ticket booth, watching us with frank curiosity. One of them sported a purple dinosaur tail.

"Yeah, yeah," I said. "Secrets-R-Us."

5

I awoke earlier than usual the next day, prodded even by my subconscious to get up and start to work. By the end of the previous night, the concession stand had looked as if it had been cleaned out by a T. rex with a sweet tooth. And everybody in Eden County who hadn't seen *The Lost World* last night would want to see it this weekend. That meant a trip to the concession supplier in downtown Columbus, which always put a large hole in my day. On the other hand, I had more money to count and deposit than usual, so that cheered me up.

At the end of every night, we stashed our proceeds in a safe up on the second floor—a souvenir from the days when the building next door to the original theater, and now incorporated into it, had been a bank.

I'd been quiet coming up the stairs, suspecting that Faye, a budding documentary video maker, had fallen asleep over her editing table, as usual. Officially, she was spending the summer with Clara, her grandmother; unofficially, she, like Duke, lived in the old dressing rooms on the second and third floors of the theater. When my back had been turned, she'd moved in enough cameras, lights, sound, and editing equipment to shoot and cut *Lawrence of Arabia* on video. Most nights, she worked upstairs after the theater closed. Most days, I moved quietly. Today, I had an impulse to wake her up and make her recount the money. I wanted to share my excitement with someone, and Duke was out helping Todd, another of our student employees, move into a new apartment. Of course, we'd had the box office figures ready last night, as we did every night, for the ten-o'clock call from the Entertainment

27

Data Institute. But that wasn't the same as counting the cash, and it didn't take concession sales into account.

I tried sharing my excitement with the bored secretary on the other end of the phone at the distributor, but her lack of enthusiasm told me that she was accustomed to hearing higher numbers than mine daily.

There were ten phone messages waiting on the answering machine. Four were requests for donations. Two were inquiries about promotional slides. One was from a Little League baseball team whose sponsor had abruptly gone out of business; they wanted to know if we'd take over if they changed the name on their shirts with marking pens. One was from our booker.

One was from Gloria. "Gilda?" she said. "Listen, I've been to see Shirley Mayer in the hospital and she's desperate to find a nurse for Leo. She's afraid she won't be able to handle him when she gets home, and I guess her daughter isn't working out too well, but that's another story. And anyway, who can blame the daughter, when he's only her stepfather, and he's got three sons of his own, not to mention the daughters-in-law, who ought to be doing something for him besides complaining about what Shirley's doing. And the daughter has her own problems, or so I hear. But I seem to remember that Peachy has a friend or a relative or somebody who's a nurse, isn't that right? Somebody who specializes in geriatrics?" I heard a voice in the background. "So if—oh, yes, well that's one way to look at it, I guess. Oliver says somebody who specializes in keeping old farts in line. So if you could just call Peachy and ask her, I'd be so grateful. Oh! No, Oliver, I won't tell her that. Well, good-bye, dear."

I sat and stewed. This was so typical of my family. Gloria knew Peachy Gower, my best friend from high school. As the only funeral director in Eden, Ohio, Peachy knew everybody and everybody knew her. But could Gloria just pick up the phone and call Peachy herself? No, because everyone in my family seems to think of me as his or her personal assistant, adviser, go-between, and gopher. You'd think that the Paradise was a clearinghouse for Liberty family business rather than a movie theater. Val wanted me to talk to Clara. Wallace wanted me to talk to Clara. And now Gloria wanted me to talk to Peachy.

I listened to the last message on the answering machine.

"It's me. Look, I know you're deep in dinomania over there in Paradise, but if you get a minute, call me. It's about Leo Mayer." The voice belonged to S. Styles, private investigator.

About Leo, not Shirley? I thought. Had the poison been intended for him instead of Shirley? Or was Styles working on something totally unrelated?

I called Styles, but her answering machine answered. "I'm not here. Leave a message," it snarled.

I hung up and dialed the Gower Funeral Home. "Lunch?" I asked when I finally heard Peachy's voice.

"Not Hamburger Heaven," she said. "My clothes are getting tight."

"Has to be quick," I said.

"Pick me up," she said. "We'll go to Peg's."

Peachy, as usual, was stylishly attired, and managed to keep her silk pantsuit spotless while she attacked a messy Italian salad. I acquired a streak of mustard on my T-shirt as soon as we sat down to eat. We were almost through eating when I got around to asking about a nurse for Leo and Shirley Mayer.

"Gloria says you have a relative that specializes in geriatrics," I said.

She nodded. She was holding a pepper between her impeccably manicured thumb and forefinger. The color of her fingernails matched the color of her pantsuit. "That's James. You know James."

"Your *cousin* James?" I asked incredulously. "The wild man? He's a nurse?" I dunked a corner of my napkin into my glass of water and began rubbing the yellow stain that decorated my right breast. The napkin shredded and the stain grew.

"Well, a nurse's aide," she said. "He's studying to be a nurse. Matter of fact, he needs a new patient. One of his former employers just died, and his last one just went into a nursing home. He's kind of down in the dumps."

James down in the dumps must resemble Tina Turner on speed, I thought. I gave up on the shirt.

"The last time I saw James," I said, "he was dancing on a table at your sister's wedding."

"Mm-hmm, I believe he gave the Southern Baptists in the family enough to pray over for years."

"He sure had the moves, all right."

"And the energy," she added.

"And the nerve. Unless we think he just didn't notice the way your Aunt Bea was looking at him."

"He doesn't miss much," she said. "Not James."

"So James is going to be a nurse," I said. "Would he come nurse me when I'm old? I'll bet he's a lot of fun to have around."

"Patients seem to think so," Peachy observed. "Of course, for some people, he takes some getting used to. What's Shirley Mayer like?"

"I haven't the foggiest," I said.

As we were leaving, she paused before she put on her sun-glasses, looked at me, and tapped at the corner of her mouth. I swiped at the corresponding spot with my tongue and tasted mustard, then rubbed it with my thumb until she nodded approval. I don't know why she hangs out with a slob like me. It's a testament to her immaculateness that she comes away from our encounters unmarked.

While I restocked the concession stand later in the afternoon, I called Gloria with James's name and phone number. Now it was out of my hands, I figured.

At some point during that crazy weekend, when the main theater sold out for every showing of *The Lost World*, Ruth Hernandez mentioned to me that Lillian had told her that my mother had called to say that Gloria had reported that Shirley Mayer was delighted with James West, and had hired him. I was glad to have been of service. I was also reminded that I needed to find a place to live outside the bosom of my family. Antarctica came to mind, but the commute was impractical.

At any rate, I thought my conscience was clear. The Mayers

were taken care of; I checked them off my mental "To Do" list. I forgot to call Styles back again.

That was my big mistake.

6

I was awakened early Monday morning by a pounding on my bedroom door.

"Gilda!" Ruth bellowed. "Wake up and answer the phone! It's Styles and she sounds funny."

"Funny funny or mad funny?" I asked groggily into my pillow. If it was the latter, I wasn't about to answer the phone.

"Just funny. Pick up yourself and see."

I rolled over and regarded the telephone with sleepy annoyance. Reluctantly, I lifted the receiver.

"Yeah?" I said.

"It's me," said a voice that sounded as if it were making its way up from underground.

"Styles? Where are you?" I asked. "I can hardly hear you. You sound like you're in a tunnel, and whispering."

"I'm in the hospital. A tunnel would be more entertaining. Also more comfortable."

"The hospital?" I started guiltily. "Does this have anything to do with the Mayers?"

"Your relatives, the Mayers? Do bears shit in the woods?"

"*Distant* relatives, Styles," I corrected her. "So distant I can't even figure out how we're related."

"Know how I figured it out, cookie? It came to me in a flash, as I was flying through the air: yep, these folks sure are Libertys. It was my last conscious thought before I woke up in the hospital with a shaved head."

"What happened?"

"I don't want to talk about it on the phone," she said.

"Okay," I said. "I guess I can squeeze you in between the post office and the bank. You at Eden County?"

"Yeah, and I'm in no condition to be squeezed."

I heard a voice in the background.

Styles raised her voice from a whisper to a croak, and turned away from the phone. "Would you get out of here? I'm talking on the phone! My sorry butt will still be in this bed five minutes from now, so take a hike! Jesus!" she swore into the phone. "These nurses are getting on my nerves!"

"I'll bet you have their vote for Miss Congeniality, too. I'll be there in about half an hour."

Forty-five minutes later, I met a nurse coming out of Styles's room.

"Better not go in without protective gear," she warned me.

"You mean earplugs?" I asked. "It's okay, I'm used to her."

Nothing had prepared me for the shock of seeing Styles flat on her back in a hospital bed. She looked smaller than usual lying there in a pastel print hospital gown that showed none of the sartorial eccentricity that made her immediately recognizable as S. Styles, private investigator. She appeared to have her left leg elevated under the sheet. Her arm on the same side was in a sling. An IV tube was taped to her other wrist. But the biggest shock was her face. The right side was badly swollen, her right eye bloodshot and almost shut. Her short dark curls emerged from either side of a large bandage wrapped around her head like a modified turban.

If I'd been asked to identify the body, I thought morbidly, I would have had to look twice to be sure it was Styles.

She skewered me with her remaining eye. "Big day at the post office," she commented. Her voice was softer than usual, but the bite was there.

I was fighting to control my expression. "Not bad," I said. "I brought you some flowers." I held out my floral offering for her to see.

"Oh, goodie," she said, eyeing it with distaste. "Something to stir up my allergies."

"I'll bet the nice nurse will put them in water for you." I pulled a chair close to the bed and sat down. I laid the flowers on the table beside the bed. On the other side of the faded green curtain at my back, somebody was snoring.

"I'll bet she'll save 'em for my funeral, and dance on my grave," she retorted. She pressed a button, and the bed raised her to a sitting position. She looked like Dracula sitting up in his coffin.

"So what happened?" I asked.

"I was headed down to the basement to look for Leo's computer, and I tripped on a wire—"

I held up a hand. "Hold on."

"One."

"What?"

"I see one hand," she said. "How many are you holding up?"

"One."

"That's a relief. The doctor I had last night looked younger than Doogie Howser, so I told him he was holding up twelve fingers just to check on his knowledge of basic anatomy."

"Back up," I continued. "I don't even know what Shirley hired you for."

"Well, she didn't hire me to commit suicide. And she sure as hell didn't warn me that her house was booby-trapped."

"So somebody had used the old wire-across-the-stairs trick, and you—"

"Fell for it. Yes, indeedy. Give me a month or two, and I'll see the humor in it myself."

"Styles, I thought this martial art you study, this aikido, was supposed to train you to take falls." I wanted a cigarette, but I couldn't have one, so I picked up that plastic tube thing they give you after surgery to test your lung capacity.

"We're trained to take falls on cement," she said irritably, "not stairs."

"If this was a basement, wasn't there cement at the bottom?"

Her one eye glared at me. "I wouldn't know," she said. "I don't remember that part." She watched me fidget, then urged, "Go ahead. Test your lung capacity. Give me something to feel superior about."

I set the contraption down.

"So what did Shirley hire you for?" I asked.

"She hired me to find somebody named August or Auggie," she said, shifting uncomfortably.

"Who's he?"

"No idea. Somebody Leo talks about, worries about. She thinks maybe an army buddy, somebody he knew during the war. Leo keeps bringing him up, wants to talk to him, gets all upset about it, but can't tell her who he is."

"Have you tried to ask him?"

She started to nod, then thought better of it. The hand trailing the IV line touched her forehead. " 'Leo,' I said, 'I'm going to find Auggie for you. Can you give me some help?' He got very excited, said, 'I have to talk to Auggie.' 'I'll go get him for you,' I said. 'Where is he? Where's Auggie?' He said, 'I have to talk to Auggie.' That's pretty much how the whole conversation went."

"You asked if Auggie was in the army?"

"Every way I could think of. Does Auggie fly planes? That's what Leo did in the war—he served in an Air Force bomb squadron. Does Auggie live with you? Is Auggie an officer? Does Auggie have a jacket like yours? Is Auggie on KP? Is Auggie AWOL? Now I know a hell of a lot about what Auggie isn't and doesn't do. Another five years and I might find out who he is by process of elimination. The only thing I know for sure is that Leo is desperate to talk to him."

"Styles, when Leo wandered into the theater last week, he thought he was going to see a Ronald Colman movie. For all we know, Auggie could be dead."

"Sure he could," she agreed. "Especially if he's visited the Mayer house lately."

"So you know about the poisoned swimming pool," I said. I wanted reassurance that my failure to warn her hadn't resulted in the human wreckage before me. I didn't get it.

"What poisoned swimming pool?" Her one eye narrowed.

"I thought Shirley hit her head or had a ministroke or heat stroke or something."

"Apparently not," I admitted. I avoided her eye by glancing around the room as if taking in the decor. There wasn't any to speak of, just a large, probably mass-produced, possibly computer-generated abstract painting in colors best described as soothing. "Dale says somebody had dumped copper cyanide in the pool water."

"When exactly did Dale say this?" she asked suspiciously, putting her fingers to the bandage on her head again.

"I did try to return your call, Styles," I protested. "You weren't there."

"I didn't get the message."

"You want me to leave you a message about somebody trying to kill Shirley Mayer by dumping cyanide in the swimming pool?"

She sighed deeply. "Babe, I get stranger messages than that all the time."

The woman on the other side of the curtain stirred and coughed.

"Styles, *I'm* not even supposed to know," I said. "Dale just wanted you to be careful, that's all. So he told me to tell you."

"They don't have phone books at the Eden P.D.? We're in worse shape than I thought."

"Styles, everybody who wants to tell anybody anything tells me," I complained in exasperation. I leaned forward, elbows propped on my knees, palms up. "What is it I do that invites these confidences? Do I look like a secretary? What? If you know, tell me, and I'll quit doing it, I swear."

"Beats the hell out of me," she said testily. "Me, I have the opposite inclination. I don't want to tell you anything for fear I'll find out something I don't want to know."

"Doesn't it seem a little weird to you that Shirley would go to all the trouble of hiring you to find this guy Auggie, who may be long gone, when she's got somebody trying to kill her in her own backyard?"

"She called me before the pool accident," Styles said. "Then she had to call me back and change the meeting place from my office to her hospital room. It seems more than a little weird to me that she didn't mention that somebody was trying to kill her. About the other thing, it's hard to say. If she's got the money, why not? People will do a lot for dying loved ones. And there's no question that Leo has a bee in his bonnet about this Auggie person. Shirley said it seemed little enough to do to make him happy. She hasn't known him all that long, and for all she knows, this guy is his oldest and best friend or his long-lost brother."

"Leo may not recognize him if he was an army buddy," I pointed out.

"Yeah, she knows that, too. I'd say she's pretty realistic about the whole thing, but she says she'd never forgive herself if one day this Auggie showed up on her doorstep, looking for his buddy, and she had to face the fact that she could have brought them together and didn't."

"And why do we think she didn't tell you that somebody had just tried to kill her?"

Styles tried to shrug, and grimaced. "Who knows? Some people are embarrassed to admit they're so unpopular in certain circles that somebody'd try to eighty-six them. Or maybe she thinks murder is an indelicate subject, though she didn't strike me as especially prim. Or maybe she's afraid the family's involved. She didn't encourage me to expect a lot of help from two of Leo's three sons, so I gather there's friction there." She grimaced again.

"I should go," I said. "You look tired."

"I was sleepy when you came in," she said. "Now that my meds are wearing off, I hurt too much to sleep."

"Oh, I brought you another present, too," I said. "Close your eyes."

The only one open rolled around, then closed.

I wound up two little windup dinosaurs and put them on her table.

"Okay, you can look."

Something like a smile tugged at the available corner of her mouth as the lizards tap-danced across the level surface.

"Better than flowers," she said, "but you still owe me big."

I was closing her door when I was approached by two tanned, athletic-looking women with muscles the size of soccer balls under the skin of their forearms. I assumed they were players from Styles's softball team.

The two women looked at me. One of them was carrying a box. Neither of them was carrying flowers.

"Is Sammy in there?" one asked.

"What's left of her," I said.

From inside came an angry croak.

"Goddamnit, why can't somebody give me some meds when I need them for a change?"

The other woman nodded. "Oh, good," she said. "She's still got her voice."

7

I went home to eat lunch and work on our ads for the week. Afterward, I called Gloria for the Mayers' number, and then dialed it. The voice that answered sounded too young to belong to Leo, and it said, "Mayer residence."

"May I speak to James West?" I asked.

"This is he," the voice said, all business.

"James? It's Gilda," I said.

"G-il-l-l-da!" he trilled. "I don't believe it! It's been ages! Leo, you'd better catch me if I fall in a faint."

"I know you can't talk," I said. "But how's it going?"

"Fine, fine," he said. "Me and Leo just ate some Spaghet-tiOs, and then we felt like some potato chips and beer, so we had that. I don't know what we'll feel like next, but I'm kind of hoping to take a little walk around the neighborhood. Then

Leo promised to show me his photo albums." I heard a low rumble, and then James's voice, away from the phone. "Yes, you did, Leo, don't you remember? You said you'd show me some pictures of when you were in the army. Yeah, that's right, you remember that, don't you?" To me, James said, "He loves to talk about the army."

"Movies, too," I put in.

"Is that right? Leo, Gilda says you like movies. Oh, yes, I got a big smile on that one." More background noise. "Oh, you don't like movies as much as Gladys, huh?" In a low voice, he said to me, "Who the hell's Gladys? I don't think she's on the cast list Shirley gave me."

"A former wife, I think," I said. "Look, James, I need to talk to you in private. Would that be possible?"

"Of course! You can come over right now if you want to. Shirley's at the doctor, and talking in front of Leo's the same thing as talking in private. He won't remember a word you say."

"No, I don't think we should meet there," I said. "What time do you get off?"

"Not till six. Want to meet me at Oscar's? I haven't been there for years."

"Okay," I agreed. "I can't stay long, but there's something I need to talk to you about." I already had Styles on my conscience; I didn't want any further injuries to the unprepared.

"Okey-dokey," James said, "but I hope you're not planning to dish dirt on Leo and Shirley. I'm practically a member of the family already."

As I was hanging up, I heard that wistful voice again, the words distinct now: "I used to be in pictures."

James was a good-looking young man in his early thirties, with medium brown skin, a slight build, and muscles that stretched his sleeves tight. In college, he had been a hurdler and an intermural volleyball player, in spite of his small stature. He had an expressive face. Since I had last seen him, he had peroxided his hair and acquired diamond studs above the small silver rings in his ears. He wore a nurse's scrubs:

teal shirt over fuchsia pants. His tennis shoes were trimmed in glitter.

"Gilda!" he greeted me enthusiastically, as he threw open the door of Oscar's. All along the main aisle, heads popped out of booths to stare at him.

"James," I said, grinning. "Fashionable as ever, I see."

"Don't you love it?" he agreed complacently, opening his arms wide in a pose. "If I'd had to wear white all the time, I would never have taken up nursing. I'd have probably been a flight attendant, or a short-order cook, or something."

He folded his arms around me, and I hugged him back. Like me, my friend Peachy had some relations who were real doozies, but James was one of my favorites.

We sat down in a booth and ordered beers. I knew Duke would give me a disapproving look when he smelled it on my breath, but it wasn't as if I was projecting, and I thought one beer might actually enhance my performance at the ticket booth.

"How many beers did you and Leo have today?" I asked James.

"One between us," he said. "Leo thinks he had one, but I drank about half of it."

"So how are you really, James?" I asked. "Peachy says you've been down in the dumps."

He sighed. "It comes with the territory, Gillie," he said sadly. "It's not like my patients recover, most of them. Oh, sometimes I take on a short job—somebody like Shirley, usually somebody who fell and broke a hip or sprained an ankle. But most of my patients get worse. Nothing I can do about it but make them comfortable and keep them clean."

"How far along is Leo?" I asked, curious.

"Oh, I'd say he's in the early middle," James said, smiling at the waitress who set our beers on the table. "You can still hold a conversation with him, and you can still understand what he's saying. He may think you're somebody else, or that you and he are living fifty years ago, but he still speaks in full sentences, mostly. Sometimes he can really get going. Eventually, he won't be able to put the words together. When that happens, it's like a telephone conversation with a lot of static on the line, and you're only getting every fourth or fifth word. His voice will probably get softer, and after that—"

A swig of beer slipped past the lump in my throat. "After that?" I echoed.

"He'll stop talking altogether." He looked down at his glass, then looked up again. "Nothing wrong with his vocal cords now, though—he can cuss a blue streak when he gets mad. Shirley says she didn't even know he knew some of those words. It affects some of them like that, you know—the Alzheimer's. I had a patient, little bitty thing she was, and a pillar of her Southern Baptist church. Sweet as the day is long, until you crossed her, or she thought you did. Her daughter kept apologizing, kept following Ida Mae around the house, lecturing her about her language. I told her it wasn't anything her mother had any control over, but some people just can't understand the change."

"Does Leo ever talk about somebody named Auggie?"

"Yes, there was something about Auggie today. Let me see." James frowned and pursed his lips. "He wanted me to find Auggie so he could talk to him."

I leaned forward. "Did he tell you where to find Auggie?"

"Nope. We didn't get that far. I knew Auggie wasn't one of the kids, 'cause he wasn't on my list from Shirley. Like Gladys wasn't. I figured he was somebody from the past— you know, a friend from the old days.

"If you ask me, though, Shirley's doing the right thing, and she knows what she's doing," he said. "A lot of spouses can't accept the inevitable." He leaned back against the wall so that he could keep me in view while scanning the room for any other long-lost friends. James lived in Columbus now, but he probably still knew a lot of people in Eden.

"What do you mean? What's she doing?"

"She's trying to get all their affairs in order, she says. She knows all about Medicaid and nursing home coverage, and she even knows she hasn't got much time."

"What do you mean?" I said again.

He looked at me over his beer mug. "Girl, I thought you were in insurance. Isn't that what Peachy told me?"

"Property, mostly," I said. "Don't know beans about medical."

"Well," he said, with an air of taking me into his confidence, "if you want to qualify for Medicaid, to pay for the nursing home? It used to be you had to go into poverty to qualify—you know, spend everything you had? Well, that left the spouse with nothing for her old age, or his. You used to hear about Medicaid divorces, where the one who was well divorced the sick one just so the sick one would qualify for Medicaid. You can't imagine what that did to people. Anyway, now the government lets the spouse keep some assets and income—don't ask me how much; I don't know. And 'well' is a relative term, here, since sometimes the spouse is sick, too, just not sick enough for a nursing home, or else they don't want to leave their house. Meanwhile, you can do what people used to do—give away your assets to your kids or whoever so you can qualify. But here's the hitch: you have to do it more than three years before the patient enters the nursing home. Any assets you had within three years of the time the patient enters the nursing home count against you for Medicaid."

"So, wait." I leaned over the table. "What you're saying is that financially speaking, people should plan more than three years in advance to go into a nursing home, or put their spouse in a nursing home."

He nodded. "Just like Shirley's doing."

I glanced at my watch.

"Look, I have to leave," I said. "I have a date with some dinosaurs and if I'm not in the ticket booth on time, there'll be hell to pay from Duke. What I wanted to tell you was to be careful. Did Shirley tell you what happened to her?"

"In the pool?" he asked. "She almost drowned, I know that."

"Yeah, well, after the poison got to her, she almost drowned," I said, annoyed. If Shirley wouldn't tell James what was going

on, I had to, no matter what Dale said about confidentiality.
Shirley wasn't being fair to him.

"Poison?" he repeated, eyebrows lifting.

"Yeah, and then a detective she'd hired tripped on a wire
somebody had stretched across the basement stairs. The detective is still in the hospital. So keep your eyes open. And
don't tell her I told you."

"Wire?" he repeated. "Across the basement stairs?"

"And if you see anything suspicious—" I paused, picturing
Styles recumbent in her hospital bed. I sighed. "Call me."

8

"Gilda, I know Wallace asked you to speak to your aunt
Clara," Adele said.

She had found me in the four-car garage out behind Liberty House, where my Honda Civic rubbed fenders with a
Duesenberg, a Packard, and a Rolls. I was changing the spark
plugs on the Civic. She leaned in under the hood until her
cologne almost suffocated me and I was forced to withdraw
from the engine, spark plug in hand, coughing. Her bright orange hair glowed in the dark, and I could have used the extra
light if I could have given up breathing. But I didn't want her
dropping a false eyelash into the fuel injector.

"Adele," I said cautiously, "I haven't really had a chance—"

She cut me off. "The whole thing's ridiculous, of course.
She'll never do a horror film. She'll think of that godawful
movie Bette and Joan made together. Dreadful sets."

Translation: I could have done better.

"So you don't think—" I began.

"The problem with Wallace is, he doesn't think like a

businessman," she said. "In today's market, you can't expect to make a movie solely on the basis of a good script, now, can you?"

"Uh, I guess not," I said, leaning against the car and fishing a cigarette out of my pocket. If she was going to start lecturing me on the state of Hollywood today, I was in for a long wait.

"Of course not!" she insisted indignantly. "You have to know what's hot, as they say. That's why I did a little research. Do you know that there are *two* films slated for production that are set in Elizabethan England and feature Elizabeth as a character?"

"No," I said unhappily. I could see where this was headed, and I didn't like it.

"Two!" she reiterated. "Now, don't you think Clara would make a splendid Elizabeth?"

"I don't know, Adele," I admitted. "I never really saw Elizabeth as gamine."

"Of course you didn't!" she agreed. When she opened her eyes wide, her false eyelashes brushed her bangs. "That's because you always see her played as a shrew, stiff and commanding. Yet we know that Elizabeth was passionate." She raised a braceleted arm and pointed a finger at me. "What was she like behind closed doors? Who was she to her lovers in private?"

"Bette Davis?" I ventured.

"Clara Liberty," she corrected me. "Little Clara, with all the weight of her queenly duties pressing down on her shoulders." She pressed on her own polyester-clad padded shoulders with hands weighed down by rings. "And yet—in the privacy of the queen's closet"—she pronounced "privacy" with a short *I* for the sake of authenticity—"she abandons herself to the last great passion of her life."

"Wallace?" I inquired.

She looked at me, and a look of exasperation passed over her features. "Certainly not! He's not the right type at all, though I suppose he could play an evil minister. No, I was thinking of perhaps Mel Gibson or Robert Redford. What do you think?"

I focused my attention on the tip of my cigarette. "Do you, by any chance, have a screenplay for this romantic extravaganza?"

"I'm working on it," she affirmed. "I've already told Tobias I'm willing to share the credit with him if he'll go over it when I'm done."

"I'm sure he appreciated your magnanimity," I observed. "And the sets?"

"Gilda!" She grabbed my wrist. "Do you remember the sets I designed for Claudette Colbert and Alan Hale in *The King's Paramour*?"

I didn't, but she didn't notice.

"I love the Elizabethan period!" she enthused. "So challenging! All that dark wood and tapestry. The trick is to design a set that looks authentic, and yet facilitates the lighting."

"So have you talked to Clara about your idea?" I asked, crushing my cigarette out under the toe of my sneaker.

"Not yet," she said. "I thought since you were planning to talk to her anyway, you might lay the groundwork."

I sighed. "Wallace wants me to—"

"Oh, I know what Wallace wants," she interrupted. "I'm not saying you can't tell her about his idea. I'm merely suggesting that you offer her several options. And be sure to mention that Tobias will be working with me." She sniffed. "Wallace thinks that after one class, he can write a screenplay all by himself. I know better. I know mine will need some cleanup, perhaps a little work on the dialogue."

"Mmm," I said noncommitally. I turned back to the car with determination and bent over the engine. "Okay, I'll mention your script to Clara, Adele."

"Thank you, Gilda." She stuck her head under the hood to give me an uncharacteristic peck on the cheek, then withdrew in horror when she spotted a smudge of black against the riot of color in her flower-print blouse. She retreated, holding her arms out stiffly so that the contamination wouldn't spread.

No news is good news. At around five o'clock that afternoon, the phone rang at the theater and I made the mistake of answering.

"I'm collecting," said a hoarse voice on the other end.

"Styles?" I said. "Collecting what?"

"I need you to check out the stuff in the Mayers' basement," she croaked softly, sounding like a Mafia hit man reporting in code.

"After what happened to you?" I protested. "If you think I'm going down there, you're nuts."

"Look at it this way: you're not going to trip over a wire on the stairs."

"No, I'm the one who'll find the bomb in the toolbox."

"I'm not interested in the toolbox," she said. "At least, I don't think I am. I'm interested in files, papers, photographs, and Leo's computer."

"Styles," I said, and repeated a phrase I'd often threatened to have tattooed on my forehead, "I have a theater to run."

"Fine, babe," she rejoined acrimoniously. "Be that way. If it weren't for you, I'd be out doing my job, too, instead of lying here popping painkillers and living on Jell-O and banana pudding. Do you know what it's like to be immobilized and forced to listen to daytime television and Trinity Broadcasting? But if you don't have two hours in your busy schedule to help one of your own relatives—"

"What's the address?" I asked curtly.

"Twenty-two eleven American Eagle Drive."

"American Eagle?"

"It's a very patriotic subdivision."

"You'll have to let Shirley know I'm coming."

"She knows," Styles said, and hung up.

9

Shirley Mayer met me at the door wearing a flowered muumuu. The colors were so bright they hurt my eyes, bleary from too many hours at the computer working on ad layouts. Shirley was taller than Leo, and possibly younger, but it was hard to tell. She wore her black hair pulled back in some kind of knot, a style that showed off dramatic streaks of white that swept back from her temples. Her skin had the color, but not the texture, of faded leather, as if she had spent a lot of time in the sun before her confinement in the hospital. She had intelligent black eyes behind stylish gold-framed glasses. She was a handsome woman, and I was gratified to see that she was smoking.

"Gilda, I'm Shirley." She saw my eyes light on her cigarette, and held up her other hand. "Don't tell me; I don't want to hear it. I had seven smoke-free days in the damn hospital, and now my lungs will just have to deal with it." She stepped back from the door. "Come on in, and excuse the mess."

"How are you feeling?" I asked.

"Hah! Better than I felt in the hospital, that's for sure," she said, leading me into the living room.

James and Leo were watching *Days of Our Lives*. Or rather, James was watching *Days of Our Lives*, and Leo appeared to be watching James, as if James's expressions would give him a clue to what was happening on the screen. James's colors today could best be described as lime green and turquoise.

"Leo, how much you want to bet me that the shady-looking dude in the coffee shop was the redhead's first husband?" James was saying, pointing at the television screen.

Leo's head swiveled toward the screen, then back to James. "I don't know," he said. His eyes shifted in our direction. "Is he?"

"Let's go in the kitchen, and leave the boys to their soaps," Shirley said. She gave her husband's shoulder an affectionate squeeze as she passed.

"When's lunch?" he asked.

"You already had lunch, sweetie," she told him.

"Yeah, you did, Leo," James affirmed. "Don't you remember? You had a big old ham sandwich with lettuce and tomato and a pickle on the side and some ice cream for dessert."

"Oh, yeah," Leo said.

"Hey, Leo," I greeted him. "Remember me? I'm Gilda. I own the movie theater downtown. You came to see me the other day."

He flashed me a toothy grin. "I love movies. I used to be in pictures."

"You told me that," I said. "I'd like to hear more about it sometime."

"I can imitate Cary Grant."

"Okay, let's hear it."

Leo scrunched his face up and held up a hand pistol. "You dirty rat!" he said.

James and I exchanged looks.

"That's amazing," I said.

"Sometime you'll have to do James Cagney for us, Leo," James said.

"Who?" Leo said.

Shirley and I went into the kitchen and I sat down at the kitchen table, which was located in an alcove that looked out over the backyard and a small swimming pool.

"Want something to drink? Coffee? Tea? Martini?" Shirley asked. She opened the refrigerator and studied the contents. She looked at me over the refrigerator door. "Milk and cookies?

James made some jam thumbprint cookies yesterday. Well, Leo made the thumbprints."

"No, thanks," I said.

With the toe of one of her gold metallic scuffs, Shirley kicked the bottommost of several boxes labeled "Kitchen" that were stacked against the wall. "I'm still not unpacked," she said. "I'm thinking about holding a yard sale, and selling off everything that's in boxes. I figure if I haven't found it and used it by now, I don't need it. What do you think?"

I thought about all the boxes piled in the basement at Liberty House—boxes containing my old life, the one I shared with Liz. Maybe Shirley was on to something.

"Sounds good to me," I said.

"Say, I wanted to thank you for sending me James. He's a real kick in the pants, isn't he?" She snagged an ashtray—SOUVENIR OF THE FLORIDA KEYS—and set it, along with a packet of cigarettes and a lighter, on the table between us as she sat down.

I was beginning to get the idea that Shirley herself was what my grandmother would have called a pistol.

"I didn't have that much to do with it," I confessed, firing up a cigarette of my own, "but I'm glad you like him."

"He's great with Leo," she said. "I'm thinking of adopting him. I like him better than Leo's kids. Hell, I think I like him better than my own kid." Her black eyes glanced at me. "Don't quote me."

"I know what you mean," I said.

"That Styles is another one," she said. "Got quite a mouth on her. But smart as a whip, you can tell. So, you're helping her out. I felt terrible about her accident." She shook her head sadly.

"Well, it wasn't exactly an accident, was it, Shirley?" I observed. "Any more than what happened to you was an accident." Directness, especially on touchy subjects, went against all of my childhood training. But I'd already had occasion to discover that when I was standing in for Styles, unexpected things came out of my mouth.

She looked surprised. "Who told you that?"

"It doesn't matter," I said. "The point is, somebody's trying to kill you. Or Leo."

She froze, cigarette halfway to her lips. "Not Leo," she said. "Why would anybody kill Leo? He's harmless."

"Why would anybody kill you?"

She shrugged.

"Is it about money? Leo's kids? Your daughter?"

"Why do you say that?" She frowned.

"Shirley, unless your house was on the home and garden tour, who else would have access to it? I think we can rule out your bridge club, if you have one; I think they'd have noticed if the dummy had excused herself to go rig a wire across your basement stairs. Who else has a key? Is your plumber mad at you? Do you owe money to your cleaning service? Did you accumulate a big Bingo debt down in Florida before you skipped town?"

She sighed. "The cops questioned my son-in-law," she admitted finally. "But I don't think he did it."

"Why your son-in-law? Does he have a motive?"

"Leo loaned him money to start his business, and he's—well, he's fallen behind on the payments. I don't want to bankrupt my daughter's husband. Well, they're separated, but even if he becomes my daughter's ex-husband, I'm not out to ruin him. But I need to get our finances—Leo's and mine—in order. So I told him I'd give him to the end of the summer to catch up. Summer's his busy season, so it shouldn't be a problem for him. But they don't live within their means, never have. That's one reason I came down hard on him. They've got credit card debt you wouldn't believe. And it doesn't seem to bother them. My daughter's just as bad as he is."

"What business is your son-in-law in?" I asked.

"Pool maintenance."

"Oh."

She nodded at me and tipped her ash into the ashtray. "Yeah, so that's why the police are so interested in him. It's even worse than that, actually, because my daughter, Pauline, has a small picture-framing business that she runs out of her basement."

"And the wire was picture wire?" I guessed.

She nodded ruefully. "But I really don't think he did it. If I were the suspicious type, I'd think somebody was trying to frame my daughter—maybe not intending to kill me, but trying to turn me against her."

I didn't comment on this theory. In my book, anyone willing to use cyanide wasn't messing around. It was true that Shirley had been rescued in time, but her survival seemed to me completely fortuitous, especially given her age and, I had to admit as I took a puff on my own cigarette, the probable condition of her lungs. And on those grounds, I wasn't willing to delete Shirley's daughter from the list of suspects.

"Tell me something. Is Pauline in your will? I mean, if you died, what would she stand to inherit?"

"Well, everything. Leo told me he didn't need the money. He didn't want me to leave him anything, so I didn't, though now that he's sick and our finances are so iffy, I was thinking that maybe I should change my will so that if something happens to me, he'll be taken care of. It may not be necessary but that's what I'm trying to find out."

"Is Pauline in Leo's will?"

"Yes, he's left her a small bequest. But you surely don't think my own daughter is trying to knock me off!"

I didn't bother telling her that I considered it a possibility; instead, I said, "If your daughter comes into some money before she divorces her husband, then that money becomes part of the assets to be divided between them—or, at least, it could.

"Does Leo swim?" I asked. "Does he use the pool?"

"He goes in the pool. He doesn't really swim anymore, but he still likes the water."

"So he could have been the intended victim?"

"He doesn't go in by himself—I mean, he doesn't just go down there by himself and take a swim the way I do. I'd always be with him, either in the water or watching from the side."

"So the killer could have been after you or Leo or both of you."

"It could have been an accident," Shirley insisted. "The police said there's a chemical kind of like the one they found in the pool water—copper something or other that looks like the poison, only it's used to keep the pool clean. Alan, my son-in-law, says that's right."

"And does Alan think that it would be easy to switch the two by mistake?"

"Well," she conceded, "not really. He's never seen this cyanide stuff, claims it isn't anything a pool service would stock."

"I met your daughter—Pauline, isn't that right? Is she your only child?"

"That's right. Just Pauline."

"What about Leo's kids?" I asked. "Do you have a good relationship with them?"

She paused, and I could see that she was considering what to say. It was one thing to criticize your own kids; it was another to criticize your husband's.

"I have a pretty good relationship with Curt, the middle son. He at least seems willing to give me a chance. The other two, Larry and Milt—I'm not sure they really approve of me. Sometimes I get the impression they think I married Leo for his money—that I could see what was coming, and figured to make off like a bandit when he died. I'm probably just being overly sensitive, though, because we're—oh, just not the same kind of people, if you know what I mean. And there's the whole stepmother thing. They're polite to me, but kind of cold.

"It wasn't that way with me and Leo, of course, if that's what they think. We didn't know he was sick when we got married. I mean, he wasn't any more forgetful than I was at that point. Anyway, it just shows what they know about Alzheimer's if they think I'm going to come out of this ahead of the game."

"You said Leo didn't need money. Is he wealthy?"

"He's well off, as far as I can tell," she said. "His oldest son

Larry has been handling all of his finances. That's caused some friction, too, because I'm trying to find out what Leo has and I'm stepping on Larry's toes to do it."

"And I take it the other kids are on Larry's side?"

"I don't think the boys are especially close," she said slowly, tapping her cigarette on the side of the ashtray, "but they unite against me. Well, Milt and Larry do. And even Curt thinks I should let Larry handle Leo's finances and leave him alone. I'm sure Larry's doing a fine job, and I don't mean to insult him. It's just that I have the nursing home expenses to think about."

"You know that Leo will need a nursing home?" I asked.

She nodded. "Unless he dies first," she said ruefully. "And in the beginning it was hard enough to get the boys to admit that there was anything wrong with their father. I understood their resistance, but it didn't make things any easier. Now if I talk about planning for nursing home care, Larry acts like I'm plotting to dump Leo and run off with his money. Milt, he's the youngest—he's Leo's stockbroker. So every time I try to get a handle on Leo's finances, I'm stepping on toes there, too. But Leo could live in a nursing home for a long time; some A.D. patients do."

She sighed, and stubbed out her cigarette. "The government counts back three years when they calculate Medicaid eligibility. That means I should make arrangements now to divide up Leo's estate. You'd think the boys would be all for it. They'd get their money sooner rather than later. They'll have to pay taxes on anything over ten thousand, and Larry objects to the tax liability, but that's better than waiting until all Leo's money has been spent on the nursing home, and getting nothing, don't you think? And by getting the loans paid up, I'm just trying to be fair to everybody. But they're so suspicious!"

She shook her head. "I don't know why I'm telling you all this. I don't believe for a minute that they had anything to do with the poison in the pool or the wire on the stairs."

"They had a motive," I summarized. "Did they have an opportunity? Anyone could have poisoned the pool, but the wire on the stairs was different. Somebody had to get into the house to do that."

She shivered. "I gave them all keys to the house in case of emergency. Well, that makes sense, doesn't it? I didn't have James around when we first moved in, and anything could happen. I could drop dead of a heart attack, and Leo wouldn't know what to do. Or I might just run to the store while Leo was napping if I needed some milk, and get into a traffic accident."

"And Pauline has a key?"

"Yes."

"So any of Leo's kids or your daughter or son-in-law could have gotten into the house while you were away," I said. "Anyone else? Cleaning service? Housesitter?"

"Well, Margie, Oliver's sister—she has one," she said, thinking.

I was beginning to wonder if everybody who was remotely related to Shirley had one.

"And do you have a key hidden outside in case you get locked out?"

"Yes, there's one under the flowerpot on the front porch," she replied. When my face fell, she added, "This is Eden, Gilda, not Miami. You don't expect burglars to come looking under your flowerpots here. Look at all the lovely porch furniture people put out right in the middle of town, and nobody ever walks off with it. Anyway, the police are investigating, and I'm being careful."

"What about business interests? Does Leo still have any?"

She thought. "He still owns part of the company he started, but I don't think he has many official obligations. He attends board meetings once a year, but in the last year or two I think they just went out on his partner's boat. Bernie—Bernie Cutter, that's Leo's partner—Bernie knows he can't contribute, but they hold these so-called board meetings so that he can feel like he's still involved. It's sweet of them, really, and I'm grateful. Bernie's son runs the business now. Leo used to get calls sometimes when we were first married—he was serving as a kind of consultant. That's what he said, anyway; for all I know, they might have been asking where to find the key to the washroom."

"What exactly did Leo do?"

"He made television commercials. He had done other things before—educational and training films, I think. But from the fifties up until the time he retired, it was television commercials."

She focused her gaze on me. "Do you think these incidents could have something to do with Leo's business?" she asked hopefully. "I can't really think what it could be unless it has something to do with Leo's moving back into the area." She was talking herself out of it already. "Anyway, everybody knows he has Alzheimer's. How could he possibly pose any kind of threat?"

"I don't know. But the danger to you and Leo is real. You might start by getting the locks changed," I proposed.

"Oh, Gilda!" She sighed. "It's just not practical to live in a fortress when you have an Alzheimer's patient. James is here during the day, but he goes home at night, and I'm all by my-self with Leo for sixteen hours. People have to be able to get in if I'm incapacitated. Pauline used her key to let herself in the other day while I was busy drowning in the swimming pool."

"Okay," I said. "James knows."

To my surprise, she looked relieved. "That's good. I know I should have told him, but I couldn't quite bring myself—well, you understand. I mean, what do you say? Watch out for death traps around the house? If he had any sense, he'd tip his hat and ride off into the sunset. I wouldn't blame him."

"You have to warn anybody who spends time in the house," I said, not letting her off the hook.

"All right," she agreed. "My daughter knows, and she's the only other one in that category. The boys avoid their father. Well, Curt comes sometimes. Larry and Milt have been here two or three times, never with their families. Leo would love to spend time with his grandchildren, I know. We moved back here to be around family, but the family doesn't want to be around us. They'll be sorry when he's gone—that's what I tell myself."

"The boys live in Eden?"

She shook her head. "In Columbus. But it's only a forty-minute drive, for heaven's sake—less than that for Milt. My daughter lives here in town. Maybe I was being a little selfish moving closer to her than to them, but I don't think it would have made any difference in the frequency of their visits. And the way it's turned out, I'm lucky to be so close to her."

"Do you have any other family here?"

She made a face. "My ex. I don't have anything to do with him anymore, though Pauline sees him, of course. If he died, I might attend his funeral. Or I might just send an insincere note to his widow."

"Does he feel as hostile toward you as you do toward him?"

She laughed. "I wouldn't call it hostility, Gilda. I honestly couldn't care less about him. I think he feels the same way— if he ever thinks about me at all."

"Would he benefit in any way if you died?"

"Like I said, everything I have goes to Pauline." Sensing that she'd turned my attention back to an inconvenient target, she added, "Believe me, Gilda, it's not worth killing me for. And it'll be worth even less if I have to spend it for Leo's nursing home care."

"But if Leo predeceased you, you'd be worth more, right?"

"Well, yes, he insisted on leaving me something. I really don't know how much—I haven't seen his will. But he was adamant that he wanted to take care of me. He's really an old sweetie, Gilda. I wish you could have known him before."

"Me, too, though I think he's an old sweetie now."

I didn't know what I was fishing for, and I wished Styles were here to do her own detective work.

"I don't suppose you have any high-stakes business interests that would give somebody a motive to kill you?"

She grinned. "Not unless they know something I don't know. Maybe I'm about to win the Publishers Clearing House Sweepstakes."

I shook my head gravely. "No, my aunt Lillian claims she's going to win it."

James stuck his head in the door.

"Me and Leo are going for a walk around the neighborhood," he said. "Do you know where his jacket is?"

"Oh, it's on the table in the front hall," she said. "The phone was ringing when we came in and I forgot to hang it up." When he disappeared, she said to me, "I know it's eighty-something outside, but he's so attached to that damn jacket, and I figure, what the hell? If he dies of heat stroke, he dies of heat stroke. At this point, that's looking like the best we can hope for."

10

Shirley paused to light another cigarette, and expelled a breath of smoke. "Anyway, you didn't come here to talk about the accidents, you came to look through Leo's things."

"Yes," I said. "What can you tell me that might help me? You think Auggie was an army buddy?"

"Oh, that's just a guess," she said. "He's fixated on the war. That's the time he seems to keep returning to—the forties. He was attached to a bomber squadron in the Pacific theater— Burma and India. He's mentioned India a few times, seeing India." She made a wry face. "I'd do anything to make him happy, but that's clearly out of the question. Leo's traveling days are over. The move nearly killed us both, he was so confused and anxious and upset. I never heard him mention Auggie until about six months ago, and now he talks about Auggie all the time. If I can find Auggie for him, it seems little enough to do."

"What does he say when you ask him who Auggie is or where to find him?"

She laughed. "He says, 'Yeah, yeah, Auggie. I have to find Auggie. I need to talk to him.' Or he looks guilty and clams up, like a little boy with a secret. Once he said, 'Auggie doesn't know I'm sick. I have to tell Auggie I'm sick.' "

Pity clutched at my heart. "Leo knows he's sick?"

"Oh, sure," she said. "He doesn't really understand what's wrong with him, but he knows something is. He gets really depressed sometimes. One morning I found him sitting on the edge of the bed in his boxer shorts. 'I'm just no good anymore, Shirley,' he said. 'You shouldn't have married me.' He can be frighteningly lucid at times."

"What did you say?"

"I told him that there was nobody in the world I'd rather spend the rest of my life with. His eyes teared up, my eyes teared up, and we both sat there and bawled for a few minutes. But then he forgot why we were crying, and we went and ate breakfast."

"Where was Leo from originally?"

"The Dayton area. His family used to have a big place outside Dayton—a farm. Leo still owns it—leases it out to tenants, I believe. Larry would know. His brother died about ten years ago, so if he has any family left, I don't know them. He has Inez's family. Inez was his second wife, Oliver's cousin, the boys' mother. She died of cancer. In fact, we're invited to a family picnic on the Fourth. James is coming along. Leo's boys will be there. I know they won't approve of me taking Leo; he'll embarrass them. But they'll just have to put up with it. This is the only family he's got, and he ought to be able to see them while he still recognizes them."

"James is going?" I asked. "I'm surprised. There's usually a big Gower-West family shindig out at his uncle's."

"Ours starts at noon," she said, "and we'll only stay an hour or so, if Leo lasts that long. James said his barbecue started in the late afternoon. Honestly, Gilda, I'm already dreading the long weekend without James, so I'm really grateful that he's willing to give me a few hours on Friday. After taking care of

Leo on my own for so long, it's such a relief to have help. And I'm not quite my old self yet, either."

The Libertys, of course, had their own version of the Fourth of July family extravaganza, stage-managed by my aunt Adele and her daughter Greer. At Liberty House, Ruth Hernandez had already started blowing up red, white, and blue balloons, which had been bouncing around the dining room for the past two days. Boxes of matching tableware, cups, glasses, and paper tablecloths had already shown up in the kitchen.

"I'll ask about Auggie at the picnic," Shirley said, "unless you find him in the basement this afternoon."

She stood up. I followed her to the basement stairs, and winced when I saw how steep they were. It was worse at the bottom, where the cement had cracked, probably prior to contact with Styles's head, though I couldn't be sure; I couldn't see any blood, except for the dark rust-colored vein where it had seeped into the crack.

She caught me staring at it.

"You will be careful down here, won't you?" she said.

11

"Start with the computer," Styles had advised me over the phone from her sickbed. "It could be as easy as that. Shirley says Leo used to use e-mail, but she doesn't know how to use it herself. She doesn't even seem to know if she's still paying for an Internet server, since Larry pays most of the bills. I don't think it's occurred to her that she could probably ask her daughter to try and find Auggie on the computer. If we find him that easily, I won't charge, unless it involves a major hack."

"Styles," I said doubtfully, "I'm no computer whiz."

She had armed me with a list of passwords to try if I wanted to check his e-mail, including the names of his kids and his wives.

"If that doesn't work, bring the computer to me," she'd said, "along with any disks you find."

I found the computer under a tarp in the corner, along with more packing boxes and an old army footlocker. On the footlocker was stenciled "Pvt. Leo F. Mayer." It called to me, but I dutifully dragged the computer over to a sturdy wooden workbench and plugged it in. I breathed a sigh of relief when it played the Windows 95 theme song, and was even more gratified to see a shortcut to AOL on his desktop. That was when it occurred to me that I needed a phone line. I'd told Styles I wasn't a computer whiz, but that was an understatement; I was generally acknowledged to be the Charlie Chaplin of machinery by everyone who knew me, including my coworkers at the Paradise and Dale Ferguson.

I went to the bottom of the stairs and looked up. No wires had appeared since I'd come down. I saw no buckets of water overhead. No visible booby traps. I went back to the computer, disconnected all the cords, and carried the box upstairs to the kitchen table.

Shirley saw me coming. "Oh, Lord, let me make sure James has Leo down for his nap. If not, he'll want to play on his computer."

It struck me that she sounded like she was talking about a toddler. I watched her leave the room, pondering the insight that must come early to the loved ones and caretakers of Alzheimer's patients: Leo was growing backward. His mental tapes were on rewind. That was what James had been describing, too, when he said that Leo's language would deteriorate, from sentences to words to silence. Except that babies were only silent before they were born.

I went back to the basement for the monitor and keyboard,

again taking the stairs carefully and listening for the sound of impending disaster. There was nothing.

I plugged in the phone line, and clicked on the dial-up icon without much hope. I heard the modem dialing. Then the moment arrived when I would have to come up with a password. I started with the list Styles had given me, and came up dry. With Shirley's help, I tried other things—Leo's brother's name, his mother's first name and maiden name, the name of his former dog, the name of the street they lived on in Florida.

Exasperated, I was about to turn the whole thing over to Styles and her hackers when I had another thought. I typed in "Auggie."

"You've got mail!" Mr. AOL announced cheerfully.

" 'Auggie' is his password," I told Shirley.

She looked at me, then at the computer.

"He must be important," she said softly.

"Yes," I agreed.

But important or not, Auggie had not sent any mail to Leo that I could find, nor had Leo sent any mail to Auggie.

"Does Leo ever talk about his childhood?" I asked, flexing my keyboard-cramped fingers.

"Sometimes," Shirley said.

"So what do you know about it?"

She thought. "Not much, really. His mother died when he was young—six or seven, I think. He had an older brother, Shelly. All the stories I've heard are pretty typical kid stories."

"He grew up on a farm?"

"Not a working farm, I don't think; they just called it 'the farm.' "

"What did his father do?"

"I really don't know, isn't that funny? I know he was a businessman of some kind, but I don't know what business he was in."

"Shirley," I ventured, " 'Auggie' couldn't be the name of a beloved pet or something, could it?"

"You mean like 'Auggie Doggie'?"

She started to giggle. Then I started. Then the giggles turned into gales and we were clutching our chests and choking on laughter. That brought James on the run.

"What is it with you two?" he demanded. "Shirl, baby, you don't have the lungs to sustain this kind of carrying on. What's so funny?"

Shirley looked chastened. She lowered her chin and made an effort to control herself. She mumbled something.

"What?" James asked, leaning forward.

"Auggie Doggie," she repeated in a louder voice, and then we were off again. Tears streamed down our cheeks. Shirley coughed.

James, normally the first to laugh at anything, shook his head over us.

"Shirley, you'd better make up your mind if you want to laugh or smoke," he admonished her sternly. "You're going to pass out if you try to do both."

"Aw, go suck an egg, James," she said, surprising both of us into fresh peals of laughter.

"Yeah, James," I said, gasping. "Don't be such a party pooper."

"P-p-party pooper!" Shirley exploded.

"You dames are nuts," James said dismissively. "I'm going out to stick my feet in the pool. Leo's taking his nap. Call me if y'all need CPR."

We wiped our eyes and blew our noses. I signed off AOL. Somebody would have to read through all the mail in Leo's files for any mention of Auggie, but that seemed like a good job for a bedridden detective with one hand available for mousework and one eye available for reading. I had a theater to run, and would soon have a house full of kids running up and down the aisles and sticking their gum to the bottoms of their seats during that outburst of hilarity and mayhem known as the kiddie matinee.

I came close to losing it again when Shirley set a plate of jam thumbprint cookies on the table. They looked like a collection of cartoon eyes. I sneaked a peek at her. The edges of her mouth were twitching.

"Leo had trouble finding the center of the cookie," she said.

I did everything I could think of to search the computer for a file with Auggie's name on it or in it. I couldn't find anything. I turned the computer off.

There were still the boxes of papers in the basement—and the footlocker. I had high hopes for that footlocker.

12

When I opened it, the footlocker released that distinctive aroma of the past when it has been locked away for safe-keeping. Here was a collection of mementos from a defining moment in Leo's life, and in all their lives—my parents, all my aunts and uncles, the young people of their generation.

On top of the pile was a small box I recognized by its size and shape. Inside was a Purple Heart. Under the box lay two faded patches. One was in the distinctive chevron of the military: a roaring tiger above an eagle carrying bombs in its talons. The other was round, and showed a death's head superimposed on a pair of aviator's wings.

There was a packet of black-and-white photographs, most labeled. The first one of Leo as a young man took me off guard. How old was he in the picture? I wondered. He looked about fifteen. But it was the same smile, the same Leo, behind the boyish nonchalance. There were pictures of men relaxing in front of barracks, men clowning around, men digging latrine trenches, men posing in front of planes, men posing with local people who did indeed look Indian. There was even one of Leo inside the plane, sitting in front of a gun of some kind. And there were, as it turned out, dogs. There were three of them captured for posterity, and they all must have been mascots. But if I was reading the labels correctly, there was a Buster, a Bomber, and a Snafu, but no Auggie.

From the papers, including Leo's discharge papers, I gathered that he had been a member of the 490th Bomb Squadron of the 341st Bombardment Group, which operated in the CBI, or China-Burma-India theater. Someone had obviously written a short history of the unit in the days before e-mail, and had photocopied this typewritten document and sent it to his old pals, or maybe distributed it at a reunion. I gathered from this history that Leo's unit was nicknamed the Burma Bridge Busters. I resolved to search the Web later for a site devoted to the 341st. Perhaps it would have a roster I could scan for somebody named "August."

There were other memorabilia, too. There were leaflets in a script I didn't recognize but guessed might be a Burmese language. There was a notice, apparently posted in the plane, listing the people who had bought war bonds to support the troops; at the bottom, it said, "They Ride With You." There was even a bill for a local movie theater called the Imperial, a "House of Comfort and the Best Pictures," that promised "You'll agree with us that Every picture of the programme is Entertaining and Smashing Hit ever offered, so folks Come one Come all—It's a chance of your lifetime!"

I was considering whether we were underselling the Paradise in our own ads when I heard a step on the stairs behind me and turned to confront the vision of Leo in his boxer shorts and brown bomber jacket, barefoot and hair mussed, standing at the foot of the stairs. He started toward me with his shuffling gait.

"Leo," I greeted him in surprise. "Where are James and Shirley?"

"I don't know," he said. "I was asleep."

The logic of this response impressed me. Leo definitely had some brainpower left, even if he used it sparingly.

"That's my footlocker," he said, pointing, "from the army."

"I know," I acknowledged. I now had a rare opportunity for a guided tour through the locker's contents, albeit with an inarticulate guide. Should I go check on Shirley and James? I felt torn.

"My pictures," he said. He squatted and picked up the bundle.

"Have a box," I said, catching his arm and guiding him to sit down on the box next to the one I was sitting on.

He began to go through the pictures. His expression was blank at first. Then he gave a small cry of recognition.

"Oh, there's—" He pointed at the man in the photograph and frowned. "He was a bastard," Leo declared suddenly, to my amazement. "Don't fly with him," he cautioned me.

"I won't," I assured him.

"There's old Finney," he said when he saw the next picture. "Good old Finney. He had a dog."

"Bomber?" I ventured.

"Bomber," he repeated. "Finney would hold up a piece of meat, and that dog would dance around on his hind legs. Then Finney would say, 'Sing for your supper,' and he sang." Leo flashed me an impish smile. "It didn't sound very good, but maybe to another dog, it did."

I studied his face as he went through the rest of the pictures, making occasional comments. I wondered if certain stories had been told so often that he could repeat them, right through the punch lines, far more easily than he could invent new stories with new words.

"Latrines," he said, and made a face at me.

"Did you have to dig latrines, Leo?"

"They made Shorty do it," he rejoined enigmatically. "Shorty mouthed off, and they made him do it. He was always mouthing off."

Another picture stirred him into a state of excitement. "Look!" He pointed at a picture of a field. In the foreground, several people who looked Indian were facing the camera and pointing off to their left. But Leo was pointing at the field in the background. "That's where it happened! Right there!" He looked at me, as if to make certain that I was following him.

"What happened, Leo?"

"It was Madison," he said excitedly. "Right there! He went

in low, took a hit in the right wing. And then, right there—Smoke, there was a hell of a lot of smoke. But Madison, he was the only one. It was right there!"

He looked at me again. I nodded and picked up the photograph to reveal the one under it: this one showed a downed plane, burning.

"Madison," Leo said sadly. "He didn't make it."

I couldn't tell if the field in which the plane was burning was the same field as the one in the background of the previous shot, but I thought it probably was. Once again, Leo's memory was outrunning his words.

"Look!" He said excitedly. "The Last Resort! She came there!" He tapped the figure of a woman. She appeared to be performing on a stage, with a microphone in front of her.

I leaned closer. "Is that Ann Sheridan?"

"Ann Sheridan," he repeated, nodding.

"Was the Last Resort a USO canteen?"

"Red Cross," he said. His face changed suddenly: his brows knit, his lips pressed together, his eyes grew unreadable. "The minstrel show," he said softly.

In the photograph were several figures in blackface performing on a small stage before a large audience.

To my amazement, he tore the photograph in half and dropped the pieces in his lap.

"Why'd you do that, Leo?" I asked gently. "Don't you like minstrel shows?"

"I don't like minstrel shows," he repeated, and went on to the next picture.

The last shot in the pile was of a plane on a short runway, its propellers blurry with motion.

"Glip," Leo said.

I thought I'd misunderstood him. "Glip?" I echoed.

"How we took out the bridges," he said clearly. He held up one hand, palm down, fingers low, and swooped in a shallow dive over the footlocker. "You have to glide in low. Stop the Jap supplies."

"Were you a pilot?"

He shook his head. "Tail gunner." He smiled wryly. "Last man out."

"And you got hit? Is that how you got your Purple Heart?"

He looked down and pulled back the right side of his bomber jacket. With his other hand he pointed at two faint scars over his lower ribcage.

"Christmas present. Song Hoa," he said. "That bridge was a son of a bitch."

"Was Auggie with you?" I asked. "In India and Burma?"

"Auggie?" he repeated. I thought for a minute he didn't know who I meant. Then he said, as if making a mental note to himself, "I have to talk to Auggie."

"Was Auggie in the war with you?" I persisted.

"No," he said.

"Auggie wasn't in the war with you," I reiterated, just to confirm what he was saying.

"Not in the war," he said.

"Was he here at home while you were in the war?" I asked.

He looked at me, confused, so I gave it up for the moment.

"Look, Leo, here's your uniform."

I held up the shirt for him to see, and he broke into a broad smile. He patted it lovingly, then patted his stomach.

"I'm too skinny now," he said. This was a surprisingly accurate assessment of how the uniform would fit him. The young man in the photographs had not been heavy, but he had been muscular—much bigger than the diminished version before me.

Leo reached down and picked up something from the bottom of the footlocker—something that must have been under the uniform. It was a packet of letters, neatly bundled with string.

"India," he sighed. He raised the letters to his nose, and breathed deeply. "It smells like India," he said wistfully.

"May I smell?" I asked, and he held them out to me. I didn't know what India smelled like, but I did catch the faint scent of something I couldn't describe. The folded letter on the side of the packet presented to my nose was written in a decidedly feminine hand, but that's all I could tell, except that

I could make out the word "Love," even upside down, and a row of small *X*s and *O*s.

Voices overhead were calling him.

"He's down here with me, in the basement," I yelled.

Again, Leo did something odd. He glanced nervously in the direction of the stairs and then carefully returned the letters to the bottom of the trunk. I laid the uniform on top of them and gave him a conspiratorial wink. If Leo didn't want Shirley to read his V-mail from a bygone girlfriend, I would help him hide it from her. Styles would have to decide whether or not to go through them for any mention of Auggie.

Shirley descended the stairs with her hair wrapped in a towel. James was right behind her.

"How did he get past the gate?" Shirley asked.

"He probably figured out that he could step over it," James said. "I told you he would. We'll have to rig up something better."

"Shirley," Leo said, beaming at her as if her appearance were an unanticipated pleasure.

She shook her head at him. "What am I going to do with you?" she asked, but she was smiling. "What are you doing down here?"

"He was just—" I looked around at the papers and photographs, patches, medal, and memorabilia. "He was just taking me on a tour of his past."

13

I had been checking the wiring on one of the speakers behind the stage on Thursday; Duke had detected a slight buzz coming from that direction the night before. I am hardly, as

I've already made clear, the family electrician, but I figured I could spot a loose wire as well as Donald Duck. When I turned off the backstage lights, the theater was dark, since I hadn't bothered with the house lights. Duke had a thing about saving electricity, and I was sufficiently cowed to go crashing around in the dark half the time, reluctant even to switch on my flashlight unless I sensed imminent peril. I didn't sense it this time.

An odd hiss issued from the speaker just in front of me, and I dropped the wire I was holding. The hiss resolved itself into a long, drawn-out whisper: "Gil-l-l-l-da-a-a."

A light hit the screen, and in the center of it, the unmistakable silhouette of a Tyrannosaurus rex.

"Very funny, Uncle Ollie," I called in the direction of the projection booth. I heard a muffled snickering coming from the speakers.

I met him in the lobby.

"How did you know it was me?" He chortled, wiping his eyes.

"Between you, Citizen Kane, and a genuine T. rex, you seemed the most likely suspect," I said dryly.

"Aw, Gillie, you have to admit, it was good," he said cheerfully. "You know, you ought to get more fun out of life! Loosen up a little!"

This was Uncle Oliver's constant refrain where I was concerned, and there was just enough truth in it to sour my disposition even further.

"You're not still upset over—you know," he said, his features rearranging themselves in a worried expression. "Are you?"

"Liz?"

He nodded uncomfortably.

I had to admit that whereas most of my family chose to deal with tragedy—real tragedy, the kind that couldn't be stage-managed—by ignoring it, Oliver at least tried to talk about it. In this way, he showed genuine concern, and I was touched.

"Liz who?" I said, though I choked a little on the "who."

"That's the spirit," he said, clapping me on the back. I

flinched as I always did when Oliver tried to touch me. He was a veteran hand buzzer, and you literally never knew what he had up his sleeve, even when he was in a tender, avuncular mood. He'd been known to forget he was armed.

But now that my eyes were adjusting to the brighter light of the lobby, I could see quite clearly what he had in his hand. It was a bundle of papers, standard size, more than two inches thick, rubber-banded together.

"Say, Gillie," he said, attaching himself to my elbow, "I hear you've been talking to Clara about her comeback."

"To tell you the truth, Uncle Ollie, I haven't had a chance yet," I admitted reluctantly.

Why I feel compelled to honesty where my family is concerned baffles me. They are all of them, in their hearts of hearts, scriptwriters, which makes them all, with the possible exception of my father, fundamentally dishonest people. They don't see it that way, of course. They lived too many years of their lives in a world where past and future were fluid, almost infinitely revisable up to the final cut, and even, sometimes, beyond, if the previews went badly.

Oliver beamed at me. "Well, that's fine, Gillie," he said approvingly. "That's just fine. The truth is, I was hoping you'd put in a good word for my own humble effort." He hefted the script up in case I'd missed it.

"That's a humble effort?" I asked. "It looks like King Kong's doorstop."

"Do you think it's too long?" he responded. He regarded it like a fond but worried father.

"Not for *Shoah*," I said, "but it might run a bit long for a comedy."

"I put everything I had into it, Gillie," he confessed.

"Well, maybe you should save some for Clara's second movie," I suggested.

"Why, that's a very good idea," he said. "Thank you, Gilda."

"De nada." I was hoping he'd be in a hurry to start rewriting, but apparently not.

"Would you like to hear the plot?" he asked hopefully.

I lit a cigarette and sat down at one of the small tables near the concession stand. Oliver set his opus on the table but remained standing, no doubt in order to act out the more hilarious scenes. He took a deep breath and raised his hands as if holding a basketball, or maybe a crystal ball in which we could both see his film as it would play at the premiere.

"Keep it short, Ollie," I warned him. "It's Thursday."

"Thursday! Right!" he said, nodding.

Thursday was the day when films changed, if they were changing, and I had a new one to make up for the side theater—a dismal also-ran from Miramax that would be out in video next month. Before she'd died, my aunt Maesie had trained the family to regard Thursdays as sacred days when she was not to be disturbed.

"The short version," Oliver agreed. "Clara plays the grandmother of this girl who's getting married, Julia Roberts or Gwyneth Paltrow—"

"Clara will never agree to Roberts or Paltrow," I put in. "They'll upstage her."

"Okay, so she's the grandmother to this girl who's getting married, but the thing of it is, the family has never met the groom until the week before the wedding, see? And he turns out to be a fabulously wealthy, titled count from Monaco—"

"Why Monaco?"

"Well, to tell you the truth, Gillie, I don't know much about European aristocrats these days, so I picked a country nobody else would know anything about, either," he confessed.

"People know about Prince Rainier and Princess Grace," I pointed out. "They may be the only titled aristocrats in Monaco."

"You think I should have picked Luxembourg?"

"Go on."

"So he's a wealthy, titled count from Luxembourg, handsome, and about twenty years older than the girl."

I made circling motions with my hand to indicate that he should pick up the pace, though I knew that if I wanted the short version I should quit interrupting him.

"He falls in love with the grandmother."

"With Clara?" I said.

"Yes, but you see, there's another complication."

"The difference in their ages?"

"No, now wait, Gilda," he said, watching my face eagerly. "His father arrives for the wedding."

"And *he* falls in love with the grandmother," I guessed.

"Well, yes, but it's not quite like that, because he was in love with the grandmother before, you see." He sliced the air with one hand. "He was her first husband." He delivered this pronouncement proudly.

"So who does the girl marry?"

"The father's valet."

"Who's he?"

"The valet? He's just a valet."

"He's not somebody's first, second, or third husband? Not a formerly famous film director?"

"No, he's just a valet. But he's very nice."

"And handy around the house. And who does the grandmother marry?"

"The father, her former husband."

I counted on my fingers. "The son? Who does the son marry?"

"Oh, this is the really good part," he said, rubbing his hands. "It turns out he's gay. He runs off with the male stripper from the girl's bachelorette party. But before that, there's a lot of funny stuff about both the father and son flirting with the grandmother, and getting jealous, and all that. Well, what do you think?"

"It has real possibilities—sort of a cross between *My Best Friend's Wedding* and *Philadelphia Story*," I heard myself saying. I hated to admit it, but it was true. Oliver's story had enough in it of what was selling these days, and Clara would get to play a romantic lead, which would tickle her no end.

"Do you think that giving the grandmother a pet leopard would be over the top?" he asked anxiously.

"Over the top," I agreed.

The phone rang and I went to answer it.

"I think you should go to this picnic," said the voice on the other end, recognizable, after consideration, as Styles's.

"What picnic?" I was still wondering if there were counts in Luxembourg, and if so, if the counts had valets in this day and age.

"Shirley's family picnic. Fourth of July," she said.

"As what? Her bodyguard?" I quipped.

"Well, I wouldn't carry a six-shooter unless you're a fast draw, babe, but I think you should keep your eyes open," she said. "No, I want you to ask around about Auggie."

"I gather you didn't find anything on the computer disks I brought you."

"Nope. Not much there. But somebody's bound to have heard of him. And I want you to scope out the rest of the family, see if you can get a line on who wants Shirley dead."

"So what do you want me to do, walk up to people and say, 'Hi, I'm investigating murder attempts on Shirley Mayer and do you expect to inherit?' "

"You'll think of something," she said. "You're a Liberty. There were a few odd things in Leo's e-mail, though."

"Such as?"

"Why would a retired seventy-one-year-old former producer of television commercials want a supply of perchloroethylene? Well, make that seventy; he was seventy when he ordered it."

"What is it?"

"Chemical solvent, toxic, carcinogenic," she said. "Not easy to find these days. Used primarily in dry cleaning."

"Beats me," I said. "I've never seen any around here. Did he order any copper cyanide?" I asked apprehensively. What if Leo had tried to help out by cleaning the pool himself?

"Not that I can find, but I may call the chemical supply and ask. So, if I talk to Shirley, will you go to the picnic?"

"You know, Styles—"

She finished the sentence with me. "—I have a theater to run."

"Cookie, nobody goes to the movies on the Fourth of July.

In the afternoon they're watching parades, and at night the soundtrack would be drowned out by the fireworks."

"Styles," I said, "you ever hear a dinosaur roar?"

14

We made quite an entrance at the Wilcox-Devereaux family picnic. James had gone patriotic for the occasion and was dressed, for once, in primary colors: his pants were navy and his shirt appeared to be made from an American flag. With his peroxided hair on top and his glitter-trimmed tennis shoes down below, he was quite a sight.

"Where do you get this stuff?" I'd asked him, fingering the shirt. I couldn't believe that the average nurse's supply carried anything like this.

"Girl, you got to know where to shop," he'd said with a wink. "Wait until dark." He'd leaned closer. "The shoes light up."

"You'll have to come by the theater later and show me," I'd said.

Shirley wore a smock dress striped like a beach towel in colors so bright they hurt my eyes. Leo wore polyester pants in a lemon yellow I wouldn't have thought viable from a marketing standpoint, but he had a yellow-and-purple plaid shirt to match. On his head was the ball cap I'd brought him: NOTHING RUNS LIKE A DINOSAUR. Apparently, James and Shirley had succeeded in separating him from his bomber jacket for the occasion.

I was the restrained one in our party. I wore white denim shorts and a DINOPHILE T-shirt.

I was more than a little apprehensive. I'd never been around this many of my Uncle Oliver's relatives at once, and I was hoping they weren't all merry pranksters like him. If they were, I was in for a long couple of hours.

The gathering was at Oliver's sister Margie's place. Like Liberty House, it was a large nineteenth-century house surrounded by land, some of it woods and some pasture, that extended down to the Scioto River.

The day was hot, so we steered Shirley and Leo toward the shade. There were some people, mostly kids, fishing from the riverbank. A group of energetic older kids and teenagers were playing volleyball in the sun. Some of the smaller kids, well supervised, were playing a haphazard game of croquet on the lawn with plastic mallets and foam-rubber balls. Margie's husband Gus waved at us from the built-in brick barbecue pit. He wore an apron, and he was surrounded by men. The gestures and the intensity of their conversation suggested that they were debating the physics of laying the fire. Oliver was among them.

Margie introduced me to the circle of people who were sitting in the shade, most of whose names I promptly forgot, with two exceptions. Sarah Mayer, a well-turned out brunette wearing a white silk pantsuit and very dark glasses, was married to Leo's oldest son Larry. She rose from her lawn chair and gave Leo a peck on the cheek. Diane Mayer, a sturdier and less elegant blonde with her thick hair ballooning out from a ponytail, was married to Milt, Leo's youngest. Diane looked wilted from the heat, but she also stood and gave both Shirley and Leo a perfunctory hug—the kind people give when they are sticky with sweat and wish they could avoid human contact. In the game of musical lawn chairs that followed, I drew her as my nearest neighbor.

I lit a cigarette.

"I didn't know nurses smoked anymore," Diane volunteered.

It took me a minute to understand her. "I'm not a nurse," I said. "James is your father-in-law's nurse—nurse's aide, really." I nodded at James, who had made a beeline for Sarah, with Leo in tow. Like a cat, James showed an unfailing attraction to people who disliked him, and Sarah's polite smile had curdled at the edges. No doubt Sarah was also having some trouble accepting a nurse who wore an American flag and twice as many earrings as she did.

"Oh," Diane said. "But you're wearing white."

In a manner of speaking, this was true, though I couldn't remember when I'd seen a nurse trotting the hospital floors in a dinosaur T-shirt.

"I don't think nurses are required to wear white anymore, except in hospitals, maybe," I said. "Private nurses probably follow their own rules."

"Well, call me old-fashioned," she said, smiling, "but I still think it's strange that a man would want to take up nursing, unless he's—" She let it trail off.

I considered showing my annoyance; after all, if I remembered correctly, I had been gay when I'd last had a sex life—a time that was rapidly fading into the mists of memory. But I was too hot. I was also determined to be on my best behavior. Some people's best behavior is better than other people's, I thought self-righteously.

"I'll have to introduce you to Spike some time," I said.

"Spike?"

"He took up nursing when his boxing career ended. He claims to have a girlfriend named Lulu." When last I saw him, Spike, whose scrubs ran to muted colors like beige and khaki, had backed Styles's father up against a wall to take his temperature. He'd had an arm like a ham planted like a restraining bar across Jake's chest.

Two girls in shorts and crop tops interrupted to ask if they could go down to the river and stick their feet in the water. They were given permission, suitably cautioned, and raced off, ponytails flying.

A smaller urchin in a checkered sunsuit approached me solemnly, carrying a half-full plastic cup of pink lemonade. "Here," she said, thrusting it toward me.

I took it and thanked her. She retreated for a whispered conversation with Sarah, whom I took to be her mother.

She returned with another half-full plastic cup. I thought perhaps it was my other half.

"I already have one," I said, holding mine up to show her.

"Chin-chin," the cup-bearer replied soberly, reaching up with her cup to bump mine.

"Chin-chin," I responded.

That seemed to satisfy her, and she went away.

"That Bethie is a cutie pie, isn't she?" Diane said.

"Yes. She belongs to Larry, I take it? I'm eager to meet Leo's sons," I told her.

"I haven't seen Curt yet," she said, craning her neck to check out the growing crowd, "but Milt and Larry were with Gus the last I saw of them. You know," she said, leaning in confidentially, "it's so hard for them to see their father like this. Milt gets so upset! Leo was brilliant, you see, not educated, I don't mean that, but a very successful businessman." She sighed, gazing discreetly at her father-in-law. "You'd never know it now, would you? Milt says to me, 'Honey, if I ever get Alzheimer's, just shoot me and put me out of my misery.' "

Not knowing quite how to respond, I tried a sympathetic smile and excused myself. I ambled over to where the men were gathered. Why men considered charcoal lighting and outdoor cooking a sacred male rite mystified me. As I approached, there was a *whoosh*, and a tongue of flame leapt from the grill. Everyone stepped back. The man in front of me landed on my foot.

"Yow!" I cried.

"Sorry! Didn't see you there!" he said. "You all right?" He put his hands on my arm as if I might now need help walking but I brushed him off with a reassurance more polite than I wanted it to be.

Gus introduced me to everyone. The man who'd stepped on my foot was Larry, Leo's oldest, a gray-haired man with glasses and a mustache. He had Leo's eyes, behind tortoise-shell glasses, and forehead, but not his million-dollar grin. He looked tan and healthy. Milt, Leo's youngest, looked more like his brother than like Leo, though his hair was blond, probably styled, and he had the intense green eyes that can only come from contact lenses. Milt sported a natural tan, as well, and muscles that probably owed their definition to the weight room at a gym or health club. He had a kind of restless energy about him; he never seemed to stand still. Sunglasses dangled from a cord around his neck. I was hoping for an opportunity to cut Larry and Milt out from the herd, but they did it for me.

"Ever been here, Gilda?" Larry said hospitably. "Let me show you around." He took my elbow and steered me away before I had a chance to say that I'd been to Margie and Gus's place on numerous occasions with my side of the family.

Milt tagged along. As we headed into the sun, he put his sunglasses on. They were blue metallic wraparounds. Then he took out a handkerchief and blew his nose.

"Summer cold?" I asked.

"Allergies," he said, and grinned.

"Your father seems to be enjoying himself," I observed, looking toward the group under the trees and catching sight of Leo's magical smile.

Larry looked in Leo's direction. "Yes, he does. Let's hope it lasts."

We had started down the hill toward the river when we heard a shout behind us. The man loping toward us was stockier than either of the two men I was with. He had a corona of brown hair, and he was smiling—a wide, toothy, boomerang smile.

"It's Curt," Larry said as we waited for the other man to catch up.

Curt was sweating heavily. When he reached us, he leaned over, like a sprinter who has just finished a race, and planted his hands on dimpled knees that showed under his plaid Bermudas.

"Whooh!" he gasped. "It's a good thing that was downhill."

He straightened, removed a handkerchief from his pocket, and mopped his forehead. There were dark rings under his arms.

"This is Gilda," Larry said. "She's Gloria's niece, but she came with Dad and Shirley."

Curt beamed at me and applied the handkerchief to his palm before offering me his hand to shake. It was soft and moist.

When Curt had caught his breath, we walked on. We stopped to watch some people fishing in the river. Milt picked up a stone and skimmed it across the water.

I asked, "Has Shirley asked any of you about Auggie?"

I knew she had, but I wanted to see what they'd say.

"Yes, she has," Larry replied, "but none of us knows who he is."

"He was probably an old army buddy of Dad's," Larry went on. "Dad was in the Air Force—the Army Air Force is what it was in those days. I guess it was pretty important to him—first time off the farm and all that. He saw the world. This Auggie guy was probably somebody he knew in the Air Force."

"Have you ever heard him mention Auggie?" I asked.

"Only in the past few months," Larry said.

Milt shook his head as he blew his nose. He was circling us like a retriever, eyes on the ground, looking for more stones to skim.

"Is it true she's hired a detective to find this Auggie person?" Curt asked. "Do you know, Gilda?"

"Yes, I think she has," I responded.

"Now there's a waste of money," Larry observed, folding his arms. "Understand, I wouldn't be opposed to it if, say, Dad was in his right mind and had an old buddy he wanted to find and knew the guy's first and last name. But we don't even have a surname for this Auggie person, or any information about when and where Leo knew him. That's like searching for a needle in a haystack. This detective is going to rack up a lot of hours and come up with zilch."

"It's some girl," Milt said. He had given up on the stones and picked up a stick, which he twirled between his fingers. "The detective, I mean. That's what Shirley told me. I don't know where she dug this one up."

I doubted that Shirley had called Styles a "girl." I doubted that anyone who had encountered her had ever called Styles a "girl."

"Probably the same place she dug up the nurse," Milt added. Larry shot him a look of reproach.

"You guys catching anything?" Curt asked the fishers, who were mostly teenage boys.

He received several humorous and contradictory responses to this question. We started back up the hill, Milt swiping at the occasional tall weed with his stick.

"We're a little concerned about some of the decisions Shirley's made, that's all, right, guys?" Curt favored me with another smile, although he was puffing a little. "The nurse seems a little strange. Oh, he's probably got credentials, but he doesn't really look like he could handle Dad."

It was a hot day. The grass on which we stood shone a dazzling green, and in the woods and fields around us, cicadas buzzed. I turned toward the volleyball court, where James and some of the other men had joined the game. As I watched, James served a hard, fast ball that whizzed past some buff athletic types on the other side of the net.

"I don't know," I said reflectively. "He looks pretty powerful to me."

"You know, Gilda, there are a lot of people out there who prey on the elderly," Curt said. "We just don't want Shirley to be taken advantage of."

"It's not the money," Larry said.

The other two murmured assent.

"I don't know what Shirley's told you, Gilda," Larry continued, glancing at my face, "but there's been some friction between us. You have to understand our perspective. We've known Dad a lot longer than she has."

"We're family," Milt put in.

"Two of us, Milt and I, we work in the financial area," Larry went on. "We're professionals. We've been managing Dad's finances for a long time. My accounting firm pays all of Dad's bills, and Milt oversees his portfolio. He had complete faith in us. Now Shirley wants to take over." He spread his hands, palms up. "Shirley thinks it's a personal thing. She thinks we hate her or resent her for marrying Dad. But it's not personal. What does she know about estate planning or managing a stock portfolio? We know that Dad's going to incur some big medical expenses, and we're planning for that."

"I was under the impression that Shirley was only trying to reduce the estate now so that Leo would qualify for Medicaid when he had to go into a nursing home," I said. "It sounds to me like that would be in your best interests as well."

"Yes, that's what she thinks, but it's complicated," Larry said. "We're going to end up paying a lot of taxes on what we inherit, and believe me, Gilda, accountants hate to pay the government any more than we have to. She's going about it the wrong way. If she asked me, I could do it for her. But she wants to do it herself. For example, she's calling in loans that don't need to be called in—something Leo would never do if he were healthy."

"She's calling them in or asking that the payments be up-to-date?"

"Well, the latter, but it's totally unnecessary," Larry replied. "And it's going to be a hardship on us and even on her own daughter."

"Can't the two of you work something out together?"

"Larry's more than willing to do that, Gilda," Curt cut in, "if you can get Shirley to agree."

Larry nodded. "She hasn't really been very interested in working with me, I'm afraid."

"She's probably got some crackpot lawyer or financial adviser who's been feeding her some line," Milt said. He was bouncing on the balls of his feet like a runner preparing for a race.

"See, that's what we mean, Gilda," Curt said. "She can so easily be taken advantage of. She's really vulnerable."

"I know what you mean," I agreed. "After all, somebody has tried to kill her twice, which kind of fits in the category of being taken advantage of." I glanced at their faces. They exchanged looks.

"She told you that?" Larry asked.

"Not in those words, no," I said.

"It's true there have been some unfortunate accidents," Curt conceded. "The police came to talk to all of us about Shirley."

"Accidents are what happens when the cause is unintentional," I objected. "Are you saying that the poison in the pool and the wire on the stairs weren't intended to cause harm?"

"I didn't see the wire on the stairs," Curt said, "but the poison in the pool—"

"Well, we know who did that," Milt said, grinning under his blue shades, red cords loosely looped over his ears. "We just don't know whether it was an accident or stupidity."

"Are you suggesting that Pauline's husband did it when he serviced the pool?" I asked.

"We don't really know anything for sure, Gilda," Curt acknowledged. "It's just that Alan Kline serviced the pool the day before Shirley . . . well, had her accident."

"But why would he want to kill his mother-in-law?" I asked.

"Why would anybody want to kill Shirley?" Milt expostulated. "The whole thing's ridiculous."

"It could have been an accident," Curt said. "I understand that this copper cyanide stuff looks a lot like some other chemical they use to keep the pool clean."

"Alan's no Einstein," Larry agreed. "We're pretty sure he's literate, but frankly, we could be wrong."

We had drifted close to a picnic table on which lay a bowl of salsa and a bag of chips.

"I happen to know that Leo loaned Alan some money to get his business started," Larry said. He frowned as Milt crammed a handful of chips in his mouth. Milt caught the look and grinned at him. "And now Shirley is pressuring him to pay up. Not that I really believe that the guy is a killer. The wire on the stairs sounds like kid stuff to me—you know, like a prank."

I flashed on Styles in the hospital bed.

I decided to change tack. "How long have you been Leo's accountant, Larry? I think it's really great that you've been looking after all his financial affairs for him."

Milt snickered through a mouthful of chips, and said nastily, "Daddy's little helper, that's our Larry, eh, Curt?"

Larry ignored him. "Well, it makes sense, really. When Dad moved to Florida, he didn't want the responsibility anymore, and I'd been doing his taxes and giving him advice for years, so we just arranged things so I could administer his finances for him."

"You mean you set up a trust?" I didn't understand what that meant, only that some older people did it.

"Something like that," he agreed amiably.

"Only Shirley doesn't trust him," Milt put in. Larry ignored him.

"So you're the only one who doesn't work in the financial area?" I asked Curt. "What do you do?"

"I'm in industrial supply."

Milt was patting his pockets. "Say, I left something in the car. Gilda, nice meeting you! Catch you later, bros."

Larry and Curt decided to go find Larry's family, leaving me to look for Leo and Shirley.

Leo was taking a walk in the garden with Shirley and a tall white-haired man I didn't recognize. From a distance it struck me that Shirley was moving as slowly as Leo was. They both appeared old. They were admiring Gus's tomatoes when I caught up with them and introduced myself to their companion. The white-haired man turned out to be Glenn Wilcox, brother to Inez, Leo's second wife.

"Leo and me go way back," he said. "Used to be old fishin' buddies. You remember that, Leo? When we used to get away from the women and go up to the lake and fish?"

Leo grinned at him. Eyes twinkling, he shook an index finger at his old friend. "You never caught anything," he said.

Glenn laughed. "Why, you old so-and-so! I did, too! Who landed the biggest bluegill ever caught in that damn lake?"

"I did," Leo said, enjoying his joke.

"Yeah, you did," Glenn conceded, and winked at him. "Just seeing if you remember."

"Some things I remember," Leo said.

"Yeah, you remember the big ones, not the little ones," Glenn said.

"You live in Eden, Glenn?" I asked.

"No, I live on the south side of Columbus," he said. "Don't

get up here much at all anymore. Haven't seen this fellow in, gosh, I don't know how long it's been. Two—three years?"

"Not that long," Shirley said, laughing. "You went fishing in March a year ago, when we were up from Florida."

"No, that can't be right!" he protested. "March a year ago? I don't think so," he said. "Did we catch anything?"

"Nothing he brought home with him," Shirley said.

"I must have repressed it," he said. He turned toward the garden. "Would you look at the size of those tomatoes, Leo? You used to grow tomatoes like that."

"No, I didn't," Leo contradicted him.

"Yes, you did, don't you remember? You liked those Rutgers tomatoes," Glenn said.

"I liked Better Boy and Beefmaster," Leo said, changing his story easily. He bent down to touch a ripe tomato.

"Those too," Glenn agreed, clapping him on the back.

"You and Glenn have something in common, Gilda," Shirley told me. "Gloria told me you used to work for an insurance company. That's what Glenn did before he retired."

We swapped company names and specialties then, as we were expected to do—a conversation that bored both of us. Shirley took Leo to watch the fishing, and Glenn and I drifted toward the beer. I spotted Curt, with Bethie riding his shoulders. Curt was red-faced and panting, but he was laughing, in spite of the grip Bethie maintained on what little hair he had left. Then he bent forward and flipped her, giggling, to the ground, setting her gently on her feet.

I asked Glenn about Auggie.

"Auggie. Auggie," he said slowly, turning it over in his mind. He shook his head. He bent over the cooler, fished out a beer and offered it to me. I shook my head. He straightened, and popped the top. "Boy, that doesn't ring a bell. I knew a kid named Auggie when I was growing up in Cleveland, but I doubt it could be the same person. Leo was from the Dayton area originally—I forget the name of the town. Sorry, I can't help you, Gilda. You know who you should talk to? You should talk to Bernie Cutter, Leo's business partner. He and Leo go way back. He might be able to help you.

"Say, did you see Leo in the parade today? He marched with the VFW, I heard."

"I didn't see it," I admitted.

"It's a damn shame, what's happened to him," Glenn said, looking off into the distance. "He was always such a bright, happy guy. He took good care of Inez when she got sick, too. I'm glad to see he's got somebody to take care of him. She seems like a special lady, that Shirley."

"I think so, too," I said. "Listen, Glenn, do you have any advice for me about where to look for Auggie if Cutter can't help me?"

He passed a hand over his face and rubbed his jaw. "Gee, Gilda, that's a pretty tall order, isn't it? He could be somebody from Leo's childhood, like the Auggie I knew. It does sound more like a kid's name."

"I don't think so," I said. "He doesn't talk about his childhood much. He talks about the war, and the times after that. What do you know about Leo's war experience?"

"Well, he was attached to a bomb squadron in Burma, I know that," he said, and took a swig of his beer. "Trained somewhere in Texas and then in India. He liked the military, stayed active in the VFW. You might check with them for this Auggie."

"He didn't go to college on the GI Bill?"

"No, he never went to college. He'd been working for his family before the war—"

"What did they do—his family?"

"What did they do?" He stared into space. "Isn't that funny, I can't remember. Getting like Leo, I guess. Anyway, by the time Inez met him, he was working for a movie company in Columbus—industrial training films, mostly. Then, he got all hepped up about television. The first time he saw one, he had to have one, and then and there he decided that television was the wave of the future. Well, sir, he went and talked this Bernie Cutter into starting a business to make television commercials." He laughed and shook his head. "It sounded pretty crazy in those days, I can tell you. It was the early fifties, and radio still ruled the roost, so to speak. I thought I was going to have to support my sister in poverty. Well, I don't have to tell you Leo was right. I expect he could have bought me twice over before he was through. Not that I begrudged him any of it! He worked hard, and he had vision, Leo did. Why, the company's still in business and still going strong—that tells you something right there."

"I understand that it's being run by the son of Leo's former partner."

"Yes, so I hear. Don? Dan? Dick? What the hell was his name? David! That was it."

"How do I find Cutter Senior?"

"Oh, you'd better call the company for that. I wouldn't know. Mayer and Cutter. It's still called Mayer and Cutter. You can look it up in the book."

"Can you think of any other family or friends I could talk to?"

"No family. His mother died when he was a kid, and his dad died during the war. Leo had a brother out west—Seattle, Portland, some place like that—but he died about ten years back. Sheldon was his name. Nice guy. Met him a few times when he came east on business. I don't know about other friends. You might find some in Florida, or high-school friends. I guess I was his best friend."

"Were you his insurance agent?"

"Yes, I sold him all his policies—life, health, home, and auto."

"Glenn, you might have heard about Shirley's accident," I said, looking up at him.

He frowned. "Yes, yes, I did hear about that. She looks pretty good to me for a woman who almost drowned, but she's not the old Shirley."

"There have been two accidents around the house," I said slowly. "Both were potentially fatal. I know it's not entirely kosher, but do you know who's named as the beneficiary on Leo's life insurance policy?"

He stared at me. "Leo's policy? Why, I haven't looked at it for ages—no reason to, and now I'm retired. But I don't remember anything unusual about it. I'm sure the money goes into his estate to be divided by the boys, though come to think of it, now that he's remarried, he might have changed the beneficiary. He would have contacted the company directly at the time of his marriage, most likely, if he wanted to make a change."

"And you wouldn't happen to know if Shirley has a life policy?"

"No idea. I was already retired by the time she came along, so she was safe from my advances." He winked at me. Then his smile disappeared. "But, say, Gilda, if you're suggesting that anyone would harm Leo or Shirley to collect their insurance—" He let it hang, waiting for me to interrupt. When I didn't, he cleared his throat and finished his sentence. "Well, I guess I have to say I think you're way off base."

"I'm glad you think so," I said.

He cleared his throat again.

"We used to go fishing together—well, you heard about that. We haven't seen each other much these past few years, but I talked to him on the phone, and then after we both got e-mail, we kept up that way." Glenn smiled at me. "He was always sending me jokes." He sobered up and looked away again. "And then—well, I guess he couldn't manage the computer anymore. I talked to him on the phone a few times." He sighed heavily. "It was pretty sad. I'll see him more often now, though."

In the distance I could see James coming our way.

"You didn't go fishing with him last year, did you?" I asked.

Glenn looked uneasy. "Well, no, I didn't. But I can't tell her that. He used to go to a hell of a lot of army reunions, I know that, so maybe she just has it mixed up. Unless—"

"—he went someplace else," I finished.

Glenn nodded. "Maybe he went to talk to Auggie."

15

"Yeah?"

"Styles?" I said a little uncertainly. I was sitting in the small office behind the concession stand at the Paradise, and the low rumble of the ice machine made me doubt the accuracy of my hearing.

"Who wants her?" The voice sounded like a good imitation of a Hollywood mafioso—not Brando, but someone lower down on the food chain.

"Spike?" I asked, startled.

"Yeah. Who's this?"

"Spike, it's Gilda. What are you doing there?"

"Gilda!" he said with enthusiasm. "Hey, how you doin'? The old man sent me up here to look after Sammy for awhile."

"Jake sent you?" I grinned. So Jake Styles had retaliated. When Styles's father had returned from a recent hospital stay expecting a lovely Latina named Carmen in a sexy white nurse's uniform, he'd found himself in the care of a hulking former boxer named Carmine, a.k.a. Spike.

"Yeah, well, he was getting along pretty good, you know, and Sammy didn't have nobody to stay with her," Spike explained. His voice dropped. "Say, Gilda, she's worse than her old man. I don't like to get physical, but jeez, she's askin' for it. I had to hide the damn crutches! She don't have no business running around with a concussion, but you can't tell her nothin'! Was she like this before she cracked her head?"

I assured him that she had been stubborn before, and that her disposition did not improve upon acquaintance, in my limited experience. "How are you getting along with the animals?" I asked. Spike loved animals, and animals loved him.

"Aw, just great, Gilda," he said. I could tell he was smiling. "Matter of fact, I got one of my little helpers on my shoulder right now. Here, say hi to Bogey. Bogey, it's Gilda."

If Bogey said hi to me, I didn't hear it. Then Spike was back. "Aw, isn't that cute? He's purring at you! Claws are kinda sharp, though."

"He gets that from his mom," I said. "The purr must come from his dad."

"You want to talk to her? She's banging away on the computer. Don't worry; I take it away from her every couple hours."

I heard a growl in the background that drowned out Bogey's purr.

"What did I do to deserve this?" Styles grumbled in my ear.

"You sicced Spike on your dad," I reminded her. "It's payback time. Have you found anything on the computer?"

"I'm following a few leads," she reported. "Mostly I've got a lot of inquiries out to people who used to correspond with Leo on e-mail, and to his Air Force unit. Nothing so far."

"Is this just about Auggie, or about who wants to kill Shirley?" I asked.

"Both," she replied. "I've run credit checks and security checks on all the kids—Shirley's as well as Leo's."

"You can do that?"

"Cookie, not only can I do it, I earn a living doing it."

"I thought you earned a living by following people around with a camera hidden behind your tie clip."

"That too."

"So what did you find out?"

"All the Mayer boys are clean, though Milt seems to have had some trouble about ten years back."

"What kind of trouble?"

"Bad credit. His dad probably bailed him out. Pauline and Alan Kline appear to have Daffy Duck for a financial adviser. Alan also did some county time twenty years ago for assault and battery—typical macho barroom bullshit, from the looks of it.

"Leo's own finances are going to take a little longer to sort out. There's nothing wrong with his credit rating, but I'd like to take a look at his bank accounts and stock holdings. I have a hacker working on compiling the raw data, based on some account numbers Shirley dug up. I might have to bring in a financial consultant to translate it."

"You can find out that stuff?"

"Welcome to the nineties, sweetheart. Of course, that's assuming that all of his accounts are really at the banks Shirley's identified for me and all of his stock is handled by Milt's brokerage. There may be other accounts she doesn't know about."

"Milt has his own brokerage?"

"No, no, he works for a place called Johnson and Cramer. He's just a broker, unlike Larry, who's a vice president at his firm."

"Styles, what if Leo had a secret life?" I proposed.

"As what? A dry cleaner?"

"You're still hung up on that chemical he ordered—"

"Perchloroethylene."

"Whatever. But I found out that Curt's in the industrial supply business. Maybe Curt ordered it, or Leo ordered it for Curt."

"Possible," Styles conceded. "I'm willing to entertain all possibilities, babe."

"When did he order it?"

"A year-and-a-half ago. I found the order in his electronic trash bin."

"It's not used for anything besides dry cleaning?"

"Lots of things. It's a solvent, a degreaser. Actually not used for much of anything anymore, because of its toxicity. It's getting harder and harder to find."

"So Curt might have recommended it to clean some piece of equipment Leo had. Did he buy a lot of it?"

"Five gallons. That doesn't sound like a lot to me, but if the stuff is highly toxic, it's probably enough."

"Enough for what? To wipe out the Ft. Lauderdale checkers club?"

"He didn't have it shipped to Florida," she said. "He had it shipped to Pleasant Ridge, Ohio."

"Pleasant Ridge?" I repeated. "Is that near Dayton?"

I heard a rustle of paper on the other end. "The way I read the map, it's not near anything, unless you count Xenia, Beavercreek, Wilberforce, and Yellow Springs. But yeah, the closest big city is Dayton."

"Shirley seems to think that he still owns the family farm. People seem to think it wasn't a working farm, but maybe this solvent he ordered is used on farm machinery."

"In that case, I hope they're farming truffles. This shit is expensive—seventy-five big ones for five gallons."

"Or maybe he liked to fix up old cars or something, and he did it there because he had more space and his wife wouldn't let him take up the garage," I suggested. "And speaking of chemicals, what have you found out about copper cyanide? Who's likely to have it lying around?"

"It's a germicide, like the copper sulfate they add to pool water to keep it free from algae. It's also a preservative. Used in paints and in electroplating."

"So is it the kind of thing an industrial supply house would have on hand?"

"Depends on the type of industrial supply house we're talking about. Curt works for Guilford Supply, which specializes in cutting tools and abrasives. My sources say that it's unlikely they'd carry copper cyanide. Or even perchloroethylene, for that matter, though that would be more likely. Want to go on a field trip?"

"Right. Like I'm really going to waltz into an industrial supply place in my shorts and sneaks and ask if they have two unrelated but highly toxic chemicals in stock."

"Babe, where's your sense of adventure?"

"I run an independent movie theater," I told her. "It's all used up."

"Well, I want to hear about Leo's secret life."

I grunted. "You're just saying that. You probably already know more about it than I do."

I told her about the fictional fishing trip. "I talked to Shirley afterward," I said. "She said he used to go off to army reunions by himself, and sometimes back here on Mayer and Cutter business. Sometimes he went to Dayton to Wright-Patterson, she says, as some kind of consultant on a museum there, which sounds pretty unlikely to me. She always wanted to see where he grew up, and he promised to take her sometime, but then they never got around to it. She got the impression he never really wanted her to go for some reason, so she didn't push it. She thought maybe he didn't want her chatting up the locals and hearing stories of his misspent youth."

"Did he have a misspent youth?"

"She doesn't know. She's guessing."

"She must've picked him up at the airport. She know for sure where he went on these trips?"

"Not exactly where, only the airports. When he was going to Wright-Pat, he flew to Dayton. Otherwise—Chicago, Atlanta, Dallas."

"Hub cities."

"Right," I agreed.

"Army reunions, huh? And she believed him?"

"Says she had no reason to doubt him."

"Can you get a list of dates from her? Airports, if she remembers them?"

"I don't think it would be very accurate," I said doubtfully. "And anyway, whose case is this?"

"I'll go halfsies with you," she offered.

I snorted. "That'll be the day!"

"There's some other stuff in his e-mail I'd like you to look at," she said. "Movie stuff, I think. Meanwhile, somebody should go to Pleasant Ridge. I'd do it, but Spike stole my crutches."

"Auggie might be there," I agreed. "You know, Styles, we might be barking up the wrong tree for Shirley's would-be killer. Maybe he or she is related to whatever Leo was doing in Pleasant Ridge."

"Right. And there's still the business partner to talk to. What's his name? Bernie something?"

"Bernie Cutter."

"Yeah, Cutter."

"I still like the kids for it, though," she said. "Any of the kids. Murder usually is a family affair."

"I don't know," I told her. "If Larry's finances are solid, and he's a legitimate accountant, which he seems to be, I guess I can understand why he wouldn't want to hand everything over to Shirley to manage. I kind of sympathize with his perspective, even though I like Shirley better."

"You're just a sucker for a guy with a big spreadsheet," Styles commented. "Anyway, the important thing now is to make sure nothing else happens to Shirley."

As it turned out, we were already too late.

16

Nobody answered the phone at the Mayers', and since it was Sunday morning, I concluded that they might be at church. According to Styles, Leo was a nonobservant Jew but Shirley was a Methodist. I was uneasy. The would-be killer was probably ready to strike again. I left a message asking Shirley to call me.

I had been relying on Styles, I realized, to do most of the brainwork in this case. She was the professional, and besides, my mind had been on other things—giant lizards in particular. But now I realized that there was some truth behind all of Styles's whining. She was not operating to her full mental capacity. The concussion and the drugs had taken their toll. Whether I liked it or not, if I wanted to keep Shirley and Leo safe, I was going to have to do more thinking on my own, and I was going to have to think the way Styles would if she were really thinking. But I was due at Clara's for brunch at noon, where I could have a nice, private talk with her about her comeback plans.

I went down to the kitchen for a cup of coffee to accompany my first cigarette of the day. I was sitting on the back porch, enjoying the peace and quiet, when Lillian, dressed in full gardening regalia, rounded the corner of the house. She had never grown accustomed to wearing pants, so she wore a cotton shirtwaist, along with what my mother would have called "sensible shoes" and a venerable straw hat. She was carrying a large basket, and appeared to be using her cane to crush any offending weeds in her path. Ruth Hernandez, wearing peach-colored slacks and a print polyester blouse, followed behind her, carrying a small stool. As usual, they were arguing.

"I told you if you put those lobelias in the front by the daylilies they'd be toast by July, but you wouldn't listen," Ruth was admonishing Lillian.

"The tag said full sun, and the hanging baskets at the nursery were in the sun," Lillian retorted. "It's not the sun that's the problem. You must have forgotten to water them last week."

"Lilly, I'm a cook," Ruth shot back. "I know the difference between baked and stewed. Those plants got plenty of water!"

Lillian mounted the steps to the porch and set her basket down. "Morning, Gilda," she said with the air of a martyr. She settled herself on the porch swing.

"Morning, Gilda," said the long-suffering Ruth, sitting beside her.

"I understand you're lunching with Clara today," Lillian said.

"They're going to talk about Clara's comeback," Ruth added.

"You don't have a script?" I asked apprehensively, eyeing the two of them.

"A script?" Lillian looked at Ruth, puzzled.

"A script you want her to use for her comeback?"

"Why would we have a script?" Lillian asked, clearly baffled. "We're not writers."

"That hasn't stopped anybody else," I said morosely.

"Wallace has that vampire movie he wants her to do," Ruth told Lillian. "The one about the widow who gets bit and grows pointy teeth. I told him, 'Clara doesn't want to play a vampire at her age, biting people's necks like a mosquito! It's not dignified. Plus, it's messy.' "

"Well, you can set your mind at rest, Gilda," Lillian pronounced. "I have no script, with or without vampires. No, what I wanted to mention to you, now that you've settled in at the theater and things are going so well with the dinosaurs and all—what I wanted to remind you about was the retrospective."

"The retrospective," I echoed. I spotted more trouble ahead. Lillian's original proposal had been for a retrospective of the films of her late sister Mae Liberty, Academy Award-winning actress and former owner of the Paradise Theatre. That might not seem like a controversial idea, but in my family, all ideas generated controversy.

"Of Maesie's films," Lillian said.

"Just Maesie's?" I inquired.

"Just Maesie's," Lillian said firmly.

"We're not talking about every Tom, Dick, and Harpo, Gilda," Ruth put in. "If the others want their own retrospectives, let them do the work. Me and Lilly, we want to work on Maesie's."

This had been the sticking point. As soon as the word "retrospective" was uttered, it opened a door through which every Liberty attempted to rush simultaneously—not just Wallace and Oliver and Clara with their movies, but Adele with her favorite set designs and Gloria with her favorite hairstyles. Even my mother was not wholly immune to its power. But maybe Clara's new scheme to stage a comeback would distract them enough to stem the tide.

"I think it's a great idea," I said. "When did you have in mind?"

"I thought perhaps fall would be appropriate," Lillian said, "so that the college students would be able to attend. Young people are so fond of old movies."

I doubted the accuracy of this statement, but I didn't contradict her. The only young people I knew who liked old movies were Faye and Duke, and they didn't have a choice.

"Why don't you draw up a list of films for me?" I suggested.

"We already did that," Ruth told me. "It's on your desk in the study."

"Great. I'll get right on it," I promised.

They stood, apparently prepared to continue their contentious garden tour.

"Now, Gilda," Lillian lectured me in her most authoritarian voice, "don't let Clara bully you."

Clara, caught up in her project, was in a very good mood, but she had every intention of bullying me.

"Sit here, Gilda," she said, patting the sofa, and I knew she was arranging me to sit on her good side. Brandishing her cigarette holder, she turned to give me the benefit of her surgically altered profile and fished for compliments.

"I really think this new beauty mask I've been using has done wonders for my skin," she said. "Can you see a difference?" She stroked her cheek.

Clara, at seventy-one, was the youngest of the Liberty siblings. She had always looked younger than her years, even before the two plastic surgeries; she had always dressed and acted even younger. Today she was wearing another dropped-waist dress draped over her slight frame and boyish figure. She'd probably been to church so that she could enlist God as her press agent.

"I don't know," I said. "How long have you been using it?"

"Four weeks." She used a hand to fluff her dark brown curls. She cocked her head coquettishly and waited.

"Well, uh, now that you mention it, you do have kind of a healthy glow—"

"That's it!" She crinkled her eyes at me and glowed harder.

"You know, Gilda, when Grosvenor died, I thought my life was over."

As an actress Clara had always overplayed her scenes. I didn't doubt that Clara had been upset when Grosvenor had been murdered. I gave her credit for a certain amount of grief. And, to be fair, how I felt about him was irrelevant. But I'd never harbored the least anxiety that Clara was planning to follow him to his grave. Now, he was barely cold in his grave, and she was planning her comeback.

"But I know he would have wanted me to go on. You remember how excited he was about our plans for my—for the resumption of my career," she continued, allowing her eyes to mist up just enough to make her point without dissolving her eye makeup. She allowed a quaver to creep into her voice. She got it just right; I could still understand what she was saying, in spite of the tremolo.

"And I *will* go on," I said to myself, as if watching *Casablanca* or *Citizen Kane* or *The Wizard of Oz* for the five hundredth time.

"And I *will* go on," she said. "For him—for Grosvenor!" She straightened her back. Her eyes flashed. Her cigarette holder trembled in her hand, which I thought kind of spoiled the effect. Not that I am antismoking, of course; it just wasn't right for the scene.

Brother, I thought. I hope she's not planning to write her own script.

I lit up a smoke of my own and settled back. I wished I could fast-forward through this part of the monologue.

She wound down at last. "I do miss him," she said for the umpteenth time, as if convincing both of us, "but it's nice not having to cook dinner."

"That is nice," I said. Once I'd gotten my toe in the door of the conversation, I thrust my leg in behind it. "So, Clara, here's the thing: Tobias doesn't want to write a script for you, but Wallace and Oliver have written scripts they want you to read, and Adele is working on one."

She looked flustered, as if I'd switched scenes on her in the middle of a take. "Oh," she said. "But I really think that a Tobias Norton script—"

"Forget about it. He doesn't want to do it." I had often found that directness worked best with Clara. If you didn't knock her over the head with reality, she ignored it and you and continued to play out whatever fantasy she was living in.

"But he hasn't won an Oscar yet," she protested.

"He doesn't care about an Oscar. Not everybody does."

This statement amounted to heresy in my family, and Clara's face registered the skepticism of the devout believer.

"Perhaps if I wrote something up—" she began.

"No. N-O, no. No Himalayan musicals, nothing. He's not really a screenwriter, and he doesn't want to work on a screenplay, not even *your* screenplay. Period."

"If I talked to Val—"

"No."

She frowned at me as if I had just spit on her parade. Then her expression changed to something more calculating.

"You were always a good writer in school, weren't you, Gilda?" she asked thoughtfully. "You published a short story in the literary magazine. I remember."

"I published three short stories," I said, pride getting the upper hand over judgment, "but I am not a screenwriter, and I am not interested in becoming a screenwriter. Clara, you have three prospective scripts waiting in the wings. Won't you at least take a look at them?"

She tossed her curls. "I suppose you think I'd make a good vampire. Is that what you think?"

"I think you'd make an interesting one," I said.

A "hmph" escaped her, but she was considering, I could tell.

"And Oliver has some godawful slapstick comedy he wants me to do," she said. "I suppose you'd like to see me make a fool of myself."

"It's screwball, not slapstick," I corrected her.

She rolled her eyes.

"Clara, *My Best Friend's Wedding* is screwball. You could at least read them," I urged. "Then if you don't like them, you could contact that writer Ron is married to. She might be able to help."

In the end, she graciously consented to read all screenplays presented for her consideration, but told me again that her heart was set on a Tobias Norton script—a point she emphasized by placing both hands over the organ in question. I told her that it would be a cold day in hell before Tobias would write her a screenplay.

When I returned home, I found another bundle of paper making a considerable crater in the middle of my bed. The first page read: "*Widow's Walk* by Wallace A. Liberty."

17

About twenty times a day I received these kinds of unsubtle reminders that I needed to put some distance between myself and my family and reclaim my privacy. I couldn't change the locks on my bedroom or study doors in Liberty House, but I could change my place of residence. I sat down with a newspaper and scanned the ads for apartment rentals. They all looked dismal.

In my brief experience as an apartment hunter, I'd learned something about how to play the game. "Charmingly decorated" meant wallpaper that featured either geese with bows around their necks or scenes of Tara. "Cozy" meant too small to turn around in. "Artistic" meant the walls were painted in garish colors. "Ideal for children" meant that there were roller skates on the stairs, sticky handrails, plenty of noise, and a pint-sized salesperson at your door every week with a brick of chocolate or a box of hideous greeting cards to sell you. "Quiet" was the adjective reserved for apartments that had no other virtues to recommend them.

I gave up and went to work.

My aunt Gloria found me there around two-thirty. Todd called me to the phone.

"Gilda, something terrible has happened!"

My family runs to melodrama, so I wasn't immediately worried. I hoped she meant that the computer had eaten Ollie's screenplay.

"Shirley's son-in-law Alan was killed," she wailed.

I sucked in a lungful of air. "How? What happened?"

"Shirley's car needed some work done on it, and Alan is kind of an amateur auto mechanic, I guess, so he picked up the car and was going to drive it down to Columbus for a part. I don't really know the details, but anyway, he took 415 to Columbus, and I guess—well, Shirley says he's a fast driver. She doesn't really like to ride with him. Even Pauline says he drives too fast, and she's a pretty fast driver herself, Shirley says—"

"So he was driving fast," I prompted, hoping to speed her up and get to the finish line.

"Well, I guess he was. We don't really know. But somehow he didn't quite make one of those turns and he went flying and crashed into a tree." She lowered her voice to a respectful whisper. "They say he was killed instantly. And, Gilda—he had a girl with him."

"A girl?" I knew she could be alluding to a thirty-five-year-old matron.

"A girl! Pauline didn't even know who she was! Isn't that awful?"

"Didn't Shirley meet his copilot?"

"No, he came by when she wasn't home. She just left the car key under the floor mat—you know, the way mechanics always do."

"When did this happen?"

"Oh, I think just after noon. You see, we took Shirley and Leo out to lunch. When we came back from lunch—that must have been one-thirty or thereabouts—Shirley had a phone message waiting from Pauline. Of course, she didn't return the call until after we'd left, and that's when she found out." She stopped to take a breath. "I just feel so bad for her, Gilda! And for Pauline, too, and their kids. But poor Shirley's had so much trouble lately! We're at Shirley's now. As soon as we heard, we got right back in the car and came over. We're about to take her over to Pauline's."

"Has Shirley talked to the police investigating the accident?"

"I don't think so. But I was wondering if she should contact them and tell them about the other accidents, and tell them to call Dale. I mean, I don't know who they are, but they won't be Eden police, will they?"

"Probably state troopers," I guessed.

"They told Pauline it was a strange accident to have in clear weather unless he was, you know, on something. They haven't been able to talk to the girl yet; she's still unconscious. So do you think somebody could have done something to Shirley's car?"

Gloria had never been the most nimble-witted of the Liberty siblings, so I was a little surprised that she'd made the connection so quickly. Then again, life with a practical joker may have predisposed her to more sinister interpretations of seemingly random events.

"I think it's very possible, Gloria," I said with a sigh. "I'm sure the state police will have the car checked out, but you'd better tell them to call Dale."

"I will. What, Shirley? Oh, Shirley's asking if you'll call Miss Styles."

I would, but I wasn't looking forward to it.

"Oh, and Shirley says you left a message on the answering machine. She wants to know what you wanted."

Styles's initial reaction to the news was unprintable. Spike took the phone away from her and told me he was hanging up till she calmed down. I didn't hear from her again that day.

After the early show started that evening, I went to see

Shirley. There were several cars parked out front, and a cluster of people I recognized from the Wilcox-Devereaux picnic were milling around in the den. Gloria was in the kitchen making coffee. Curt was out on the patio with several other men. Conspicuously absent were his two brothers, Larry and Milt.

From down the hall I heard Leo's voice raised querulously. "Why don't they all go home?"

I heard two voices murmuring, and headed in that direction, looking for Shirley.

She sat on the bed next to Leo, holding his hand and stroking his forearm. James sat on the other side of her, with his arm around her shoulders. Her eyes were red; her cheeks, swollen. James was dressed in khaki Dockers and a pale olive shirt with a dark damp spot at the shoulder.

"I still don't know why you're crying," Leo said, studying her face with a troubled frown.

James looked up and saw me in the doorway. "Tell you what, Leo," he said. "Let's us go out and sample some of that lemon pie I was telling you about."

"Okay," Leo said affably. He stood up and took a few shuffling steps, then turned back. "Shirley?" he said softly.

"Go on with James, Leo," she said gently. "I'll be all right."

I sat down on the bed and put an arm around Shirley.

"Oh, Gilda," she whispered, "I wish I could take back every mean thing I said about him! I just . . ." Her voice trailed off, then started again. "Why did it have to be him? It was supposed to be me!"

She began to sob and I put my other arm around her, holding her to me and stroking her back.

"It wasn't your time, Shirley," I said soothingly. "It just wasn't your time. Besides, Leo needs you."

"But I should never have let him take the car!" Her wail was muffled. "I should have thought! I just didn't think! After everything that's been happening—Pauline will never forgive me, and I wouldn't blame her if she didn't. It's worse, you know, because they were separated."

"Shirley, there's only one person truly at fault here, if it turns out that the car was sabotaged, and that person is the one who sabotaged it. Right?"

Shirley sniffled and blew her nose. "I understand what you're saying, Gilda, but I should have seen it coming. I don't think I'll ever be able to forgive myself. He was—he was doing me a favor, and . . . I'll never be able to forgive myself."

I patted her shoulders like a sculptor trying to reshape wet clay.

"Sure you will," I assured her.

My aunt Gloria came to the door. "Pauline's on the phone, Shirley. She needs to ask you something."

I gave Shirley a few final pats of encouragement and left the room.

In the hall I ran into Leo.

"Is Shirley crying about what happened?" he asked.

"Yes, Leo," I said, taking his arm and turning him back toward the den. "She's sad."

"I don't understand it," he said.

I gave his arm a squeeze. "Neither do I, Leo."

But he had something else on his mind now.

"I'm sick," he said. "I don't know how it happened, but I got sick. Now Shirley—" He swallowed and put a hand on my arm. "I'm no good anymore," he said, and I felt the sudden burning eruption of tears. "Shirley needs help," he confided. His own eyes filled with liquid.

I put my hand over his. "I'll help her, Leo," I said. "I promise. And James will help her. We'll all help her. Don't worry, Leo. We'll take good care of Shirley."

Tears slowly dribbled down his cheeks.

"I got old," he said. "One day, I got old."

18

On Monday morning, I called my booker, Russell Wong, with the list for Mae's retrospective.

"I'll see what I can do," he said. "Some of these titles may not be available."

At first, I didn't think anything of it; most of the titles we wanted, most of the time, were not available to the Paradise because they'd been conferred on chain theaters by the powers that be. Our luck had improved since the Eden Square Theater had burned down in May, but we still considered it a major coup when we snagged a *Lost World* anywhere within a few weeks of its national release. It was only after I'd hung up that I wondered whom we'd be competing with for a 1938 B movie. If other indie movie houses around the country were holding Mae Liberty retrospectives, I hadn't heard about it.

I was hungover and woozy from lack of sleep, and that put me in a foul temper. I'd stayed up much too late reading Uncle Wallace's screenplay, driven by a fascination with its relentless progression from bad to worse. I'd finally decided that it might improve if I drank as much while reading it as he had while writing it.

I sat at my desk at Liberty House and did paperwork until my eyes ached, then went in to the theater to clean. Concern about Shirley and Leo distracted me until I found myself wiping the concession counter for the second time. Was I developing early-onset Alzheimer's? The thought sent a hot flush of panic along nerves and blood vessels and my heart thumped wildly. Menopause, I reminded myself, gripping the glass I'd just cleaned twice, also increases forgetfulness. It was just my hormones acting up; what estrogen I had left was probably weakened by lack of sleep or chemically altered by combination with gin.

Two phone requests for donations were met with a surly, unenthusiastic assent. No one had the misfortune to cross my path in person until Duke arrived in the late afternoon from his computer gaming club. I went around the corner to the Fig Leaf to wake myself up with coffee.

When I returned, Duke told me that Styles had called.

"Just what I need—a counterirritant," I said. "What did she want?"

"She's holding a council of war tonight at her place at eight. She wants you to come."

"Did you happen to mention—"

"That you had a theater to run? Yeah, I told her. She said, 'Be there or be square.' " Duke pushed his glasses up on his nose with his thumb. He followed me into the small office where the ice machine lived. "She said to tell you that she was calling in Jake."

"Calling Jake? Well, I guess that might be helpful."

"She didn't say *calling* Jake," Duke corrected me. "She said *calling in* Jake."

The meeting took place on Styles's patio, a cement slab that had cracked, heaved, and sunk as if tormented by a series of earthquakes or the tunneling of some subterranean monster, like the atomic ants in *Them!* The patio overlooked Styles's weedy, overgrown backyard. Rustling sounds and fissures in the mass of weeds charted the progress of Waldo, Styles's bloodhound-basset mix. We sat on an eclectic collection of rusted lawn chairs, most of which didn't look capable of bearing any weight at all without collapsing. Spike had surrounded us with bug repellent candles, and the air was redolent with citronella. The day's heat was receding; the sun, low on the horizon.

Spike, who'd been put in charge of the refreshments, was serving nacho-flavored tortilla chips, salsa, Little Debbie snack cakes, and beer. He'd stepped cautiously over Bogey, the black cat, who lay sprawled like roadkill in the dead center of the patio. James, in mufti, was pinching his lips together as he selected a snack cake with the concentration of a master taster and set it on the paper towel draped over his lap.

"I like Hostess better," Spike apologized, "but the Hostess truck didn't come today."

Bravely, James bit into a jelly roll. "Delicious," he said.

In deference to her condition, Styles had been given the only chair with all of its plastic webbing intact—a venerable lounge chair that wobbled on the uneven paving. Her leg, wrapped in velcroed neoprene like a taco, was propped on a couple of telephone books. Her face under the bandage across her forehead was an interesting mix of white, green, and purple hues, but both eyes were open, as was her mouth.

Shirley's chair was only missing one of its plastic strips. Mine was missing so many that I felt as if I were sitting on a spider web that might break at any instant; Jake's looked like its twin. When Spike sat, he turned his around backward. It wasn't easy to sit backward in a lawn chair, but he managed, and his position seemed to have the advantage of settling most of his weight on the metal frame rather than the frayed plastic strips.

I studied Styles's face and wondered what it had cost her to ask her father for help. Normally, she kept her distance from Jake, an attitude born of longstanding resentment about his history of abandoning her.

He jumped up now and rubbed his hands together. "Okay, Sammy," he said, "whatta we got here?"

"The main thing is to keep Shirley and Leo safe," Styles said. "Our killer has made a lot of mistakes, just none that are any use to us in identifying him."

"Or her," I said in an undertone. I hadn't been happy to learn that Pauline was staying with Leo tonight, but I knew it would take some doing to convince Shirley to be suspicious of her own daughter. I only had Shirley's word for it that Pauline didn't want her husband dead, and even if that was true, I didn't know whether Pauline knew about the arrangements for Alan to pick up the car. As far as I was concerned, the only person I'd eliminated from my list of suspects was the dead one, Alan. On the other hand, if you were a speed freak who wanted to commit suicide, driving 415 with the accelerator floored was a good way to go. But I didn't honestly think Alan's death had been a suicide.

So far, though, the killer had preferred indirect to direct action, and seemed to be targeting Shirley, so I thought Leo was probably safe with Pauline.

"In fact, about the only thing the killer has done right so far," Styles continued, "is to wear gloves and not leave behind any clues to his identity—hasn't dropped any matchbooks, high school rings, credit cards, cell phones, not even a goddamn button. But he's oh for three in the attempts on Shirley's life. That means we should be able to outthink him. And we need to because he's shown a degree of persistence, and had the kind of limited success that will encourage him to try again."

"Plus, Shirley's about to raise the stakes," James said.

We all turned toward Shirley.

"I'm going to court to get control of Leo's finances," Shirley said quietly. "I see the lawyer on Thursday."

"You're asking the court to revoke Larry's power of attorney?" I asked.

"Yes." Her glasses caught the reflection of the setting sun as she turned her head. "I don't feel that he's left me any choice."

"So," Styles continued. "If we're right that the motive is financial—"

"*If* we're right," I repeated. "But then there's the whole question of Auggie—"

"Who might play a part in the financial motive," Styles interrupted.

"Who might play a part in the financial motive," I agreed, "or who might relate to some other motive we don't even know about yet. We know Leo had secrets."

"We know he had secrets from *me*," Shirley emphasized.

"From you and from the person who claims to be his best friend," I reminded her. "His former brother-in-law and fishing buddy, Glenn Wilcox."

"Guys don't keep secrets from their fishing buddies," Spike assured us.

"That means whatever he was hiding was so important that he didn't want his best friend to know. He didn't even ask Glenn to cover for him," I said.

"He might have forgotten," Shirley pointed out.

We couldn't help it; we smiled.

"Point taken," I said.

Styles returned to her argument. "We also need to look more closely into Leo's business affairs. But if the motive is financial, somebody might not want Shirley holding the purse strings."

"You're saying that Larry is the killer?" Shirley asked.

"It could be Larry or it could be somebody who's used to dealing with Larry," Styles said.

"The Three Stooges, you mean?" James asked.

"The Three Stooges?" Styles echoed.

"That's how I think of them," James said. His tie-dyed T-shirt glowed warmly in the evening light. "Larry, Curly, and Mo. They're the sorriest-looking trio of dim bulbs I've ever seen. They don't know how to behave. I asked Leo, 'Why didn't you teach your boys some manners?' Know what he said? He said, 'Their mother won't let me spank them.'"

Shirley smiled. "Leo said that?"

"Yeah, so you got it from the horse's mouth that those boys are messed up," James said. "And he doesn't even know about little Milty's nose condition."

"Milt said he's got bad allergies," I remarked casually.

James rolled his eyes at me. "Gilda!"

"What?"

James pressed one nostril and sniffed.

"Oh." I felt my face flush.

"I didn't know what James was talking about either when he told me, Gilda," Shirley confided.

"Are you sure?" I asked him. He gave me a look. "Never mind," I mumbled.

"So the problem is that we can see trouble coming, we just don't know where it's coming from," Styles summarized.

"Then the problem is protection, right, Sammy?" Jake said. He sat down again and rubbed his thighs. His full head of white hair reflected the light. He still had the good looks that set female hearts pattering in the Golden Buckeye crowd.

"Protection and surveillance," Styles amended. "It would be nice to catch the guy when he makes his next move. Otherwise, we got a problem on our hands that could last indefinitely."

Jake nodded. He rubbed his mustache thoughtfully. "Yeah, you got a problem, all right." He looked at Shirley. "You got a security system, doll? Alarms, keypads, stuff like that?"

Shirley started. It had evidently been some time since she'd been addressed as "doll."

"Shirley's got an open door policy is what she has," Styles groused. "Next time I go there I expect to bump into Snow White and all the cute little animals."

"I guess I have a few holes in my security," Shirley admitted in an injured tone.

Styles snorted.

"That would be a 'no,' " I told Jake in order to move the meeting along. My chances of making it back to the theater for the late show were looking slim.

"Sammy can give you the name of a good security service," Jake said to Shirley. "Not one of these low-class rip-off artists, but a good, reliable service. Can you afford that, doll?"

"I don't know," she confessed anxiously. "How much will it be? My late husband left me pretty well off, but now I have to think about the future. Larry pays all the bills—the major bills, that is. He deposits something in Leo's account every month, but I don't think it will cover a security service."

"Demand a raise. And don't worry, sweetheart," Styles said. "Jake's donating his services."

Jake looked at her in apparent surprise. He opened his mouth to speak but I stepped in. "Send Larry the bill," I said.

"You're going to have to change all your locks, Shirl," Styles said, "and stop giving away the keys like Cracker Jack prizes."

"Ask James to help you plan for emergencies," I suggested. "I'm sure he has plenty of experience."

"Glad to," James acknowledged.

Shirley lit a cigarette and then frowned at it. "These security systems," she began. "Don't the alarms go off a lot by accident?"

"Shirl, it's the nineties," Styles said dryly. "Adjust."

"Sammy's right, doll," Jake said. "We gotta move with the times." He pumped his arms, bent at the elbow, and wiggled his hips. He didn't look like he was moving with the times, he looked like he was imitating Chubby Checker.

"Hey, you guys!" a voice called.

A vision in red was making her way across the yard from the side gate. She wore red shorts cut just below her crotch, a red scarf looped around cascading black hair, and a red shirt tied under her breasts for a Lana Turner look. A small gold cross dangled tantalizingly in her cleavage. She wore red platform shoes and stepped gingerly along a path worn through the weeds and dog droppings. Over her elbow she carried a boxy white basket painted with red strawberries.

"It's Lulu," Spike explained. "We're going out later. Hey, sugar!" He rose and put an arm around her waist.

"Hi, Spike! Hi, everybody!" the young woman said cheerfully. She raised a hand studded with red talons and waved.

We were all introduced, and Lulu was settled awkwardly into Spike's chair with a can of beer and a Little Debbie. Waldo sidled up and sniffed her kneecaps.

"Now just sit here, hon, and enjoy your snacks," he told her. "We'll be done in a little while."

James beamed at her. I could tell he was admiring her ability to match that shade of red from head to toe. Now that I saw them up close, I realized that her nails weren't red, they were red-and-white striped with a white star on navy blue tips.

Spike stretched out next to Bogey, the only one present who had not acknowledged Lulu's arrival. He began stroking the cat's long back with a meaty paw the size of an *Encyclopædia Britannica*, and murmuring, "Who's a good boy?

Huh? Who's Spike's good boy?" The resulting purr was probably disrupting cell phone transmissions all over Eden County.

"Who does she tell that she's changing the locks?" I asked, dragging my own attention and everybody else's back to the matter at hand. "And when?"

"That's what I love about you, cookie," Styles said. "You cut to the chase. If she tells all the people who have keys now—"

"Who happen all to be on our list of primary suspects," I interjected.

"Right. So it narrows their window of opportunity to get into the house and sabotage it," she finished.

"Which narrows the amount of time we gotta run surveillance," Jake added. "We hope."

"And gives us an opportunity to set a trap," I said.

"Am I the bait?" Shirley asked. She had a can of beer in one hand and a cigarette in the other. She didn't sound nervous, just curious.

"Yes and no," Styles said. "Can you arrange to leave town for a few days?"

"Realistically? No," Shirley answered. "Sam, Alzheimer's patients need consistency—a familiar routine and familiar surroundings. Leo's just now getting used to the new house. If I move him, it will upset him, and he'll lose ground. Ask James."

"She's right," James agreed. "Leo needs to stay put."

"But you take him around town, don't you?" Styles asked. "You don't stay home all the time? If you did, the wire on the stairs would never have been there."

"Oh, sure, I take him on errands with me," Shirley said. "On Friday we have an appointment at OSU to see about participating in a drug experiment."

"So are you going to watch the house twenty-four hours a day?" I asked Styles.

I saw Spike open his mouth to object but Styles beat him to it. "Me and whose army?" she said. "You may have noticed I'm not in prime condition. No, we haven't got the manpower to run that kind of surveillance. It'll have to be electronic—CCTV."

"How many cameras do you have?" I asked doubtfully.

"Not enough," she conceded. "The best we can hope to do is cover the entrances, and check the tapes several times a day. We can hook up our equipment to your computer monitor or your television, Shirley, and show you how to check."

"The cameras won't tell us what an intruder did inside the house or the garage once he went in," James said. "How will we know what to look for inside? Shirley could get killed on the way to the television."

"That's why she needs an alarm system," Styles said. "See, an alarm system would prevent our killer from entering the house. That's good, but if he's determined to kill Shirley, he'll just find another way to get at her."

"What do you mean, another way?" James asked.

"Well, he might get into her purse, for example, and substitute some kind of poison for any prescription pills or aspirin she might be carrying around."

The sun had dropped below the horizon. I glanced at Shirley, who appeared pale in the diffused light.

"It's always possible, of course, that he's already thought of that, given his track record inside the house," Styles continued. "So Shirley, be careful what you put in your mouth."

Shirley nodded.

"Meanwhile, if he goes near the house, we want him on tape," Styles said. "If he hasn't made his move before the alarm is installed, we'll have to keep the cameras in place. Even after the alarm is installed, if he doesn't know about it and tries to get in, we want to see who he is. If he hears the alarm and runs away, we'll at least know who we're dealing with. Until the alarm is installed, we'll have to figure out another way for Shirley to tell if the house has been entered."

"The old hair-in-the-door trick always worked for me," Jake offered.

"Just remember, I'm an old lady with bad eyes and a bad back," Shirley said. "I can't be down on my hands and knees, crawling around my porch looking for a hair. Leo will have *me* committed."

"Excuse me," said a new voice. We all turned to regard Lulu, who was waving one patriotic hand. "I don't mean to interrupt," she said shyly. "But what if he's wearing a mask?"

We stared at her blankly.

"You know, like they do on TV?" she said, searching our faces anxiously for comprehension. "That's why I thought about it—because you said she could watch those tapes on TV, and then y'all would know who the intruder was. But on TV a lot of times they wear these stocking masks so you can't see their faces. Well, you can see them, but they look all twisted and disgusting. It's not like anybody can recognize them in a lineup later." We were still staring at her. "I just thought I'd ask," she finished contritely, and ducked her head to take a swig of her beer.

"Damn it, she's right," Styles said finally. "We'd feel pretty stupid if we ended up with somebody on tape we couldn't identify. The image will be black and white. We might be able to tell something from the guy's build and height, but if he's wearing a stocking mask, we won't even be able to tell much about his hair."

"It's too bad y'all can't use one of those exploding dye packs, like they have at the bank," Lulu said into her beer.

"Maybe we could," Styles said thoughtfully. "Gilda, do you think Val could rig up something like that that would be triggered if you opened the door?"

"It doesn't sound electrical, but he probably could," I said.

"The way I see it, the big question is whether you want evidence you can use in court," Jake volunteered. "A perp who gets hit with an exploding dye pack isn't going to hang around and set himself up for murder one, know what I mean? It's your call, Sammy. What do you say?"

"It's not my call, it's Shirley's," Styles replied.

"What happens if he gets in and sets something up?" Shirley asked. She was looking down. Her fingers smoothed the fabric of her dress over her lap.

"Once we know somebody's been in, Sammy and I can go

in and look around," Jake said. "We'll find the sabotage, whatever it is."

"Yeah, she did last time." I gestured at Styles's leg.

She glared at me.

Shirley looked up. "In that case, I say we go for broke," she said with decision. "I'd hate to see one of Leo's kids on trial for murder, if that's how it turns out. But if that's how it turns out, it means they not only killed my son-in-law, they endangered their own father." Her voice broke, and she swallowed.

"Just so you understand, Shirl," Styles warned her, "it's a long way from the collection of evidence to conviction."

"I know that!" Shirley said, sounding a little miffed. "I watched the O. J. Simpson trial! I know the perp might walk."

She spoke the last sentence tentatively, as if she were using unfamiliar words. I smiled to myself. Everybody's an amateur criminologist these days, and given recent developments, I had to count myself among them.

"And," she continued, eyes shining, "I also know that if he's convicted, it probably won't be for my son-in-law's death."

"Just show me who the guy is," Spike proposed through a mouthful of Little Debbie. "I'll bust his ass for you."

Lulu giggled.

"Not without me you won't," James said.

"Okay," Spike said agreeably. He licked his fingers and turned to Jake. "Me and him'll take care of the guy. He won't bother Shirley no more once we're through with him."

"I love it," Styles muttered. "Nurse vigilantes."

"You'll have to admit it would do a lot for the image of male nurses," I said.

"So let me get this straight," Jake said. "Are we nixing the exploding dye packs?"

"Phosphorescent paint!" I exclaimed suddenly. "That's what we need! Something that will mark him without his noticing. Something that will come off on everything he touches. Maybe we can put it on the door handles."

"Won't he notice?" James said doubtfully.

"No, Gilda's on to something," Styles said. "Only it's

fluorescent ink or dye we need—the stuff they use on re-admission stamps sometimes at concerts or bars. It's only visible under a black light. If we could mark his gloves, and then get it to rub off on everything he touched—"

"That stuff dries pretty fast," Spike said, shaking his head. "How we going to get it to come off?"

"There's fluorescent paints and chalks," Lulu interjected. "We used to use them in this theater I worked at. Once we painted scenery with some fluorescent paint, and used chalk on some of the costumes. You couldn't see it till they turned on the black light, and then it was just beautiful!"

We grinned at each other. Now it was dusk, and the fireflies had come out.

"I hate to mention it at a time like this, Sam," Shirley said softly, "but Alan's funeral is on Wednesday. People will come back to my house afterward. I thought—well, it would be better for Pauline and the kids not to have all that confusion at her house. People won't be tracking fluorescent chalk dust all over the house, will they?"

Styles and I exchanged glances.

"Okay," she said, "hair in the door until after the funeral, plus camera surveillance. Better yet, somebody home at all times. If you can't be there, or James, call me and Spike or call Gilda. We'll all be there after the funeral to keep an eye on things." She stared Spike down. "I'll ask Ferguson to alert the patrol cars in your neighborhood. Let's just hope the bastard has the decency to wait until after the funeral to make his next move."

19

Monday night before I went to sleep I sat in bed and read through copies of e-mail that Leo had received and Styles had retrieved. Leo's America Online handle was just "leo." "Leo" had received three letters from a "moviemad," who signed his or her notes "DJ" or just "D."

The first one read: *"Desperately seeking OM's THE EXILE. Any chance? Do you have anything of his? Any Norman or Lincoln? DJ"*

The second one read: *"Did you get my last e-mail? Still need prints of THE EXILE. I'll meet you anywhere, anytime. You say when and where. D."*

The third one read: *"Are you there? Holding out on me? Consorting with the enemy??! Still looking for OM, especially THE EXILE. Yes? No? Maybe? D."*

Was *The Exile* a training film? A commercial? It didn't sound like either. And DJ was "moviemad," not "tvmad."

Curious, I got out of bed and retrieved a copy of Leonard Maltin's video guide on the assumption that moviemad DJ was looking for videos or movies that he thought Leo, who "used to be in pictures," might have. There was one film entitled *The Exile*, a 1947 Max Ophuls film starring Douglas Fairbanks, Jr. There was no film called *Lincoln*, although I knew there were several biopics about Lincoln, including D. W. Griffith's *Abraham Lincoln*, starring Walter Huston. The only *Norman*s I came up with were that low-budget Redd Foxx comedy, *Norman . . . Is That You?* and an Australian comedy called *Norman Loves Rose*. But the wording of the note suggested that "Lincoln" and "Norman" might be the names of individual directors, or even production companies.

Why was somebody "desperate" to find *The Exile*? And why did he think Leo might have it? Maltin hadn't liked it much; he'd only given it two and a half stars. But surely a film that matched up Ophuls and Fairbanks Jr. would be easy enough to find. After all, if it appeared in Maltin's *TV Movies and Video Guide*, that meant it was easily available. Maybe that was the key, though. Maybe there was another film called *The Exile* that couldn't be seen on television or video.

But surely Max Ophuls was "OM." He should be "MO," but hadn't the writer reversed his initials? Maybe he was following some convention practiced by users of alphabetized databases. How common could that particular combination of letters be? I couldn't think of anyone whose initials were O. M. I turned out the light and spent the next hour with O. M. on my brain.

Over breakfast the next morning, I looked through several of Mae's film encyclopedias, but I found no reference to Lincoln or Norman.

The title had been given in English and the possessive strongly suggested that O.M. had been an actor, director, or producer. In my sleepless hours the night before, I'd come up with a limited collection of names, either male or female, that began with an O: Oscar, Oliver, Oswald, Osmond, and Otto for the men and Olive or Olivia for the women. In Maesie's books, I found only two people whose initials were O.M. One was Oswald Morris, the cinematographer who had won an Academy Award for *Fiddler on the Roof*. The other was an Italian actress, Ornella Muti, none of whose films I'd seen.

In addition to the Max Ophuls film, I found a 1917 Maurice Tourneur film called *Exile* and a 1980 film from Niger called *L'exile*. The first starred Olga Petrova and the second was directed by Oumarou Ganda—two "O" names I hadn't thought of—but neither of these O's was matched up with an M, and DJ had typed "OM" twice.

All of my research and cogitation tended to assure me that my first conclusion had been right. But why was someone asking Leo for a copy of Max Ophuls' *The Exile*? Did Leo have an extensive collection of obscure movies on video?

A thought struck me. Had Leo been duplicating films illegally and selling them? The market for pirated videos nowadays was immense, especially overseas. Had there always been a market for illegally obtained copies of Hollywood movies? I put down my spoon and let my cereal get soggy as I pursued the implications. Leo had already been in the moviemaking business shortly after the war when he'd married Inez. That meant his own production in those days was in either thirty-five millimeter or sixteen millimeter. If he was making training films, then probably he'd been working in sixteen. Afterward, he'd made television commercials. Eventually, that would have meant video production, but was that what it meant in the fifties? I didn't know enough about the technology, but Leo seemed to have been well-positioned to get in on the ground floor when the video market exploded in the eighties, especially if he had previously been duplicating Hollywood movies on either sixteen or thirty-five millimeter. What he'd said to me was, "I used to be in pictures." If Leo had in fact been one of the first in the tidal wave of movie pirates that continued to erode Hollywood profits, he might well possess a fortune worth killing for.

An illegal business might explain some of those mysterious trips Leo had taken. But it didn't explain why we only had copies of three requests, unless Leo had another e-mail address we didn't know about, and these had been sent to his regular address by mistake. It would make sense for him to maintain a separate account for business purposes, especially if his business was illegal. It would make even more sense if he normally received requests and orders in another way that was more secure and private—by fax, for example. This didn't seem like the type of business he could conduct over the Internet.

Of course, Leo might have been a legitimate distributor of films on either sixteen millimeter or video. But if so, why had nobody mentioned it when talking about his business? Had it been an insignificant sideline? Or perhaps he'd merely been a kind of collector of old movies—not somebody who went looking for customers, but somebody known to have some special titles in his private collection. I doubted, though, that a Max Ophuls film would be that obscure.

I cast about for another explanation that would fit the facts as neatly as this one did. The only other one I could come up with was the possibility that Leo had made pornographic videos as a sideline to his regular business. That could also explain why he kept secrets from Shirley. But *The Exile* didn't sound pornographic, either, unless my imagination— or my memory of sex—was failing me. And "Lincoln"? I shut a mental door on a sudden image of a bearded porn stud dressed in a frock coat and tall hat copulating with a babe in hoop skirts. No, video piracy made more sense than that.

I tried to summon the righteous indignation I should feel when contemplating such a crime. I told myself that video pirates helped to drive up prices at the box office, making movies virtually unaffordable for people with young children who couldn't pay for tickets and a babysitter. But it was a little like trying to get worked up because someone was slapping an Air Jordan logo on Korean knockoffs and cutting into Nike's and Jordan's profits.

I'd have to ask Shirley if Leo had an extensive video or film collection stashed away somewhere, since I hadn't seen anything like that around the house. And I found myself wanting to talk to Leo's former business partner, Bernie Cutter.

Styles, it turned out, had reached the son, David Cutter, who said that his father lived in a house up on Buckeye Lake and spent most of his time on his boat. She was eager to have me talk to Cutter in person. She gave me a phone number to call, and I agreed to arrange a visit. When I dialed Cutter's number at the lake, he didn't answer, as predicted, and I left a message, hoping that Shirley's name would motivate a quick response.

Otherwise, Tuesday passed without incident, except for a discouraging series of phone conversations, beginning with a call from my booker.

"What are you telling me, Russ?" I asked him. "I gave you

a list of twelve films and you can only locate four of them? This is Mae Liberty we're talking about! She was an Academy Award winner, not somebody who played handmaidens in De Mille's biblical epics."

"I know, Gilda, I know," Russ said placatingly. "But if the films aren't available, there's nothing I can do about it."

"What do you mean 'not available'?"

"There aren't any prints in circulation."

"Look, we'll settle for sixteen millimeter if we have to."

"No good, Gilda," he said. "I checked that, too. I knew you wanted these for a retrospective of your aunt's work. Honest, I tried!"

"So what do you suggest?" I asked in exasperation. "Do I contact the studios directly, if they still exist, and get the films from their archives?"

"Most of them don't archive films that old anymore," he replied. "I'd try the major film archives—Eastman House, MoMA, UCLA, and the national archives at the Library of Congress."

"Will they let me borrow films for showings?"

"Depends," he said. "Depends on what shape the film is in, whether it's been restored or not—"

"And who's asking."

"There's always that," he admitted. "As Mae Liberty's niece, I'd say you have a good shot. Have you got anything to bargain with? Memorabilia, say?"

"Nothing that Mae's sister will let out of the house."

"Well, see how it goes," he advised. "Maybe you can offer them something after Lillian dies. It is Lillian you mean, right? Played with Mae in *Within These Walls*?"

"You sure know your film history," I said.

I hung up and then called directory assistance for D.C. I picked the Library of Congress on the assumption that my taxpayer dollars were underwriting the collections, so I could legitimately claim co-ownership. At the national archives, I was transferred to somebody's phone mail, and left a message. I took the cordless phone into the men's bathroom to change a washer on one of the sinks. I hadn't actually done this before; all of my sink experience had involved stem assemblies, not washers.

My first try resulted in a bigger leak than before. I swore to myself as the water spread.

"That's impossible!" I complained. "That washer fits, I crammed it in tight, and screwed down the top. You're fixed."

I often talked to household contraptions when I was working on them. They never responded, not even with the least bit of friendly cooperation. On the up side, this one didn't squirt me in the eye.

The phone rang.

"Ms. Liberty? I'm John Pogue at the Library of Congress. What can I do for you?"

I told him what I wanted and why. I went through the list of titles, and he wrote them down.

"Off the top of my head, I can tell you that we own copies of three of those eight, and one of them is scheduled for restoration," he said. "I doubt any of them is available but I'll check. I might also be able to save you some time on the others. We keep a database of what's in the public archives. Let me call you back on this."

I took another whack at the sink and this time managed to fix it. Then I took a can of paint out to the front entrance to touch up the dinosaur footprints we'd painted on the sidewalk.

Duke descended from his third floor penthouse while I was down on all fours with my butt in the air.

"You should have called me, Gilda," he protested, pushing his glasses up. "I would have helped you with that. I was just messing around on the computer."

"I should have called you when I was fixing the bathroom sink," I said. "This job is a picnic compared to that."

"I wouldn't have helped you with that," he admitted. "The only plumbing skill I have is flushing the toilet."

"I don't think that counts," I observed. "Or putting the seat down, either. Tell you what, you can blow up Trix."

Trix was our nickname for the inflatable dinosaur foot we'd had hanging over the ticket booth ever since we'd heard that we'd succeeded in booking *The Lost World*. She was always losing air until she looked more like a giant green condom. If the dinosaurs had been as flimsy as Trix, they wouldn't have survived long enough to leave fossils, much less inspire movies.

I needed to deliver tickets to some local day care centers who were bringing their charges to the Wednesday kids' matinees the next day, but I was reluctant to leave until John Pogue called back. I was recounting to Duke my problems with Mae's retrospective when the phone rang. It was Pogue.

"I wish I had better news for you, Gilda," he said, "but none of our titles is available for exhibition right now. MoMA has a sixteen-millimeter print of *Fair Game* that's available, but their print of *Never Say Never Again* isn't available. Both the Eastman House and the Academy Film Archive have *Edith's Folly*, but neither of those prints is available. Nobody has prints of the other two. I'm sorry."

"When you say 'not available'—" I began.

He cut me off. "MoMA's the only archive with a circulating collection," he said. "You might be able to talk some of the others into letting you have a print if they had multiple copies, but only because you're a theater owner and Mae's niece."

"So if I were a senator from Ohio, your three unavailable prints would be available?" I asked.

He laughed. "No, you misunderstand. When I say they aren't available, I really mean that they're in no condition to be shown. Even if we let you have them, they wouldn't make it through your projector."

"Well, there must be prints somewhere," I said.

I heard something like a small sigh from the other end of the phone.

"That's what everybody thinks, but it ain't necessarily so," Pogue said. "We estimate that less than half of the movies made before 1950 survive today."

I was stunned. He must be putting me on.

"You're telling me we've misplaced thousands of movies?" I asked incredulously.

"Not misplaced," he said. "We just didn't take care of them. They weren't stored properly. The film stock deteriorated."

"They got old," I said softly.

"That's exactly what happened," he confirmed. "Nitrate stock was really vulnerable to heat and humidity, plus it was downright dangerous to store because it was so combustible. But even safety film deteriorates."

"But surely it was in the studios' interest to preserve their own films?"

"That's a historian's perspective, Gilda," he pointed out. "After all, in the old days, there was no television, no video, no DVD. A movie got made, it got shown, maybe even overseas, and that was that. There was no percentage in keeping prints around. Disney was the only studio holding movies for rerelease, and even Disney didn't take especially good care of them. It was partly ignorance on the part of the studios. People didn't know enough, but they also didn't especially care. Once they closed the books on a film, it didn't matter what happened to it."

"You're a real ray of sunshine, John," I said.

"Tell me about it," he said. "I have one of the few jobs in the movie industry that's even more depressing than owning an independent theater."

I had a thought. "Say, are you sitting in front of a computer database that tells you what prints are still in circulation?"

"Yep. Got another one you want me to try?"

"How about *The Exile*? It's a 1947 Max Ophuls film."

"The Exile." I heard the soft click of computer keys. "Nope, not in circulation. Eastman House has a badly damaged copy, but that may be the only one."

"But if Leonard Maltin lists it in his book—"

"It's possible that Turner owns an old copy that's been transferred to video for television," Pogue said. "They may or may not have the master they took it from."

"Can you think of anybody who might be desperate to get their hands on it, either a clean copy on video or a thirty-five millimeter print?"

"Well, Eastman might be, if they wanted to restore their print," he said. "But there are lots of private collectors, too."

"Video collectors, you mean, or film collectors?"

"Both," Pogue said. "Some of them specialize. For example, somebody might be collecting Douglas Fairbanks, Jr., or Max Ophuls. Or maybe it's somebody like you who's putting together a retrospective."

"I see." I paused, considering how much to give away, then gave a mental shrug. "Suppose somebody had been involved in film and video piracy for a long time, and owned pirated copies of old films—you know, old pirated copies of old films. If such a collection existed, what would it be worth?"

There was a moment of silence on the other end.

"Are you telling me that such a collection exists?" Pogue asked.

"I'm really not sure," I admitted. "It's just a theory I'm testing."

"If somebody owned a collection of lost films, even on video, and if those videos were first generation masters in good condition made from a good quality master print of films that no longer exist, it would be worth a great deal of money," he said slowly. "But you really couldn't put a price on the value to film historians."

"Try."

"Megabucks."

20

Bernie Cutter, Leo's former business partner, returned my phone call on Wednesday morning and agreed to see me on Thursday. He sounded happy to help out—any friend of Leo's, and so on.

Wednesday afternoons filled me with dread. The staff and I had greeted with enthusiasm Duke's idea about showing kids' movies on Wednesday afternoons in the summer. It would bring in some extra income and give us some good publicity with their parents. What we'd overlooked was that none of us was especially fond of children as a class of people.

Faye turned out to be even worse than I was.

"I feel like Gena Rowlands's Gloria," she said after the first matinee. Her punk hairstyle had wilted, and her nose ring was askew.

She behaved more like Miss Hannigan in *Annie*.

"This whole idea could bite the dust fast if we let her handle the kids," Duke said morosely when she went to help Todd clean up the theater. "If she has her way, they'll feel like they're in boot camp watching VD films."

"Then she should project and stay out of the way, and you and Todd can handle concessions," I said.

"Me?" he responded, palms to his chest, his face registering horror. "You know I'm a behind-the-scenes man, Gilda."

"You're good with kids," I said, "you and Todd both."

Todd was our champion child-handler, a cross between Danny Kaye and Mary Poppins. Kids loved him. He had one more year at Eden College, and I was already having anxiety attacks about what we'd do when he graduated.

My own rapport with the little rugrats was minimal. Duke's was better, but I knew he was anxious about his dinosaur kitsch, and I worried that if one windup stegosaurus got stepped on, or worse yet, if a kid spilled orange drink on a pile of T-shirts, he'd lose it. I suggested we put the stuff away while the kids were there, but he refused because he knew it would sell if we left it out.

So on the Wednesday of Alan's funeral, I took the coward's way out: I offered to stay home with Leo while James and Shirley attended the funeral. To my relief, they accepted my offer.

"Does Leo know what's going on?" I asked James, who

was nattily dressed in a dark suit and a pale yellow shirt that matched his peroxided hair. His tie was so conservative, I wondered whether he'd borrowed it from his father. Or Peachy might have given it to him; she kept some in stock for funeral attenders who arrived unsuitably attired. Or it might have been one of Leo's. James had spent the last two nights in the house, guarding Shirley and Leo.

"Sort of," James said. "He knows Shirley's sad about something, and sometimes he remembers what it is. He's been told that we're going to the funeral, but he may not remember once we're gone. He's had breakfast, in case he asks, and you can tell him that we'll have lunch when Shirley comes home. He'll understand that, though he might ask you a couple hundred times when she's coming."

Shirley entered the room leading Leo by the arm. Her face sagged with weariness, and her eyes were pink. She still moved like a recent invalid. She was dressed in a nicely tailored black suit with a wide white collar.

"People will be coming here after the funeral, as you know, Gilda, so the women from church will probably be here before we get back. Leo's just been to the bathroom, so he should be okay for a few hours," she was saying. She let go of Leo's hand to cough. "This darn cough. I can't seem to shake it." She rooted around in her purse, extracting a handkerchief and a pair of sunglasses. "If he wants a snack, he can have one. If he gets nasty, it's best to just ignore him or try to confine him to the back part of the house. Sometimes the child gate still works." She turned to Leo. "But he'll be good, won't you, sweetie?" She gave him a kiss and smoothed his hair.

"I'll be good," he promised. "You smell nice, Shirley."

She pinched his cheek. "Ah, Leo, you always knew how to turn on the charm."

When they were gone, I lit a cigarette and sat down on the couch with one of the photo albums from the coffee table. I patted the couch next to me. "Want to show me your pictures, Leo?" I asked.

"Okay," he said, and sat beside me. But before I could get

the album open he changed the subject. "Why is Shirley crying? I don't understand what's going on."

I turned to face him. His eyes, open and troubled, were on mine. His forehead was creased with concern.

I picked up one of his hands in both of mine. "Leo, Shirley has been sad because her son-in-law Alan died in a car accident. Do you remember Alan?"

"Alan," he echoed. "He likes to work on cars. He was rebuilding a Porsche—a red one."

"Was he?" I said, surprised. I expected so little of him that it amazed me when Leo remembered something.

He nodded. "Pauline says she won't ride in it. Alan drives too fast."

"Alan died in a car accident, Leo."

"That's terrible!" he said. "How did it happen?" He was frowning with concentration.

"We don't know," I told him. "Maybe he was driving too fast."

"Maybe he was," Leo agreed. He thought for a minute. Then his mouth began to tremble and his eyes watered. "Something happened to Shirley, too. She wasn't here. Pauline was here."

"Shirley was in the hospital, but she's all right now," I assured him, stroking the back of his hand.

"I love Shirley," he said softly. His eyes, bright with tears, pleaded with me to understand. "She's my girl."

"I know you do, Leo," I said. "Shirley's sad now, but she's going to be all right. We won't let anything happen to Shirley, I promise. Okay?"

"Okay," he whispered. He passed a palm across one wet cheek. He raised the other hand and touched my shoulder. "I can't help Shirley."

"Sure you can, Leo," I told him. "You help Shirley every day just by being yourself. You make her happy."

In his eyes I saw doubt.

"You make her happy," I repeated, and I knew that this, too, was true. "Okay?"

"Okay."

I opened the album and spread it across our laps. "Let's look at pictures," I said.

In spite of James's reports, I was surprised how long the pictures held his attention and surprised all over again about what he remembered. I saw his kids grow up on film in what appeared to be a happy, normal family. Inez, their mother, was a pretty, slightly plump, blond woman with an unembarrassed smile for the camera. They lived in a suburban ranch house with trees in the yard, a car in the driveway, and bikes on the front porch. A mottled brown mutt Leo named as Jack appeared often.

In another album I found some more army pictures, as well as pictures of Leo as a young bachelor-about-town. Leo couldn't name most of the young women who hung on his arm or sat on his lap or posed with him in a wide range of settings.

"Where's Gladys?" I asked. "Can you show me Gladys?"

"Gladys," he repeated. He bent over the album and turned a page or two, studying the fading black-and-white images. "Gladys isn't here," he announced finally.

"She's not?" I asked. "Are you sure?"

"Yes," he said, looking at me and not the album.

He might be mistaken, or Gladys might have been expunged from the permanent collection, either by Leo himself or by one of her successors. I didn't think Shirley was a likely candidate. She was the third wife, after all, and both she and Leo had lived other lives before they met. She hadn't tried to hide the pictures of Inez; in fact, she'd put them out where he could look at them often.

"What about Auggie?" I asked. "I'd like to see a picture of Auggie."

"Auggie?" Leo frowned. His gaze traveled over the four photograph albums spread around us. Then he said, "I need to talk to Auggie."

"I know you do," I said. "But where *is* Auggie?"

"I don't know," he replied. An idea seemed to come to him. "Ask Shirley."

"Shirley doesn't know, Leo," I said. "How can she find Auggie?"

"Shirley doesn't know about Auggie," he said, as if reminding himself about something.

"No, but she wants to help you find him. Can you help us?"

"No," he said, shaking his head. "I don't know."

"Was Auggie in the army with you?" I asked.

"I have to tell Auggie—"

"What? What do you have to tell Auggie?"

He looked at me blankly, then reached for one of the albums on the table. "Auggie," he repeated, and sighed. But he didn't find Auggie's picture in the album he picked up, or if he did, he didn't tell me.

"Hey, Leo, your shirt's unbuttoned." I pointed to where his shirt gaped in the middle of his chest. "Can you button it back up?"

"Yes," he said, and his hands went to the button. His fingers worried at the button, then dropped into his lap. The shirt was still unbuttoned, but he seemed to have forgotten about it.

"Here, let me help you." I buttoned his shirt and gave him a pat.

"Thank you," he said.

"De nada. Do you remember my name?"

He looked at me, then shook his head a little sheepishly. "No."

"It's Gilda."

A smile spread over his face like an undercranked sunrise. "Gilda. You own the movie theater."

"Very good, Leo. You used to make movies, didn't you?"

"Oh, sure. Movies and television commercials."

"Do you have a lot of videos?"

"A lot."

"Do you have movies on video? Like old movies?"

"Old movies and television shows and commercials. But it wasn't like now."

"It wasn't?"

"We didn't have—" He groped for a word, then gave up. "We didn't have them. Not like now. We had a Kinney."

I assumed that "Kinney" was the name of a long-defunct manufacturer.

"Do you remember a movie called *The Exile*?"

He shook his head. "I don't know."

"It had Douglas Fairbanks, Jr., in it."

"Douglas Fairbanks! He was a handsome devil!" Leo sat up straight with the memory. "He was a swashbuckler!" To my amazement, he slashed at the air with an imaginary sword. "He married that girl—"

"Mary Pickford."

He shook his head. "The other one. The mean one."

I realized he was talking about the son, not the father, after all. "Joan Crawford, do you mean?"

He narrowed his eyes. "I never trusted her."

"That was probably a good policy. Do you remember a film he was in called *The Exile*?"

"No." He blinked, uncertain.

I decided to try him on Auggie again. "Say, does Auggie like movies?"

"Auggie likes funny movies."

"Really? Who does Auggie like? The Three Stooges? The Marx Brothers? The Pink Panther?" I stopped there and told myself to be patient. I could already tell I'd given him too much information to process.

"Auggie likes Donald Duck," Leo said at last.

"Auggie is a little boy," I said, trying to contain my excitement.

"No, he's not so little," Leo said.

"How old is Auggie?" I asked.

"I don't know," he said. His gaze wandered the room and settled on the doorway into the hall.

"What is it, Leo? Do you want to show me something?" I stood up and moved in the direction of the hall. He didn't seem to notice. From the doorway, I peered into the dimness lit at one end by the bedroom and at the other, past the entrance to the basement, by the kitchen. Mounted on the wall was a gallery of framed photographs.

"More pictures," I said aloud, more to myself than to Leo.

I turned on the hall light. Leo came, his shuffling slippers making a low susurration on the carpet, and stood beside me.

"Is Auggie here, Leo?" I watched him study the pictures.

Then he sighed and his shoulders slumped. "He's not here," he said sadly.

"Leo." I touched him on the arm and turned him toward me. "Did Gladys have a baby?"

"Gladys?"

"Yes, did she have a baby? Was Auggie your baby?"

"Auggie's not a baby," he said.

I felt very close to something. But Leo turned away and moved down the hall.

21

The doorbell rang, cutting short my fishing expedition with Leo. I went to open the door to several women from Shirley's church.

"They've gone on to the cemetery," reported the woman in the lead, her glasses steamed over a casserole dish. "Harriet, don't forget the rolls!" she called to someone behind her. "It was a lovely service, dear, very moving."

No one ever criticized a funeral service to a stranger. If you were talking it over with friends or family, that was different, as long as you weren't speaking to the person who'd arranged the service. The Libertys were veteran funeral critics, since they weren't usually consulted on the production. When they all got involved, the result was the kind of extravaganza that had constituted Aunt Maesie's send-off. As a longtime friend of Peachy's, and a behind-the-scenes observer at the Gower Funeral Home, I had my own standards of tastefulness. But by avoiding funerals, I congratulated myself that I was avoiding the occasion of sin.

The casserole lady spotted Leo in my wake.

"Leo, how are you?" She spoke loudly as if Leo were deaf rather than senile. "It's Bess Holcomb, from church."

"Fine," Leo said gravely. "How are you?"

"I'm fine, dear, but very sorry about Alan." She patted his shoulder.

"Alan drives too fast," Leo told her.

The other two members of Bess's entourage put in their appearance. Between them, they were toting enough Tupperware for the leftovers from Babette's feast. I called Styles, as instructed, so that Spike could bring her over, along with Jake, and get her settled before the crowd arrived.

Between keeping an eye on Leo and helping the church women, I had my hands full. The women, having delivered the customary compliment on the funeral service, had moved on to hard-core gossip, conducted under their breaths as they sprinted from stove to refrigerator to dining room table.

"I don't see how she had the nerve to come," one said. "I know that Pauline and Alan were separated, and I truly don't believe she played any part in that, but—"

"You don't think she did?" another interrupted. "The way I heard it, he was always fooling around."

"I think it was an act of God, what happened," Bess declared piously. "If you leave things in the hands of the Lord, he'll see that justice is done."

"Well, I guess if you think she deserved—"

"You know, it would be one thing if she could have come incognito, like they say. But with that big old brace on her neck, you couldn't help but know who she was."

I found their talk entertaining, but hardly informative. As the house filled up, Jake, Spike, and I circulated through the den, living room, kitchen, and patio. The object was to keep the whole house under surveillance while people were milling about. We kept an especially close eye on Curt, the only one of

Leo's sons in attendance. Styles sat enthroned in a recliner, keeping an eye on everything in her line of vision. James stayed close to Shirley, as planned, and Leo was usually with them.

I got my first look at Pauline since her husband had died. She had that glazed look I remembered from Clara under similar circumstances—the air of someone whose artificial serenity had come out of a small bottle. I expressed my condolences succinctly, and she thanked me, a little too brightly. I took her over to introduce her to Styles.

"Pauline, can you think of anybody who has it in for Shirley?" I asked her.

She looked at me without focusing, eyebrows raised in surprise. "Who'd want to hurt Mom? I can't think of a soul."

"We heard she asked you and Alan to catch up on your loan payments," Styles said.

"That was just her way of trying to make us more responsible. I know she means well, and we intended to get paid up. As it turned out—well, if we'd gotten divorced—" Her lip trembled, and she dabbed at one eye with a handkerchief she held crushed in her hand. "There'll be money from the life insurance, but Mother doesn't want that. She said not to worry."

"What about Leo's boys?" I asked. "Do you think they feel the same way—about the loan payments, I mean?"

"I really wouldn't know anything about that," she said. Her eyes wandered across the room to where Curt was squatting on his haunches, talking to two little boys. "I've only met them a few times. I stay out of their way. I don't bother them and they don't bother me." She rubbed her hands together and looked down at them. Her eyes seemed to snag on her wedding ring and I saw her chest heave.

I fought the answering stab in my own chest. When your lover dies, there's a funeral. When your lover leaves you, there's nothing. I felt a hole opening in my heart and if I paid it the least bit of attention I'd fall into it.

"You don't get along," I said. My voice quavered only slightly.

She shrugged. "I don't see them to get along with." She

looked up and nodded across the room in Curt's direction. "Curt's not so bad, though. He's the best of the bunch."

"Do you know why anybody would have wanted to set you up for Shirley's murder, you and Alan?" Styles asked.

"I thought of that. The pool, the wire, and the car—they're all connected to us, aren't they? Specifically to us. Of course, anybody can buy picture wire, so if you ask me, that's a pretty stupid way to—what do you call it?—implicate us. I mean, the police would have to think I was a moron to use my own picture wire to— Well, anyway, I wouldn't kill my own mother, that's crazy. As for who might want us blamed for everything, I just don't know. There are people I get along with and people I don't, like everybody, but why would somebody kill Shirley just to get back at me? It doesn't make sense."

She was becoming restless, and I knew we'd kept her too long from the other guests.

"Is your father here?" Styles asked. "We'd like to meet him."

She shook her head. "He came to the funeral, but he and Mom don't get along, so—" Something caught her attention on the other side of the room. "Sorry, will you excuse me?"

I squatted down next to Styles. "What about Shirley's ex?" I asked.

"Better ask James if he met the guy," she said. "Meanwhile, I think that's Curt headed down the hall."

I stood as quickly as my knees would let me and followed him to the hall, then paused nonchalantly in front of the family photo gallery when he disappeared into the bathroom.

I wasn't too worried about what he was doing in there. James had sealed every bottle of medicine with a drop of wax so that we'd know if anyone had opened anything. We'd considered and rejected the idea of wedging a hair in the door to the medicine cabinet. "This is a funeral, after all, and a family gathering," James had said. "There's a good chance somebody will be looking for aspirin."

When Curt came out of the bathroom, he joined me in front of the photographs.

"Shirley's big on pictures," he observed. "Pictures on the wall, pictures all over the den, photo albums—you name it. She says it's good for Dad, helps keep his memory alive. I don't know if it helps him at all myself, but he does like to look at pictures. We should be grateful she's not the kind who wants to bury his past because it didn't include her."

"Have you ever seen a picture of Gladys, Leo's first wife?"

"You know, I don't think I have. Hard to believe—he's got pictures of everything else. But I can't remember seeing one of her."

"It was nice of you to come to the funeral."

"Well, I wanted to come for Shirley," he said, turning back to look at me. "I didn't know Alan well at all; I only met him casually a few times at family affairs. Listen, I hope you don't think badly of my brothers for not coming." He fingered his tie. "Milt was called out of town last night, and Larry's busy at work. But as I say, we didn't really know him."

I wondered what kind of business called stockbrokers out of town. In this day and age, surely they weren't seized by sudden urges to visit Wall Street. But I didn't ask.

"I'm doing my best to work things out between my brothers and Shirley, Gilda," he said, "but everybody's feelings keep getting in the way. I understand how they all feel, I even understand how Shirley feels, but if they could all just behave like responsible adults who want the best for Leo, we might get somewhere." He turned to face me fully. "You don't have any advice for me, do you, Gilda?"

"I don't know the parties well enough, or the circumstances," I said. "But it seems to me the main thing is to win Shirley's confidence. If Larry opened the books to her and satisfied her that he was acting responsibly on Leo's behalf, it would pave the way for a more open discussion, seems to me."

He sighed and held out his arms. "That's what I keep telling him! But he's got too much pride for his own good. You'd think an accountant would be capable of recognizing where his best interests lie. But he's acting like a little kid about this. And Milt encourages him! I don't know what to do with them, I honestly don't."

As we entered the den, Shirley caught my eye, then shifted her gaze to Curt. She excused herself to the group she was with and crossed the room to intercept her stepson. She put one hand on his elbow, said something to him, and led him out of the room. Styles and I exchanged glances. Curt was about to become unhappier. Shirley was having a little heart-to-heart with him in which she would tell him she was seeing a lawyer and possibly filing a suit against Larry. She was also supposed to mention in passing that the new locks and a security system would be installed on Saturday. One down, two to go. Of the brothers, Curt would probably be the easiest to talk to, but that didn't make Shirley's job easy. When Shirley and Curt reappeared, he was frowning, but he put a hand on her shoulder and smiled at her as they separated.

James dragged me into a corner with Leo.

"Gilda, I'm telling you it was a three-ring circus." He dropped his voice conspiratorially as he scanned the room.

"Who's watching Shirley?" I asked.

"Jake is. So, anyway, the Other Woman was there." He let me hear the capitals in the words "other woman" and cocked an eyebrow at me. "Neck brace and everything. Plus you got the deceased's family on the other side of the aisle—the mother and stepfather and sisters, I mean, not to mention the mother's ex—and they're all looking daggers at Pauline because she and the dear departed were separated, though one look at Miss Neck Brace and you just knew it wasn't all Pauline's fault." He paused to catch his breath. "Then you got Shirley's ex. You got nothing to worry about there, Leo," he told his charge. "She definitely married up when she married you."

Leo grinned, maybe because he could tell he was supposed to, maybe not.

"And you got Pauline's son, who looked as if he'd just as soon spit on his father's coffin as bury it, and her daughter with a couple of giggling kids who should have been left at home. And there's Pauline, who ought to sue her pusher for malpractice. And I can hear somebody in a snit behind us because I'm sitting in the family pew with Shirley, though how this biddy knew I wasn't family I'll never know. But Shirley's holding onto my arm like a pit bull to a dachshund. I got the bruises to prove it." He had already shed his coat, and now he pulled up one sleeve and held out his arm for Leo to inspect. "Look at that, Leo. That girl's got muscles."

"I know," Leo said. He gave James a rueful smile.

"Oops, Spike's giving me the high sign. I better drag my mangled body over there and see what he wants. You coming, Leo?"

"Okay," Leo said agreeably.

Leo's conviviality lasted until everyone had had a chance to eat dessert. Then he stood in the middle of the den and announced loudly, "When are they going home, Shirley? Why don't they go home?"

People smiled and laughed nervously, but the crowd melted away like ice on a summer sidewalk. In no time at all, we were down to a core group of Shirley's protectors.

James gave Leo a high-five, and Leo grinned delightedly. He didn't know why he was being congratulated, but he was willing to accept the congratulations. He was also better able to cope with a smaller group. I could only imagine how many opportunities for testing his memory were presented by crowds of friends and relatives.

Shirley collapsed onto a sofa, kicked her shoes off, coughed, and lit a cigarette. In the background, the dishwasher hummed with the first load, thanks to the efficiency of the church women.

James held up an aspirin bottle he'd kept stashed in his pocket. "Drugs, Shirl?" he offered.

"Yeah, thanks," she said. "Can I take 'em with bourbon?"

"You can take 'em with water," James told her, "and chase it with bourbon."

Spike and Jake were already checking the house for booby traps. I could hear someone in the bathroom rattling pill bottles.

"Better make it a double," I advised James. "Double aspirin, double bourbon. I'm calling in the rest of our team."

22

Uncle Val, former studio electrician, had been drafted to help set up the cameras as inconspicuously as possible. He brought Tobias along because Toby was constantly in search of good material. Not without misgivings, I recruited Adele, the former set designer, because she had a good eye for the placement of things in a room. She wanted to bring Wallace, who claimed that his experience with phosphorescent paint would be valuable. He had also acquired the paint and chalk from a theatrical supply store he frequented.

"Okay," I'd said, "but I draw the line at Uncle Ollie. If he comes, he'll take a pratfall on the doormat, and we'll have enough footprints to light up the house."

Once Spike and Jake had declared the house safe, we began work. Doormats at front, side, and patio doors were chalked. Shirley kept chairs in front of the doors to deter Leo from walking out when no one was looking, and she claimed that it worked well. So once the doormats were chalked, the chairs were replaced on top of them. The chalk was visible as ordinary chalk, however, and we knew it might be noticed and avoided.

"If we're lucky," Styles said, "he'll think that's the extent of Shirley's defenses."

We next brushed a clear, oil-based fluorescent paint on the necks of the front and back doorknobs, as well as the knob on the basement door and garage door. The same paint went on the doors of medicine cabinets, the pantry cabinet, and the refrigerator. The paint would dry slowly, but James would reapply it every night just to make sure it stayed wet enough to rub off on anything it touched. Shirley and James would avoid touching the painted strips. There was always a chance that Leo would disturb things, but Shirley and James would try to steer him clear of the painted areas.

"Lulu says you can just leave it on after it dries," Spike told Shirley. "You won't be able to see anything unless you shine a black light on it."

"Let's hope the owners never do that," she replied, "or we'll lose our security deposit for sure."

Val placed the surveillance cameras inside wrought-iron sconces at the front and back doors and connected a receiver unit to Leo's computer, which he set up in the guestroom while James took Leo for a walk outside.

While Val was working, I retired with Shirley to the den, where Styles was fidgeting in the recliner; Spike had carried off her crutches when he left the room. I told them my theory about film piracy.

"What do you think?" I scanned their faces.

Styles had one eye shut. Her head was cocked to the purple side of her face, and she grimaced. "Let me get this straight. You telling me that somebody is desperate to find a video of an old Douglas Fairbanks movie I never heard of?" she asked. "Not even a Douglas Fairbanks movie, but a Douglas Fairbanks, *Junior*?"

"I know it sounds unlikely," I said apologetically. "But if you'd talked to the guy from the Library of Congress, it might seem more plausible to you, too. Maybe this film doesn't exist anymore, like some of Mae's movies. Or maybe it exists in more than one version—you know, a director's cut and the version that the studio released. Max Ophuls was a highly regarded director. It's always possible DJ is a collector, or has a customer who is. If, for instance, Leo happened to have been one of the first video pirates, he might have some videos of films that don't exist anymore in any version."

"Well," Styles conceded, "I guess if people will pay thousands for palm-sized mass-produced beanbag animals, they'll buy anything. What's your take on this, Shirl?"

Shirley shook her head slowly. "It's possible. I mean, I could see Leo bending the law."

" 'Bending the law'?" Styles repeated. "Shirl, we're not talking about driving fifty in a forty-mile-per-hour zone here."

"It's not like he'd ever steal a television set or a stereo, or rob anybody. But I could see him enjoying the adventure of—well, ripping off the big Hollywood studios. It's kind of boyish, don't you think? Like sneaking into the circus for free."

"More like sneaking in several hundred thousand people for free," Styles said.

"Mind you, I don't know of any large stash of movies or videotapes, but I suppose that could be anywhere, couldn't it? If he had a business, he might have had an office somewhere that I didn't know about—or even just a storage locker."

"If he's got thirty-five millimeter instead of video, that would be a hell of a storage locker," Styles commented.

"If he had something like that, a locker, the rental bill would go to Larry though, right?" I asked.

"I suppose so," she said. "I certainly haven't seen one for any kind of rent."

"Wait a minute!" I exclaimed. "What if he didn't pay rent?"

Styles rolled one and a half eyes at me.

"He still owns the family farm, doesn't he?" I continued. "Maybe he ran the business out of Pleasant Ridge. If it really was a farm, he'd have plenty of space. Why pay for more?"

"Alternatively, if Leo had a bootlegged movie business, his partner could have been in on it," Styles said. "The other stuff they did could have been a front."

"I'm supposed to see Bernie Cutter tomorrow. I'll see what I can find out."

"You going to ask him if his son inherited the video piracy business?" Styles asked.

"Hey, give me some credit, will you? If you don't think I can handle it, fine! Just don't call me next time you need someone to run errands."

I turned my back on her. To Shirley, I said, "What if Larry took over the business? What if he doesn't want to open Leo's books because it will expose his and Leo's illegal activities?"

"Or perhaps only Leo's illegal activities," she mused. "It is possible that Larry found out what his father was doing, and is trying to protect him—and me."

"It's possible," Styles said without conviction.

"If I take him to court, and it turns out that all this time he's been protecting us, I'll feel awful," Shirley said. She sat down in an armchair, dragged an ashtray across an end table to position it at her elbow, fumbled in her pocket for a lighter, and lit a cigarette.

"In that case," Styles said, shifting uncomfortably in her chair, "all he has to do is come clean with you."

"I suppose," Shirley said sadly.

"We could try asking Leo whether he had a sideline in pirated videos," Styles said. "I think we'll leave that to you, Shirley, since you seem to think it's like asking him if he ever peed in the pool when he was a kid."

"Or you could ask DJ," I said.

"You mean, ask DJ if he or she is attempting to acquire an illegally produced copy of a movie?"

"Why not just come right out and ask what DJ wants it for?"

"Same thing. If I sell three-quarter-inch Phillips-head wood screws, and you want to buy three-quarter-inch Phillips-head wood screws, I don't ask what you want them for." She thought a minute. "Maybe I'll ask what DJ's offering for it."

Shirley was frowning in concentration. "Would this illegal business, selling pirated videotapes, if that's what it is—would it be very lucrative?"

Styles and I exchanged glances.

"Oh, yes," she said. "Yes, indeedy."

I went out to the patio for some fresh air and a cigarette to

foul it up, and my uncle Wallace followed me. I could tell he
was following me because the scent of Adele's perfume faded
and the smell of Jack Daniels replaced it.

"Say, Gillie," he said awkwardly, catching up to me and
putting a heavy hand on my shoulder, "I was wondering if
you'd had a chance to read my screenplay yet."

I turned toward his hopeful pink eyes.

"I've read about half of it," I conceded. "I haven't had a
chance to finish it." I paused. He waited. "It's, um, compelling in its own way. It—it has a lot of—" I stopped,
searching for the right word.

"Suspense," he supplied.

"Well, yes, it has that. But what I meant to say was that
maybe there are too many, um,—"

"Characters?"

"Vampires."

He cleared his throat. "Well, Gillie, you know, it *is* a vampire movie." He avoided my eyes, as if embarrassed on my
behalf.

"I know. And I'm probably not the right person to evaluate
it. It's just that I kept getting everybody mixed up, like the
young woman who's run away from home to get away from
her abusive stepfather and the one who's run away from home
because she's pregnant by her high school math teacher."

He looked relieved. He raised an index finger for emphasis. "That's good, Gilda! You've picked up on something
very important. Those characters are doubles, you know? It's
the old doppelganger motif. According to Tobias, Hollywood
movies always have doubles."

"How many do they always have?"

"Why, the more the merrier is the way I look at it." He
opened his arms as if to embrace a Pharaoh's army of doubles.

"Oh. Well, in that case, you have a very merry screenplay."

He pursed his lips. "Too lighthearted, do you think?"

"Nooo," I said slowly. "Only at the very beginning. As soon
as the master vampire sinks his fangs into the widow's neck,
the mood shifts, and things go downhill from there. Unless

you have a happy ending?" I glanced at him through the haze of cigarette smoke and whiskey fumes.

He smiled mysteriously, eyebrows raised, and waggled a finger at me. "Now, now, Gillie, I'm not going to give it away. The only thing I'll tell you is that I haven't forgotten the possibility of a sequel. I'm an old dog, but I can still learn a few tricks." He tapped his temple and winked.

"Well, Clara promised to read it, that's the best I can do for you, Wally," I said. I dropped my cigarette butt on a flagstone and crushed it out with my foot.

"I'm not worried." Grinning, he punched me lightly in the chest. "Compelling, eh?"

"In its way, Wally," I said. "In its way."

Inside, Jake was explaining to Shirley how to check the surveillance tapes. Val had also installed a simple burglar alarm at each of the doors.

"These are just battery-operated switches I rigged up," he explained. "When the door's closed, the circuit's complete. When the door is opened, the circuit's broken, and this little metal pin drops. That's what you check for when you come home, Shirley. I've painted them white to match your doors and trim and mounted them at the bottom so that they're as unobtrusive as possible."

We retired to the den, satisfied with our work.

Adele brought up the rear, pausing in the doorway to survey the room through narrowed eyes that threatened to entangle her false eyelashes.

"Now for the setting," she announced. "We need to create just the right ambiance."

I sighed. This was what I had been afraid would happen. She'd want to redecorate Shirley's house.

"It's not supposed to look any different from what everybody's used to, Adele," I said. "It's just supposed to look ordinary, everyday."

"Exactly," she agreed, nodding. She put one hand to her cheek and tilted her head as if to give her a better angle. "You have no idea how hard that is to accomplish."

We all looked at each other.

"But that's how it looks now," I insisted.

"It's not bad," she admitted, drawing her words out to indicate that a "but" was in the offing. "Wallace, do you remember that set I designed for *House on the Corner*? I remember Eve told me she always felt right at home in that living room."

"I feel right at home in this one," Val said. He leaned back in a recliner, twin to the one Styles lay stretched out in, and put his feet up to demonstrate.

"Honey, I think they're right," Wallace ventured. His gaze swept the room. "It looks okay to me."

"What do you know about it?" she snapped. "You did all of your work in Transylvanian castles and crumbling Victorian mansions! What do you know from ordinary?"

Shirley stepped in. She spoke in a tired but placating voice. "I really appreciate the offer, Adele," she said. "I'm sure you could do wonders with my whole house. The problem is that Leo doesn't adapt well to changes of any kind. Change upsets him. I'm afraid we'll just have to make do with what we have."

Adele gave in reluctantly. "Well, I see your point. All right, then. We'll just have to keep our fingers crossed."

James smiled at Leo and winked. Leo's boomerang smile flashed across his face like an epiphany.

23

On Thursday morning, earlier than a theater owner should reasonably be expected to operate a motor vehicle, I drove down to Buckeye Lake to see Bernie Cutter, Leo's former business partner. The sun shone, the birds twittered in the trees, the lake glittered and exuded a slightly fishy smell. Outboard motors split the morning air like buzz saws and added an acrid petroleum smell to the general bouquet.

I found my way to the marina, parked my Honda, and ambled out onto the dock. The *Boardroom*, moored at slip twenty-eight, was a big white cabin cruiser. I didn't know how big; I didn't know anything about boats. It wasn't the biggest boat in the neighborhood, but it wasn't the smallest, either. It looked expensive.

There was a good-sized man down on his hands and knees doing something to the deck. My angle on him was not flattering. There was a large white mop next to him, so maybe he was doing what they called "swabbing the deck," though I had always thought that was a task performed upright, preferably dancing. I had visions of Gilbert and Sullivan.

"Hi," I said; I couldn't bring myself to shout "Ahoy!" "Are you Mr. Cutter?"

He sat up on his haunches and turned to look at me, a broad smile under his sunglasses and yachting cap. He was a study in pinks and reds—pink polo shirt over pink pants, matching pink socks under Top-Siders, a florid complexion crowned by a head of bushy gray hair still showing a fair amount of its original red. The mop next to him sat up, too, and started yapping.

"You must be Gilda!" he boomed. "Come on aboard!"

He got up and gave me a hand as I clambered over the side. In his other hand he held a glistening paintbrush.

"Don't mind Skipper there," he said jovially.

I would have minded Skipper less if he, she, or it hadn't been snapping at my ankles.

"We were just doing a little work on the deck, me and Skip, eh, boy?" he said, waving the brush in the direction of a small can of something that had the heady smell of an oil slick. Then he gestured toward the front of the boat—the stern? the keel? I couldn't remember. "Well, what do you think of her?"

Whenever someone uses a personal pronoun, and particularly a feminine one, to refer to an inanimate object in their possession, I think it safe to conclude that they're expecting admiration, so I delivered. In any case, at this point I could muster more enthusiasm for the boat than I could for Skipper, who was trying to unravel my socks.

"Oh, hey, it's great!" I looked around. "I don't know anything about boats," I hastened to add before my ignorance became apparent, "but I think it's beautiful!"

This was the right response, I could tell. He beamed at me. It was probably the right response on two counts: it expressed the admiration his boat was due, and it presented him with an opening to educate a nautical ignoramus.

He recapped the small can and carefully set his brush down on top. "Come on! Let me show you around! Just step around that wet spot there on the deck." He reached out a hand to guide me. "Skippy, now you behave yourself! Gilda is our guest."

Skipper's eyes were virtually hidden behind hair, but what I could see of them looked beady.

Cutter took me on a tour of the boat's amenities, and I made cooing noises and ran my hand respectfully over various surfaces.

"Want to go for a spin?" he said at last.

"Well, I don't want to put you to any trouble."

"No trouble at all! I want you to see this baby in action. Then you'll really appreciate her!"

Skipper disappeared. No doubt he had gone to the back of the boat to wave good-bye to his buddies on the dock.

Moments later, Cutter was backing the boat out of the slip when he asked, "You swim, don't you?"

"Like a fish," I said. I didn't say what kind of fish. I hadn't actually been called upon to demonstrate my swimming skills for years—not since I'd traded my youthful not-quite-slenderness for middle-aged spread. The fish I had in mind was a bottom-feeder, a flounder, maybe.

"Get seasick?"

"Not much. But just for my information, is it illegal to throw up in the lake or just a breach of boating etiquette?"

"I'm teasing you," he said, raising his voice now to be heard over the motor. "We've got a nice, calm day. Don't worry."

I looked out across the water as the wind whipped the hair across my eyes. Gilda Liberty, theater owner, adventurer, girl detective. Skipper was back, standing shoulder to shoulder with me on top of some kind of storage compartment, barking into the wind. I sincerely hoped that this interview didn't have to be conducted in a shout.

"How do you like her?" Cutter shouted.

It occurred to me that if I acted as if I couldn't hear him, he might slow the boat down so that we could talk. "What?" I yelled.

"How do you like her?" he roared. "The boat?"

I gritted my teeth in what felt like a moronic grin and nodded.

"Skippy loves it," he reported, nodding affectionately at the dog. "He's a natural-born sailor." I couldn't see anything of Skippy's eyes now. His mouth hung open in panting position and his tongue fluttered in one corner. I suspected that some of the spray I was catching was coming from the old canine salt, himself.

"How's Leo doing?" Cutter shouted. "I've only seen him once since he moved back. I live down here now, all summer. It was quite a shock to see him, I can tell you. Hard to believe that a guy as bright and quick as Leo could get that way. I told Shirley, I said, 'Listen, Leo's family. If you need anything, just give me a buzz.' And I meant it."

"Do you see much of Leo's sons?"

"Who?"

I drew in a big breath. It scorched my lungs on the way out. "Leo's sons! Do you still see Leo's sons?"

"Oh, the boys. No, I don't see them much. Larry I see from time to time, of course. The other two—we exchange holiday cards, you know, so I keep up with them that way. And I think Davey sees them more than I do."

"Your son?"

"Right. I think he keeps in closer touch than I do. Well, I'm down here for five months out of the year, so I'm really cut off. But I've got to tell you, Gilda, I like it that way. Retirement should be retirement, know what I mean?"

There were plenty of other boats on the water, most of them powerboats, but a few rowboats near the water's edge and a sailboat or two. I didn't know how they could all peacefully coexist—the jet skis and the cabin cruisers and the rowboats and the sailboats. We were churning up a considerable wake, and we weren't the largest craft on the water. I watched a small sailboat bob up and down in the wake of a powerboat pulling a water-skier. I wondered how Skipper kept from toppling overboard.

Then we cut across a substantial wake ourselves, hitting the top of every wave like a steeplechaser hitting every bar. I found out how Skipper managed to keep his balance when his paws scrabbled for purchase on the slick surface of his perch and he found my arm. You don't normally think of dogs having claws, or at least, I don't, but this one definitely had something sharp at the end of those fuzzy little feet.

"Say, want something to drink?" Cutter bellowed in my ear. "I've got some beer and soft drinks down below."

This I took as a hopeful sign that he might cut the engine, and I wasn't disappointed. The roar died down, and he disappeared below deck. Skippy and I regarded each other with mutual suspicion.

"Why don't you go take another nice little doggy nap?" I asked him in a low voice. "When you wake up, I'll just seem like part of a bad dream."

He yawned as if he were suggestible, but he was only raising false hopes. He jumped down from his pedestal and trotted over to stand at the doorway through which Cutter had disappeared, looking expectantly down the steps. Cutter emerged soon after with two beers and a doggy dish containing a suspiciously amber foamy liquid. Maybe the beer would put us all in a more convivial mood. By the time we got back to the dock, we'd be arm-in-paw, singing "Yo-Ho-Ho and a Bottle of Rum."

I accepted a beer and settled on a bench.

"Tell me something, Mr. Cutter—"

"Bernie, please." He set the dog dish on the deck, and Skippy began to lap noisily.

"Tell me something, Bernie. Does Leo still have anything to do with the business? I mean technically. Does he still own a share?"

"Yes, he does, as a matter of fact." He sat down across from me, his beer can resting on one pink knee, where it made a dark circle. "We offered to buy him out when he moved to Florida—well, Davey did. But he couldn't make up his mind to sell out. It was his brainchild, after all. Hard to let go. I told him, I said, 'Leo, don't rush into anything you might regret later. If you don't want to sell out, don't. Davey can take care of everything here, and once or twice a year, why, you can come back here for a board meeting and Davey can fill you in if you like. If you don't want to come, we'll talk on the phone, what the hell.' "

"So Leo trusted Davey to run the business?"

"Oh, sure! Worked together for years, those two; they got along fine. Oh, they had their disagreements, didn't always see eye to eye on things, but then the same was true of me and Leo. Or me and Davey, for that matter. With Davey, though, it was like a generation thing—you know, sometimes I think he saw Leo and me as a couple of old farts who didn't appreciate innovation. But hell, Leo wrote the book on innovation, and I wasn't far behind. But Leo had the vision, you know? As soon as television came along, why, Leo saw where the future was headed. 'It's going to be big, Bern,' he told me. 'It's going to have everything, even movies. You'll see.' Hell, I'm just glad I listened to him. I'd still be running some nickel-and-dime operation if Leo hadn't come along with his big ideas. Damned shame, what's happened to him. A guy ought to be able to enjoy his retirement, you know? Leo sure earned his."

"Did you use videotape in the early days?" I asked. "How did that work?"

He batted a hand at me. "Nah, this was before. We had a thirty-five-millimeter kinescope when we started. A 'kine,' that's what we called 'em."

So Leo hadn't been talking about a brand called "Kinney," but about a kinescope.

"Ampex came along in the midfifties with the first VTR for magnetic recording—the Mark Four is what it was called. We didn't get our first quad until fifty-nine or sixty, somewhere in there—they were called 'quads' because of the four heads—and don't you know, Leo wouldn't be satisfied unless we got color. So we got us an RCA color VTR. Man, we thought we were hot stuff! And you know something?" He leaned toward me. "We were."

I found myself wondering if I could have given such a detailed account of the early years of my own career, down to the brand and model of typewriter I'd used. I thought not.

Now that we were standing still in the sun I was hot. Skippy seemed to notice this and planted his hairy behind next to my foot so that he could lean his hairy body against my leg. I tried to shift away from him.

I considered which of the many threads woven into Cutter's narrative I would worry at first.

"What kinds of things did Leo and Davey disagree about?"

He expelled a puff of air. "Everything from ad concepts to music to pricing, at one time or another. They didn't fight, you understand; they just disagreed."

"So Davey never became so angry that he threatened to—oh, say, quit and start his own company?"

"No, nothing like that. Mayer and Cutter was the best in the business—everybody knew that. Even Davey knew he could never compete with us."

The comment made it sound as if Davey might have given the prospect some thought.

"So how does the business work now?"

He took a contemplative pull on his beer. "Davey does it all. Oh, we had our last board meeting last year. Even then, we were sort of humoring Leo by having him attend. He couldn't really contribute anything, poor bastard, but we wanted him to feel like he could. Hell, the meetings had gotten pretty informal anyway. We held 'em here on the boat—that's how come I re-named her the *Boardroom*. That was our little joke, you see. Now we deal with Larry when we need something—he has Leo's power of attorney, you know."

He squinted at me to see if I was following the intricacies of corporate organization and practice. Skipper heaved a deep sigh, as if bored to tears by the elementary nature of the explanation, and collapsed in a heap on my right foot.

"I expect this year we'll invite Larry to the real board meeting, such as it is," Cutter continued, gazing thought-fully at his dog. "Then we'll probably have Leo and Shirley out for a little excursion around the lake so we can pretend again that Leo attended the annual board meeting. It'll make him happy, eh, Skip? We'll have to remember to mention it to Davey, eh?"

If the dog recognized his name, he made no sign.

"Has Larry been easy to work with?"

"Oh, sure, Larry knows his stuff. He doesn't try to interfere."

"It's interesting that none of Leo's sons went into the busi-ness," I observed. I decided to promote goodwill and bent down to scratch Skipper behind the ears, but I couldn't really find anything readily distinguishable as an ear to scratch, so I patted him on the head. He sprang up, yipping. I retracted my arms hurriedly and showed him my palms.

Cutter grinned fondly at the dog. "No, the boys weren't really interested. Well, Davey wasn't interested when he was younger. Didn't have any intention of following in the old man's footsteps. He worked for us summers some years—all the boys did. But Davey did it right through college, and de-cided after he graduated that he liked it well enough to stay on."

"Do all the boys get along well, then? Davey and Leo's sons?"

"Oh, sure, they grew up together. They were never best friends, you understand. Went to different schools. But they were friends."

Skipper had retreated from the dog molester and sat down next to Cutter. I was hot, out of beer, and increasingly out of sorts, but I soldiered on.

"Bernie, did your company ever have anything to do with showing movies on television? What I mean is, did you own a film library of any kind?"

"No, nothing like that," he said easily. "Now what we did, we would produce the commercials—the local ones, I mean— that would air during, say, *Sci-Fi Theater* or *The Late Show*. But we didn't have the movies; the stations had those."

"The reason I'm asking," I said carefully, setting my beer can down on the deck, "is that somebody e-mailed Leo and asked him if he owned a copy of *The Exile*. Does that ring a bell?"

He thought. Then the corners of his mouth curled down in exaggerated denial as he shook his head. "Never heard of it. That a movie?"

"From the forties."

Again he shook his head. "No, I can't think of any reason why Leo would have a thing like that, unless he had it on video. But anybody can buy movies on video at Blockbuster. Why would he ask Leo for it? Did he want to borrow it?"

"I don't know. I was hoping maybe you could help me. I even wondered if Leo was making video copies of movies back in the—gee, I don't know. When did videotape come in?"

"Well, we had videotape back in the fifties; matter of fact the first cartridges were introduced in the late fifties. But that was strictly television technology. It's not like now, when practically everybody owns a VCR. Wouldn't have been worth much to copy movies onto videotape back then because there wouldn't have been a market, you see?

"And technically, that would be illegal, but you don't need me to tell you that. Of course, people do it all the time now, even when they're not supposed to. Copy things off of television, too. Hell, everybody does it; that's why they sell so many VCRs." He grinned at me.

Skipper heaved a deep sigh that seemed to raise his whole body like a levitating balloon and then drop it.

I took a breath myself. "I was wondering if Leo had been copying movies and selling the copies, maybe not on video at first, but later—in the eighties."

He laughed. "You think Leo was a video pirate?" He seemed to find this idea very amusing. "I doubt it, Gilda. I'm not saying he wasn't; he could have been into all sorts of things I didn't know about. His mind was always working, you know? And I wouldn't want to give you the impression that Leo was any kind of schoolmarm. He could skate pretty close to the edge sometimes, if you know what I mean. But I don't see him as a video pirate. Not Leo."

He reached down to scratch Skippy's invisible ears and the dog moaned in contentment.

I told him about the battle being waged over Leo's finances and asked him for his opinion.

"Well, now, I call that a real shame, Gilda," he said. "Larry hasn't said anything to me about it. But when families start bickering over money, it's too bad."

A passing boat tooted at us, and Cutter turned around and waved. Turning back to me, he said, "To tell you the truth, though, Gilda, I'd have to side with the boys on this one. Don't get me wrong; I think Leo picked a real winner when he married Shirley. Hell, I guess Leo always picked winners, except for that first time, but that didn't last long, I hear. Inez was a wonderful woman, though. And Shirley's a wonderful woman, too. But she doesn't know the first thing about high finance, and here she's got an accountant and a broker in the family and she doesn't want to take advantage of that?"

"I think she just wants to know where things stand."

"Understandable, perfectly understandable. And Larry ought to be able to explain it to her. Sounds to me like the way she asked him maybe got his back up, eh? That's what it sounds like to me. Maybe she made him think she didn't trust him."

"I think she's worried about nursing home expenses for Leo."

"Listen, you don't have to tell me about nursing home expenses. My mother's in a nursing home, and it's the biggest darned racket I ever saw! Extra charges for just about everything you can think of except flushing the toilet! Shirley's right to worry. But she's not right to make Larry think she doesn't trust him to look after his own father's interests."

"How big are Leo's interests, if you don't mind my asking? I don't mean in dollars, I just mean, well, is he what you might call affluent?"

"I haven't seen his portfolio, of course, but unless he's made some bad investments—yeah, sure, I'd call Leo affluent. He was never one to waste money. Didn't have any bad habits—women, drugs, gambling, skiing." He grinned at me. "I said that last one because Leo used to tease me about skiing. My whole family loves to ski, and Leo, he never could see what we saw in it. I have to laugh every time I think about it." He demonstrated with a throaty chuckle. "See, in the first place, Leo never liked the cold. Then there was the expense involved. He never could see why anybody would spend that kind of money to fly off somewhere where they could tie two sticks on their feet and slide down the side of a mountain. That's how he put it." He shook his head, and I suddenly realized that there was a tear gliding down one cheek. I peered at him and realized that the water in his eyes was not caused only by merriment. "That Leo," he said, and sniffed. "He was a hell of a funny guy."

Cutter extracted a handkerchief from his pocket and blew his nose, then smiled at me a little sheepishly.

"He still is," I said gently. "He still makes jokes sometimes."

"Still is," Cutter amended, and cleared his throat. He looked around. "This used to be Leo's boat, did you know that?"

I shook my head.

"Yep, bought her from him. Always lusted after this boat. He always said, 'Bernie, if I ever decide to sell her, you'll be the first one I'll call.' And he did, too."

"You said that you renamed this boat," I recalled. "What was its name when Leo owned it?"

"She was the *India*. I guess you know that Leo was stationed in India during the war."

"It seems to have been an important time in his life," I observed.

"It was for all of us," he said, gazing into the distance. "All the boys of my generation—hell, some of the gals, too. Most of us left home for the first time, and that was back in the days when you didn't leave home unless you got married. We traveled around the world, saw new people and places we'd never even imagined. Why, I'll bet for some kids, it was the only time in their lives they left the county they were born in. And, of course, most of us saw death for the first time—death and destruction on a scale we never anticipated. It was a hell of a time, Gilda, a hell of a time. Young people today have no idea."

"Where were you stationed?"

"I was in the Navy, cruising around the South Pacific," he said, and he set down his beer and pulled up his sleeve so that I could get the full effect of his Navy tattoo. "I've got some other little souvenirs I won't show you to save us both embarrassment." He grinned at me and patted the seat of his pants. "Little mementos from when we retook Corregidor from the Japs in forty-five."

"I have one more thing to ask you about, if you don't mind," I said. He had stood up as if restless to crank up the engine and get moving again. "Leo keeps talking about someone named Auggie, someone he seems desperate to talk to. Do you know who that is?"

"Auggie," he repeated thoughtfully. "Doesn't ring a bell."

"Are you sure?" I persisted. "Auggie, or it might be August. Or I suppose it might even be Augusta." The feminine possibility had only just occurred to me.

"Augusta. No, sorry."

"Any ideas how I might find this person he's talking about?"

"I suppose you asked the boys?"

"They haven't heard of him."

"That's a tough one. I wouldn't even know where to start. Leo's what? Seventy-one years old? And his brain's not working too well. So Auggie could be his best friend from kindergarten, right? Sounds to me like looking for Auggie would be like looking for a needle in a haystack, that's how it sounds to me. Care for another beer? I want to take you up a ways before we head home." He winked at me. "Might as well get your money's worth."

Skipper clambered up to his former perch, stepping on my foot in the process.

"Watch this!" Cutter boomed as soon as he'd cranked up the engine. Then he shouted, "Cast off! Ay, ay, Skipper!"

The dog gave three short barks.

Cutter beamed at me.

The beer and sun took their toll on my tolerance for being slammed against the surf, and I disembarked considerably queasier than I had embarked. I managed to thank my host.

Skippy raced up and down the deck, yapping in my direction.

"That's right, Skipper! Tell Gilda good-bye," Cutter instructed him heartily.

I suspected that a more accurate translation of Skipper's yaps might be, "Good riddance, bitch!"

24

In the afternoon Duke and I were caught up in the reconstruction of the movie that was opening that night in the side theater: *Spawn*. It was about an assassin who is killed, goes to hell, and makes a deal with the devil to return to earth.

"The devil must have been in charge of breaking this film down," Duke groused. "Look at this thing, Gilda!" He held up a badly chewed section of film.

"The hounds of hell," I agreed. "I met one of them today; his name was Skippy. I hope this movie doesn't jinx us. I'm going to unpack our latest box of goodies."

I left him to it and went down to the lobby. After less than two weeks of peddling dinobilia, we'd found ourselves low in stock and forced to reorder.

The box was heavy. What had Duke ordered that was so damn heavy? I crouched down, slit the top, reached in, and extracted a large, smooth, egg-shaped piece of stone. Obviously a life-sized replica of a dinosaur egg, it must be intended to be a giant's paperweight.

We'd better sell these, I thought; I don't want to have to ship them back.

I heard nothing from Shirley or Styles. A handful of the leather crowd turned out for *Spawn*, clinking as they walked and looking down their pierced noses at the moms and dads bringing their kids to see *The Lost World*. The moms and dads, for their part, eyed the punks nervously, while their kids gazed wistfully at the purple and green hair. The teenaged girls who were headed for the teenpic in the balcony watched the punks discreetly from behind curtains of hair, whispered together, and giggled.

"Just one big happy melting pot," I said to Duke, "that's us."

"Dinosaur kitsch doesn't exactly attract a crossover market, does it, Gilda?" Duke observed. "I should have stocked some demonic merchandise as well."

"Yeah, so we could get picketed by the Catholic Legion of Decency," I said, "and draw lots of free publicity."

"Maybe I could get my hands on some death's head earrings on short notice," he mused.

I turned to look at him. I wasn't sure whether he was serious or not. I saw that he wasn't sure, either.

"You could take your scissors out on the sidewalk and pierce ears," I suggested. "If you could get people to lay their earlobes down on the cement, all you'd have to do would be position the scissors, and then whack 'em with a dinosaur egg."

"Hey, yeah! I could do tongues, too! Noses might be tricky, but I could give it a try."

Faye's voice cut in. "Insurance risk," she said shortly, as if taking us seriously.

"Well, jeez, Faye, what the hell?" I said. "Everything's an insurance risk. I mean, if anybody drops one of those dinosaur eggs on their foot, we may lose all of our *Lost World* profits in a lawsuit."

The late crowd for *Spawn* was even stranger.

"The early show, that was the wanna-bes," Faye observed sagely. She spoke with the authority of someone whose own hair was spiked, whose own nose was pierced, and whose own neck was draped in chains and padlocked to her shoulders. "That crowd, they have, like, real jobs. They can wash the dye out of their hair by nine o'clock in the morning."

"And the nose rings?" Duke asked with genuine curiosity.

"Clip on."

"Ouch!" He rubbed his own nose.

That explained in part why Faye was working for us this summer: apart from the free space upstairs for her editing equipment, we had the appeal of no dress code.

At nine-thirty, I broke down and called Styles. Spike answered.

"She's real crabby today, Gilda," he warned me in a whisper.

"You've seen her when she wasn't?"

"She don't like to admit she overdid it yesterday, but you can tell she's sore today. Y'know, Gilda, between Sammy and her old man, I'm kinda hoping my next patient is a sweet little old grandmotherly type."

"I think they're obsolete," I said. "I don't know any."

Styles came on the line. "Are the dinosaurs still winning?"

"Last I looked."

"Good."

"I don't suppose you've heard anything from Shirley?"

"Cookie, if I'd heard anything from Shirley, your family would know every last fucking detail by now," she said irritably.

That was true. Gossip in my family moved faster than the speed of sound.

"Meanwhile, DJ wants to know if I really have *The Exile* and what did I have in mind? Seems to think I know that 'our resources are limited,' as he says. Asked me how good the sound was, and whether the dialogue was audible throughout the film."

"And what did you say?"

"I said the sound was fine. Then I thought maybe he wouldn't believe me, so I said that the dialogue was a bit muffled in two or three scenes, but you could still hear what was being said."

Something about this exchange made me uneasy. "You did call around to find out whether or not *The Exile* was readily available?"

"I called every video store in Eden and Columbus; nobody had it. Then I checked on-line. None of the on-line video stores had it, either."

"So I guess it is pretty rare," I mused.

"And speaking of who knows what and who has what," she went on, "my hacker turned up jackshit on Leo's assets. Apart from the property in Pleasant Ridge, I don't know what he's got where."

I raised my eyebrows. "Does that mean he doesn't have any?"

"No, it means that none of the account numbers Shirley got off old records was valid. It means that all those accounts were closed, possibly at the time Larry took over Leo's finances, and no new accounts were opened at those banks in Leo's name."

I whistled. "Any accounts in Larry's name?"

"Nope," she said. "Larry's accounts could be anywhere. You ask me, they're in the Caymans."

I hesitated. "I suppose you could argue that Larry and Leo closed out those accounts and opened new joint accounts at Larry's own bank or S and L to make things more convenient for Larry."

"Maybe. But if I were Shirley, that would make me nervous."

"We'll find out all this stuff about Leo's finances if Shirley sues, right?"

She snorted. "If she survives that long, we'll find out."

"Say, Styles, can you trace Leo's first wife, Gladys, through the computer?"

"If I had her maiden name, I might be able to. Why? Are you thinking about Auggie again?"

"Yeah. Maybe she knows who he is."

"It's worth a try," Styles agreed. "But first I have to see if anybody knows what her maiden name was. Doesn't sound like they were together very long. What we really need is for somebody to go to Pleasant Ridge."

"Somebody meaning me."

"What's the matter, Nancy? Aren't we having fun yet?"

25

The call I'd been expecting came at around four o'clock the next afternoon.

"It's show time," Styles said.

"I'll be right there," I said, and hung up.

I glanced at the clock. Shirley had taken Leo to see a doctor at the university medical center in Columbus at one that afternoon. She had taken pains to inform Pauline and the Three Stooges. No one had entered the house while she was at the lawyer's office yesterday, so today had been their last clear opportunity to get into the house before the locks were changed. After today, the options would be severely limited.

But I couldn't turn down Shirley's street because the road was blocked by police cars, their flashers glinting feebly in the hot July sunshine.

My heart lurched. I switched off the ignition and hit the ground running. I left the Honda parked in the middle of the street.

There seemed about the scene before me no particular air of urgency, however. A small crowd of people, including kids, was scattered around. Two cops, a man and a woman, were standing to one side talking to a stocky man in a short-sleeved sport shirt and a drooping tie.

The thud of my running footsteps on the pavement made them turn around.

"What's going on?" I asked breathlessly. I peered down the street to where a fire engine, two unmarked but official-looking cars, and a plain white van were parked in front of Leo and Shirley's. I sniffed the air but I couldn't smell smoke, and I saw no fire hoses on the ground. "Was anybody hurt?"

Before they could answer, I heard my name being called, and turned to see Spike waving at me. He stood near an old Dodge Dart, red in color. Sitting on the hood of the car, her back against the windshield, was Styles. Her foot was propped up on a toolbox to elevate her broken leg, and her arm was still in a sling. She was wearing dark shades. A Cleveland Indians cap was perched rakishly over the bandage on her head, and she appeared to be hanging out, catching some rays. James sat on a front fender. My uncle Val stood with his back to me, arms folded, deep in conversation with James. Tobias leaned against the driver's side door; he smiled and waved.

I glanced back down the street, then made my way through the crowd to the Dodge Dart. The cops had already gone back to their conversation.

"What's going on?" I demanded. "Do those flak jackets say 'ATF' on the back? Where are Leo and Shirley?"

"It's okay," Spike reassured me, taking my arm and guiding me closer. "They're with your friend Dale over there." He nodded in the direction of a cruiser parked behind the barricade about halfway down the block. "Everybody's all right, but the cops got a bomb to deal with."

"A bomb?" I fumbled for my cigarettes.

" 'Incendiary device' is what they're calling it. Bomb squad got here just before you did," Val reported.

"Do we know who yet?" I asked.

Spike shook his head. "Nəah, we don't know nothin'. Shirley did just like we told her to—she called the cops and didn't go in."

"I gave them your black light from the *Austin Powers* premiere, Gil," Val said. "Worked like a charm. Led them right to the goods."

James hopped down off the fender. "Here comes Shirley now," he said.

Shirley was leading a very agitated Leo in our direction.

"James, can you—" She gave James a pleading look, but he didn't need an explanation.

He put an arm around Leo's shoulders and steered him our way. "Come on over here with us, Leo," he said. "It's too noisy over there where you were."

Leo put a hand tentatively to his ear. "It was noisy over there," he conceded. He turned his head anxiously to watch Shirley's retreat. Then he complained, "I don't know what's going on. Why are all these people here? Why can't we go home?" His voice rose a notch with hysteria.

James patted him on the back. "You can go home soon, Leo. We're just going to hang loose here for a little while."

"Hang loose," Leo echoed. He looked around at us, frowning.

"Hey, Leo," I said, waving my cigarette at him. "Remember me? Gilda?"

"Gilda!" His smile broke his face wide open. The petulant lines in it receded like waves at low tide. "The movie lady!"

"That's right."

"I used to be in pictures," he said, focusing all his attention on me.

"I heard that."

"But then I got old," he said, and some of the shadows returned. "I'm too old for pictures now."

"Why don't you tell us about your pictures, Leo?" Styles suggested. She was still lying back against the windshield, not looking at Leo. I couldn't tell whether her eyes behind the sunglasses were open or closed.

When Leo didn't respond, James prompted him. "Sam wants to know what kinds of pictures you made, Leo."

"All kinds," he answered unexpectedly, flapping a hand at James. "Why, we made all kinds—westerns and suspense and romance." He smiled reminiscently. "India—" He broke off and you could see his eyes change.

James looked at me. I looked at Styles.

"You made movies in India?" I asked. Had he confused his venues? Or had the troops shot home movies, as they had taken photographs, just to amuse themselves and record the moment? I remembered the program from the Imperial— "House of Comfort and the Best Pictures." Was Leo confusing a time when he'd watched movies with a time when he'd made movies? Or had he simply misunderstood the question?

His expression had gone blank, and I repeated the question.

"No," he replied. "Not in India. That was during the war."

"But you made pictures after the war," I said.

Leo was distracted by the arrival of a new carload of onlookers, a mother and two boys. Like me, the mother was noisy until reassured, then her boys were noisy.

"You made pictures after the war, didn't you Leo?" I asked.

"Oh, we made a lot of pictures," he said. "There was always something to shoot."

"Thirty-five millimeter?"

"We had a kine," he said.

"And then later you used video."

He nodded. "We had an RCA VTR. The color wasn't very good."

"Where are all the films and videos now, Leo?"

He shrugged. "God knows," he said, surprising me again.

"*You* don't know?"

He shook his head with a sheepish expression, as if accustomed to apologizing for what he didn't know or didn't remember.

A kid who was clowning around bumped into him, hard, and his mood changed.

"I want to go home," he said querulously. "Where's Shirley? Who are all these people? Why don't they go home?"

There was a ripple of nervous laughter around us as James tried to soothe Leo. Leo rubbed his crotch and a small crowd of boys near us burst into giggles.

"Tell you what, Leo, let's go for a ride," James suggested, catching my eye. "Would you like that?"

"No, I want to go home," he insisted.

But we got him into my car and I drove to my aunt Gloria's. By the time we arrived, Leo's pants were wet, as was the seat under him.

He seemed deeply humiliated. "I can't get out," he told James hoarsely. "I'm wet."

"Tell you what, Leo," James said cheerfully. "I'll walk in front of you and we'll borrow some dry pants from Oliver, okay?"

I went on ahead to spare Leo further embarrassment. Oliver was home by himself, and for once seemed to apprehend the seriousness of the situation. He produced a pair of pants for Leo, and when Leo and James emerged from the bedroom, Leo seemed to have forgotten the incident entirely. Kindly, Oliver took him down to the basement to distract him with a model train set he had been working on for years. Given the state of things, I went back to the theater to await developments.

At around ten o'clock, I was standing in front of our display of dinosaur kitsch, selecting items to stash in my bag for a talk I was giving the next day at a kids' summer program sponsored by the local parks and recreation department. I don't like to carry a purse if I can avoid it, but when I do, the purses I favor are open bags large enough to accommodate a brontosaurus pup. Duke was standing by, literally egging me on.

"No way!" I was protesting, backing away from the two eggs he was extending in my direction. "I'll dislocate my shoulder."

"C'mon, Gilda!" he wheedled. "They're really cool! They look really authentic, and the kids will be amazed at the size of them."

"Duke, if I drop one on the head of an average-sized six-year-old, we'll have a lawsuit on our hands for a sum that will rival Steven Spielberg's annual income."

That was when Todd called me to the phone for Styles's latest installment.

"Care to guess whose mug was on the security camera?" she asked slyly.

"Eenie, meenie, minie. I guess Larry's."

"You win the donkey instead of the new living room suite. It was Milt's."

"That was going to be my next guess. He struck me as cocky and not too bright. Not too brave, either, and the killer was always trying to strike from a distance."

"This dipshit doesn't have the brains God gave an armadillo, I swear. Dale says we should've seen his face when they pointed the black light at him and his ear lit up."

I wished I'd seen it. Crooks wear gloves so that they won't leave fingerprints at the scene of the crime. What they don't expect is that the scene of the crime will leave marks on them. Milt wouldn't have been able to feel the paint through the gloves, and wouldn't have been able to see it there, either. I pictured him standing in the front hallway, holding a bomb in one hand and scratching his head with the other while he tried to decide where to put it. Even if he'd felt anything at that point, he wouldn't have had any reason to guess what it was and wouldn't have seen anything in the mirror if he'd looked.

"And get this: Dale thinks he's a user."

"That's what James says. So did he really plant a bomb? That sounds like kind of a difficult operation to manage when you're on drugs."

"Technically, an incendiary device," Styles said. "It was tricked out to look like an ordinary package—typed address label, the works. It wasn't a particularly complicated one. Dale said anybody with a modicum of mechanical skill and a good set of instructions could have put it together. He might not have been high when he made it, *if* he made it."

"I'm sure he has a perfectly reasonable explanation."

"You bet he does," she said. "First he denied ever handling a package. Then, once his ears and face started glowing in the dark, his memory came back in a rush and he said he found it on the porch and brought it in. He couldn't explain why he'd left it in the basement, but I'm sure when his lawyer gets through with him, he'll have a perfectly reasonable explanation for that, too. And get this: he also couldn't explain why his hands didn't glow, and why there weren't any fingerprints on the back doorknob, even though he let himself in that way using his key."

"Cops find the gloves?"

"Not yet. Maybe never."

"How's Shirley?"

"Fit to be tied. She keeps saying, 'His own father! He was willing to kill his own father!' Meanwhile, James and Spike keep flexing their muscles and popping their knuckles like they're the Terminator's sparring partners or something. Milt's already out on bond, of course, but he'd be safer inside. I'm liable to take a swing at him myself if I get half a chance."

"Same here." I was laughing, but I was conscious of a small caterpillar of doubt making its way up the back of my neck. "How'd you get all this information, anyway? Dale isn't usually that forthcoming."

"He didn't have any choice. None of the cops could figure out how to replay the security tapes."

That caterpillar was really bothering me.

"Say, Styles—"

"Yeah?"

"What if Milt wasn't in this alone?"

"You mean, what if he had an accomplice? One of the other brothers or Alan and Pauline?"

"I just think Larry has to be in it somehow. He's the one who signs the checks."

"You're just a sore loser. But seriously, I think we have to consider the possibility," she said, not laughing now. "Dale's worried because ATF didn't find any bomb-making materials in Milt's house—nothing obvious, anyway, like a stash of fertilizer and fuses in the basement. They'll go over it again, and over the bomb itself, of course, but unless they can prove Milt made the damn thing, he could walk."

"Did Dale look for drugs?"

"Not covered by his warrant," Styles said. "And he didn't happen to trip over any, sad to say."

"I gather Milt's not talking, except to say that he picked up the package and brought it in the house."

"That's right."

I thought back to the Fourth of July cookout, and the man I'd met there. Milt had not seemed the type to hold his tongue.

"He's been well coached," I observed.

"Quite likely," she conceded.

"Maybe even set up."

"Quite possibly."

I sighed. "So what do we do now?"

"I called the home security company again; they'll be at Shirley's in the morning. We'll leave the other security measures in place for a few days, including the cameras, although now everybody will know they're there. James offered to spend the night tonight, but Shirley said no, she didn't want to upset Leo's routine any more than she had already. I gather he's pretty agitated. She's really had her hands full."

"I'll call her and offer to help her clean up tomorrow," I said. "I'll bet the house is a mess, with all the fingerprint dust and the fallout from the hordes of cops and firefighters and feds and technicians who traipsed through there today."

But when I called Shirley, it became apparent that our day wasn't over.

She picked up on the sixth ring, breathless. In the background I could hear television noises.

"Oh, Gilda!" she wailed when she heard my voice. "I can't talk now. Leo's out!"

"Leo's out?" I echoed. I couldn't think what she meant.

"He got out of the house!" she said. "I don't know why; he's never done it before—not since I put the chairs in front of the doors. And I put them back after the police left; they were all in place. I was on the phone, and I thought he was watching television, and when I got off the phone and went into the den he wasn't there!"

"He's not in the basement?" I suggested.

"I looked. Listen, I have to go."

"I'll be right over," I told her. "In the meantime, don't panic. He's wearing an ID bracelet. Somebody will find him and bring him home."

I rushed to pick up my bag and nearly pulled a muscle lifting it.

"I'm going over to Shirley's to help her look for Leo," I threw at Todd and Duke, who were leaning on the ticket counter, talking. At the door, I hesitated, and then glanced back at them. "Call Styles for me, will you?"

26

I took every shortcut I knew. I had a bad feeling about this.

In the first place, Milt was already out on bond. People with resources, and especially white men with resources, almost never spent a night in jail. And even if Milt was home in the bosom of his family, there might be an accomplice, or even a garden variety opportunist, who had decided that this would be a good night to make a move.

Was the killer still after Shirley? Or had he or she decided that killing Leo would accomplish the same goal? I didn't know enough about how probate worked to know whether that could be true or not.

I turned into Shirley's street on two wheels and then swerved to miss two luminous eyes in the headlights. I proceeded more cautiously, blood beating in my ears, scarcely able to breathe.

Shirley's door was standing open when I pulled into the drive, leaking the sounds of canned laughter. A quick, frantic search of the house revealed no bodies, dead or otherwise, strewn about. I turned on the pool and patio lights, but saw nothing.

"Hello?" a voice called tentatively from the open front door.

I trotted back through the den to confront a handsome middle-aged woman with frosted hair.

"Are you looking for Shirley?" she asked.

"Yes. Have you seen her?"

"She was looking for Leo," the woman said helpfully. "I just saw her headed toward the end of the street, where the field and the woods are."

"Thanks." I pushed past her.

"Anything I can do?" she asked.

"Answer the phone if it rings," I shouted. "Wait for reinforcements."

I jogged in the direction the woman had indicated. Shirley lived on the edge of a recently built housing development that seemed to end abruptly with a cul-de-sac, as if the developers had suddenly run out of money. Beyond the cul-de-sac was the dark region outside the comfortably lit familiarity of the suburban neighborhood. My shoulder bag whacked me painfully in the hip every other step.

I stopped to listen. Directly in front of me was a field, moderately overgrown with weeds. To my left, perhaps a hundred yards away, tall, dark shapes marked the edge of the wood.

Around me I heard the chittering of night insects, saw against the blackness sparks of light from fireflies. I heard the faint sounds of a radio playing behind me. Then heat lightning flickered overhead, but I couldn't see anything else. I breathed deeply to calm my own blood, and listened intently, fearful to close my eyes or call out. The object was to rescue Shirley and Leo, and to do that I had to stay alive.

Now I heard the soft snap of a twig coming from the woods. I moved forward.

I remembered what Styles had taught me, the principles of her martial arts training: breathe deeply, stay centered. I stepped carefully, keeping my weight evenly distributed and placing each foot flat on the ground. I didn't want to be caught off balance.

I could now distinguish, I thought, two sets of sounds in front of me—two animals, an animal and a person, or two people. If the latter, please let one of them be on my team, I prayed. Then I heard a cough—Shirley's cough—some little distance away. My eyes were slowly adjusting to the deeper darkness when another flash of heat lightning lit up the scene before me and showed me a dark silhouette, definitely human, on the other side of a clearing in front of me.

What I couldn't tell was whether the figure was facing me. But I thought I saw that it was holding something in its hand. I wasn't sure I wanted to find out what that was.

The shortest distance between two points is a straight line. My night vision had been disrupted by fulguration, so I couldn't tell what the ground was like in the clearing. But the long way around, while less exposed, was more likely to be strewn with noisy twigs and obstructed by roots. I had to decide quickly, in case I'd been spotted.

I dug in my bag and found the small plastic box I was looking for. Taking a deep breath, I pressed the button and flung it across the clearing and to the far right of the place where the figure had been standing. As the dinosaur began to roar, I crouched and ran through the clearing, bearing left, dodging imaginary bullets like Harold Lloyd in *Grandma's Boy*. My hands fumbled inside my bag.

The startled cry gave me my bearings, and I switched on the dinosaur flashlight and aimed it at the sound. The figure turned as I launched myself at it, flinging the flashlight away. An explosion went off in my ear. I fell on top of something soft that grunted. The grunt guided me to its head, and I slammed my bag down, bringing the full weight of two dinosaur eggs down on its skull. There was a gratifying crack and a groan. Then the mass under me heaved, and I felt a hand in my face, on my throat.

"Gilda!" someone shouted.

My ears were ringing and I tried to hit the head again, but it slid out of my reach. Then the woods exploded with sound.

The pressure on my throat eased. Something lifted me up and I felt myself flying through the air. I lay on the soft ground, gulping in air that smelled of humus and watching the light flicker overhead. I was vaguely conscious of grunts and thuds and shouts and roars like background noise to the roaring of my own blood.

After what seemed a long time, I rolled over and found the flashlight a foot from my nose. I picked it up and pointed it at the noisy shapes across from me. Even with the dinosaur silhouette blocking most of the light, I could identify the two men who stood on either side of a figure on the ground. For one thing, the colors they were wearing nearly blinded me.

"The Blues Brothers, I presume?" I squawked.

"Bring that light closer, Gilda," James said, bending down. "Let's see who we have here."

I didn't move. "Who has the gun?" I asked.

The dinosaur roared on.

"I got it," Spike said. "But I don't think he's going to wake up any time soon. What'd you hit him with, Gilda? He's bleeding like a son of a bitch."

I stood carefully. My legs still seemed to be working, more or less.

"Can't you shut that dinosaur up while you're at it?" James asked. "That thing is getting on my last nerve."

I searched around in the brush and located the little plastic box. I switched it off, and blessed silence descended.

"Gilda?" Shirley stood on the edge of the clearing with Leo in tow. In her other hand she held a flashlight. Leo's bomber jacket was draped over her arm. Her eyes were wide with fear, her hair mussed and decorated with a leaf and a twig. She looked from me to where James and Spike were standing, now turning the flashlight on them. "Is everybody all right?" she asked.

"Everybody but him," James said, looking down.

"I hope he ain't planning to have no more kids," Spike said. "James gave him one hell of a karate kick in the nuts."

"Yeah, but that was after you took out his kidneys," James observed.

"And that was after Gilda clobbered him with—" They turned to look at me.

"Dinosaur eggs," I said.

"Maybe that will teach him to respect his elders," James suggested.

"Who is it?" Shirley asked, approaching. James and Spike propped up the gunman. She shone the flashlight on the top of a bloody bald head.

"I'm afraid it's another son-in-law, Shirl," James said. "Or was."

27

But the two nurses confirmed that Curt still had a pulse, and after wrestling with their professional ethics, decided that he shouldn't be moved. They stayed with him while we went for help, which turned out to be waiting for us at the end of the cul-de-sac in the form of two patrol cars. They had been summoned by neighbors obviously unaccustomed to hearing gunshots on their quiet street—or bomb blasts, either, I thought.

I stayed with the cops and sent Shirley and Leo back to the house. Leo was completely confused; he kept asking what had happened to Curt. Shirley was hanging on by a thread. I advised her not to enter the house through the door Leo had used when he left. Clearly, Leo had had help; leaving had probably not been his idea. I doubted that the police would find anything to prove that, but it would be better to preserve the scene as best we could, even if there had been some coming and going since.

It was nearly midnight when we returned to Shirley's to check on her. On the way, I asked how James and Spike had happened to arrive together.

"We was over at Sammy's," Spike said, cocking a thumb over his shoulder. "James ordered me some new scrubs from this supplier he has, and he brought 'em over for me to try on."

"Yeah, Gilda, you haven't commented on Spike's new threads," James said. He nudged me in the ribs with an elbow.

"They're stunning," I said, looking Spike over. He wore a bright orange shirt and maroon pants with a thin orange stripe in them. A clutch of mangled tags hung from one sleeve. "Positively electrifying."

Spike grinned loopily. "I like 'em, too. They're more cheerful. James says there's no reason why us nurses got to be drab." He looked down at his shirt and frowned. He lifted the tail. "I got blood all over my shirt, though."

"Not to worry," James said, winking at me. "You can soak it when you get home, and it'll come right out in the wash." He seemed to have a sudden thought. "Of course, there's Lulu to consider."

"You don't think she'll like 'em?" Spike asked anxiously.

"Oh, I think she will," James reassured him. "It's just that her own wardrobe appears to run to primary colors. We may have to coordinate."

"That was just for the Fourth of July," Spike said. "She don't wear red all the time."

Shirley had put Leo to bed and was sitting out on the patio, drinking a gin and tonic and smoking a cigarette. She was wearing a cotton snap-front bathrobe and smelled of soap.

James made me a gin and tonic and fetched beers for Spike and himself.

Shirley's voice was thick with swallowed tears.

"I've done everything wrong," she said. "I should never have brought Leo back here. I should never have tried to take control of his finances. Sometimes I think I should never have married him, but then who would have taken care of him? The boys would probably have put him in some cut-rate nursing home by now, and he would have declined even more." She sniffled. "Or he'd be so doped up he wouldn't know what was happening. But Alan would be alive. I don't know! I've made such a mess of things!"

"You've done the best you could for Leo," I said, stroking her hand.

"It's not your fault if his kids are screwed up, Shirl," James put in.

"Yeah," Spike agreed. "You been really good to Leo. You couldn't have expected his kids to be killers, Shirley. Nobody expects that."

She sniffled. "But they make me feel so stupid to have been so trusting."

"How did you know where to look for Leo?" I asked.

"His jacket was lying at the edge of the cul-de-sac. I guess Curt must have dropped it there to—" She swallowed. "To lure me into the woods. And he was the nicest one of the bunch! I trusted him more than the others!"

"Well, you didn't trust 'em with Leo's money," James pointed out. "You weren't that stupid."

She laughed a little.

"I just want it to be over," she said wistfully. "I hope this is the end of it, but I see myself in court for the rest of my life."

"At least you won't have to be afraid in your own house," Spike said soothingly.

My heart caught. Milt was already out on bond. Curt probably soon would be. They would be foolish to try again, but they seemed impervious to risk. And then there was that other little problem.

"You said you were on the phone when Leo walked out," I remarked to Shirley, trying for a casual tone.

She nodded. "I was in the back bedroom so I could talk without the television noise. But the air conditioning makes it hard to hear sounds in the rest of the house, so I never heard the front door open."

"Who were you talking to?"

"Oh, Larry called. He was trying to talk me out of the lawsuit. He kept saying, over and over, 'I'm sure I can find a way to satisfy you. I'm sure we can work this out.' But the trouble is he's all talk and no action. I'd be satisfied if he just opened the books, or whatever you do when you're looking at the finances of a person rather than a corporation. But he won't do that."

I was staring off across the yard to where heat lightning was dancing on the surface of the pool.

Larry. It was Larry who kept her on the phone while Curt invited Leo out for a walk. It always came back to Larry.

28

The next afternoon I located Styles at a softball field. I heard her voice as soon as I got out of the car.

"Home plate is that little white vinyl mat where the batter's standing, you moron!"

She was sitting on the second row of the bleachers behind her team's dugout. A small green cooler sat next to her, and her crutches leaned against it. Her leg was propped up on the first row on top of a box that was nearly crushed flat. Once again, she wore her cap and sunglasses. Waldo greeted me by sniffing my shoes.

"Styles, what are you doing here?" I remonstrated. "Where's Spike?"

"Out with Lulu," she replied shortly, intent on the game.

"Didn't he lock you in?"

"Can't lock me in. Took my crutches, though."

I stared at the pair of crutches leaning against the bench next to her.

"So where'd you get these?"

She still hadn't made eye contact. "Blondie," she said. "Just stole second." Then she belted out, "Way to go, Blonds! Make 'em work!"

I turned to look across the field. A blond woman about my height wearing a peach-colored Gower Funeral Home T-shirt and a peach-colored cap was standing on second, dusting off her jeans. The opposition was wearing maroon Oscar's regalia. The irony was, of course, that Styles and her teammates spent more time at Oscar's Bar and Grill than at the Gower Funeral Home. But presumably if any of them died on the field, they'd patronize Gower's and Peachy would give them a good send-off.

I sat down in the bleachers next to Styles.

"Aw, c'mon, Ramon!" Styles shouted. "Whaddya want her to do, grow tentacles, for chrissake?"

Ramon Hunt had been two years ahead of me in school. He'd played college baseball, and now he was umpiring for the Eden City League. He'd never been a particular pal of mine, but you had to admire his guts. It's tough to umpire in a town where everybody knows your history. He also owned the local Wendy's franchise, but I guess he felt safe from the vicissitudes of public opinion; nobody's going to boycott hamburgers on the basis of a bad call at the plate.

"Heard anything from DJ?"

Styles shook her head.

"You check today?"

Styles nodded. "That's the way to do it, babe!" she called. "Make her walk you."

Styles was not wearing her Gower Funeral Home T-shirt, perhaps to give her more leeway to criticize the umpires. On the other hand, Ramon probably knew whom she played for, and the other ump looked familiar, too, though I couldn't quite make him out at this distance. Instead she wore a white muscle shirt and a pair of short cutoffs that had been slit on the right side to accommodate her cast, then safety-pinned together. On her feet she wore unlaced high-tops.

"You going to Pleasant Ridge?" she asked.

"We'll see," I said, feeling taken for granted. "Maybe Monday." I lowered my voice. The stands weren't filled, but they weren't empty, either. "Styles, I'm still worried about Shirley." My eyes were on the game now, too.

"You think we haven't heard the last from the boys?"

"You should have seen this boat that used to belong to Leo," I said. "I don't know what it costs to buy and maintain a boat like that, but seeing it kind of made the whole thing concrete, you know? Like there could be a lot of money involved."

"There better be a lot of money involved," Styles growled. "I don't want anybody thinking they can eighty-six Shirley for pocket change. That would really worry me.

"Pick out a good one, Tess! Right field's got her mind on her portfolio!"

This last nearly shattered my eardrums, pitched as it was to carry to right field. I noticed that the left fielder and center fielder shifted right.

"Don't you think Larry has to be the brains behind all this? He's the one who controls Leo's money. So it all comes back to Larry."

She glanced at me and smiled. "And they call me cynical."

"On the other hand, if Larry's playing the sugar daddy, he doesn't need to do his own dirty work; he can bribe or blackmail the other two to do it for him. After all, Shirley's threatening their source of revenue if she's threatening him. He'd probably rather they succeeded in eliminating her without getting caught, but if they do get caught, it's no big deal. He'll get them a good lawyer. Maybe he even figures that conviction will cut them out of Leo's estate. Isn't there some law that prevents them from profiting from their crimes? If Milt or

Curt were convicted of killing Leo as well as Shirley, wouldn't they be cut out of the inheritance?"

"Evidence, babe. Where's the evidence?"

"You think I'm right," I said, studying her face.

"I do. But how are we going to prove it? If we could set it up so that the cops could find bomb-making materials in Larry's basement, that would be one thing—"

"Jeez, do you think we could?"

She shook her head. "Not unless they're already there. They can't be just any bomb-making materials, you know; they have to match the stuff that was actually in the bomb. I mean an exact match; you can't find out they used fertilizer, for example, and go stash a bag of Frank's Premium Brand in Larry's basement expecting it to match the Wal-Mart brand in the bomb. Doesn't work that way. Best case scenario: Larry built the bomb himself and handled some component bare-handed. Or Milt built it somewhere other than at home."

I considered this. "So you think they did build the bomb themselves?"

She was distracted by a line drive to left field. She couldn't stand up to shout, so she bounced excitedly and projected her voice to make up for her disadvantaged position. When the dust cleared, the Gower Grrls had brought in two runners.

I repeated my question.

She shrugged. "These days anybody can. They can download instructions off the Internet, or mail order 'em from any one of a dozen right-wing paramilitary supply houses that cater to paranoid psychotics. What usually trips them up is the small components. They have trouble handling them with gloves on, so they take the gloves off, figuring the fingerprints will be too partial to provide evidence. Sometimes they're wrong. Not always, but sometimes."

"Will the cops get around to searching Larry's house?"

"No probable cause. Milt and Curt were the ones arrested."

"Yeah, but—"

"Listen, cookie, would you have wanted your room searched after your Aunt Lillian was picked up for B and E in a house that burned down a few hours later?"

Unfortunately, she was not making up this situation, and I had to concede that I would have been incensed if the cops had proposed to search my room. But I didn't admit it to Styles. "Maybe they could find my missing gray sock. That was my favorite pair."

"Until the court forces Larry to turn over all of Leo's financial records, we've got nothing on him," she insisted. "It's not like we can mark some money with fluorescent paint and wait for it to show up in Larry's pocket—or Milt's or Curt's. Getting them to take it out and show it to us under a black light would be a challenge, but doable if that were the kind of thievery we were dealing with, but it isn't."

"But what if the court doesn't side with Shirley?"

"Then we've got nothing. But at least she's out of danger. Oh, hell!"

"What?"

"Pop fly to center field. That's our third out."

She stretched, arching her back. She'd lost the sling on her left arm, but it was still encased in a brace and she shifted her shoulders gingerly. The right side of her face had faded to a pale lavender. When I looked around, I noticed that Waldo was lying on the bench in the Gower Grrls' dugout, wearing a small peach-colored cap with slits cut in it for his ears. He had his head in somebody's lap.

"Look, babe, the new security system will make it a lot harder for anyone to get to Shirley," Styles said. "Anyway, Milt and Curt would be stupid to try again while they're out on bail."

"They might be stupid not to," I pointed out. "They're about to rack up some heavy legal expenses. And Larry's not out on bail. And let's face it, these guys are not that bright."

"What do you want me to do?"

"I don't know," I admitted. "Think of something. Come up with a way to get Larry."

"I'll think about it," she promised. But she looked tired.

"I also think I should go talk to David Cutter," I said. "I don't know what he can tell me, but I don't feel like we have the whole picture yet. He's running Leo's business, after all."

"And he's Larry's brother-in-law."

"No!" I was dumbfounded.

She nodded. "Larry's married to Sarah Cutter, Dave's sister."

"How come nobody told me? How come Shirley didn't? Or Bernie Cutter?"

"Maybe they thought you already knew."

"Jesus! How could I know if they didn't tell me? How long have you known?"

"I don't know, a week?"

This pissed me off. If the people on my own team were going to leave out crucial information, then what was the point of talking to anybody? I'd get better results with a Ouija board.

"I thought you knew," she said. She was as close to apologetic as Styles ever gets.

"I have to go," I said abruptly.

"I know, you have a theater to run. Don't leave in a huff."

"I'm not," I said huffily. "This is a snit, not a huff. Furthermore, it's a snit I'm fully entitled to, so don't try to talk me out of it."

"Okay, be that way. I guess you don't care if the Grrls win."

"How can they not win with you mouthing off from the stands? You knew that batter was going to hit to left field, and you made them think she'd pull to the right."

She grinned at me. "That's the game of psych-out. You have to figure out what they're expecting you to do, change their expectations, and then score off their confusion."

The brainpower on our side was at a low ebb, I thought glumly, what with Leo on the permanently disabled list and Styles and Shirley on drugs. It would take some doing to be more confused than we were.

29

"How'd it go last night?" my father asked.

I shrugged. "We had a film break right in the middle of the jeep scene. On the up side, we sold two dinosaur eggs. They could have been the ones I used on Curt. Hard to tell. You seen one dinosaur egg, you seen 'em all."

"I'll bet their mother doesn't feel that way."

I was having lunch with my parents on Sunday. Every now and then they would complain that they didn't see enough of me—this in spite of our almost daily contacts. But it was true that we usually saw each other in crowds—of relatives or moviegoers or both. Not that my parents ever discussed anything that couldn't safely be discussed in a crowd. They weren't big on intimacy and self-revelation. My father made more of an effort in that regard. Criticism of and advice to me was my mother's specialty, though I noticed she'd toned it down since I'd moved back home. She must be mellowing in her old age, I thought.

We were sitting on the sunporch, a breeze from a fan curling the paper napkins and ruffling our hair. From where I was sitting I could admire the bright colors of my mother's midsummer garden—the golden coreopsis and helianthus, the orange marigolds and calendulas, the purple loosestrife just coming into bloom, and a riot of zinnias and snapdragons. A deep breath brought the heady scent of lilies and summersweet to mingle with the aroma of warm blueberry muffins.

I felt a deep contentment that I had rarely known since Liz had walked out the door. There was something to be said for living in a small town, even a small town where your parents lived, as long as they were behaving themselves—even a small town overpopulated with your relatives, on those rare occasions when they weren't in your face.

"Clara asked Douglas for advice on her new film," my mother said.

"What did you tell her?" I asked my father.

"Oh, I told her my tastes were too old-fashioned," he said, buttering a muffin. "I wouldn't be any use to her."

"She asked him if he would talk to Tobias about writing her a screenplay," my mother said.

I shook my head. "She never gives up."

"Well, I'm happy for her," my father said. "She needs a new interest."

"You mean she needs an interest, period," my mother retorted.

My father smiled at her. "You have a point, Flo. My baby sister has never been much for hobbies. Grosvenor was the one with all the hobbies, so until he died, it was easy to miss the fact that Clara didn't have anything to do."

"Driving her kids crazy," my mother observed, stirring her coffee. "That was her hobby."

"Well, I finished Wallace's screenplay last night," I said. "I don't think Clara will go for it. Too messy."

"Too much blood?" my mother guessed.

I nodded and helped myself to another muffin. "There's no percentage in a close-up if you have fangs and your face is smeared with red."

My mother grimaced. My father said placidly, "You'd think Wallace would know her better after all these years."

"Adele wants her to play Elizabeth," I reported.

My mother frowned. "Elizabeth who? Elizabeth Taylor? She's still alive." She looked at my father and a note of anxiety crept into her voice. "Isn't she?"

"Last I heard," he reassured her, patting her hand. "And I get weekly updates on the state of her health from the tabloids."

"Elizabeth the First," I said.

"God help us all," my mother said. "Just think of the opportunities for overacting. At least if she overacted in a vampire movie, nobody would notice."

"Ollie was telling me about his script at dinner the other night," my father said. "It doesn't sound half bad."

"That's what I thought," I agreed.

"Kind of Erich Von Stroheim, I thought," my mother said, "with European counts or dukes or whatever. But who knows if it would go over nowadays."

"I don't know, Flo," my father mused. "If you could get someone like Sean Connery to play the count—"

"With an Irish accent?" My mother was skeptical.

"Liam Neeson, then."

"I don't think he's old enough, Douglas. And if Clara's going to play a romantic lead, she'd better pick somebody close to her own age to play it with, or the audience will be thinking it's comedy."

"Yes, but Clara looks good for her age, Flo, you have to admit."

"She ought to look good for her age. She's paid her plastic surgeon enough to look twenty-two."

"Say, speaking of the elderly," I interrupted, "do you guys remember an old movie called *The Exile*? It had Douglas Fairbanks Jr. in it. Max Ophuls directed."

"Max directed it? What was it about?" my father asked.

"Leonard Maltin says it's a swashbuckler about a king who falls in love with a commoner."

"My God, Gilda, I must have seen a hundred movies with that plot line," my mother protested, "including that one with Marilyn Monroe." She turned to my father. "What was that called?"

"The Prince and the Showgirl," my father supplied. "But that was Olivier, and I wouldn't exactly call it 'swashbuckling.' "

"The thing is, somebody asked Leo if he had a copy—e-mailed him, I mean, and said he was 'desperate' to find it. I was wondering if there was anything special or unusual about it that would make it rare or hard to find."

"Well, a lot of older films have deteriorated so badly that for all intents and purposes, they don't exist anymore," my father said.

"Yeah, that's what I found out when I tried to track down films for Maesie's retrospective. And an archivist at the Library of Congress says *The Exile* is out of circulation. But I just wondered if there was something special about it, if it had some kind of historic significance that would make somebody want it so badly."

"We could check the IMDb," my mother proposed.

"What's that?" I asked.

My mother looked surprised. "You don't know about the Internet Movie Database?"

"Mom, I don't have a lot of time to spend surfing the Net," I said, a little defensively.

While all my other relatives had been taking Tobias's screenplay writing workshop, my parents had been attending a computer class. It had been a beginning class for senior citizens, and they had taken the plunge into cyberspace with all the enthusiasm of a pair of kids with new light sabers. They knew more about the Web than I did—a lot more—and they were always eager to show off their skills. We adjourned to the study.

My dad typed, and my mother and I hung over his shoulders. In no time, he had the search results for *The Exile*.

"Which one did you want?" he asked.

The search had located four titles: two *Exiles*, one in 1917 and one in 1994; one *L'Exile*, the film from Niger by Oumarou Ganda; and two *The Exiles*, one from 1931 and one from 1947.

I put my finger on the screen.

"It's the one from 1947," I said.

He clicked on it, and a new screen came up.

"Hmm," he said. He tilted his head back to find the right part of his glasses to look through. "Not much here. No standouts in the cast except Fairbanks."

"Maria Montez," my mother pointed out. "Maybe somebody's doing a Latina retrospective."

"In that case they'll need to include the woman you're named after, eh, Gilda?"

"It doesn't look like they have any more information," my mother said.

"Want to try 'Ophuls' or 'Fairbanks'?" my father asked.

"No, wait," I said. "Can we look at those other *Exiles*?"

"Sure." He returned to the list of titles. "Which one?"

"Well, he asked about the quality of the soundtrack, so that probably eliminates the 1917 version, unless it was a soundtrack recorded later," I said. "Let's try the 1931 film."

A new screen appeared. My heart thumped.

"My God, there he is," I said softly. "O. M. Not Max Ophuls, Oscar Micheaux."

"Who's Oscar Micheaux?" my mother asked. "I've never heard of him. Have you, Douglas?"

"I don't think so," my father admitted. He clicked on "combined details."

"I've never heard of anybody in the cast, either," my mother complained. "Eunice Brooks. A. B. DeComathiere. Who are these people? It must have been a poverty row production."

My father shook his head and pointed at the screen. "Take a look at the tagline," he said.

"Mighty modern all talking epic of Negro life," she read. "It's a race film."

"In 1931 it must have been an early race talkie," my father remarked.

"What do you know about race films, Dad?" I asked him.

"Not much," he admitted. "They were made for colored theaters in the North. I really don't know if there were colored theaters in the South but I expect there must have been some. That's what they called them in those days—colored theaters."

"Race films showed in segregated theaters in the North, too," my mother said. "I think there was a special time set aside for black audiences to watch black films. Seems to me it was late at night."

"And they were made by all-black companies?"

"Now that I couldn't say," my mother replied. "Douglas?"

"I don't know, either," he said.

I tried to think of a connection to Leo. "Were they ever shown on television in the fifties?" I asked.

"I don't know that, either," he said, "but we might be able to find out some of this stuff. Let's look at Oscar Micheaux's bio."

But the only thing the biography reported was a spouse, Alice Russell, whose dates were represented by question marks on either side of a dash.

"Well, that's helpful," my mother said. "Gilda, I thought you took a film course when you were an undergraduate. Didn't you ever study race films?"

"That was ages ago, Mom," I objected. "Film professors were still as ignorant as every other white teacher. Come to think of it, I'll bet that's why I didn't find Micheaux in Maesie's reference books. They were all too old to have thought to include him."

"Unless he's really obscure," my mother said.

"We're about to find out," my father said.

Twenty minutes of surfing the Web brought enlightenment. Oscar Micheaux wasn't merely a black filmmaker, I found out; he was the most prolific black filmmaker who had ever lived. His filmography rivaled that of many studio directors, in spite of his constant battle to stay afloat. He'd declared bankruptcy once in the late twenties, when everybody went bankrupt, and come back to make the first black talkie—*The Exile*. He had also been a homesteader in South Dakota, as well as a novelist.

He was praised on all sides for his entrepreneurial genius. Whereas the Hollywood studios had a well-developed system for distribution, starting at the top with studios like MGM and Warner Bros. and RKO that owned their own theater chains, there was no such system for race films. Instead, Micheaux and his agents had toured the country, especially in the South, selling films and seeking investors for films as yet unmade. In this way, he managed to produce more than forty films between 1919 and 1948. Not bad for a former shoeshine boy, farm worker, and Pullman porter.

He was buried in the town where he had homesteaded, which had hosted a Micheaux retrospective last year and would again host one next month. But few of his films had survived. DJ was probably involved in the planning for another retrospective; for all I knew, "DJ" might stand for "Dakota Joe." If so, and if we could find a print of *The Exile* among Leo's possessions, I for one would have been glad to hand it over free of charge.

We would need to come clean with DJ and find out why he thought Leo might have a copy of the film. A race film, even the first talkie, wouldn't seem like a good candidate for the late movie. Perhaps a local station had featured a special late show aimed at black audiences and sponsored by manufacturers who targeted black consumers. I remembered Leo's reaction to the photograph of the minstrel show that members of his unit had staged during the war. Perhaps Leo's postwar clientele had included some black-owned companies. I would need to find out from David Cutter whether there were any storage areas on the premises of Mayer and Cutter that might house old movies. And I supposed that I would need to go to Pleasant Ridge in my nonexistent spare time, either alone or in the company of a Styles who was hobbled but not silenced.

30

Once I'm in the theater my mind is on the theater. After we open, I have no time to ruminate on the crises of family members, however near or distantly related, or friends, or on the troubles of a one-legged detective. For that matter, I don't even have time to think about my own crises, such as my abrupt transition from partnered to single status or my dissatisfaction with my living quarters.

This does not mean, unfortunately, that my family observes a moratorium on crisis generation while I'm working.

The first call was from my aunt Gloria.

"Gilda, Wallace isn't there, is he?" she asked in her usual hesitant and slightly befuddled manner. "You haven't seen him?"

"No. What's up?" I knew better than to ask "What's up," but the response is virtually automatic in someone like me who is trained to expect the worst. And in my family, people will generally tell you what's up whether you ask or not.

"Well, he and Adele had a fight over those scripts they were writing—you know the ones I mean? The scripts for Clara's comeback?"

"I know them." And how.

"Well, as nearly as I can figure things out, they were going at it, you know, when Adele got so angry she told Wallace that vampire movies were passé and nobody wanted to see them anymore except thirteen-year-old boys—"

"Ouch."

"Yes, well, so then Wallace stormed out and Adele doesn't know where he's gone. But he took the car, you see, and Adele's things are in the back—"

I heard a distant, incoherent but decidedly histrionic wail.

"Yes, well, they're materials for making party decorations, she says. I don't really know what she's talking about, but the point is she's supposed to take them up to the nursing home so they can work on them, and—"

The background voice interrupted again.

"Well, I don't think Gilda cares whether they were paper cups and crepe paper or not, Adele. It's not important. But the point is, she needs to get them back, and—"

Rumble, rumble.

"Adele, you *don't* have to speak to him, *I'll* speak to him," Gloria continued, "though I have to say I think both of you are being very childish. And anyway, Gilda doesn't know where he is, do you, Gilda?"

"Not a clue."

"What? She says she doesn't know. Well, if you see him, Gilda, will you ask him to at least bring the car home?"

"Happy to."

As soon as I hung up, the phone rang again. It was my mother.

"Gilda? I'm glad I caught you."

Where did she think I would be? But the answer to that was obvious: running errands for my relations or responding to emergencies created by said relations.

"You haven't seen Wallace lately, have you?"

I assured her I hadn't, and hung up.

My aunt Clara was the next to clock in.

"Oh, Gilda, listen, I don't have time to talk—"

I pulled the phone away from my ear and stared at it. Who had called whom?

"—but your uncle Wallace was just here and he asked what I thought of his screenplay, and I'm afraid I was just a bit abrupt because I have a tennis date with Marilyn McCready— you know Marilyn, don't you? Divorced, two teenagers, English sheepdog and a summer house on the Cape? Anyway, I told him that vampires just weren't my cup of tea, if you know what I mean, and I'm afraid it hit him harder than I expected—well, especially since I'd been telling him all along that I wasn't cut out to be a vampire, and anyway didn't want the expense of a fabulous wardrobe, never mind the makeup job and the hair, just to drip blood all over everything. You understand. So do you think you could explain it all to him in a more tactful way? Tell him I didn't mean to hurt his feelings and I'm sure somebody will want to make his movie. He should ask Jessica or Betty or maybe even somebody like Olympia or Vanessa." She stopped to take a breath.

"I—"

"Sorry, Gilda, I can't chat now. I have to run." And she hung up. She didn't say either of the magic words, but then my family has never been big on gratitude, and miserly Clara has less than the rest of them to dole out, so she reserves it for special occasions. If I ever saved her life, she might send me a note.

The phone chirped as soon as I set the receiver down. This time it was Shirley.

"I'm sorry to bother you at work, Gilda," she said. I don't know why she was sorry; nobody else was. "But Sam asked me for some letters and she said they were in Leo's foot-locker. Is that right?"

"That's right. He showed them to me when we were down in the basement together."

"Well, they're not there now. I think he must have taken them out and put them someplace else." She sighed audibly. "I'm afraid you called his attention to that footlocker, Gilda, and ever since then I've been finding him down in the basement looking through it."

"Did you ask him about the letters?"

"Yes, but he doesn't seem to know what I'm talking about. If he put them somewhere, I doubt he remembers where. This morning I found his dinosaur cap in the refrigerator."

I joined her in another sigh. Between the deliberate obstructionists and the accidental ones, we didn't seem to be making much headway.

"Did you ask Leo what happened the other night when he got out?"

"Yes, but I didn't get a very clear answer," she said. "He knows something happened and it's connected to the front door. He gets agitated whenever we're near it, and tries to tell me something. I do know he's angry with Curt. He told me last night to tell Curt's mother he ought to be spanked."

"I'd be happy to sit on Curt if Leo wants to spank him," I offered.

"You'll have a lot of company," she said. "James and Spike have already volunteered."

"Say, Shirley, do you know of any connection Leo might have to race films?"

"Race films?"

"Yeah—you know, films for black audiences."

She sounded perplexed. "I didn't know there was such a thing. I guess I never really thought about it. I've never heard Leo mention it. Why?"

"I think the film DJ wants is a race film, that's all."

"Maybe DJ has the wrong person, Gilda. Maybe he used one of those Web directories, and he's got Leo mixed up with some other Leo. I suppose there could even be another Leo Mayer, couldn't there?"

"Sure, I guess so."

"I wouldn't waste too much time on it, Gilda. But I do hope you and Sam find Auggie soon. He mentions Auggie to me all the time now. I think it's because he's upset about everything that's been going on. When he's upset, he seems to think about Auggie, finding Auggie and talking to Auggie. But he still can't tell me who Auggie is."

The next call was from my uncle Val.

"If anybody calls looking for Wallace, he's here," he reported. "Tobias is bucking him up and he's drowning his sorrows in our Scotch, so I hope somebody finds him soon."

"You need to call Adele's," I said. "She's desperate to get the car back."

"I tried. The line's always busy."

"Okay. The next person I hear from, I'll give 'em the message."

But the next person I heard from was not one of my relatives caught up in the latest episode in the family serial. This voice I didn't recognize.

"Gilda?"

It sounded wrong somehow, hoarse.

"Yes?"

"Gilda, I'm glad I found you. It's Curt Mayer."

The "hi, how are you?" died in my throat. In fact, my throat and neck were still sore from his attempt to throttle me.

"Look, I know you're mad at me, and I just wanted to call and apologize."

For attempted murder? This was certainly a novel development. I didn't think he'd been in jail long enough to have gotten religion. In fact, I didn't think he'd been in jail at all, what with his various injuries. Perhaps he'd stumbled on a twelve-step program for killers at the hospital, and he was working on whatever step it was that required you to take responsibility for your actions. Well, if he was depending on me to certify him for his Boy Scout badge in self-improvement, he had another think coming.

"You see, I couldn't see who you were in the dark, and I thought you were the killer."

Those dinosaur eggs must have really scrambled his brains, I thought. He's got us mixed up.

He sighed. "It was all a big misunderstanding. See, I was stopping by to talk to Shirley about Milt's arrest because I was afraid she was still in danger. Not from him, you understand, but from the real killer. And I'm driving down the street and I see Shirley—at least, it looks like Shirley—headed into the weeds there past the end of the street. And I notice that the door to the house is standing open. Well, I didn't like the looks of that, especially given everything that's been happening, so I took off after her."

"With a gun."

"Well, yeah, I have a gun in the glove compartment, and like I said, I didn't like the looks of things and I didn't think she should be out alone like that with this maniac running around trying to kill her. So I took the gun with me. And I followed her into the woods. Well, I guess you followed me, thinking I was the killer, and you know the rest. Man, I've still got one heck of a headache! What did you hit me with?"

"How come I didn't hear you calling her?"

"You didn't?" His voice sounded surprised. "You must have come too late. When I started after her, I was yelling my head off; I'm sure the neighbors heard. Once we got into the woods, I didn't want to spook her, so I didn't say anything."

Unfortunately, this was a plausible explanation. I hadn't called her, either, not only because I hadn't wanted to frighten Shirley, but also because I hadn't wanted to call attention to her location or mine.

"Anyway, I'm sorry I tried to choke you—"

"You not only tried, you succeeded."

"Well, you've got to admit you hit me pretty hard. I wasn't thinking too clearly. I thought the killer was attacking me."

"Where was your car? I didn't see it."

He gave what was supposed to be an embarrassed laugh. "Once I saw Shirley, I pulled over, grabbed my gun, and took off running. Like I said, I was shouting at her."

"Did you see the neighbor?"

"The neighbor? I didn't see anybody. I just ran after Shirley."

I was silent. I really hated to admit how plausible his explanation was, though it had its weak points. I'd have to find out from Dale where Curt's car had been found. And the timing was suspicious: Curt shows up just as Larry calls Shirley and Leo manages to walk out the door? Greater coincidences have happened, but it doesn't do to accept them at face value in an attempted murder investigation. Unfortunately, Leo wasn't the most reliable of witnesses, and the D.A. would have a tough time convincing a jury to convict Curt because Leo thought he ought to be spanked.

"You know, Milt's not the killer, Gilda," he added at last. "He really did find that package on the porch and take it into the house. He went down in the basement because he thought he heard a noise he didn't recognize, but it must have been the furnace or water pipes or something.

"The trouble is, the cops think they have their man, and now that he's been charged, they're not worried about Shirley anymore. But I know Milt didn't do any of those things they're accusing him of, so I think Shirley's still in danger. That's why I panicked when I saw her out at night alone and headed into those woods. Now I know that she was chasing Dad, but I didn't know it at the time. I'm worried about her, Gilda. Aren't you?"

I put a finger to my bruised throat and vacillated. I decided to give him the benefit of my own thoughts on the subject just to see what he'd say.

"You want to know what I think? I think your big brother is

using you and Milt to do his dirty work because he thinks
you're dumb enough or scared enough to do what he says
without ratting him out. I hope you realize that you and Milt
are going to be eating prison food and stripping down for
body cavity searches while Larry lives the good life off of
Leo's money. And I know that blood is supposed to be thicker
than water, but if he were my brother, I'd divorce him."

Silence. I hoped it was sinking in.

Then he said earnestly, "I'm sorry you feel that way, Gilda.
I was really hoping we could work this thing through." As if
we were talking about a spat, not attempted murder. "I mean,
I feel pretty silly now, but at the time I went charging after
Shirley like Arnold Schwarzenegger, and all I got to show for
it was a busted head, busted ribs, and sore kidneys."

"Curt," I said, "you'll never be on my Christmas card list."

"I'm sorry you feel that way," he repeated.

I hung up.

In the background, I heard the roar of dinosaurs on a ram-
page. Who says real life doesn't have a soundtrack?

31

The next day I went to see David Cutter.

The Mayer and Cutter production studios were in a building
that looked like a big warehouse off Fifth Street in Columbus.
The receptionist had me wait until someone could escort me
into the bowels of the building. On the walls were blowups of
stills from television commercials produced by Mayer and
Cutter, as well as a large photograph of this same building as
it looked when Mayer and Cutter moved here in 1969, when
the neighborhood was considerably less densely populated.

The blowups included the first television ad that Mayer and Cutter had ever produced—a black-and-white commercial for a local Chevrolet dealer that featured a family right out of *Father Knows Best*. Dad wore a suit, Mom wore pearls and carried a handbag at her elbow, and the kids were well-scrubbed. A mutt, frozen in midprance, ears flying, barked merrily at the family Chevy.

"You could say our whole company was built on that image," a man's voice said behind me.

I turned to confront a tall, slim man with a full head of salt-and-pepper hair. He wore a neat mustache cut straight across his upper lip as if with a pair of hedge trimmers and thick eyebrows manicured by the same gardener. He wore tortoiseshell glasses whose curiously shaped lenses suggested that an Italian designer had had a hand in them somewhere. His dress was in the style they were now designating as "business casual"—gray Dockers and a short-sleeved, striped navy-blue-and-gray sport shirt, no tie. He was about my age. He smiled fondly at the still photograph, hands in his pockets.

"Kind of a blast from the past, I was thinking," I said.

"Mmm." He nodded, unoffended. "It sold cars, though. We still carry that account—Markham Chevrolet. We don't use the same approach, of course. Today, unless you're selling minivans, it's all about escape. You take a drive in the car to get away from your family." He slid one hand from a pocket and offered it to me. "I'm Dave Cutter. You must be Gilda. I'm afraid we're running late on a shoot. Want to come watch?"

We passed through a heavy door and down a hallway.

"Kids and dogs," he said as if by way of explanation. "They're hell to work with, but they sell."

"You never work with cats?"

He paused at a door on his right labeled "Studio B," and shot me a look. "Please," he said. "I may be crazy but I'm not stupid."

We passed through another heavy door and into commotion. I was vaguely aware of the trappings of a television studio—lights hanging from girders overhead, two large cameras on wheels, and a sound console. But my attention was drawn to the knot of people congregated in a set that looked like a kitchen split neatly in half by a tornado. At the center of the group was a little girl in a pink dress, Shirley Temple revisited, only younger even than Shirley was when she starred in the Baby Burlesques.

"Flapjack's Pancake House," Cutter told me in a low voice. "Ever heard of it?" When I nodded, he jerked his chin in the direction of the moppet in pink. "The owner's granddaughter."

The moppet was flashing me with her Underoos. Her dress was caught in the crook of one arm, bent in the classic thumb-in-mouth position. It must be hard, I thought, to suck your thumb and scowl at the same time, but she was managing it. The hair ribbon adorning one pigtail had come untied and hung limply in her face, stuck to her damp skin by the steady drip from a big blue eye. The end of the other bow disappeared into her mouth.

Another girl of perhaps twelve or thirteen stood nearby. She was bone thin and showed off the definition of her lower ribcage by wearing a cropped T-shirt over a pair of jeans I couldn't have gotten my arm into. Her long blond hair flowed around a set of earphones, but she seemed to be paying more attention to the confrontation at midcourt than to whatever music was passing between her ears. She rolled her eyes frequently and pawed the ground with a foot encased in clunky platform sandals. A sister? Or perhaps a half-sister. Someone who had been supplanted by a new arrival and who had a low tolerance for cuteness.

Circling the group like a hyperactive comet was a small terrier, who made his own contribution to the discussion. Maybe his union contract specified a dog biscuit and a nap in his trailer at this point in the proceedings.

A harried woman knelt before Little Miss America.

"Now, Glynnie," she said, "all you have to do is say, 'Everybody flips for Flapjacks,' just like you did at home, just like you did this morning in rehearsal. And then you give Sparky his signal, just like you do at home, and he'll do his trick. Now, don't you think you could do that just once for Mother? How about it, sweetheart?"

She reached up unconsciously and pulled the thumb from the mouth and straightened the pink dress. Deprived of the thumb, the lower lip protruded ominously. The blue eyes blinked, squeezing out two fresh tears.

I could have told her what was wrong with her approach. I could have told her that kids, like dogs, can detect fear in a voice, and the mother's whine had fear written all over it. Our little pink friend had her status as top dog to defend, and any sign of cooperation would have undermined that status. There's more than one way to show who's in charge.

A gray-haired, grandmotherly-looking woman sighed heavily, set down her clipboard, and held out one hand to the pint-sized starlet. "Mind if I try?" she asked the mother.

They went out into the hall. Cutter, who had approached a bored-looking sound technician with earphones hung around his neck, now looked back at me and winked. "Watch this," he said.

A woman with a clipboard retrieved a coffee cup from somewhere and collapsed in a wooden chair. Another woman wearing a smock and a man in jeans leaned up against the kitchen counter. The teenager sprawled in another chair and examined her hair for split ends. Sparky did a series of back flips across the set and then collapsed in a heap with his chin on the linoleum.

In less than five minutes the grandmotherly woman and little girl returned. The little girl was decidedly less soggy, her expression placid.

"I think we're ready now," the woman said.

She handed the little girl off to the woman in the smock, who must have been in charge of makeup. The two went off together, and the older woman approached Cutter. He steered her toward me. I saw at a glance that she proved rather than disproved my earlier observation to James that grandmotherly types didn't exist anymore. The steel behind her glasses gave it away.

"What did you say to her?" I asked when we'd been introduced.

"Trade secret," she said, smiling pleasantly.

"She won't even tell me how she does it," Cutter said.

I watched the proceedings for another half hour before Cutter was satisfied that he could leave. Sparky was turning a seemingly endless series of back flips as we closed the door to the studio.

"Come on into my office, so we can talk," Cutter said. He ushered me down the hall, through an outer office where a secretary looked up as we passed but made no comment, and into a pleasantly furnished medium-sized executive office.

"Sorry about the delay," he said, smiling. "But I understand you come from a long line of movie people, so I don't have to tell you that productions always run behind schedule. Cigarette?"

"I have my own, thanks." I was overjoyed to see him light up; I had been craving a cigarette since I'd walked in the door, and half an hour of barking had only intensified the urge.

He passed up the chair behind his desk and sat down in one of a pair of armchairs, gesturing toward the other. "So what can I tell you? Dad said you were looking for somebody Leo's been talking about?"

"That's right—somebody named Auggie."

"Never heard of him. I'm sorry." He pulled at his mustache. "Is this somebody he worked with at Mayer and Cutter?"

"We don't know. We don't know anything about Auggie— just that Leo wants to find him."

This sounded lame, even to me, and Cutter's expression suggested he had reached the same conclusion. "So this Auggie could be anybody? Anybody Leo might have encountered in his, what, seventy-some years?"

"That's right."

He shook his head. "You have your work cut out for you."

"Got any advice?"

Again he shook his head. "Not my line of work. I wouldn't know where to start."

"How computerized are your personnel records?"

"Fully computerized from about 1988 or so. Payroll was computerized earlier, around 1983. Why? You want me to ask one of the secretaries to search the database for an Auggie?"

"I'd appreciate it."

"No problem. Glad to help. But I'm afraid I can't make the same offer for the files before 1983. You're welcome to go through them yourself, if you like, but it would be a tedious business."

"I'll pass for now, but thanks."

"You've met Leo, I take it?"

"Yes."

"Then you know his mental wires are pretty crossed." Cutter seemed to be studying his shoelaces. "This Auggie he's talking about—that could be some cameraman out of his past that he wants to talk to about an angle on the Jungle Jim commercial."

"I don't think so," I said. "Leo seems to keep coming back to things that bother him—big things, not little things. He can't articulate what's bothering him, but he seems to distinguish between what's important and what's trivial."

Cutter smiled at me, showing an attractive fan of wrinkles at the corners of both eyes. "Believe me, Leo never considered the Jungle Jim commercial trivial, but I take your point."

He let the silence lengthen between us.

"You mentioned your payroll," I said. "Mind if I ask if Larry is your accountant?"

"Sure he is. I figure my sister will keep him honest." He stubbed his cigarette out and rested a palm casually on one knee. "Seriously, though, he's a good accountant. I wouldn't have anybody else even if he hadn't married into the family. I know there's some tension between Shirley and him, but if I were you, I'd tell Shirley to relax and let him handle things."

"You would."

"Sure I would. He's not even charging anything for his services. Wish he'd offer me a deal like that."

"Well, I'll tell her what you think."

He flashed me a grin. "She won't listen. Older people like my dad and Leo, they always complain that young people don't listen. But when's the last time your parents took your advice?"

I couldn't think of a single time when *any* of my elder relatives had taken any of my advice. On rare occasions, they asked for it, but they never followed it.

My silence answered his question.

"There you are," he said.

"I understand your father wants to hold another board meeting for Leo's benefit."

He grimaced. "I thought it was about time for him to start bugging me again. Understand, I think the world of Leo, but we're not talking about a two-hour meeting here. We're talking about a full day of fishing and cruising around and drinking beer in the hot sun and listening to Bernie tell the same old stories about the past that he tells every year." He shook his head. "I don't have the time for it, but I'll make time again to please my dad and Leo."

"Leo still owns part of the company," I noted.

"Technically, yes. Larry takes care of all the official stuff that's required."

"So the board does actually meet and vote on things?"

"Sometimes. Not often."

I shifted in my chair and leaned toward him. "Listen, David, can you think of any reason why someone might want to harm Leo or Shirley? Can you think of any enemies Leo might have?"

"Enemies?" He looked surprised.

"Well, former business rivals or employees he fired or a client he had a falling out with."

"Enemies," he echoed. "I guess I can think of a few. You can't be in business as long as Leo was and not get on the wrong side of somebody. But do you mean a person who might want to harm Leo now?"

"Yes."

He expelled a small puff of air through his nose. "I can't think of anybody like that."

"Well, thanks for your time." I gathered myself together and stood up.

He stood as well and offered me his hand. "No problem, Gilda. Any time. If you can think of anything else I can help you with, just give me a buzz."

I sat in my car in the parking lot, lighting another cigarette. I felt discouraged. I wasn't sure I'd accomplished anything other than a greater respect for anybody who produced a television commercial starring a young child.

I stared out through the windshield. After a minute I realized that I was looking at the same view of the building that had been captured in the earlier photograph displayed in the waiting area. In the late sixties, the Mayer and Cutter studio had bordered a vacant lot on one side and another small cinderblock warehouse on the other,

And then the focus puller in my brain zoomed out, and I was seeing the scene in wide-angle deep focus. In the foreground was the Mayer and Cutter studio. In the midground was a taller building behind it facing another street; atop this building was a cut-out sign whose backwards lettering, when reversed, spelled out "electroplating." And in the background, beyond that building and facing me, was a vertical sign mounted on the side of another building. The sign read GUILFORD SUPPLY.

All within a few blocks. Circumstantial, I thought. But interesting, very interesting.

32

When I returned to the theater, I had a phone message to call Leo's old fishing buddy and former insurance agent Glenn Wilcox. His voice on the phone sounded troubled.

"Hey, Gilda, thanks for returning my call. Listen, after we talked, I got to brooding about what you said, thinking about all the things that had been happening to Shirley. Well, I finally couldn't stand it anymore, so I called the company to find out the status of Leo's insurance—thinking, like I said, that he might have changed it after he married Shirley or he might not have. It turns out he doesn't own his life insurance policy anymore."

"He doesn't?" That struck me as odd for a caring husband like Leo.

"Not the one I sold him, he doesn't. He may have another one by now—probably does. I hope so. But here's the thing. You know about viatical companies, right?"

"Sure. They buy life insurance policies from the terminally ill and collect the benefits upon death. AIDS patients especially use them to raise cash for their treatment. You don't mean to tell me that a viatical company bought Leo's policy."

"That's exactly what I'm saying."

"But why would he sell? He doesn't need the cash, I don't think."

"Well, I didn't think so, either. I'd be mighty embarrassed if it turned out he was in financial straits and I didn't even know about it. I would've helped him out."

I sat down to think. Next to me the ice machine hummed and exuded heat like a Franklin stove.

"Glenn, I haven't seen any evidence that Leo's in financial trouble," I said slowly, "and I think Shirley would have been candid with me if he was. But what you're telling me is that somebody has, in effect, managed to change the beneficiary on Leo's policy."

He sighed. "Yes, I guess that's what I'm telling you."

"So do you have the name of the new owner?"

"It's called Mid-Western Viatical Service, that's hyphenated with two caps. Never heard of them."

I called Styles to report this latest piece of information. She agreed to track down Mid-Western Viatical.

"And that's not all. Curt works a few blocks from David Cutter, and in those same few blocks is an electroplating company," I told her. "The electroplating company stocks copper cyanide—I checked. Is there any way a forensic lab can tell whether the copper cyanide in Shirley's pool water came from the copper cyanide stored in the yard at this particular electroplating company?"

"Dale Ferguson warned me you were lousy in high school chemistry," Styles said. "No, there's no way to trace the copper cyanide in the pool water. There is a difference between cuprous cyanide and cupric cyanide, which I can't explain except that one or the other of them is a liquid more like the stuff they use in swimming pools and the other is a powder. I'm assuming this was the liquid one they found in Shirley's pool, since they were so interested in the late Alan Kline as a suspect, and they might be able to confirm that this electroplating company you found uses the stuff. What they can't do is prove that the poison in the pool came from this company unless they can find the container it came in, which is probably long gone."

"Wait, how come *you* know so much about chemistry all of a sudden?"

"Been talking to Dale. Seems he made an A in high school chemistry."

"Don't remind me."

"Anyway, I'd agree that your observations are—shall we say, highly suggestive?"

"I'm tired of 'highly suggestive.' I want phosphorescent

footprints leading from the scene of the crime to the criminal's door."

"Doesn't everybody?"

"Styles, you say that the container's long gone. But suppose—"

She cut me off. "Forget it, babe. Even if you were willing to go Dumpster diving again, it's been more than two weeks and this is July. If the guy had any sense, he buried the container in a Dumpster and it's already busy contaminating a landfill somewhere."

"Well, how the hell are we going to get any evidence on these guys? Curt claims he was sneaking around the woods with a gun because he was trying to protect Shirley. And he says it so sincerely even I believe him. I don't know. Do you think it could be true?"

"Jesus, Gilda, you're going to have to overcome your female conditioning! Trust your instincts, for chrissake! If it looks like rape and feels like rape, then it *is* rape. You saw a guy tippy-toeing around in the woods with a gun. If he looked like a killer and felt like a killer, then chances are good, he was a killer."

"Yeah, I guess you're right. But he and Milt are both going to walk unless we get something more solid."

"There is one thing we haven't tried."

"Yeah?"

"It's illegal."

"I knew you were going to say that."

"Remember what I said at the game, about figuring out what they expect you to do?"

"They expect us to be law-abiding citizens."

"That's right."

"It just goes to show."

I could hear the grin in her voice. "So you're in?"

"I'll bring the dinosaur eggs," I said.

33

Styles called back around midnight while I was sweeping up popcorn and heavy metal from the carpet in the side theater. Every night after two showings of *Spawn* I swept the floor with a magnet attached to a broom handle—something Duke had rigged up. Stray earrings, chain links, and studs littered the floor. I could start a metal recycling center with the collection I had.

"That was fast," I said into the phone.

"Hey, babe, the autobahn is nothing compared to the information superhighway. It would've been faster if I didn't have to track Mid-Western Viatical through a chain of parent companies. It beats me why anybody would think they could hide ownership these days."

"So the result was?"

"The CEO of the parent company of the parent company of the parent company that owns Mid-Western is a certain E. A. Mayer."

"Ah. Do I know him?"

"Probably not. It's a her, by the way. I understand she's a charming little number, with big blue eyes and a collection of hair barrettes that makes Imelda Marcos seem like a casual shopper. She probably comes up to your kneecaps."

"Wait! Does the 'E' stand for Elizabeth?"

"That's right."

"I've met her."

"Was she power lunching at the time?"

"Not unless a sunsuit qualifies as a power suit in the four-and-under set. But she was serving cocktails."

"There you are. She's obviously overqualified to be an insurance agent. No offense."

"None taken. I was overqualified to be an insurance agent. That's why I moved on to a challenging new career as a theater owner."

"For which you're underqualified."

"Apparently," I said.

From where I was standing I could see Duke taking apart the cappuccino machine on the concession counter. He was shaking his head and poking at it.

"I think I broke the cappuccino machine tonight," I said.

"Again? You've only had it a month!"

"Two months."

"Then it's out of warranty, so it was probably programmed to break down. Not your fault, babe."

"I'm glad somebody sees it that way." I was in Duke's doghouse. "So what do we do about E. A. Mayer, a.k.a. Bethie?"

"You up for a spot of B and E?"

"This is going to be another Laurel and Hardy experience, right? Where you're on crutches and I can't see in the dark?"

"Getting cold feet?"

"I just want to know what I'm in for. How're you going to get past Spike?"

"Spike's decamped. He found a granny with a broken hip who needs him more than I do. But he'll be back. He promised to teach Waldo a card trick."

"So we're going after Larry first?"

"Show me the money."

"Right. He signs the checks. Tell me when so I can pencil you in."

" 'Pencil me in'? Cookie, if we make this date you better not cancel at the last minute. I don't want to be left all by my lonesome, standing on Larry's doorstep with my crutches under my arms and my picklocks in my pocket."

"All right, already. I'll be there. When?"

"They're leaving town on Thursday for a cousin's wedding—her side of the family."

Duke was the only person I told about our plans. He was

my business partner, after all, and I couldn't just call in sick on the night in question.

He kept shaking his head.

"What?"

"Remember when you first came back to town, Gilda?" he asked. "You were quiet, and kind of timid, and anxious all the time. You were scared of the popcorn machine."

"Hell, I was catatonic! The love of my life had just flattened me with her new girlfriend's Harley and squeezed my heart into an oil spot on the highway of life."

"How many months before?"

"Your point being?"

He pushed his glasses up on his nose and deftly stuffed napkins into the napkin dispenser, a feat that had taken me three weeks to master. "My point being that you now seem awfully eager to jump on your own Harley and go out and flatten somebody."

"Duke, I'm not planning for anybody to get hurt." After a brief pause, I added, "Especially not me."

He just looked at me.

"What? You think I'm compensating?"

"What do I know? I'm just a kid. I just think you've changed a lot in the past two months, that's all."

"And you liked me better as a wimp—a baby brontosaurus rather than a T. rex."

"No, I didn't like you so much as a wimp, I didn't think you gave yourself enough credit. All's I'm saying is that you should do stuff you really want to do because you really want to do it and think it's a good idea, not because Styles thinks it's a good idea or Liz thought it would be a good idea or because anybody else in the family wants you to do it, you know?" He was studying the napkin dispenser as if it held the key to the universe. "I just think you should be yourself. That's all I'm saying."

I was touched—not least because I suspected the high price Duke paid, both within the family and among his schoolmates, for being himself. I also seemed to recall giving him a similar lecture not that long ago, when he was trying too hard to step into Aunt Maesie's shoes.

"I understand what you're saying," I said earnestly. "I do. And it's true that ever since I came back to Eden—or it may be ever since I met Styles—my life has taken a turn toward the questionable, if not the downright illegal. And it may even be true that the more often I cross that line, the less drastic and—well, scary—it seems."

"You laugh in the face of danger."

"I don't think so. If I ever laugh in the face of danger, I hope you'll have me committed. But I want to see if we can get anything on Larry. And I don't want to wait until Shirley's dead to do it."

"Styles could take her dad with her," Duke objected. "They're both professionals."

I shook my head. "Not a good idea. They'll have a fight on the front porch over which picklock to use and the neighbors will have the police down on them before they get it resolved." I put a hand on his shoulder. "Hey, don't worry, okay? Nothing's going to happen to me."

I had a feeling that was partly what this was about. Duke had been abandoned by Maesie, the only person who really understood and appreciated him. I had more or less inherited that role in his life, even though I'd never achieve Maesie's status. He didn't want to lose me, too.

"It better not," he grumbled. "After all the time I've spent training you—it just better not."

"Well, look on the bright side," I said. "At least the movies aren't changing this week. We won't have to break down and make up."

"If that's the good news," he said, glancing up at a *Spawn* poster and grimacing, "I don't want to hear the bad."

34

I put in some time on Wednesday at the public library. The truth was that I wanted to call my pal John Pogue at the Library of Congress film archives, but I didn't want to sound like a complete ignoramus when I did. What I discovered was that as recently as the previous year, 1996, when the latest source I found had been published, the vast majority of Oscar Micheaux's work was being reported as lost, including the first black talkie, *The Exile*.

I doubted now that DJ's request for the movie had anything to do with our search for Auggie. It didn't matter; I was hooked. Now that I knew more about how movies "disappeared," as well as more about Oscar Micheaux, I wanted to find out if Leo really did have a cache of old movies somewhere.

I called Pogue from the theater on Wednesday afternoon. I reminded him who I was and told him I was interested in Oscar Micheaux's sound film *The Exile*.

"You and a hundred other people." He sighed.

"Then it's true there are no surviving copies?"

"Only stills."

"I understand there's a group from Micheaux's hometown in South Dakota that puts on festivals in his honor."

"The town where he homesteaded—yes, that's right. I've talked to them. They have to keep showing the same few movies over and over. Sad, isn't it?"

"Have you corresponded with anyone in the group whose initials are 'DJ'?"

"DJ. DJ." He paused to consider. "No, now what was that fellow's name? Hold on, I have it here." I heard papers rustling, a drawer opening. "No, no DJs." I heard papers rustling again. "Nope, sorry. Were you wanting to contact them?"

"No, not really."

"Because I'm guessing that this is an all-volunteer group. The names could change from year to year."

"Sure, that's possible. Tell me something, John," I said as a thought struck me. "Is there anything odd about the sound-track of *The Exile*?"

"Odd? In what way?"

"I don't know. I mean, did the sound ever get redubbed or anything like that?"

"Not that I know of. You mean, did they dub in dialogue where there wasn't any, something like that?"

Now I was puzzled. "What do you mean?"

"Well, you know that it wasn't an all-talkie, don't you?"

"Meaning?"

"Sorry, I thought you knew. Micheaux always worked on a shoestring. He couldn't afford to record dialogue throughout, only in a few scenes. The rest of the soundtrack was just a synchronized musical score. It would have been kind of like *The Jazz Singer*, if you've seen that."

I had, and I'd learned enough about the history of early sound film to know that the original intent was to synchronize a musical score, not dialogue, so that smaller theaters could compete against the first-run urban movie palaces that featured full orchestras. Warner Bros. had invested in the partnership with Western Electric so that they could compete against MGM and RKO. No one had anticipated the effect on the audience of the words that Al Jolson had added in between the songs he sang in *The Jazz Singer*.

Had DJ known that *The Exile* contained little spoken dialogue? Was his question about the clarity of the dialogue throughout the film intended as a test, to see whether we—or Leo, with whom he thought he was corresponding—were genuine? I was beginning to think it was a test, and we had failed. That would explain DJ's subsequent silence. He wasn't going to waste any more time on us, and I didn't blame him.

The image of Leo leading the vanguard of movie pirates was fast losing its credibility. I was inclined to come clean with DJ so that we could find out what he knew about Leo's movie collection. I would tell that to Styles the next time I saw her.

But the next time I saw Styles I had other things to talk to her about—personal safety issues, for example.

Larry lived in an upscale suburban house that would have accommodated four families in some neighborhoods. It was in a fairly new suburb northeast of the city, where Columbus was growing out to meet Les Wexner, founding CEO of The Limited and one of Columbus's favorite sons. I got my first view of it as we cruised past slowly. The moon wasn't providing much light but what I could see of it looked imposing. I didn't know what style it was, but I was willing to bet that a high-priced architect had designed it.

"There are motion detectors on the front and back lights," Styles reported in a businesslike tone of voice. "We're not going to worry too much about them; the light by the door will help us see what we're doing. The lot size works to our advantage—neighbors pretty far away and on the other side of a tall fence."

"Which we'll have to climb," I noted.

"Nah, we'll go through the side gate there on the right," she said. "It's not a neighborhood of dog-walkers, which also works to our advantage."

"Is it a neighborhood of dogs?"

"No dogs on either side, and no dogs at the Mayer residence. No doubt the Chairmunchkin of the Board is too busy attending to her executive duties to play with a dog. Pull over here."

We'd taken my car because a Honda, even a venerable Civic, was less conspicuous in this neighborhood than Styles's truck would have been.

"If it's not a neighborhood of dogs," I said cautiously, "why do *we* have a dog?"

We both turned and surveyed Waldo, whose grubby nose was pressed up against the window, whose bloodhound ears projected from his head and then drooped to his shoulders, and whose short, stubby basset forelegs stood on the armrest.

"We have a dog because even in a relatively dog-free neighborhood, dogs still provide a good excuse for walking the streets late at night."

"He won't make noise, will he?" I asked anxiously.

She looked at me. "He's very well trained."

I bit my tongue. Peachy had taken the same dog obedience class that Styles and Waldo had, and her reports were not encouraging.

"Well," I said at last, "ask him to keep it down, will you?"

"Waldo, you hear that?" Styles was now rummaging in my glove compartment, and glanced up at the rearview mirror to address our backseat passenger. "Put a sock in it."

She spread out a road map and turned on the overhead light.

"It's upside down," I objected.

She ignored me. So much for verisimilitude. You could tell she wasn't a Liberty.

Behind the cover of the map, she showed me another map, a hand-drawn sketch of the layout of Larry's house.

"Pay attention," she commanded. "Here's our point of entry. I open the door, you have sixty seconds to reach the panel here"—she tapped the plan with her index finger—"and punch in the security code. Got it?"

My mouth went dry, but sweat popped out on my brow.

"Styles, you know I don't do numbers! I'll screw up!"

"No, you won't. It's only four numbers. Here's the code." She handed me a slip of paper. "Don't ask me how Shirley got it; I don't know. After that, we're home free. Shirley's marked Larry's office here—first floor, down the hall to the end."

"What's Waldo doing while I'm busting my ass to get to the security panel?" I asked resentfully.

"Waldo's job is to behave like a normal dog."

"Well, that should be a challenge," I conceded. "As long as we don't get hung up waiting for him to pee on all the bushes."

I checked the mirror one more time to make sure that my hair was stuffed up under my Dinomania cap. We were both wearing loose-fitting dark clothing.

We got out of the car and Styles reached for her crutches. Stabilized, she stretched as if we'd just driven in from New Jersey. She escorted Waldo out of the back seat and clipped on his leash. We walked, or walked and hopped, back to Larry's.

"Act normal," she said. "Talk."

"I don't normally talk when I'm terrified," I said. I was definitely not laughing in the face of danger.

After a quick scan of the immediate vicinity, she headed for the side gate, unlatched it, and disappeared inside. Blinded by the sudden light triggered by the motion detector, I followed, feeling conspicuous.

Styles hopped boldly up to the back door, where the light accommodated her by turning on so that she could study the lock and select the right tool to open it. She had the door open before I was ready.

"Go!" she said.

I went, tripped over Waldo's leash, which he'd managed to wind around my ankles, and stumbled into the door frame.

"Yow!" I shouted softly.

I toed the heel of the sneaker on my entangled leg, pulled it off, stepped free and sprinted for the security panel. One eye on the code, I punched it in.

Styles trailed me nonchalantly, holding my sneaker. She handed it to me, and I tried to wedge my foot inside as I hopped up the hall after her. Home invasion by a pair of bunnies and a pooch.

Styles used a thin flashlight beam to survey the room.

"No windows on the side wall, only facing the back. Good," she said. "Shirley couldn't remember." She crossed the room to the heavy curtains covering a window and adjusted them, then said, "Turn on the light."

The light showed us a well-appointed office with wooden file cabinets that matched the wooden bookshelves that matched the large wooden desk. The wood looked like some endangered species of rain forest flora.

I fumbled in my pocket for cotton gloves.

"Resist the temptation to do the white glove test," Styles directed me. She was already going through Larry's computer disks. "You can look through the files. Thoughtful of him to provide a photocopier." She gestured to a side table where a small machine stood. "We might as well let it warm up."

Soon the room was quiet except for the click of keys on the keyboard, the rustling of paper, and the sniffing of our canine companion.

"Remember," Styles cautioned me, "we're not auditing the guy. You find anything looks interesting, make a copy and we'll take it with us." Styles was half-unconsciously rubbing her sore shoulder, and I was rubbing mine. We would not fare well in a fight.

Soon I was blithely making photocopy after photocopy. This felt a lot like an average day at the office in my former life. I resisted the urge to whistle while I worked.

Apparently, Waldo did not feel similarly constrained. His bloodhound baying cut into the low hum of the photocopier.

"Shit!" Styles expostulated. "He's probably spotted a raccoon."

I followed the sound at a run. Neither of us had noticed that he wasn't in the room with us anymore. I found him in a front window, leaving paw and nose prints all over the glass as he followed the progress of some nocturnal creature across the wide expanse of lawn. I seized him by the collar and dragged him away.

"Shush, Waldo! Be quiet! Do you want to get us all arrested?" I struggled to hold him back with one hand while with the other I swiped at the glass with my handkerchief. I wasn't sure that Waldo could be identified positively by his paw prints, but I was pretty sure a chemical analysis of the nose print would be damning.

He quieted as soon as I reprimanded him and buried his muzzle in my hands. This might have seemed a gesture of contrition but I suspected that he was drawn to the scent of duplicating fluid. Maybe he'd get high on the stuff and pass out. That would keep him quiet, but if I had to carry him unconscious back to the car it would spoil the illusion that we were walking the dog.

Styles had turned out the lights in the office.

"It's after one," I said. "Maybe the neighbors will think they dreamed about a dog."

"It's probably the kind of neighborhood where people don't give a shit unless it's their house somebody's breaking into," she offered. "Have you got enough stuff?"

"I've got a lot," I said. "I'm guessing that if we follow up on what I've got, it should be enough to incriminate him, especially if your hacker can access these accounts over the past six years."

"Same here," she said. "We'll wait for people to go back to sleep, then we'll blow this joint."

We hung out at the back door and waited. Waldo also went to sleep, snuffling in his doggie dreams.

"We don't have the whole picture," Styles said, "but assuming that Leo had something to begin with, it looks to me like Larry has pretty much transferred all of Leo's funds into his own accounts."

I nodded. "Nineteen ninety-one seemed to be a pretty good year for Larry. Same year Leo moved to Florida and left Larry in charge of his money. Funny how that works."

"Leo paid Larry one hell of a salary to be his accountant. But I'm still not convinced we've found the mother lode yet. He's got to have some offshore bank accounts somewhere to hide the income he's not paying taxes on."

"Yeah, I saw his tax returns. He's not paying that much."

"Here's hoping they'll show up on some of the disks I copied," Styles said, and glanced at her watch. "Ready to rock and roll?"

We had to shake Waldo to rouse him. Then we left the way we came, more or less; I tripped over Waldo's leash again, but managed to regain my balance without crashing into anything. I would have had a hard time preventing myself from bolting for the car if I weren't forced to keep pace with a gimp and a basset.

I fired up the engine and eased away from the curb. I let my breath out in an audible sigh of relief.

35

Over the next few days, Styles and her hacker assembled quite a case against Larry. They even hacked into an account in the Caymans, which proved to be the mother lode Styles was looking for. All Leo had at this point was a checking account, into which Larry deposited Leo's modest monthly allowance, and a money market account holding about thirty-five thousand dollars. Larry's accounting firm paid Leo's monthly bills.

"It's the greed that always gets 'em in the end," Styles said, shaking her head. "Greed and arrogance."

We were sitting at her kitchen table, an antique running to rusty chrome and scarred yellow plastic laminate. There were papers everywhere. Bogey the cat was making his own unique contribution by sprawling on top of them, disarranging what order there was every time he stretched.

"Yeah, geez, he had all of Leo's money, and he had to go for the life insurance, too?"

Styles shrugged, winced, and put a hand to her sore shoulder. "Why not? He thought he could get away with it. Until Shirley came along, he was getting away with it. Leo obviously trusted him. And he didn't think Shirley was any match for him."

"And like you said, he never expected her to behave as deviously as he did."

"Or hire someone who did."

Bogey opened his eyes on that and looked at her upside-down, chin pointed at the bare light bulbs in the overhead fixture. Styles winked at him.

"So what's our next move?" I asked. "James has been really good about staying with Shirley and Leo, but he's getting antsy, I can tell. He says the food's good, but his social life leaves something to be desired. Plus, I think Shirley keeps beating him at Scrabble."

Absentmindedly, Styles scratched Bogey under the chin. "Who's the weakest link in our little chain of murderers?"

"That's easy," I said. "Milt. He's the most volatile. Of course, we don't know what Larry's got on him, if anything."

"Or vice versa."

"Or vice versa," she conceded. "But Milt's our man. If we really want these guys to do jail time, we have to make Milt talk."

"And how do we do that?"

She looked at me speculatively. "Let me ask you another question. So far, Milt and Curt have had a pretty mild taste of the criminal justice system. They barely spent enough time in jail to dirty the towels. Now, what offense causes the cops to ignore all of your civil rights? What offense practically ensures that you'll be punished even before you're convicted?"

I frowned at her. "I don't know. Rape?"

She rolled her eyes. "Please."

"Pedophilia?"

"What offense ensures that you'll do time if you're convicted, and allows the government to seize your property even before you're convicted?"

"Drugs."

"Very good, Gilda."

"We get him on a drug rap," I said thoughtfully. "That's okay with me, I guess, considering how dangerous he is. But the property seizure law is a terrible law, Styles."

She rolled her eyes. "Spare me," she said.

"No, really," I insisted. "The feds take everything before a person is convicted, even charged, sometimes. Some people

get arrested, get acquitted, and then spend years trying to recover their property. Anyway, it applies to dealers, doesn't it?
Milt may be a user, but is he a dealer?"

"Listen to what you just said. The feds will figure out
if he's a dealer or not, after they've seized all his property. Gilda, this is *Milt* we're talking about! Milt, the mad
bomber!"

"I know, I know."

"If Milt goes down, he'll probably take the others with
him," she said. "Shirley and Leo will be safe."

"Okay," I said. "You're right. But how do we make it
happen? Dale couldn't even look for drugs when he had a
search warrant."

"Dale wasn't supposed to be looking for drugs." She stared
thoughtfully into space. "What we need is an actor. You know
any actors?"

36

Did I know actors? Did De Mille know extras? Did Disney
know dalmatians? Did Hitchcock know birds?

The more important question was whether I knew any actors who were willing to engage in an enterprise that was
ethically questionable. There again, I was in luck; since life
was one long screenplay to most of my family members, they
never anticipated consequences they couldn't handle with a
rewrite. In the end, though, we picked my father, even though
of all the clan he was probably the one most grounded in
reality.

He frowned at me in concentration as I explained the role
to him.

"Look, you're the middle brother," I said. We'd chosen Curt because he had, after all, been stalking Shirley with a gun, if you faced facts and ignored the colorful embroidery Curt had so deftly applied to them. "You're kind of an underachiever, overshadowed by your older and younger brothers. You're middle-aged, out of shape, divorced. You compensate by being very outgoing and friendly."

"It sounds a lot like Winston Sparkle, Douglas," my mother said from the kitchen, where she was fixing dinner. "You remember how you played him in *Sparkling Eyes*?"

"Oh, yes, I see what you mean, Flo," my father said. "But Winston wasn't an evil person, his surface pretty much corresponded to his core. And I gather that this fellow Gilda's talking about is a nefarious schemer, a would-be murderer. Isn't that right?"

My mother, who was stuffing a chicken, paused, one hand buried inside the bird. She looked at him over her glasses. "Then maybe he's more like Christian Bulow, your rival in *Better by Half*," she mused. "You never really played the nefarious type. This will be a challenge for you."

"It certainly will. So, Gilda, tell me again about the motivation." He adjusted his own glasses so that he could study my face.

"Basically, you're ratting on your younger brother," I explained. "On the phone, you're reluctant, apologetic, worried. Secretly, of course, you've always resented the little bastard and you're enjoying setting him up."

"Secret enjoyment," he echoed. "I can do that."

"Yes, but remember, on the surface, you feel bad about it."

"I feel bad about it. Yes, I see." He stroked his chin thoughtfully.

"And remember, if by any chance we get caught, you don't know anything about it. We told you we were playing a trick on a friend."

"A trick on a friend," he repeated. "Roger."

Late Monday morning, I picked up my father and took him over to Styles's house. She was sitting on the front porch, shooting the breeze with Momo Fazir, a graduate student in computer science at Ohio State. We shook hands.

"You're on, Dad," Styles said.

He gave me a friendly pat on the shoulder.

"Okay, Gil?"

I smiled at him and wondered if he could tell that I'd been clenching my jaw for so long that my teeth were locked together.

"In here, Doug," Momo called from down the hall.

Like her other office, Styles's home office was furnished in early Salvation Army—battered, paint-stained file cabinets, a small bookshelf listing to the right topped by three brown plants, and a large steel desk in gun-metal gray with a chipped wood veneer surface. The only thing state-of-the-art about her office was the computer, and I knew she didn't skimp on electronics. Behind the scarred closet door across from the desk, she probably had a stash of expensive surveillance equipment. The scars were explained by a torso target taped to the door and stuck with darts. Mounted to the back of the door we came in by was a small basketball hoop. Wads of paper crunched underfoot. Bogey the cat batted another one off the desk and looked at us expectantly.

"You can use this phone, either the speaker phone or the handset, it doesn't matter," Momo said. "I have it set up so that any calls out from this phone will be routed through Curt Mayer's number."

"Here's the number you're calling." Styles handed him a slip of paper. "Just tell them you want to report a drug dealer."

She perched on one side of the desk and Momo perched on the other. I sat down in an old loose-jointed wooden chair. My father sat behind the desk and studied the number. He raised an eyebrow at us and dialed.

"Yes, hello, I'd—I don't know who I should talk to. It's about a drug dealer. I want to report a drug dealer." He wiped his hand nervously across his forehead. He didn't appear to be sweating, so I suspected that he was just getting into character.

"Yes, hello, I'm calling about a drug dealer."

Silence.

"Well, yes, that's exactly what I want to do. I have some information about a drug dealer, and I wanted to report to you." He paused and took an audible breath. "It's just that—well, I'm sorry, but this is difficult for me. It's my brother, you see. I think he may be selling drugs."

He listened.

"My name? Are you sure you need that? I don't—that is, well . . . I see. As long as you won't . . . My name is Curt Mayer. No, with a 'C,' Curt with a 'C.' His name is Milton Mayer. He's a stockbroker with Johnson and Cramer. It's a good firm; I have an account there."

I was proud of my father. He had named Milt's company without so much as a glance at his crib sheet. We all had our heads bowed, the better to focus on his words.

"I can't actually say that I've seen him selling, no. That is, I haven't actually seen money change hands. But—well, I know he's a user—a 'recreational user' is what he calls it. Not that I'd call to report him for that. It's just that I've seen people stop by his house, and, well, some of them are just kids. He takes them out of the room and speaks to them for— oh, I don't know—not more than five minutes. If it weren't for the kids, I wouldn't get involved at all. But I've got kids of my own, and that makes it hard."

We knew from Shirley that Curt had three kids, two from a first marriage and one from a second. The oldest was thirteen.

"I didn't know what to do. It's kind of like being Ted Kaczynski's brother."

Three heads popped up in surprise. I was realizing, too late, that my father was, after all, an actor, not a screenwriter; maybe we should have given him a script to follow. Styles was directing hand signals at him.

"Well, maybe not like that. See, he's really a nice guy. He's never had much trouble with the law. I think maybe he's just gotten in with a fast crowd at the brokerage, you know?"

Someone was making little moans of protest. It seemed to be me.

"Yes, I understand that. If it weren't for the kids—he is my baby brother, after all." My father choked on this last sentence, and to my amazement, when I looked up there were tears standing in his eyes. "I just—I don't want to see the kids get hurt."

After that he seemed to be answering questions about Milt's address and his own address and phone number.

"Yes, all right, I understand. And he will—" My father's voice broke again. "He will get drug treatment in prison if it comes to that, won't he?"

He swallowed hard as he listened.

"Well, that eases my mind. I suppose we all spoiled him, growing up, and now it's time for us to pay for that. Well, have a nice day."

And he hung up, wiping tears from his eyes with his handkerchief.

"If that doesn't cook his goose," Styles muttered.

"What?" I asked.

"If that doesn't cook his goose, we'll have to turn up the heat."

"If there's a Plan B," I said, "I don't want to know about it."

"Cookie, there's always a Plan B," Styles said. "Plan B is what separates the professionals from the amateurs."

37

As it turned out, Plan B was unnecessary. The feds searched Milt's house late Monday afternoon and found three hundred grams of powdered cocaine in his sock drawer. Then they searched his Jeep and found another two hundred and fifty in the glove compartment.

"So does that make him a dealer?" I asked Styles. "Or just a heavy user? It sounds like a lot."

"Maybe he just ran into a fire sale," she said. "For our purposes, the important point is it makes him a guest at Uncle Sam's hotel for a minimum of five years."

"Did Dale talk to him?"

She nodded. "The DEA guys checked his record. I don't know if they called ATF, too; I gather Dale has a contact at DEA who contacted him. Anyway, as soon as Dale heard who'd tipped them off, he hustled his buns down to Columbus and found Milt still in custody. All Dale had to say was that Curt had been the DEA's informant, and after that, Milt's lawyer couldn't control him."

"So did Dale get any more evidence against these guys, or just Milt's testimony, which could evaporate once his lawyer explains the facts of life to him?"

"On the basis of Milt's statement, he got a search warrant for some property Larry owns south of Columbus someplace. They went out there last night and found the materials for an incendiary device in a shed on the property."

"Tsk, tsk."

"That was why, he said, he didn't get around to calling me till two in the morning," she said, and yawned broadly. "He would have called you, but he didn't want to disturb Lillian and Ruth."

"Did you call Shirley?"

"This morning. I told her James could go home now."

"I'll bet he's thrilled."

She yawned. "You were wrong about Larry running the whole operation, though. Milt claims your pal Curt was the mastermind. He says Curt decided that they had to get rid of Shirley and persuaded Larry to go along. Then they blackmailed poor little Milty into doing their dirty work."

"Curt," I said evenly, "is not my pal, whatever he thinks. Did anybody point out that they could have killed their own father?"

"Dale claims Milt seemed kind of sorry about that, but—"

"But Leo's dying anyway," I finished.

"We're all dying, sweetheart," she said dryly.

"Yeah, so if anybody gets it into their heads to hurry *me* along, I hope you'll nail the bastard."

"Why don't *you* nail him?" she groused. "I'm not exactly Miss Popularity myself, and my business associates come more heavily armed than yours." She yawned.

"Say, speaking of death—" I looked over at her. She was riding shotgun, her seat pushed back to accommodate her stiff left leg. She was pulling on the seatbelt where it crossed her sore shoulder. "You getting any sleep?"

She grimaced. "I can't get comfortable. I've never slept on my back before, but that's the only way it doesn't hurt. Spike says I'm using the crutches too much, putting too much strain on my shoulder."

"James says the same thing."

"It's easy for them to say. You don't catch either one of them lying around all day."

"A girl's gotta do what a girl's gotta do."

"You said it, sister."

We were on our way, at long last, to Pleasant Ridge, the town outside of Dayton where Leo had grown up. Now that Shirley was safe, we could concentrate on the hunt for Auggie. But we'd gotten off to a late start, since I had worked the Wednesday matinee and the little buggers had left behind even more of a mess than usual for us to clean up. In fact, I'd been delayed so long that Styles and I decided to wait until the rush hour traffic subsided, and then figured I might as well staff the ticket booth for the early show.

"You have dinner?" Styles asked.

I thought back. "My uncle Val brought me two Krispy Kreme donuts around four o'clock. You?"

"Cold pizza at five."

So we cruised through a Wendy's.

Styles had taken charge of the map, and I followed her directions until she said, "I don't think this is right. We're practically on the outskirts of Dayton. I think we must've missed it."

"How could we have missed it?" I objected. "What is it? Shangri-La?"

"Well, I dropped a tomato on I-75 south, but that's east of where we are, so it shouldn't matter. I still think we passed it."

I turned around.

"It has to be right around here someplace," she said about fifteen minutes later. She was scanning the shopping centers, auto parts stores, and fast-food restaurants through the side window. "But I don't see the name anywhere."

"I wish it weren't so dark," I complained. The sky had grown overcast in the past twenty minutes. A storm was moving in.

We stopped at a convenience store.

"Yeah," the clerk said, ringing up my Donettes, Snowballs, and Twinkies, "Pleasant Ridge. This is it. It's kinda been overrun by Fairborn, which has kinda been overrun by Dayton. But it's Pleasant Ridge."

"Where, exactly, is the center of town?" I asked. Styles was watching me from the car.

He thought about that for a minute. He was a guy in his twenties, a lanky redhead with sideburns cut across his jawline like hatchet blades.

"This is pretty much it. If you go up to the light and turn right, you'll see the post office."

"I'm looking for a road called Settles Creek Road."

He shook his head. "I think I heard of Settles Creek, but I don't know where that road is at."

"Is there a town hall, city offices, anything like that?"

He looked at me confused. Then he spotted somebody coming up the aisle from the beer and wine coolers.

"Hey, Mick!" he called. "You know if there's any town hall or city offices around here?"

"Like where the mayor hangs out?" I prompted helpfully.

"No, man, I don't know anyplace like that," the other young man said. He was about the same age as the cashier. He grinned and added, "I know where the cops hang out."

"The mayor's usually not too far away," I said.

"You go up here to the light and make a right. You go maybe half a mile, past an Arby's and a McDonald's and a Dairy Queen. You make a left at the Taco Bell, and it's right there. You can't miss it." He turned back to me and grinned slyly. "Or else you can just turn at the light and floor it. That way, the cops'll find you."

Back at the car, I told Styles, "Well, at least we won't go hungry if we get lost on the way to the police station." I threw the bag at her.

"What's this?"

"Dessert. Breakfast. Whatever."

Outside, the wind was picking up, and I could smell the approaching rain. The front desk at the police station was staffed by a woman officer who looked to be in her early thirties. She had a blond ponytail and freckles. I asked her about Settles Creek Road.

She frowned and shook her head. "There's a Settles Creek, but I don't know about a Settles Creek Road. Hang on, let me get a map."

She pored over the map for a while, expressionless, then laid it on the counter between us.

"Here's Settles Creek," she said. I followed a wandering purple fingernail for about an inch. I glanced at the gun she wore on her hip and wondered if it took a toll on her nails at the firing range. "That's out in the county. But there isn't a Settles Creek Road."

Maybe we were looking for Shangri-La after all.

"Could it have changed names?" I asked.

She shrugged. "Could have. I wouldn't know about that."

"May I have this map?"

"Go ahead," she said. Her expression said it wouldn't do me much good if I was looking for a road that wasn't on it.

"Is there—" I hesitated. "Is there an older person here who might have lived here longer, somebody who might remember an older name?"

"Well, Fred's here. Let me ask him."

She disappeared through a door and returned with another officer. This one was older, with the paunch and gray thinning hair to prove it. I guessed he was planning his retirement. He had a large nose like a lump of dough attached to a friendly face.

"You looking for Settles Creek Road?"

I nodded.

"That's that Tower Road extension," he said to the woman, "where they connected up the roads when they built that subdivision out by Lawson's. Hell, must've been twenty, twenty-five years ago now. Used to be called Settles Creek, part of it."

"I'm looking for a farm," I said, "on Settles Creek Road."

He shook his head. "There ain't too many farms around anymore. There's some, but a lot of 'em went under or sold up to the developers."

"The one I'm looking for belonged to the Mayer family."

"Oh, the Mayers." He nodded brightly. "I've heard about them. They were in the movie business, the Mayers."

"They were?"

"That's right." He was eager to talk about local history. "A lot of people don't know that in the old days they made pictures right here in Greene County. You know who you ought to talk to?" He turned to the woman. "She ought to talk to Noble." To me he said, "Noble Scott owns the diner up the street, the Deluxe. If you hurry, you might catch him. He's there most nights at dinnertime." He glanced at his watch. "It's getting kind of late, though. And there's a storm coming. So I don't know whether he'll be there or not."

"Did he know the Mayers?" I asked.

"Why, he worked for the Mayers, in those pictures they made. He knows all about those times."

Eager to follow my first lead before he went home for the night, I thanked them and left.

In the car, I told Styles what I learned as we headed for the Deluxe Diner.

"His family made movies?" She was as surprised as I was. "How come nobody knows that? How come he never told anybody?"

"He told me," I reminded her.

The Deluxe Diner was in a building from an earlier era. It was not an attractive building; it looked like a diner. It also looked like the sole survivor in some cataclysmic event that had leveled everything around it from its time and earlier. It was squashed between a Kentucky Fried Chicken and a Napa

Auto Parts, but the parking lot was pretty full for nine o'clock at night.

We told the young brunette who greeted us with menus that we were looking for Noble Scott.

"Have a seat," she said, glancing at Styles's crutches. "I think he's still in the kitchen."

"Y'all might as well order something and stay awhile," a waitress told us, swiping at crumbs on our table. "It's fixing to storm out there. And anyway, if you haven't tasted Edna's pies, you haven't lived yet."

She recited a list of flavors as long as the cast call for *Titanic*. I ordered black raspberry and Styles ordered strawberry-rhubarb.

Noble Scott was a short, wiry man wearing bright gold-framed bifocals against very dark skin. He had the air of a man who concealed a lot of nervous energy under a smooth exterior.

We introduced ourselves and he took a chair.

"I understand you ladies are friends of Leo's," he said. "How is Leo? I haven't seen him for a while."

"He hasn't been getting out much," Styles said.

"I'm sorry to hear that," he said. "Is he in poor health?"

"He has Alzheimer's disease," she said. "Otherwise, he's doing fine."

He looked down at the table and didn't say anything for a moment. "I've been wondering," he said finally. "The last time he was here, I thought he seemed kind of forgetful. But it was just a few little things, you know?" He glanced up at us. "It wasn't anything big. We old men, we do that sometimes. But then he never came back, and I wondered."

"So he came back pretty often, then?" Styles asked.

"I don't know what you'd call often. He came back once or twice a year." Scott rubbed the back of his hand with his thumb, as if he were massaging arthritis out of his knuckles.

"We heard that you worked for the Mayers in the movie business."

He smiled, but his eyes remained serious. "Oh, that was a long time ago, Miss Styles. A long time ago."

It occurred to me that we were engaged in an elaborate verbal dance. Styles was trying to figure out how much to tell him. And he was watching us from behind those glasses, cautious. But why?

Styles made up her mind. "Here's our situation, Mr. Scott. Leo's wife, Shirley—you know he remarried?" Scott nodded, and Styles continued. "Shirley hired me to find somebody Leo wants to talk to. I'm a private investigator." She handed him a card. "Leo keeps saying he wants to talk to somebody— seems obsessed by it. But he can't—or won't—tell Shirley who this person is or how to find him. Shirley thinks it's important enough to Leo that she wants to find this person for him. But she didn't know where to start. I never met Shirley and Leo before she hired me, and Shirley seems kind of vague about Leo's past. So far, we haven't come up with anything. It took us awhile to figure out that Leo still had ties to Pleasant Ridge. Now we're hoping that we can find the person we're looking for here, if he's still alive, or get a lead on where he might be."

"Who are you looking for?" he asked.

"His name is Auggie," Styles said. "Leo wants to talk to Auggie."

"Auggie," he repeated. "And you think this Auggie's around here?"

"We're hoping he is," I said. "Or if not, that somebody knows who he is and where he is."

He resettled his bifocals and stared off into space. A busboy rattled dishes at a nearby table. "I might be able to help you," Scott said. He rubbed the back of his hand again. "I don't know for sure. I have to ask around."

"Do you know who Auggie is?" Styles pressed.

"I'm not sure that I do," he said. "But I'll ask around. Is this the phone number I call?" He pointed at the card.

"No, we'll be staying in town," I said. "We can let you know where. We'd like to go out to the Mayer property and look around."

He raised his eyebrows. "Nothing much to see. The old farmhouse is empty—Leo never stayed there. I don't know that it's even safe to walk around in. Leo never bothered much with maintenance. Probably doesn't have electricity."

"We'd still like to see it," I insisted. "Can you tell us how to get there?"

He thought a minute, then shook his head. "It's been so long since I've been out there, and they've changed the roads all around. I'm not sure I could find it myself, not without taking a lot of wrong turns."

"I have a map," I said, and held it up. "Would that help?"

"I've never been good with maps," he said. "My wife, she says I'd better learn, the way the county's growing and everything's getting changed around. She says one day I won't be able to find my way here to the diner. I tell her when that day comes, I'll retire. She's waiting for me now," he added, a little apologetically. "I've got to go."

He stood up and we shook hands.

"I'd like to hear more about the movie business," I told him.

"Come back any time," he said, smiling.

Back in the car, we watched the lightning flicker overhead.

"He knew what you were going to say before you said it," I observed. I lit a cigarette.

"He knows who Auggie is," Styles agreed.

"Then why doesn't he want us to know?"

"If we knew that," Styles said, "we'd know everything."

I exhaled smoke. "It would be really stupid to try and find the farm now."

Thunder rumbled in the distance.

"It's late, it's dark, and there's a storm coming on," I said.

A flash of lightning lit up the sky.

"Scott doesn't want us to go to the farm. Why not?"

"There's only one way to find out," Styles said.

I pressed the cigarette between my lips and put the car in gear.

38

"If Auggie's at the farm, Scott will probably call him to warn him we're coming," I mused. "If the farm still has a phone."

"Yeah, but they won't expect us tonight," she said. "No phone at that address, I checked. But the electricity is still on. Scott was wrong about that—or lying."

She had to repeat this comment because I couldn't hear it over the latest crash of thunder.

"Maybe we should've turned on the radio, listened to the weather report," she shouted.

"Radio's broken," I shouted back.

"Figures," she said, and buried her head in the map, which she was reading by flashlight.

"Take the next turnoff you see," she said, not shouting, but cranking up the volume.

"I can't see any turnoffs," I objected. "I can't see anything."

The storm had broken and the wind was sending waves of water over my windshield. What made us think we could find a house in a thunderstorm? I thought. We couldn't even find a town when it wasn't raining.

Something exploded in front of us.

"Jesus!" we chorused.

I slammed on the brakes and we skidded sideways. We both watched the tree falling toward the windshield and then it disappeared from view. When we glided to a stop, we looked at each other, then out the back window.

I turned the key in the ignition. "I hope this was the turnoff you meant," I said, "because we ain't going back."

"We *can't* go back," she pointed out. "If we're lucky, we're on Settles Creek Road. Also if we're unlucky."

I nodded, and fumbled for another cigarette. "You know what to do in case of a flash flood?"

"Not me," she said. "I was thrown out of the Brownies for using foul language and unsportsmanlike conduct."

"No! You?"

"This has to be it," Styles said a minute later. She shone the flashlight on the rusty mailbox and stretched her neck out the car window. "I can make out something that was painted on the mailbox. There's an A-R-T, and maybe a B and an O-N something." She retracted a very wet head, wincing at the pain in her shoulder.

" 'Art' is promising," I said.

Styles shook her wet curls like a dog, spattering me with rain. "I could be wrong, of course," she said, and sneezed. "Maybe it said 'target range.' "

I aimed the Honda at a barely visible path through high weeds that were being tossed by the wind. My headlights hardly pierced the curtain of water before us, revealed intermittently as the windshield wipers struggled to clear the glass. We were both leaning forward as if proximity to glass and storm would improve visibility. Underneath us, I felt the tires slide on mud and roll awkwardly over rock. The small car bucked, dipped, and lurched forward through the watery darkness.

Then, just as I glimpsed a house-sized silhouette rising before us, the wheels spun without resistance, and the car died, and gave up the struggle. Neither one of us spoke. I sighed, turned the key, eased the stick into reverse, and pressed on the gas pedal. The wheels spun and whined. I shifted to first and got the same result. Back and forth, from reverse to first, I tried to persuade the car to move. It refused. I switched off the ignition and the lights; no point in running the battery down. I turned and stared gloomily at Styles's crutches.

"Okay," I said. "We might as well find out if anybody's home. Give me the flashlight."

"And leave me here in the dark? No way, babe."

She swung her car door open and a wet gust of wind hit me full in the face.

"You can't walk around in this mud," I objected, raising my voice to be heard.

But she was already struggling ahead, or so I gathered from the erratic movement of the flashlight and the string of curses that issued from the darkness somewhere in front of the car. I cursed, too, as I dug around in a backpack lying on the backseat and retrieved another flashlight. When I reached Styles, she was bogged down in mud some three yards from the car. I yanked on her crutch to disengage it and nearly sent her flying.

"Thanks a heap," she said.

"De nada."

The ground under our feet grew firmer, and we found ourselves on a gravel drive. My flashlight, shining weakly through the gloom, picked out a downspout, a stretch of decorative molding, a wall.

Styles grabbed my T-shirt by one sleeve and pulled.

"Over here," she said, dragging me with her as she stumbled toward a set of steps.

We found ourselves on a wide wraparound porch. The house was dark and dead quiet. The storm roared.

"You ever see *The Haunting*?" Styles shouted in my ear.

"I was thinking *Rocky Horror Picture Show* myself. Oh, look!" I said, pointing. "Here's the doorbell."

Styles rolled her eyes at me and tried the doorknob. The door didn't budge.

"The knob feels loose," she said, "but the deadbolt's holding. I'll bet we can break in somehow."

We backed up a few steps to look around. Then we heard the screech of metal on metal and froze.

I took a breath and turned. "What the hell was that?"

Several yards from where we stood, my flashlight picked out the boxy shape of a small foreign car, maybe a Nissan or a Mazda. I exchanged a look with Styles, moved down the steps and toward the car. I reached out and touched the hood.

Beneath my fingertips I could feel the faint warmth of an engine recently fired.

"I hate it when I'm right about stuff like this," I said.

I swiped one wet arm across my eyes and turned to survey the terrain. I could now make out a large barn nearby. The same metallic screech ran from my ears down my spine again, and it was coming from that direction. Probably, I told myself, it was the barn door swinging on rusty hinges.

"Let's play the glad game," Styles muttered next to me, looking more like a drowned terrier than Pollyanna. "I think the storm is letting up."

Lightning flashed and thunder set the ground vibrating beneath our feet.

"It was just a theory," I heard her say as the sound died away.

I headed for the barn. There was no point in asking Styles if she was carrying; she always struck me as astonishingly unprepared in moments of crisis. Of course, I was unprepared, too, but then I was a theater owner, not a P.I.

When I pushed on the barn door, it did indeed make a screeching sound. Within, the air smelled of mildew and damp earth and rotting wood. In a surreal moment, as I pointed my flashlight straight ahead, I found myself in a Western town, a little faded, as if it were Brigadoon materializing out of the mists of time. Then the moment passed, and I realized I was looking at a dusty facade from a Western set— one of a number of large wooden flats propped against the opposite wall. My flashlight played over stacks of furniture, an old Moviola and a rusty collection of lights, a small tractor with a flatbed wagon attached, and a hayloft crammed with boxes. Styles had followed me in. She was leaning forward, both shoulders propped on her crutches, as she directed her own flashlight beam into corners. Another crack of thunder rattled the structure and sent a shower of dirt, dust, and what was probably owl and bat shit down on our heads.

"What's that?" Styles gasped, coughing.

I followed the beam of her flashlight and bent over. I touched the dull metal object as familiar to me now as a wedding ring had once been.

"It's a film canister," I said.

I stood and followed my inclinations around the corner to a storage area with a flagstone floor. A blinding flash lit the small space through gaps in the wood holding the barn together, and something exploded. I dropped my flashlight, which shattered on the stone.

"Styles?" I called anxiously in the dark, suddenly disoriented.

"It wasn't me," she said.

"Styles?" I called again. I heard the panic rising in my voice. I held a hand out tentatively, hoping to find something solid, but my stomach lurched as I brushed cobwebs thick as lamb's wool. "It just occurred to me that if lightning hit this barn, and if there happened to be a collection of old movies inside it—"

She didn't need any further explanation. Nitrate was highly combustible. That's why people used it in bombs.

"We'd better get out of here," she agreed.

I took two steps in what I hoped was the right direction, willing my eyes to adjust to the constant flashes of lightning. Then my foot struck something soft, and I fell.

I cried out. I heard Styles galloping in my direction at a fast limp.

"What is it?" she asked, blinding me with the flashlight.

"Oh, God!" I wailed. "It's a body!" I was trying to scramble to my feet without touching the soft flesh.

"A dead one?"

"Yes—no—I don't know!" I hopped around, trying not to put too much weight on the ankle I'd twisted. Idiotically, I shook my hands as if they were contaminated. It wasn't as if the corpse was half-rotted, I tried to tell myself; it was a nice, fresh one. I could tell that much in the dim light. "I think I'm going to be sick," I announced, as Styles thrust the flashlight into my hands.

She leaned her crutches against me and crouched down.

"Not dead," she reported, her hand buried inside clothing.

"Jesus H. Christ on a raft," the corpse mumbled as it stirred, "if she falls on me again, I might be."

The moving bundle of cloth resolved itself into a woman in a rain slicker and jeans. Styles helped pull her into a sitting position and she slumped against Styles, rubbing the back of her head, which appeared to be overendowed with long, frizzy, dark blond hair. She looked a little like a silent film heroine, Lillian Gish on a bad hair day, maybe—a resemblance heightened by the way the flashlight shook in my hand and flickered over her face.

"If she's Auggie, I'll croak," I told Styles.

"Five bucks says she isn't," Styles replied.

"Auggie who?" she asked irritably. "Who the hell are you, anyway?"

"The owner sent us," Styles said. "Who the hell are you?"

"Dylan," she said. "Dylan Jellico."

"Dylan Jellico?" I echoed excitedly. "You're DJ! Hi!" I burbled, and stuck out my hand. "I'm Gilda Liberty."

She stared at the hand. "My lucky day," she said.

39

Another thunderclap made us all jump.

"We'd better get the hell out of here," Dylan Jellico said.

I got her to her feet, and the three of us stumbled out of the barn and into the rain.

"Your car or mine?" she shouted.

"Ours is standing in the middle of a bog," I said. "Unless of course it's sunk by now."

She yanked open her car door and threw herself in. Styles and I ended up in a tangle of wet clothes and crutches in the backseat. I heard the flick of a lighter and raised my head, sniffing.

"Cigarettes?" I said hopefully. My own were crushed and soggy against my left buttock.

She handed one over. Her wet hair had flattened against her head like an otter's fur. She glanced at herself in the rearview mirror and rolled her eyes. She was a tall woman and broad-shouldered. She looked to be in her early to middle thirties.

"So how did you know Leo?" I asked.

"We met on-line," she said, cracking her window and then leaning back against it. She had a hint of a Southern accent. She parked the cigarette between her lips and began to press strands of sodden hair between her fingers. "There's this movie newsgroup I subscribe to. And Leo wrote in asking for information about film restoration. I answered his letter and we started corresponding. Later on, he came to see me at work once, to see what I did."

"What *do* you do?" Styles asked.

DJ stopped dehumidifying her hair and stared at us. "I thought you recognized my name," she said accusingly.

"We know you were looking for a copy of Oscar Micheaux's *The Exile*," I said. "We don't know why."

"I work for the Conservation Center at Wright-Pat."

"The Air Force base?" I asked, puzzled.

"That's where we're located," she said. "The Air Force provides space for the Library of Congress Motion Picture Conservation Center."

"You're involved in film preservation work?"

"Restoration, mainly." Thunder boomed and she winced. "God, that hurts." She put a hand gingerly to the back of her head. "Damn, I got a lump back there sticking out like the Hollywood sign. There were these shelves, and I couldn't see what was on the top one. I put my weight on the bottom one and the next thing I know I'm on the ground and somebody's on top of me. I must've hit my head when I fell." She started as if she'd thought of something and raised a wrist to look at her watch. "Damn, I must've been out—what? A good twenty minutes."

"You must know John Pogue." Call me insensitive, but if

she was going to croak in the night from concussion, I wanted her story first.

"I've talked to him on the phone," she said. "He's in D.C., at the archives."

So why hadn't Pogue identified "DJ" with the Dylan Jellico he knew? Because I hadn't encouraged him to. I'd asked about connections with the Micheaux film festival organizers in South Dakota. I would've kicked myself except that there wasn't room and I didn't have an ankle to spare.

"Did Leo have some old films he wanted to restore?"

She raised a hand over her shoulder and flicked her ash out the car window. "Don't you know?" she asked, frowning.

"There's a lot we don't know, okay?" Styles said, a little irritably. She was rubbing her shoulder again. "Leo has Alzheimer's, so we're not getting a very coherent account from him. We were hired to find somebody from his past."

The "we" startled me, but I didn't turn my head.

"Alzheimer's?" She looked from Styles to me. I nodded. "So that explains it. Look, I don't really know what Leo had. He always played his cards pretty close to his chest. But I figured out who he was, so of course I had my suspicions."

"What do you mean exactly, 'who he was'?"

"That he was one of the Mayers—the Mayers of Ebony Art."

"Ebony Art?" Styles echoed.

"You two really don't know shit, do you?" she asked, but not as rudely as it sounds. "Ebony Art Motion Picture Company. This was their home base—right here where we're sitting."

"They made race films," I guessed.

"That's right. There were a lot of white-owned companies, and a few black-owned companies, in the business of making movies for black audiences. Most of them weren't in Los Angeles, they were in places like Chicago and Kansas City and Houston. Ebony Art was here, in between Dayton and Wilberforce."

"Where the black college is—Wilberforce College," I said. I was beginning to understand.

"That's right. Like a lot of motion picture producers, the

Mayers started out as theater owners. They owned theaters all over Ohio, and a few in Indiana. With the great black migration north during World War One, they found that they owned quite a few theaters in black neighborhoods and wanted something besides the standard Hollywood fare. So they started making their own. They used a lot of Wilberforce students over the years. It was a big problem, you know, finding trained black actors to make movies. But in a black college, students had the opportunity to develop their talent without having to take menial roles or compete with white students for major roles."

"Did Leo tell you he had some Ebony Art films?"

"Nuh-uh, he just told me he'd found some old movies he wanted to restore, but I knew he was a Mayer from somewhere in the Dayton area." She gestured with her hands. "You don't have to be a genius to figure it out."

"Didn't you offer to restore them yourself?" Styles asked. "Or to have the Library of Congress do it?"

"I offered to help him," Jellico said. "People are touchy, and they can be real possessive about anything like this that they think might be worth some money. I could tell it wasn't the money Leo was thinking about. He loved movies; you could see that. He just wanted to do it himself."

She flipped the butt out the window and pushed back her mane, half-frizzy now. "God, do you know how hard it is to let somebody do that? I mean, there was nothing I could've done to stop him. The movies belonged to him. We couldn't confiscate them and force him to let us restore them. But if I could've, I would've. Do you know how few of those early race films still exist anymore? Jesus, I thought, I hope to hell he doesn't fuck it up. But like I said, he came and watched me and he asked good questions and I even let him help me do some of the steps. So I thought he might actually be able to pull it off. And then it was like he disappeared into thin air, and I didn't hear anything from him. It did cross my mind that he'd screwed up in a big way, and was too embarrassed to tell me."

"Perchloroethylene," Styles said.

"Did y'all find some of that?" she asked. "Did you find his workshop?"

I shook my head. "We found an order confirmation, that's all. What is it?"

"It's a solvent we use in immersion printing. It's ideal for our purposes because of the index of refraction. But it's real toxic. And of course it's carcinogenic." She rolled her eyes and lit another cigarette. She held out the pack to me.

"Thanks. Why did you think he might have an Oscar Micheaux film?" I asked.

"It was a long shot," she admitted. "But after all, *The Exile* was the first black talkie, so it was the major competition for Ebony Art. I thought they might just possibly have acquired a copy."

"But it wasn't an all-talkie."

"Were you the ones who answered my e-mail? The first one, asking how much I was offering—that didn't sound like Leo at all. So I got suspicious. After all, I hadn't heard from him in a long time, and I didn't know what was going on with him. So then I asked that question about the sound track, just to see what he'd say."

"It was a trick question," I reminded Styles. "She asked whether the dialogue was clear throughout, to see if you knew that the dialogue was limited to a few scenes."

"I thought maybe Leo had died, and some greedy relative of his was trying to squeeze every penny out of his estate."

"Well, you weren't too far wrong about that last part," I told her. "But he's not dead."

"So what were you doing here tonight, in the dark, in the middle of a storm?" Styles asked bluntly. She reached out and plucked the cigarette from my hand, took a puff and passed it back.

"The same thing you were: looking for something." She eyed Styles coolly. "See, I just got back from vacation yesterday, and I picked up that e-mail this morning. When I started hearing the severe thunderstorm watches, I got nervous. I thought, goddamnit, Leo's estate is in the hands of some ignorant bastard who doesn't know shit about movies.

Somewhere out there on that Pleasant Ridge property is a stash of rare race movies. What if they're in a barn like the ones they found in Michigan? Well, those weren't race movies, but you get the picture. And those were in such bad shape, they would've caught fire and burned the barn down in five minutes if lightning even thought about striking within ten feet. I thought Leo knew better, but what if he'd died before he got the chance to move them to a safe place? This was the same storm that caused tornadoes in Oklahoma. I couldn't stop worrying about it. So finally I gave up and came out here. I'd driven by the place before when I figured out who Leo was, so I knew where it was. And it wasn't storming yet. I would've missed the storm completely if I hadn't hit my head. But I was prepared. Look!" She leaned forward and hoisted a red canister up off the seat. "I even brought along a fire extinguisher. Not that it'd do much good against a barn full of deteriorated nitrate."

The thunder had died down to a grumble, and the rain had eased into a steady shower.

"So if you didn't know about the movies, what were y'all doing out here tonight?"

"We knew there might be movies," I said, a little defensively. "We were just a little sketchy on the details."

"We're looking for somebody named Auggie," Styles said. "Ever heard of him?"

"Auggie. You were talking about him when I woke up. I never heard of him, though."

"No August Mayer in the Mayer family tree that you know of?" Styles asked.

She shook her head, bumped it against the car window, and winced. She reached up to touch the back of her head again, the way people do, as if fingering the bump would ease the pain. "Leo's dad was Solomon Mayer—Sol or Solly, everybody called him. His granddad was Samuel. His brother was Sheldon."

It seemed to me sadly ironic that Dylan Jellico knew more about Leo's family than anyone else we'd met.

"Any cameramen named Auggie associated with Ebony

Art?" Styles persisted. "Actors? Electricians? Anybody like that?"

Again, she shook her head. "He had a black grandmother," she offered. "Did you know that? Not his blood grandmother, but Samuel's second wife. Miss Leila is what everybody called her. She was their star in the twenties—Leila Nickerson was her screen name. Her name is pure gold around here, among the older folks, white and black." She gestured to take in the neighborhood. She frowned then. "Haven't you talked to anybody who knows all this stuff I'm telling you?"

"Nobody in the family seems to know it," Styles said.

"Leo's only known his present wife for about four years," I explained. "His former brother-in-law, who claims to be his best friend, didn't seem to know it. His former business partner didn't seem to know it. And if his sons know it, they're keeping it to themselves. But it seems more likely that Leo kept his own secrets, and not just from you."

She nodded. "I got that impression. I guess that's why I didn't pry when I figured out who he was. I was dying to ask him about Ebony Art. I was going to try to talk him into writing a book about the company, maybe work with a ghostwriter or a graduate student." She sighed. "I thought eventually, he'd come to trust me more. I thought I had plenty of time."

"Don't we all," I said wryly.

I said. "Maybe it embarrassed Leo to be associated with race films. I think the war provided Leo with his first exposure to full-blown racial prejudice."

I had a momentary vision of Leo, tearing up the photograph of the minstrel show staged by his army buddies. I thought that his heart was in the right place. But very few people have the courage to follow their hearts against the tide of public opprobrium.

She rolled her eyes again and blew smoke in exasperation. "Yeah, yeah, I know. Things were different back then. Times have changed, yadda, yadda. But I still don't get it."

We fell silent and gazed out at the rain.

"So what do we do now?" I asked finally.

"I vote against going back out in the rain and slogging through the mud with one flashlight among us," Styles said.

"Damn! I had a flashlight," Jellico said, and looked wistfully toward the barn.

"I also vote against trying to get your car out of the mud tonight," Styles said to me, yawning and stretching. "We'll be lucky if we can get *her* car out of here tonight," she added, raising her chin in Jellico's direction.

"You're a real ray of sunshine, you know that, Styles?" I said.

"I can give y'all a ride," Jellico said. "Where you staying?"

"Anyplace cheap, clean, and close," Styles said, closing her eyes.

In the end, we managed to retrieve our bags and stash of junk food from my car, which appeared to have sunk another inch. Jellico, or Dylan as she told us to call her, drove us to a Best Western and arranged to pick us up in the morning.

"My boss will let me off if I explain the situation," she told me. "Hell, if I come back with a trunk full of Ebony Art films, he'll go crazy."

Styles stumbled into the room, threw her crutches on the floor, pulled off her boots, and stretched out on the closest bed. By the time I came out of the bathroom she was sound asleep.

In the movies, when this kind of thing happens, somebody comes along and covers the person up, tucks them in, kisses them affectionately. I didn't do this for Styles. In the first place, for all I knew, she slept this way every night. In the second, there was always the chance she'd awaken suddenly and throw me across the room. That's the part they never show in movies.

40

"This is so cool!" Dylan Jellico exclaimed for the three hundredth time. "Look! Movie posters! Dry and everything! I bet these date back to the twenties."

"Will you get out of there?" I said irritably. "You can look at all that stuff later. Shirley will probably give it to you if you ask."

We'd worked our way up to the attic, which was downright tropical on this hot and steamy day. We hadn't found anything of interest in the barn except for my flashlight (broken) and Dylan's flashlight (intact). No collection of old movies. No workshop for restoring old movies. No Auggie. Styles had easily picked the lock on the back door of the old farmhouse in which we stood. It was a large house in utter disrepair, empty of furniture except for a few mismatched piles here and there that appeared to be former movie properties, now cozy homes to mice who rustled and scratched behind the wallpaper as we walked the house. Everywhere we encountered the flotsam of a once-vital film production company—everything but the films themselves.

"Oh, look!" Dylan said, and pounced on something. "A clue!"

She held up an old insurance company calendar, turned to August 1960, and giggled. She'd piled her hair untidily on top of her head, and half of it had fallen damply around her face. It was decorated, here and there, with cobwebs.

Styles gave her a murderous look. "She's driving," I reminded Styles under my breath.

"Not if we get the keys away from her," Styles muttered.

"We still have some outbuildings to check," Dylan said cheerfully. "Maybe we'll find his workshop in one of those."

But an hour later we hadn't found anything we were looking for. We sat on the front steps of the house, discouraged.

"The property is pretty extensive," Styles said. She had insisted that we start the day at the county courthouse, where we had acquired a copy of an old survey map of the property.

We stared gloomily across fields and woods.

"Okay," I said finally. "Let's assume that Leo knew what he was doing. Let's assume that he had some money to invest in this project. We know he had time; we know he was serious." I turned to Dylan. "What would be the optimal facility for storing film?"

"Cold and dry," she said. "We have climate-controlled vaults. Leo's seen them."

I sighed. "We haven't seen anyplace cold and dry," I said. I picked at my sweat-dampened T-shirt and peeled it away from my body.

"No, but the electricity's still turned on," Styles pointed out.

"Wonder what the electric bills run to," I mused.

"One way to find out." Styles pulled a flip phone out of her back pocket and dialed information. She got the number for the local electric company, dialed it, and handed me the phone.

"The acting's all in your family, not mine," she said.

I had plenty of time to compose myself while the recorded voice ran through my forty-three touch-tone options.

"Stay on the line," Styles coached me. "You get a person only if you're too persistent to hang up."

Eventually, I got an accounts representative.

"Oh, hi. Hi. This is Mrs. Mayer, Sarah Mayer," I said. "My husband pays all the utility bills for my father-in-law, and he's out of town right now—my husband, that is—and he's asked me to pay the bill but I can't find it. I know he has it on even billing, but I don't know the amount. I was wondering if you could tell me, and I'll mail in the check."

She asked for the account number, and I told her I didn't

have it. I read the address to her. She went away and came back and told me we owed seventy-two dollars. I felt my eyebrows lift.

"But my records show the billing address as an accounting firm," she said.

"My husband's," I said. "It looks bigger on paper. Thanks."

"Seventy-two dollars?" Dylan echoed when I reported. "For an abandoned house? He *must* have a cooled storage area someplace."

"Maybe we've set our sights too high," Styles speculated. "Maybe we should be looking for a root cellar."

"Or a bomb shelter," I said.

They both looked at me.

"That calendar Dylan found was from 1960," I pointed out. "That means somebody was living here then. Suppose you lived near an Air Force base during the height of the Cold War. What would you have done?"

Styles grinned at me. Dylan was still trying to figure it out. She was probably still trying to imagine the Cold War.

Styles was the one who found it. What we saw from the outside was a heavy metal ring surrounded by a metal frame that divided a rectangle of overgrown lawn and weeds from more of the same. Two feet away, a series of pipes protruded from the ground. Two were open at the top and then capped to keep out the elements.

"There's the intake for the refrigeration system." Styles pointed her crutch. "You can hear the compressor."

We stood still and listened. She was right. A soft hum seemed to issue from the ground beneath our feet.

I tugged at the ring, feeling a little like Dorothy in *The Wizard of Oz*. I'd never been inside an underground shelter before. The door opened more easily than I thought, and we faced a flight of concrete steps.

Dylan was dancing around in her excitement.

"Better let her go first," Styles said to me. "She's got a history of falling, and I don't want her falling on top of me."

"Look who's talking," I muttered under my breath. It

occurred to me that she wanted Dylan and me both to go first so she'd have something soft to land on.

"Oh, my God!" Dylan was saying from the bottom of the steps. "Guys, this is it! You gotta see this!"

The underground room had been a generous size for a bomb shelter before it had been subdivided. All along one wall was a series of heavy metal cabinets, not the kind you could buy at the hardware store but some industrial type. Next to them was the source of the humming sound, a boxlike unit with a thermostat mounted on the front. Each cabinet also boasted a thermostat mounted in the door, though it was clear these were not part of the original equipment but had been added by a skilled do-it-yourselfer. The room was cool but not cold; the heat produced by the machinery was offset by a vent in some ductwork leading to the cabinets.

On the other side of the room was Leo's workbench. Again, it was homemade, pieced together from scrap lumber. On top of the workbench was a large plastic container of perchloroethylene. Past the workbench another corner had been bitten out of the room by two short sections of drywall. A primitive door had been cut in one of these. I was guessing that this space was a darkroom.

Tucked into the corner nearest the stairs was a large piece of equipment that looked something like my cousin Faye's digital editor, with platters and spools and an enclosed screen.

"What are you waiting for?" I asked Dylan. "Open the cabinets and let's see if we have anything."

There was always the possibility that someone had removed everything that they contained.

Dylan swallowed. "I'm afraid to," she whispered. "Maybe we shouldn't let any air in. Or maybe we shouldn't let the cold air out."

Styles made a sound of impatience. "We have to know if there's anything to preserve."

She hobbled over, unlatched a cabinet door, and threw it open. The shelves were filled with metal canisters. Movie titles, printed in several hands, danced before my eyes. I felt faint, and realized I'd been holding my breath.

Dylan burst into tears.

Even Styles looked awestruck.

Dylan approached slowly and ran an index finger over a label.

"A Black Magdalene," she read in a choked voice. "Do you know what this is? It's from nineteen—" Her voice caught. "T-t-twenty-t-t-two!"

41

"What I don't understand," I said later, as we ate Big Macs under a tree in front of the house, "is why Larry kept paying the utility bills on this place. Did he know about the films or not?"

Styles shrugged. "Maybe it was an oversight. Maybe seventy dollars wasn't enough to call attention to itself in the grand scheme of things. Or maybe someone else in his firm did the actual bill paying. Vice presidents probably have better things to do."

"Than watch Leo's money?" I said skeptically.

"Maybe Leo warned him at the beginning not to forget to pay that bill in particular," Dylan suggested. "Maybe he made up some excuse."

"Or maybe the patron saint of cinema was keeping an eye on him," I said.

"The patron saint of cinema." Dylan laughed. "Who's that?"

"I don't know," I said. "But when I meet him, I plan to have a talk with him about our breakage rate at the Paradise."

"Or her," Styles corrected dryly. "Maybe it's Saint Mary."

"Or Saint Dorothy," I acknowledged.

"Or Saint Alice Guy," Dylan proposed.

"Well, whoever it is, I think we probably have you to thank for teaching Leo about restoration," I said to Dylan.

She nodded. "It looks like he was doing a really professional job. Of course, he didn't have all the equipment we have, but still."

"Gotta give the guy credit," Styles said. "He hasn't even been out here for at least a year, and the refrigeration unit is still running."

"And here I thought you had to vacuum the coils at least once a year," I said.

"Maternal folklore," Styles said, "dating from the days when women practiced domestic science."

"Oh, look! A kitty!" Dylan pinched off a piece of hamburger meat and held it out in the direction of a light golden tiger cat headed in our direction from across the field. He made a beeline for her. He plucked the offering neatly from her fingers and retired a few yards to eat it.

"Aren't you the pretty boy?" Dylan cooed. "Aren't you a sweetie?"

Two more sweeties emerged from the woods, a tortoise-shell and a long-haired black cat with a white nose. They were trailed by a gray kitten.

Styles and I exchanged looks.

I broke off a few pieces of hamburger. "You always said that an investment in goodwill among the locals pays off in the end," I reminded her.

She gave me a look but broke off a few pieces of meat, anyway, and tossed them to the new arrivals.

"I know I said that," she complained, "but I wasn't exactly talking about loaves and fishes."

I followed her gaze and saw two more cats running up the drive.

Styles bent down till she was eye to eye with the bawling kitten.

"You are not a stray," she said, "so don't even bother playing on my sympathy."

"They do look well kept," Dylan said.

As a matter of fact, they looked better kept than she did. Smudges of dirt mixed with the sweat on her face. Tendrils of hair clung to her cheeks and neck. One of the cats had raised up on its hind legs to sniff at the cobwebs in her hair.

Another cat shot around the side of the house, scolding and chattering.

"I wasn't that hungry anyway," I said, and divided up what was left of my hamburger. It was true; the morning's Donettes were weighing heavily on my stomach.

We still had a lot of property to explore, although it wasn't easy to tear Dylan away from the bomb shelter. There was a limit to how much we could do, or would do, on foot. Styles couldn't hike with her crutches, my ankle was bothering me, and Dylan had a headache and a sore back.

"Let's just circle the house again, farther out," Styles said, "and see what we can see."

But our lunch guests became excited when we began walking. Some circled our ankles, some ran ahead. They seemed to know where we were going. The advance guard took a turn into an old dirt road that ran between field and woods behind the house. When we paused, they stopped and turned around. They sat and looked at us, puzzled.

"I think we're supposed to follow them," I said. To Styles, I said, "You up for it?"

"Five minutes," she said, negotiating around a mudhole. "They've got five minutes to convince me we're not on a mouse hunt."

So we followed. I limped, Styles hopped, and Dylan kept a hand pressed to her back. I thought Styles would throw in the towel when our path climbed a short hill, but she just gritted her teeth and continued on. Or maybe she was scowling. Crickets buzzed in the tall grass all around us; the sun beat down, and steam rose from puddles.

Dylan was the first to reach the top of the rise. She stopped dead in her tracks.

"Holy shit!" she exclaimed softly.

We caught up with her and followed her gaze.

Below us was an Italian villa. My first thought was that it was a stage set, like the one for the Western town last night. But a second glance confirmed that it was a real, honest-to-God Italian villa. It was a huge rectangular building constructed out of something that looked like weathered white marble and featured a Mediterranean tile roof and tall windows. We were approaching it from the back garden, a riot of colorful flowers and fanciful topiaries. Even at this distance, I could tell that the back entrance—a stone path that met the path we were on—was guarded by a topiary duo, a rabbit and a cat. At the center of the garden was a Victorian maze that reminded me of the one in *The Shining*, except that this one was flooded with sunlight.

"Wow," I said.

"You said it, babe," Styles commented.

The cats were running ahead. Another cat was perched on the garden wall, watching our approach.

Close up, the topiaries were even more imposing, and we were reluctant to enter the garden without an invitation.

"*They* invited us," Styles said, gesturing at the cats.

I hesitated. "It may not be their garden."

"It certainly looks like it's theirs," Styles persisted. And it was true that the cats had scattered into the garden, where a few more of their kind were in evidence, chasing each other in and out of bushes, sprawling on the path, or sitting like statues in the afternoon sun.

We followed the garden wall around to the front of the house. At this distance, the house showed its age. The marble was cracked, chipped, and stained in many places. The gutters needed painting and hung at odd angles from the edge of the roof. A downspout we passed had lost its bottom half.

The front entrance faced a gravel circular driveway. The door, which was heavy and wooden and elaborately carved, was surmounted by a canopy of aged copper. Above the canopy was a small balcony. On either side of the door, red roses climbed broken trellises and bloomed prodigiously.

We stepped under the canopy. We found no bell, so Styles lifted the door knocker, which was shaped like a woman's hand.

"You there!" a voice called out.

We looked around and saw no one, not even a cat.

"You there!" the voice repeated in a peremptory tone.

I backed down the steps and looked up.

Standing on the balcony was a small elderly woman. She was dressed in a tan-and-black caftan and wore a turban to match. Dark glasses covered her eyes. Rings and bracelets glinted in the sunlight.

"If you've come about the home, you can turn right around and go back where you came from!" she announced imperiously. She had a well-modulated voice, a trained voice, I thought, that projected well. As she spoke, she pointed down the driveway in a theatrical gesture. I had occasion to know about theatrical gestures.

"We haven't come about the home," I said, playing a hunch. "Leo sent us."

She gazed at me in silence for a moment.

"Why hasn't he come with you?" she asked, suspicion in her voice.

"He wasn't able to," I said gently. "He's ill. May we come in and talk to you?"

She took a minute to decide, as much for effect, I thought, as from indecision. Suddenly, I found myself on familiar ground. The pause was required for suspense, and to emphasize the degree of her magnanimity when she yielded to our request.

"Very well," she said, and stepped back from the balcony.

She opened the door herself a few minutes later and ushered us regally into a drawing room that my aunt Adele would have drooled over, even if it was a bit threadbare and faded. She indicated seats for us that were more decorative than comfortable, and for herself she selected a wood chaise lounge shaped like the front of a gondola.

Our host had removed her dark glasses. We were looking into intelligent brown eyes that took their measure of us. She had pale skin, remarkably smooth for her apparent age, and if she wore makeup, it wasn't obvious except for the bright red lipstick that covered her bow mouth. There were small indentations in her cheeks, barely visible, that threatened to turn into dimples if she let her dignity slip. She appeared to be sitting erect, but her shoulders were hunched slightly from osteoporosis. She wasn't wearing a wedding ring, I noticed, and she had slightly swollen knuckles that suggested arthritis.

Styles introduced us, and she acknowledged the introductions with a regal inclination of her head, but made no offer to reciprocate.

"You say that Leo is ill?" she said.

"He has Alzheimer's," I told her gently. I saw something shift behind her eyes, and added, "I'm sorry."

"His wife Shirley doesn't let him travel alone," Styles said.

"But you said Leo sent you," she said, looking from Styles to me. "How can that be if he has Alzheimer's disease?"

"He wants to see Auggie," I said, "but nobody knows who Auggie is or where to find him. Shirley hired Ms. Styles to find Auggie." I studied her face. "I think you can help us."

"And why do you think that, Miss . . . Liberty, did you say your name was?"

"Because I have a feeling you might be Auggie's mother," I said.

She said nothing.

"Was Leo his father?" I asked softly.

"You did say your name was Liberty?" she said at last. "I suppose you come from film people?"

I nodded.

"And do you know who I am?" she asked.

"I'm just guessing," I said apologetically, feeling put on the spot. "I think your name might be India."

"India?" Dylan gasped. She stared at our hostess. "*India Williams?* Oh, my God! Are you really India Williams?"

The woman smiled then, a little sadly, perhaps a little bitterly. "Your friend seems to know who I am."

"Well, sure!" Dylan enthused. "You were Ebony Art's biggest star in the forties. I've only seen two of your pictures, though," she added apologetically. "*Madam Satan* and *The Black Diamond*. You were great! I heard you did musicals, but I've never seen one." She leaned forward eagerly.

"I was a trained dancer," Williams acknowledged. "I danced with a Liberty once at an NAACP charity ball—Douglas, it was, of the Dancing Liberties."

"He's my father," I said. "Florence is my mother."

"They were wonderful dancers," she said. "Your father had that rare quality that Fred Astaire had, of making it appear as though tails were specially designed for dancing. Your mother was splendid, too. And their daughter is a—what? A private investigator?"

"Styles is the investigator," I said. "I'm just helping out."

"And I can see that Miss Styles is not so graceful on her feet," she said, fixing her eyes on Styles's crutches. She shifted her attention back to me. "What do you do?"

"I own a small movie theater in Eden," I said. "I inherited it from my aunt Mae."

"Mae Liberty was a fine actress," she said. "The most talented, I think, in your very talented family." She turned to Dylan, who was frozen in an attitude of reverence. "That leaves you, Miss Jellico. What do you do?"

I glanced anxiously at Styles, worried that, with her usual social insensitivity, she would wrench the conversation back to Auggie, but she just raised her eyebrows at me and folded her hands on her knees.

Dylan started. "Me? Oh, I work in film preservation and restoration. I'm with the Library of Congress Motion Picture Conservation Center at Wright-Pat." She paused and took a deep breath. "Miss Williams, do you—would you—I mean, is it possible that you might have copies of some of your films?" she stammered, and then blushed furiously. "We'd love to—um—"

"Get your hands on them?" Williams smiled. "That was Leo's department—film preservation and restoration." Her eyes lifted. "I'm guessing from the state of your hair that you've already been to the barn, possibly even to the house.

It's not very secure, not secure at all, I imagine, for someone of Miss Styles's capabilities. Did you find anything?"

"We found Leo's storeroom and workshop," I told her. "So we did find his film collection, yes."

"The films belong to Leo now," she told Dylan. "So you'll have to ask him whether you can have them or not. Or his wife—Shirley, isn't it?"

"Were you and Leo married, Miss Williams?" Styles asked abruptly.

"What an impertinent question!" she responded, arching an eyebrow in Styles's direction.

Styles suddenly grinned at her. "Now there's a word you don't hear much anymore—impertinent."

"Indeed. And if *you* don't hear it, Miss Styles, then it assuredly has fallen into disfavor. I should think it a word peculiarly useful in conversation with you." I worried for an instant that we'd lost her, but then a smile played on her lips and her dimples threatened to make an appearance. "I suppose, Miss Styles, that that is your specialty as a private investigator, asking impertinent questions. I played a detective, once or twice, you know, and thoroughly enjoyed it. I am something of an aficionada of mystery novels. But to answer your question, yes, Leo and I were married. He was my first husband. And, before you ask, I was his first wife."

"Was Auggie your son—yours and Leo's?" I asked.

"Yes," she said simply.

"How old were you?" Dylan asked. "You must have been young."

Dylan didn't sound impertinent; she didn't sound like she was prying. Hers was the voice of youthful curiosity—she was interested, even fascinated. I was fascinated myself, but I couldn't convey quite the same quality of hunger for the details of this woman's life. Dylan was irresistible.

"We were very young," Williams affirmed softly. "Young and foolish. Although in point of fact, I was an older woman." The dimples finally appeared as she smiled wryly at Dylan. "Leo was seventeen at the time, and he was very handsome, very charming. I was twenty-one. I should have had more sense than he; I'd grown up partly in the South and partly in Cincinnati before I came to this area to attend college at Wilberforce. But Leo had never lived anywhere else. And Pleasant Ridge, in those days, was a special place. Ebony Art made it special."

"How did you come to work for Ebony Art?" I asked.

"I joined the Wilberforce Theatrical Society, and took part in some of the dramatic productions at the college. Leo's father, Solomon Mayer, used to attend many of the college plays and recruit actors for his movies. He saw me in a production of *Midsummer Night's Dream*—I have always thought that was rather prophetic—and asked me if I wouldn't like to play in motion pictures. As you can imagine, I was thrilled. Eventually, movies became my life, and I dropped out of Wilberforce. As you can also imagine, my parents disapproved, although they couldn't help but be proud when they saw me up there on the silver screen. One didn't, of course, make a living in motion pictures—not unless one was a contract player at a Hollywood studio. But there was always work available in those days for a young lady with typing skills."

"And you met Leo," I prompted when she fell silent.

She sighed. "Yes, I met Leo. He was a cocky young cameraman, energetic and funny and headstrong. Seventeen was older in those days than it is now, you understand. And then the war broke out, and he planned to enlist but he wanted to get married first. One giddy moonlit night, we eloped. It wasn't anything we'd planned, it just happened. We woke up married and immensely pleased with ourselves."

"What did your families think?" Dylan asked. She was leaning forward, elbows on knees, chin in hands, rapt.

"My parents were shocked, but determined to make the best of a bad situation. They liked Leo very much, but an interracial marriage? It just wasn't done in those days. They feared that we'd both be made miserable by public disapproval."

She stopped herself, and seemed to focus on something distant.

"No, it was more than that," she corrected herself. "They

were terrified that we would become the targets of racist violence."

"And Leo's family?" I asked.

"Oh, Leo's family was wonderful, but then his grandmother, Miss Leila, was Negro. So you can see how naive Leo was. He had no way of knowing that the world beyond Pleasant Ridge was a very different place. Oh, Ebony Art sometimes made pictures about racism, and even about racist violence, but that wasn't real to Leo. And I let him talk me out of my own misgivings."

She broke off. "This is getting to be a long story, and I've neglected my duties as hostess. May I offer you some tea?"

Dylan glanced at us anxiously.

"Unless you'd care for some," I said, "I think we're all too interested in hearing the rest of your story to stop now."

"Very well," she said. "Where was I? You see, I'm getting as forgetful as Leo. Soon they'll put us both in a home and we can spend the rest of our lives going mad together."

She delivered this line like a professional actress caressing a favorite line from a script.

"In any case, Leo went off to war."

"To India," I couldn't resist putting in.

"Oh, yes, indeed, to India," she said. "He thought it terribly romantic, that little coincidence. We wrote each other madly passionate letters, and I thanked God he couldn't see me as I was then, pregnant and sick to my stomach and ill-tempered."

"Did he know you were pregnant when he left?" Dylan wanted to know.

"No, though he must have suspected something might have come of—well, all that spooning we did."

Styles couldn't contain a snort, and Williams pretended to frown at her.

"There's not much more to tell," she continued. "Leo came home a different man, and he came home to a different woman. We still loved each other, but we had both changed in other ways. Our experiences had damaged our youthful romanticism. Like so many other young veterans in those days, Leo was restless. He couldn't stay in Pleasant Ridge, he

wanted to move to a city. I had been living in Cincinnati with
my parents during the war, but I didn't want to live there with
Leo. Much as we loved each other, we both began to see how
impractical we'd been. And then, of course, there was the
baby."

She stood slowly and moved to the window to look out.

"I sent Leo away," she said softly. "It was one of the
hardest things I've ever done. But it was the best thing for
both of us. I still believe that. Leo went to Columbus and
made movies there, and later, he became involved in television production. He met his second wife, Gladys, and married her on impulse, divorced her six months later. But then
he met Inez. From everything he said about her, I believe she
was a wonderful woman. They raised a family together and he
was very happy.

"And I came back to live here in Pleasant Ridge. I rented a
small house in town and made some movies. But the movie
business had changed, too, and television was coming in.
Samuel had died during the war, and then Solly died, too—in
nineteen forty-nine, I believe it was. Shelly, Leo's brother,
had moved away, and Leo had, and there was no one left to
run the business. Oh, Leo's cousin Max tried to keep it going
for awhile, but the market for our films was shrinking. I remarried twice, both times to men of my own race, and had
other children."

"You never considered moving to a city with Leo and
passing for white?" asked the impertinent Miss Styles.

Williams turned her head to glance back at Styles.

"No. I have never denied my race, nor would I wish to," she
said with dignity. "I was raised by people who were proud of
who they were, Miss Styles. That's what Ebony Art films
were all about—pride in the Negro race. And I wanted my
son to be proud of who he was. Neither of my husbands
wished me to accept money from Leo. They liked him well
enough, but they were proud men. Leo used to pay Auggie's
school bills, and give him extravagant presents, but that was
where my husbands drew the line."

"But when you were widowed? You *were* widowed?" I asked.

She nodded. "My second and third husbands left me well provided for, I assure you. And there's a trust fund at the local bank for Auggie." She looked around the room and smiled wryly. "Needless to say, neither of my husbands was planning for maintenance on a house of this scale."

"So how *did* you come to be living in an Italian villa out in the middle of no place in southern Ohio?" Styles asked.

She smiled again. "It used to be in the middle of no place; I wish that were still true. I have housing developments and shopping centers encroaching on all sides."

"The villa?" Styles prompted impatiently.

"The villa was a gift from Leo's cousin Max," she said. She had moved to a grand piano that seemed to dominate the room from its corner. She brushed its gleaming surface lightly.

Styles whistled. "Some present."

"In the late sixties, when my third husband died, I was rather at loose ends. Miss Leila was still living at the Homestead then, but she was in her nineties and needed looking after. I'd refused the invitation twenty-odd years before, when Leo and I broke up and I moved back here, and the family invited me to live at the Homestead—that's what we called the old house. Miss Leila and I had always been close, so I moved into the Homestead to take care of her. She died in nineteen seventy." As if drawn there irresistibly, Williams stepped to the piano bench and seated herself. We waited, and she began playing softly. "The house was getting old and needed many repairs. Max insisted that I couldn't live there anymore, that the house wasn't worth repairing. Once he'd asked me what kind of house I'd most like to live in, and I'd said an Italian villa. Not that I knew anything about them, you understand, except what I'd seen in the movies, like everyone else."

From where I was sitting, I could no longer see her; she'd disappeared behind the piano. I only caught an occasional glimpse of the top of her turban as it moved to the music. I felt a sense of déjà vu, as if we were replaying a scene from an old melodrama.

"Marble"—her disembodied voice rose sternly over the music—"is shockingly cold in the winter. Of course, I'd never breathe a word to Max. It might hurt his feelings."

"Or he might build you another house," Styles observed dryly.

She sighed. "There's always that possibility. I think he wanted to shame Leo. You see, he insists on believing that Leo used me cruelly, that Leo abandoned me and my child. It does no good to tell him otherwise; that's what he wants to believe." She sighed. "He proposed to me many times, but I've always said that one interracial marriage in a lifetime is enough. He has always looked after me, though, and I'm very fond of him. He and Leo have never gotten along.

"My children," she added after a brief pause, "think this house is too much for me. They want me to move into one of those retirement places, where old people play cards all day—'the home' is what I call it. They keep threatening to send a representative to call on me—a salesman, that's what those people are. Oh, they have all kinds of euphemistic names for those places nowadays, but I still say they're old folks' homes, and I don't want any part of one."

After a short pause, Dylan asked, "Have you ever considered making movies again?"

The piano music shifted into ragtime, a Scott Joplin tune.

"Good heavens, child, who'd want to see an old dinosaur like me when they've got Angela Bassett and Lonette McKee and Robin Givens and Whitney Houston?"

"And Ruby Dee and Maya Angelou and Cicely Tyson," I couldn't help adding. "And who was that wonderful actress who played the grandmother in *Daughters of the Dust*?"

"Cora Lee Day," Dylan supplied automatically.

"Not to mention Jessica Tandy and Lauren Bacall and Anne Bancroft and Ellen Burstyn and Sophia Loren," Styles put in. "Old ladies are hot."

"Did you know Edna Mae Harris and Nina Mae McKinney and Laura Bowman?"

The turban moved in what might have been a shake of the head. "We didn't live in the same part of the country, and people didn't travel in those days the way they do now. Colored film companies like ours weren't concentrated in one place, like Los Angeles, so Negro actors didn't often meet, unless they went to New York to do theater. I did see McKinney on stage once, in Louisville, but I never met her."

"The Black Garbo," Dylan said reverently.

"The Black Garbo," Williams repeated. "But Fredi Washington was my idol. I thought she was so beautiful and elegant. And she had the most cultured voice. I wonder if she's still alive."

"She died a few years ago," Dylan said. "And Edna Mae Harris died just last year."

"Ah," Williams almost sighed.

Realizing her mistake, Dylan said clumsily, "But Lena Horne is still going strong, and she must be older than you are."

Williams played for a minute without speaking—a melancholy tune I didn't recognize.

"So will you tell us where to find Auggie?" Styles asked abruptly.

She stopped playing and stood up. "He's in the greenhouse," she said. "Would you like to meet him?"

The greenhouse assaulted our senses. It was oppressively warm, the air thick with humidity. I half expected General Sternwood to be wheeled into view at any moment. Vibrant greens and occasional splashes of other colors dazzled our eyes. The air was fragrant with the heady perfume of some exotic flower in bloom. Spiked leafy fingers brushed our skin and hanging tendrils touched our hair as softly as fallen spiders.

India Williams pushed aside a curtain of green and led us down a path through the wilderness. At the far end, his back to us, stood the gardener, bent over a tall workbench and humming a tuneless tune. He was dressed in faded and patched denim overalls and a plain cotton undershirt. A parrot perched on his shoulder, preening itself. One cat wound around his ankles. Another stood on the bench, watching what he was doing, tail switching. A brown puppy worried the tail as it flicked back and forth. A third cat was curled in a large ceramic bowl on the ground. Nearby a large lop-eared rabbit was standing on its hind legs, its forepaws on the rim of a large pot, munching some rabbit delicacy. And astonishingly, squatting on a bench that overlooked the rabbit was a small raccoon with a splinted forearm.

"I think you just found Snow White," I whispered to Styles.

But when the man turned toward his mother's voice, we could see that he wasn't white at all. His skin was a rich medium brown.

"Auggie, dear, we have visitors," his mother said. "They're friends of Leo's."

He smiled. And now there was no mistaking his parentage. His cheeks expanded to accommodate the width of his mouth. His chin dropped to complete the triangle and expose gleaming white teeth, the top ones protruding slightly over the bottom ones. His eyebrows arched in an almost comical expression of delight.

But there was something about him—I couldn't put my finger on what it was. Not the width or the shape of his forehead below the receding cap of black curly hair heavily interspersed with gray. Not the ears that protruded a little too noticeably from the side of his head, nor the slight droop at the outer edges of his eyes. But the effect of the whole was, though not displeasing, a little surprising, like a mismatched set of dishes.

"Leo? Is Leo here?" he asked.

His voice was slow and slightly thick, and I understood. Auggie was mentally handicapped.

"No, dear, Leo's not here, but these are his friends," his mother said.

His gaze, which had drifted over our shoulders to catch sight of his father, moved to his mother and back to us. The wattage of his smile wavered, and his eyebrows began a slow descent into puzzlement or distress.

"Where's Leo?"

"Leo's at his house, but he sent his friends to see you," Williams insisted gently. "Isn't that nice?"

Eager to make up for his father's absence, I stepped forward with my hand out. "Auggie, I'm Gilda. It's nice to meet you."

His right hand rose automatically, holding a pair of open pruning shears. Looking down, he realized the problem and remedied it by offering me his left hand instead.

"Nice to meet you, Gilda," he said politely as I took the empty hand and grasped it warmly.

"Don't worry, Auggie," I told him. "Next time we come, we'll bring Leo."

I was nearly blinded by the smile.

42

We kept our promise. A little over a week later, on August first, we attended a birthday party in Pleasant Ridge—Leo, Shirley, Styles, James, and I. Leo, wearing his brown bomber jacket, grew impatient and agitated on the car trip, but when he began to recognize the scenery outside the car, he became excited. He wasn't the most articulate of tour guides, but we all caught his enthusiasm.

"There—right there!" he'd say, pointing out the window at some aged brick building that might once have housed a bank or a small department store, or at a street corner, or at a weathered Victorian house. "And I was—but then he said, 'You *should*, you know, you son of a gun'—but I couldn't.

Shelly never liked him, because of band practice. And then later, when he told Jeannette—but it was right there!"

Again I had the feeling that we were tuned in to a radio station from Alaska while driving a city freeway. We seemed to be missing the crucial information—or if not the crucial information, the smaller pieces that would help us make sense of it.

But when we pulled into the circular drive in front of the old Italian villa and Shirley unlocked Leo's door, he bolted from the car and ran at an awkward lope that represented top speed for him now. At the door to the house, he met India Williams and threw his arms around her.

We all glanced anxiously at Shirley. Her eyes were filled with tears, but she was smiling.

"It's all right," she reassured us. "It's all right if he loves her. He loves me, too." She took a deep breath. "I'm an old woman," she said. "I'm willing to share."

Then Auggie rounded the side of the house, scattering cats, that silly parrot bouncing along on his shoulder. He raced up the steps and threw himself into his parents' arms.

We held back for a few minutes until India Williams broke away and led the two men down the steps toward us.

"You have to introduce us to Shirley, Leo," she was telling him. She had spoken to Shirley on the telephone when the two of them had arranged this event, but now they would meet face to face for the first time.

Reminded of Shirley's presence, Leo looked at her delightedly, and the smile he sent her was reward enough for giving him this moment. He held out his free hand to his wife, and stood between the two women, tears catching on his smile, overcome with his good fortune.

And even I got my reward when Auggie shouted, "Gilda! The movie lady! Hi!" and ambushed me with a hug that tangled a squawking parrot in my hair. "You brought him, just like you promised! You brought Leo!"

Everybody was introduced to everybody, including the nonhuman contingent. There would be another party that evening for the rest of the Williams family, but Shirley and India had decided not to spring them all on Leo at this point.

India Williams was wearing a different caftan, this one a wine color shot with gold, and another turban. Shirley wore a blue pastel polyester pantsuit. Williams greeted her with genuine warmth and thanked her for reuniting the family. Shirley blushed, embarrassed, and said that she had only wanted to make Leo happy.

India, as we now called her, suggested that Auggie show us the house and grounds. Auggie complied eagerly, dragging his father in the direction of the garden. We followed at a more leisurely pace.

We knew by now that Auggie had lived most of his life in a school for the mentally retarded, and that India had brought him to live with her when the school had closed in the seventies.

"My other children thought I should have sent him to live in a group home then," she'd told us. "They weren't being mean-spirited," she'd reassured us. "They loved Auggie and visited him often. But they thought he'd be too much for me to take care of in my—in my declining years. And Auggie, as you can see, has always been sociable. We were worried about how he'd adjust to life in comparative isolation. But, as you can see, he simply made new friends." The sweep of her arm had taken in a veritable menagerie of animal housemates.

Now, as she watched her son in the garden with Leo, she said, "I could never have taught him the many things he learned in school." She paused by a topiary cat that guarded the entrance to the garden from this side like a leafy sphinx guarding a royal tomb. "He learned gardening and animal care there. Actresses, as I'm sure you know, Miss Liberty, know a very little on many subjects—the ones that have been covered by one script or another—but not enough about anything to be of much general use to anybody."

It was a bittersweet day all around. India hadn't seen Leo for at least a year, and I often noticed her sad eyes fixed on him. It must have occurred to her, as it did to all of us, that Leo had in some ways descended to Auggie's intellectual level. In fact, because Auggie's memory was unimpaired, Auggie often seemed more intelligent than his father.

Even Leo sensed this. He had not forgotten why he had wanted to see Auggie again, and we overheard him in the greenhouse, trying to explain an illness he himself didn't understand.

"I'm sick, son," Leo told Auggie, who was frowning with concentration as he listened. "I got old. I don't—I can't think so good anymore." We heard the quaver in his voice. "You must ask your mother. I'm no good anymore."

"Yes, you are, Leo," Auggie protested loyally. "You're still good."

Auggie put his arms around Leo as if the embrace could protect his father from self-doubt as well as the disparagement of others. Perhaps Auggie himself had been on the receiving end of such embraces all his life and knew their healing power. Auggie patted Leo's back awkwardly. India stepped forward and scooped the irate parrot off of Auggie's shoulder in time to hear Leo's muffled voice say, "Shirley. Shirley will take care of everything."

India Williams exchanged a tearful glance with Shirley Presser Mayer. Then she swallowed and said, "Time for lunch, Auggie, and then cake and ice cream."

Auggie and Leo broke from their embrace, diverted from their pain by the promise of pleasures yet to come.

"And then presents!" Auggie shouted gleefully.

Styles and I had gone in together on a small collection of Donald Duck videos. I threw in a dinosaur egg because I was still trying to unload the damn things. Curiously enough, though, the dinosaur egg was a big hit with Auggie. But then, everything was a big hit with Auggie. He made Shirley sit down on the couch with him and look at the pictures, one by one, in the topiary book she'd given him. James gave him a documentary video on cats, and it was all we could do to drag him away from it for a round of croquet.

"Auggie beat the pants off us!" James complained as we rejoined India and Shirley in the solarium. "Didn't he, Leo?"

"I didn't mean to, Mom," Auggie said, in some distress. "James, I didn't mean to."

"It's okay, kid," Styles said, punching the fifty-four-year-old Auggie on the shoulder as if he were a teenage boy, "you just don't know your own strength." To India, she said, "He plays a mean game of croquet."

"You should talk," I muttered. Styles had improved her own game by running her mouth whenever James or I was playing, and by using one crutch as a hockey stick when she thought she could get away with it.

"It *is* your birthday, Auggie dear," India said dryly. "I think your guests will survive the humiliation of their defeat." And she gave Styles an arch look.

Leo clapped Auggie on the back. "You should have seen him, India! Why, he knocked my ball way over into the bushes!" He smiled proudly at Auggie.

Auggie returned the smile with interest. "You knocked my ball, too, Leo! I saw you!"

Strictly speaking, it had been James's hand on the mallet that had guided Leo's ball into Auggie's, but nobody contested Auggie's version. Truth was a small price to pay for a good story, and in my family, we paid it without a moment's hesitation or the slightest twinge of conscience.

And truth, after all, was slippery. It so often depended upon your point of view. Why had Leo kept the secret of his first family for so long? Had he been ashamed of them? Or ashamed of his own failure at marriage, not once but twice before he met Inez? Or had the subject been too painful for him? Or did he think it would be too painful for Inez and the boys? Perhaps he had always intended to tell, first Inez and then Shirley, when the moment was right, and then the moments had somehow slipped away. We would never know now. We might know India Williams's version of Leo's truth, but that, too, would be only one point of view—hers and not Leo's.

I looked at Leo and his son, smiling at each other. That it had all come out all right in the end seemed a quirk of fate, unless we could credit a Capraesque God who liked happy endings as much as the average moviegoer.

Later, as we prepared to leave, Leo and Auggie saluted each other in the front hall. As we drove off, Auggie ran after the car for a few yards, waving, but my last view of him was of an erect figure, saluting.

On the way home that evening, Shirley told us that she'd talked to India about moving to Pleasant Ridge.

"I made the offer," she said, "and told her to think it over. The decision is hers, either way. Perhaps it would be too painful, for her and especially for Auggie, to watch Leo deteriorate." She laid a hand along Leo's cheek, but he was asleep and didn't wake up. "If she says yes, her children will object, of course, and so will Pauline—two old ladies taking care of an Alzheimer's patient and a mentally handicapped man between them. And it will throw Leo off at first, perhaps, but he's still unsettled by everything that's been going on since we moved, and at least the neighborhood and India's house will be familiar to him. And we can still commute to Columbus for the OSU drug study, if we're accepted. Who knows? The drugs might work. Maybe he won't deteriorate. Anything's possible."

And at that moment, with the warm glow of sun on our cheeks as it dropped toward the horizon, I thought perhaps she was right.

43

I was leaning over the ticket counter when my uncle Oliver appeared before me.

"I thought you'd be interested to know, Gillie," he said, "Clara liked my screenplay."

Two steps behind him was another uncle, preceded by the aromatic scent of Scotch. "She liked mine, too," Uncle Wallace said, "even though it wasn't quite her cup of tea, as she said."

"She's going to use them both," Oliver reported, one hand resting chummily on Wallace's shoulder now.

I blinked. "Both?" I echoed. "You mean she's going to make two movies?"

"No, she's going to put them together—combine them," Wallace said. "Wonderful idea, eh?"

I looked from one to the other. "A screwball remarriage comedy and a horror movie?" I asked skeptically.

"See, the bride's mother's going to be an actress," Oliver said, planting an elbow on a turquoise Tyrannosaurus in his eagerness to explain. "And in the middle of all the wedding plans, she's making a movie, see. And this movie, well, it's—"

"A horror movie about a widow who becomes a vampire," I said. "I got it."

I looked at their eager faces. The wrinkles, pouches, and discolorations of age were softened by the glow of excitement.

"More power to you," I said. "Sounds like a winner."

They grinned sheepishly at each other.

"Yeah, we think so, too," Oliver said. "So as soon as Tobias can fix up the script—"

"Say, Gillie," Wallace interrupted, laying a hand heavily on my forearm, "do you think you could talk to him for us?"

Further Acknowledgments

A major resource for this book was Tom McGreevey and Joanne L. Yeck's book about film conservation and restoration, *Our Movie Heritage* (Rutgers University Press, 1997). Other resources included Thomas Cripps's *Slow Fade to Black: The Negro in American Film, 1900–1942* (Oxford, 1993) and Larry Richards's *African American Films Through 1959* (McFarland, 1998), as well as the following Web resources: the National Film Preservation Board Web site, the Oscar Micheaux Society Web site, Martin J. Keenan's material on Micheaux at the Great Bend History Web site, Jean-Jacques Peters's "A History of Television" at the DVB Web site, Jerry Whitaker's "Milestones in the Evolution of Technology" at the Technical Press Web site, the Web site of the 341st Bombardment Group, and, as always, the Internet Movie Database.

The Movies

The recent revival of Billy Wilder's 1950 masterpiece *Sunset Boulevard* as a Broadway musical has introduced it to a new generation of moviegoers. It was one of a series of successful collaborations between Wilder and veteran screen-writer Charles Brackett and won them their second Academy Award for Best Screenplay. But its scathing portrayal of the Hollywood Dream Factory may have lost it the Best Picture Oscar, which went instead to Joseph Mankiewicz's *All About Eve*—a film with which it had a great deal in common.

The film was plagued with casting problems, initially be-cause no one wanted to play an aging actress; Mae West and Pola Negri declined, and Mary Pickford wanted too many changes to suit Wilder. Almost fifty years later, it is inter-esting to reflect that Gloria Swanson at age fifty-two was playing a has-been, an actress who couldn't hope to return to her former glory, although her former director, Cecil B. De Mille, is depicted in the film as active at age sixty-nine. (In fact, De Mille died nine years later, and Swanson outlived him by twenty-four years.) Norma Desmond's bridge partners, other actors who played themselves—Buster Keaton, Anna Q. Nilsson, and H. B. Warner—were all from De Mille's genera-tion, not Swanson's. Another of Swanson's former directors, Erich Von Stroheim, plays her butler in the film. William Holden, who plays Norma's young lover, landed the role when Fred MacMurray and Gene Kelly declined it, and Mont-gomery Clift abandoned it two weeks before filming began.

Sadly, F. W. Murnau's *The Last Laugh* (*Der letzte Mann*, 1924) is relatively unknown today except to students of film history. In it, the great German actor Emil Jannings plays an aging doorman who is devastated when he is declared too old for his job and demoted to washroom attendant. Desperate to maintain his status in the eyes of the world and his family, the former doorman steals back his splendid coat, emblem of his past glory, but the exposure of the truth brings him public hu-miliation and private misery as he is abandoned by his wife and children. Here the film would have ended had not the German studio UFA insisted on an ending that would give the old man, in the words of the American title, the "last laugh."

The Last Laugh is a tour-de-force not only on the part of Jannings, but also because of the dazzling innovation of its cinematography. Cinematographer Karl Freund and Murnau created a fluid camera in a time when camera movement was reserved for emphasis. Moreover, theirs was the most elaborate use to date of subjective camera, permitting the audience an opportunity to see the world through the eyes of the old man. So effective was this cinematic storytelling when combined with Jannings's performance, it is easy to overlook the almost complete absence of titles.

Working as art director at UFA while Murnau was making *The Last Laugh* was a twenty-five-year-old Englishman named Alfred Hitchcock. *The Last Laugh* would influence not only Hitchcock, but also Orson Welles, Max Ophuls, and Kenji Mizoguchi, among others, and establish the moving camera as a significant component of cinematic storytelling.

ACROSS

1 Harold's girlfriend, played by veteran actress Ruth Gordon.

4 Federico Fellini's nostalgic evocation of the Italy of his youth.

9 Popular singing partner of Jeanette MacDonald in films of the forties (initials).

10 Acclaimed Indian director whose last film, THE STRANGER (1991), was released in his seventieth year.

12 The character played in various films by Margaret Rutherford, Angela Lansbury, Helen Hayes, and Joan Hickson would have been given this at the vicarage.

13 Eight years before his death in 1998, Akira Kurosawa made this film, a series of vignettes featuring haunting surrealistic images and dazzling color.

15 Lauren Bacall played Barbra Streisand's mother in the 1996 film, THE MIRROR ___ TWO FACES.

18 Only one of this prolific Irish novelist's books has been made into a movie (A SEVERED HEAD, 1971); her husband of over forty years recently

published an elegy for the woman he lost to Alzheimer's disease (initials).

19 It coupled Audrey Hepburn with George Peppard; in West Germany, this 1962 Blake Edwards film was released under the title, FRUHSTUCK ___ TIFFANY.

20 This actress specializes in playing assertive older women such as the title character in MADAME SOUSATZKA (1988) and GUARDING TESS (1994).

22 Nickname for the filmmaker who made 13 across.

23 The kind of "citizen" who is over sixty (abbreviation).

24 Victor Laszlo tells Rick, "If we stop breathing, we'll ___. If we stop fighting our enemies, the world will ___."

25 Battling cancer himself, the Duke played this character, a dying gunfighter, in his last film.

31 Federal agency with which Shelley Levene (Jack Lemmon) and his desperate coworkers have to deal if they want to be "closers" rather than "losers" in GLENGARRY GLEN ROSS (initials).

32 A former stage director whose fourth film was NOW, VOYAGER (1942) and whose last film was BORN AGAIN (1978) (initials).

33 She won Tonys for her roles in MAME and SWEENEY TODD, among others, but she's best known today for her role as sleuth Jessica Fletcher (initials).

34 Edith Evans and Margaret Rutherford played in the 1952 Anthony Asquith adaptation of Oscar Wilde's THE IMPORTANCE OF BEING ___.

36 Best known for her role as Brigid O'Shaughnessy in THE MALTESE FALCON (1941), in 1964 she joined veterans Bette Davis, Olivia de Havilland, Joseph Cotten, and Agnes Moorehead in Robert Aldrich's HUSH, HUSH, SWEET CHARLOTTE (initials).

37 Veteran horror actor (53 across) who died while playing in Ed Wood's PLAN 9 FROM OUTER SPACE (1958) (first name).

38 Wearing a toupee, thirty-two-year-old Sean Connery launched his film career in 1962 as the sophisticated James Bond in DR. ___.

40 Last initials of the Indian-British producer-director team famed for their lush adaptations of classic novels, including REMAINS OF THE DAY (1993).

41 Best remembered for his role as Grandpa Walton, he had a long and distinguished career as a character actor.

43 She played Apple Annie in LADY FOR A DAY (1933).

46 British-born actress and director Lupino, who made one last film, MY BOYS ARE GOOD BOYS, in 1978.

48 Whitty and Robson; Marsh and Harris spelled theirs differently.

50 Professional designation for Joan Blondell in MISS PINKERTON (1932) and Brooke Adams in TELL ME A RIDDLE (1980) (abbreviation).

51 In his last big screen role, he played a victim of Alzheimer's disease in ON GOLDEN POND (1981) (first initial, last name).

53 Actor described in 37 across (last name).

56 Ingrid Bergman starred in the 1958 film about a woman's life and loves in China, ___ OF THE SIXTH HAPPINESS.

57 In 1926, before teaming Oliver Hardy with Stan Laurel, Leo McCarey featured Hardy in a comedy called ___ YOUR AGE.

58 The result of addition—child's play to Walter Matthau's Albert Einstein in I.Q. (1994).

61 The voice of Darth Vader and CNN, he played the reclusive sportswriter Terence Mann in FIELD OF DREAMS (1989).

62 Katherine Hepburn's autobiography.

63 He once played Stephen Foster and Alexander Graham Bell, but won an Academy Award for his role in Ron Howard's COCOON (1985).

64 The other half of 49 down.

65 Her eight Academy Awards for costume design make her the most Oscar-decorated woman in film history.

DOWN

1 Controversial president of Disney who had bypass surgery in 1994 and fired Jeff Katzenberg the same year (initials).

2 If old age is not ripe, it is ___.

3 She made her first film in 1939; she has starred in film versions of A RAISIN IN THE SUN (1961), GO TELL IT ON THE MOUNTAIN (1979), I KNOW WHY THE CAGED BIRD SINGS (1984), and two Spike Lee films.

4 Perhaps best remembered for hanging out with Mr. Ed in the early 1960s, he played in BEVERLY HILLS COP III (1994) (initials).

5 She won an Academy Award for Best Supporting Actress in David Lean's A PASSAGE TO INDIA.

6 Basketball abbreviation for, say, HOOSIERS has-been Coach Norman Dale (Gene Hackman).

7 When he's not doing one-handed push-ups, Jack Palance needs a pair of this item to control his horse.

8 Title for Peggy Ashcroft, Judith Anderson, Wendy Hiller, Diana Rigg, and Judi Dench, among others.

10 He studied karate under master Pat Morita (initials).

11 The recent adaptation of William Faulkner's classic novel about the death and attempted burial of Addie Bundren, ___ I LAY DYING.

13 Once Norma Desmond's—and Gloria Swanson's—director, he made his first film in 1914 and his last in 1958.

14 Cesar Bernal and Martha Stella Calle starred in a 1973 adaptation of this Carlos Fuentes novel about an elderly sorceress.

16 Actor Pacino.

17 Edmund Gwenn played this genial gent in MIRACLE ON 34TH STREET (1947).

19 Place from which exit lines are frequently delivered.

21 Elizabeth Taylor plays a woman who attempts to recapture her youth in the 1973 film, ___ WEDNESDAY, which also features 51 across.

25 Distinguished cinematographer Nykvist; he won Academy Awards for CRIES AND WHISPERS (1972) and FANNY AND ALEXANDER (1982).

26 George Burns lived more than a decade after his last appearance as God in the ___, GOD! films—long enough to pass his hundredth birthday and prove that the Almighty has a sense of humor.

27 She plays Em, once the lover of her friend's artist husband, in HOW TO MAKE AN AMERICAN QUILT (1995).

28 Whitty, and in the remake, Angela Lansbury, vanished from here in THE LADY VANISHES (1938, 1979).

29 America's most famous Alzheimer's disease victim.

30 He played the chauffeur to Jessica Tandy's Daisy in DRIVING MISS DAISY (1989).

33 As a young man, 51 across played American president ___ Lincoln.

35 In 1943, he starred with Janet Blair in SOMETHING TO SHOUT ABOUT, and sang the Cole Porter song, "You'd Be ___ Nice to Come Home To."

39 Last two letters of initials for a Web site indispensable to film buffs.

42 This director's 1992 film, THE PLAYER, opens with a long take during which a studio executive, played by Tim Robbins, laments the decline of the long take (initials).

44 Director who made TOKYO STORY (1953), a classic about an elderly couple.

45 The kind of house Broadway

star Margo Channing (Bette Davis) hoped to play to in ALL ABOUT EVE (1950) (abbreviation).

46 Lindsay Anderson, who directed THE WHALES OF AUGUST in 1987, made this classic about a revolution at a boys' school in 1968.

47 3 down played the character Mother Sister in Spike Lee's 1989 film, ___ THE RIGHT THING.

49 Half the name of a best-selling sisterhood of old friends, soon to appear on the silver screen.

51 In a dramatic courtroom speech in AMISTAD, former president John Quincy Adams (Anthony Hopkins), says, "The natural state of mankind . . . is freedom. And the proof is the length to which a man, woman or child will go to regain it once taken. He will break loose ___ chains. He will decimate ___ enemies. He will try and try and try, against all odds, against all prejudices, to get home."

52 Most of the early experiments with synchronous sound, were not optical sound but sound-on-___.

53 Actress Horne is best known to American film for CABIN IN THE SKY (1943) and STORMY WEATHER (1943), but she also played Glinda the Good Witch in THE WIZ (1978).

54 In her last film, THE WHALES OF AUGUST (1987), her irascible sister was played by Bette Davis.

55 12 across is commonly drunk this way in the land of Miss

Daisy, the Threadgoode sisters, and Miss Jane Pittman.

57 In one of Harold Lloyd's most popular films, he was GRANDMA'S ___ (1922). He also played Granddaddy.

59 At twenty-six, Mary Pickford co-founded this film distribution company. (abbreviation).

60 One of the alternative spellings in 48 across, this actress joined D. W. Griffith's company in 1912; her last film was DONOVAN'S REEF in 1963 (initials).

62 Jane Darwell played her in the 1940 John Ford adaptation of Steinbeck's THE GRAPES OF WRATH.

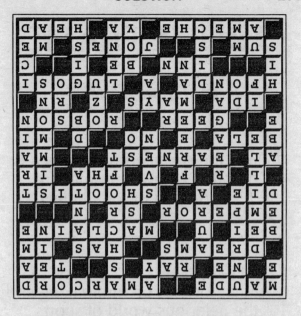

Notes on Age and Aging in Film

ACROSS	DOWN
9 Nelson Eddy	1 Michael Eisenberg
18 Iris Murdoch	4 Alan Young
23 Senior	10 Ralph Maccio
31 Federal Housing Administration	39 The Internet Movie Database
32 Irving Rapper	42 Robert Altman
33 Angela Lansbury	45 Standing room only
36 Mary Astor	59 United Artists
50 They are nurses.	60 Mae Marsh

FREEZE FRAME

by Della Borton

Gilda Liberty's headstrong niece is
shooting a new film in town.
And it's going to make a killing. . .

"FREEZE FRAME is a breezy, fun
read that focuses on filmmaking and
the nefarious world of sports
recruiting. Borton provides us
with a lively story. . ."

—*Romantic Times*

———◆———

If you enjoyed this Gilda Liberty mystery,
why not go back to where it all began . . .

FADE TO BLACK

by Della Borton

———m———

When eighty-two-year-old film legend and
Oscar-winner Mae Liberty ascends to that big
movie studio in the sky, her funeral in Eden,
Ohio, draws raves—not to mention the threat of
blackmail, a case of arson, and an uninvited
corpse.

"If you're hooked on the American Movie
Channel, you'll welcome Gilda Liberty and
her crazy movie-loving family. . . .Just relax
and enjoy the glitter and the glitz.
Hooray for Hollywood!"

—*Meritorious Mysteries*

Published by Ballantine Books.
Available at bookstores everywhere.

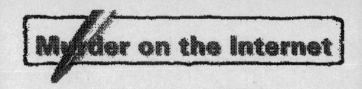